LET ME SEE THE STARS

Pearl Bell was born and brought up in the North East of England where she still lives with her husband. She has a daughter, son in law and two grandchildren.

LET ME SEE THE STARS

PEARL BELL

For my daughter Sally.
You have climbed many mountains
and there are many more ahead.
You will succeed.

PROLOGUE

"Open the curtains and let me see the stars," my father murmured.

My mother sat quietly by my side; she had told me earlier in the day that tonight she wanted to be with him. She looks so fragile, so helpless, what is that look on her face? Not sorrow, not sadness. "What is she thinking?" I ask myself. "Why that look, why not sorrow, why no tears?"

I opened the curtains and settled in my chair, a chair used by hundreds of people before me. What stories could they tell? How many had gone, their story left untold? I closed my eyes, disturbed only by the irregular breathing of my father and the now familiar sounds of a hospital ward at night. The muffled voices of nurses, a cup clattering onto a saucer, mutters, moans, all sounds I had become accustomed to. Noises, which had at first upset me, now part of my nightly vigil.

I drifted back to another time, another place. Christmas Eve, the clock on the mantelpiece chimed twelve times.

"By we've had some Christmas's afore but never one as bad as this." The good looking man said as he warmed his hands in front of a roaring fire. "We didn't join in the celebrations last month an' now this, Sarah's had her fair share o' trouble since she married me."

The good looking man's father stood with his back to the fire. He turned to face his son. "Aye lad," he said, "but y'll just have to mek the best o' it an' see the lass alreet, she's your daughter an' my granddaughter, we'll not let her down. Folk are blamin' the war for everythin' an' there's many a lot worse off than us, at least we're all alive an' still in one piece. The Kaiser might have fled to Holland, but think o' poor Hannah, the signin' o' the armistice on the

eleventh day o' the eleventh month didn't end the war f'
her. One lad back wi' only one leg, an' here's six months on
an' still nee word o' their John."

In the room upstairs a young girl, barely sixteen years
old, lay in her parent's bed, the bed in which she had lain
since the clock had chimed twelve times the night before.
She wished she would die, both her and this baby she was
having. She did not want a baby; no one else wanted her to
have a baby.

"It would be better if a was dead," she thought. "Ne
more rows wi' me Da, ne more havin' to hide away from
the rest o' the world."

The pain was more than she could bear. Why was that
stupid woman in the white pinny shouting at her?

"One last push an' it'll all be over."

"One last push an' a'll be dead," the young girl thought.

But no, what was happening? She was still alive and
splitting in two, she was being tortured to pay for her sins.
Her Ma had said she would suffer for what she had done.
She had not thought she was being a bad girl, and he had
said he loved her and one day they would be married. She
remembered how she had cried when he married a lass from
Durham. Her mates had said it was a posh weddin' 'cos her
Da was well off. Mary, her best friend, had told her they
had a baby boy now and he was three months old.

"It's a good job he's married her," Mary's mothers had
said, "'cos he wouldn't be alive t' tell the tale if he hadn't."

It was over; the baby was born. She turned her head to
face the wall; staring at the washstand with the marble top
she wondered if life would ever be the same again. The
midwife was speaking but the young girl ignored her.

"It's a fine healthy lass, no need to hang this one up by
the ankles an' gi' it a clout."

Meg took her first breath and cried. Her tiny wrinkled
face was topped with sticky, black curls.

"My, she'll be a beauty when we get her topped an' tailed," the midwife said as she handed the little bundle to Sarah, who had never left her daughter's side during the last twenty four hours.

Sarah looked old.

"Old enough to be her husband's mother," the neighbours would say.

Some sympathised with her, others condemned Sarah.

"She's not the only one who's had problems, others have had t' mek the best o' it. She's got two fine lads, an' the two lasses, but you never see her smile an' the' say she likes nowt better than a glass o' beer or port. There's a pair o' them in that house that likes the drink," they gossiped.

As the kindly, if rough, midwife completed her care; Jane's thoughts were not on the child. She did not care if it was a boy or a girl or how many fingers or toes it had.

"After all", she thought to herself, "a didn't want a baby, but me Ma's here wi' me now, so she still must care about me a bit. Maybe a won't die? Maybe me Ma will keep the baby? She said a'd made me bed an' a could lie on it, but she wouldn't be wi' me now if she'd meant it."

Jane had been born in the same bed, in the same room where she now lay. Her father worked at the pit and times had not been all that bad. At least they were better off than many of the miners' families. There was always food on the table and Jane had never been without a pair of good strong boots. Her clothes were often shabby but always clean and warm.

"Me Da's different from me Ma," she thought, "he's always crackin' jokes an' mekin' me laugh, at least he was until the night me Ma told him a was gannin' to have a bairn."

Ever since that night, he had not spoken to her. He had gone to the Bay Horse and when he came home drunk, he did not speak; he just walked straight past her as if she was

11

not there. Her Granddad had come the following weekend and she had been told to stay upstairs while he talked to her Ma and Da. She knew they were talking about her and when her Granddad shouted for her to come downstairs for tea she could tell her Da had been crying.

Jane loved her Granddad; he went to the chapel and did not drink like her Da did. Her Granddad had worked at the pit but he was retired now. He did not like her Da to drink and she laughed every time her Granddad said to him.

"Dan you've turned me hair grey."

Her Da would wait, until her Granddad was not looking, and turn and wink at her.

A gentle tap on the door startled me.

"Is everything alright?" the pretty young nurse asked.

"It's my sixth night on the trot," she had told me earlier when I commented on how tired she was looking.

"Tonight's my last shift and then three lovely nights in bed," she continued.

"Everything is fine", I told her, and off she went to see to the needs of others in her care.

I stared out of the window, I could not see the moon but the stars were twinkling, surrounded by a black velvet sky and one star seemed to be shining more brightly than I had ever seen a star shine before. They were the same stars and it was the same sky that had towered over my parents, my grandparents and my great grandparents, no matter when or where they were. Maybe they had also seen that same bright star?

When I was a child my father had told me stories about the stars. On clear nights he had taught me how to find the constellations, the seven sisters and the great bear. I had really believed those seven pretty little girls lived up there and were safe from that great big bear. When we were lucky we sometimes saw a shooting star and we would make a wish and promise never to tell what we had wished for.

Where had I been for the last hour? It was as if I had witnessed the birth of that child, but it was not possible, it had happened long before I was born. It was one of the stories my mother had told me, not make believe, this story was true. Maybe if I closed my eyes I could return to that other time, that Christmas long ago. Would it help me to understand that look on the face of my mother?

14

CHAPTER 1.

When he left school Dan started working at the pit. He was the eldest of three boys and they, like their father and grandfather before them, had no choice but to take the only jobs available and carry on the family tradition of mining. Dan was born in a terraced house in the middle of the rows built for the families of miners and the families of the men who worked at the local ironworks.

As a young boy he played with his friends in the back streets, but when the opportunity arose his favourite places were either the back of the brewery or outside of the Penny Gill. He would hide around the corner of the street hoping his parents were not looking.

"A'll cop it t'night o' me Da," Dan would tell his mates, "but let's away up the Penny Gill an' see if some drunk's lost a ha'penny."

The Penny Gill was one of two public houses nearby. It was the only place in the area where a gill of beer could be bought for a penny and had been purposely built at the top of the ironworks road. The men would call for a gill of beer at the end of their shift and Dan and his mates would watch for the workers who needed more than a gill to quench their thirst. Sometimes they would be lucky and would head to the shops to spend their ill-gotten gains. The front street shops provided the iron workers and the miners' families with their every day needs but when Dan and his mates had a prosperous day the shops provided their black bullets and gobstoppers.

Dan's favourite day was market day. He would gaze in amazement at the pot-man's stall as he banged his wares to attract attention. Sometimes, if he had been lucky, he would buy a half-pennorth of bullets from the stall that, he thought, sold more sweets than he could have eaten in a lifetime. Hiding behind the stalls, he would breathe a sigh of relief, when his mother appeared.

"Phew, me Ma didn't see me this time, me Da'd 'ave killed me t'night."

Little did he know his mother never once missed seeing him, she would smile to herself and Dan's father never heard about his escapades.

Dan's father and uncles worked at the colliery that was only a short walk from their home. Dan was only seven when there was an explosion at the mine and thirty -seven men and boys were killed. Fortunately his father and uncles were in back shift on the week of the disaster but many of their relatives and friends were not.

The mine was said to be one of the safest in the county but many of the miners had been uneasy for some weeks before the explosion. Dan never forgot the time he was playing with his brother, Harry, on the clipping mat in front of the fire. His mother, sitting on her favourite chair at one side of the fireplace nursing George his baby brother, his father squatting on the three legged cracket facing her. He was absorbed in a game of pop allies with Harry and taking very little notice of his parent's conversation until he heard the name `Fortesque`.

Mrs Fortesque had been at their school gates the day before telling him and his school friends to warn their fathers. She told them to tell them not to go to the pit, but to stay at home, as there would be a disaster in six days time. They had all laughed at the cranky old woman especially when the local bobby arrived and told her to go home and leave the lads alone.

Dan listened intently to his parents.

"Mrs Fortesque's always predictin' some tragedy hinnie," Dan's father continued. "The's nowt t' worry about. A've heard the stories but it's the explosions at

Seaham an' Trimdon pits that's mekin' the men uneasy an' not that silly woman."

"Why are some o' y' marrers not goin' in then?" Dan's mother asked.

Dan's father had no answer; he just shrugged his shoulders and turned away. After six days nothing happened at the colliery and the miners who had stayed away from the pit returned to work. Two weeks later there was a massive explosion in one of the seams at the pit. It was half past one in the morning; a drizzling rain was falling, and Dan was still awake. He had a sore throat, his chest hurt when he coughed and he could not breathe through his stuffy nose. The bed suddenly shuddered and Dan heard a loud boom. There was a clatter down in the kitchen and then he heard his mother and father hurrying down the stairs. His brother was still sleeping soundly and Dan knew there would be trouble if he got up. Curiosity soon got the better of him; he quietly opened the bedroom door, careful not to wake Harry, and crept down the stairs. The sneck was not caught onto the kitchen door; a slight push was all it needed, yes, if he closed one eye he could see what was happening over beside the fireplace. His mother was picking up the pieces of the two china dogs that had stood at each end of the mantelpiece for as long as he could remember. His mother said they had belonged to her mother and her mother before that. His father was already dressed and as he tied his pit boot laces he turned to Dan's mother.

"The's nowt y' can de hinnie," Dan heard his father say. "Get yersel' back t' bed wi' the bairn, it must be the pit; a'll away now an' see what's happenin'."

His father fastened his muffler round his neck and ran his fingers through his tousled hair before putting on his old and trusted cap, a present from his father many Christmases ago. This was a signal to Dan to return to bed before his mother spotted him. He tiptoed back up the stairs and jumped back into bed with his brother, the bed was warm but his head hurt, he tossed and turned but he could not settle. His head was full of thoughts of Mrs Fortesque, her tales of doom and disaster, and the two china dogs that had belonged to his great granny.

He heard his mother climbing the stairs, she settled the baby and then went straight back down to the kitchen.

"Somat's up," he thought to himself, but he was tired now and feeling his eyes closing mumbled. "She's lightin' the fire in the middle o' the night." Within seconds he was fast asleep.

Dan heard the full story two days later as he listened intently to his tired and bleary-eyed father and uncles telling his mother the tragic story of the events at the mine. He learnt just how many of their relatives, friends and neighbours had lost, husbands, fathers, sons, uncles and cousins.

Dan's father was a God fearing man, as were his brothers, they attended the Methodist chapel with him every Sunday and his father had taken the pledge, at least that is what Dan's friend Johnny had told him.

"Y' Da never drinks o' gambles like mine," he confided. "Me Da drinks like a fish an' sometimes he owes all his pay afore he gets it."

Dan's father had just returned from the mine and as he spoke he rubbed his tired eyes, smearing the coal dust on his blackened face.

"It's the first time in me life that a ever doubted whether the' was a God," he told Dan's mother as they sat around the kitchen table, the men with pint pots of tea, Dan's mother drinking from her china cup which, they all knew, was hers and hers alone.

Dan's father was doing most of the talking and Dan had been told to go out and play. Usually he did not need telling twice, any opportunity and he would be off, but on this occasion news about the explosion was far too interesting to miss. He hid in the pantry and, sitting on the cold cement floor, listened to the full story.

"How could there be a God, a' thought, that could tek so many o' me marrers?" his father continued. "A soon realised there must be mind, 'cos wi' out faith how will we be able to cope wi' the sorrows o' this tragedy."

Dan sat with bated breath willing his father to continue. His mates had told him some of the gory details but he wanted to know the full story. When he left school he wanted to work down the pit and, if he was to be a good worker like his father, he needed to know everything that had happened.

Dan's father was not an educated man, he could read and write, but his knowledge or interest did not extend farther than his own family and those people or things that had a direct bearing on him or his. As a local preacher, on Sundays, he would take the service at the local chapel and was often invited to preach in the neighbouring villages. Dan sometimes accompanied him and was so proud of his father, standing up in the pulpit looking down on Dan and the rest of the congregation, not just reading from the bible but telling them things in his own words, words they could understand and relate to their everyday lives.

Dan was proud of his father for other reasons. He was not just a pitman, he could write beautiful poetry, and often after Sunday tea he would read it to the family. It was about the people and the places they knew, the pit, the shops, the chapel, his school and best of all about the things Dan and his father saw when they went for walks in the surrounding countryside. They described the beauty of the trees, the flowers in the fields, the fish in the rivers, the birds in the sky and the animals in the fields. Some of his poetry was funny especially the ones about some of the people they

19

knew; they would all have a good laugh until his father told them sternly, with a glimmer of a smile, to shush.

Dan's father wiped the back of his hand across his cheek; it wiped away a single tear. Dan had never seen his father cry and was upset at seeing him looking so sad.

"When we got t' the pit," his father continued, "it was only about three quarters o' an hour since the explosion an' the' were ready t' gan down the shaft. A just managed t' get int' the cage wi' our Jack an' Will an' then we were nearly at the shaft bottom when it jammed. It was dangerous, but we had nee choice, we had t' get out an' slide down the guides t' the bottom. A couldn't believe me eyes when we reached them, we found one after the other, some alive, some dead, some weren't injured at all. A can't describe the look o' them that had been burnt. A can still hear the screams, some o' them had broken arms and legs, an' a couple o' them were all twisted and must have broken their backs. Mercifully the'd passed out. There's been a fall o' stone an' it`s all ower, it'll tek us a long time t' get them all out."

Dan was surprised when his father stopped talking; it was not often he let his younger brothers intervene. His uncle continued; his father too upset to continue.

"The' say the' was nearly five thousand folk at the pit head t' see what was happenin', seems a lot, but that's what th' say.The manager telt some o' the bank lads t' mek' a mortuary out o' the fittin' shops."

Dan thought his uncle was going to cry but after a few seconds he continued.

"We've got a lot o' them out but we'll have t' be away back when we've had a couple o' hours sleep an' a bite to eat."

It was two days later before all of the casualties, and the last of the dead, were brought to the pit head. The following morning, after his father had slept, Dan heard the rest of the story.

"It was hard work hinnie," his father told his mother. "Replacin' the stoppins an' cuttin' through falls o' stone but we finally reached the ponies. Out o' eighty three the' was only fifteen left alive. We found two young lads, still alive, wi' a dead pony 'atween them. Some 'o the dead, poor souls, were charred from head to foot but the last job we had t' de was the worst. We brought the dead up t' the pit head an' a doctor examined them. All we could de was wrap them in waddin' an' flannel an' put them in temporary coffins. Th' own families 'll have carried them home by now; a think."

That night was a turning point in Dan's life. The tragedy made such an impression on him that his attitude towards the future changed. Once more he lay awake, but not because of a cold, his head was full of the sorry tale his father had told. By the time he fell asleep he had made up his mind.

"A'm not gannin' down the pit like me Da, so a'd better not grow up like me Da."

Dan became a rebel; he played hard, did the least he could at school and hated going to chapel. Unfortunately, when he left school, he had little choice but to do as his father bid and he started work at the pit.

"Well," he thought to himself, "me Da can mek me gan down that black hole but he can't mek me like it."

By the time he was twenty Dan had married Sarah. Her family were builders and her grandfather and his brothers had seized the opportunity when new mines were being sunk in the surrounding countryside and a need had arisen for housing for the miners and their families who were moving into the area. Sarah lived with her parents only two miles from Dan's home but the difference in their families was so great it might have been two hundred miles. Her father owned the house they lived in, as did others, in the neat terrace that was so strikingly different from the rows built for the miners and the ironworkers.

Her father was not happy with her choice of husband, but Sarah was strong willed and determined to have her way. Her family had helped build the houses that sprang up like mushrooms in the developing town and the shops in the front street where a bustling weekly market thrived. They helped with the building of the railway station, places of entertainment, ballrooms and public houses and as the community grew they became involved in the building of a Town Hall and a theatre.

The miners at that time thought they were prosperous but not to the extent of Sarah's parents. Some earned as much as a pound a day as more collieries opened and the furnaces at the iron works were in full blast. As the families all came to the town to buy their provisions the shops prospered. Unfortunately these years of prosperity were not to last. Prices soared and the people rose in revolt. During 1892 the workers came out on strike and every industry in the area was silent for thirteen weeks, some for several months more.

It was during this year that Sarah's grandfather died and her uncles and their families left the area. Some moved as far away as London where the lucky ones were eventually to make their fortunes. Sarah's family stayed, someone had to look after her grandmother who was a strong willed old lady and Sarah's father often told Sarah when they had their numerous arguments.

"Y're just like your Granny."

Dan and Sarah spent the first three years of their married life living with Sarah's parents. They had the downstairs front room, comfortably furnished with a double bed, two upright chairs and a small table, which Dan's grandfather had given them on the day they were married. They took their meals with the rest of the family but Dan knew that he was never really accepted. He was a miner and Sarah's family had always felt themselves a cut above the miners and their families who, they thought, always lived for the day and never thought about the future. Dan was a regular worker but he still did not like the pit. Whilst the other miners respected it, and its hidden dangers, Dan still feared it.

When Harry and George left school they, like Dan, started working at the pit. They liked the work but neither could remember, as Dan could, that fateful week of the pit explosion.They were the apple of their father's eye, worked hard and went with him every Sunday to chapel. They had done well at school and their father saw a great future for them at the new bigger pits that were soon to open throughout the county. Harry idolised his big brother and hated to hear his father chastise him but George did not really care; as long as he was not on the wrong side of his father it did not matter to him who was.

Dan was not the son his father wanted him to be, he enjoyed a night out at the institute, frequented the many public houses in the town and was often the worse for wear after a night out on the booze and he only went to chapel for funerals or weddings. Harry and George had heard their father telling their mother that before he married Sarah Dan had been seen in the ballroom at the back of one of the public houses.

They had been married for over three years and Dan and Sarah could not believe what her father was saying to them.

"Old Hood owes me a favour."

As her father warmed his back beside the fire Dan could not hide his impatience. He understood that Sarah's father was a proud man and that times were not as easy for him

23

now as they had been; but he did ramble on. Dan could not wait for him to get to the point.

"A don't like askin' f' favours an' the's not the money around the' was; we're all scramblin' f' what little buildin' work there is, but y' Ma persuaded me to ask him."

He did not tell them that an argument with Sarah's mother on the rights and wrongs of asking for favours to be repaid had forced him to make a decision.

"If we don't see them settled in their own place soon an' gi' Dan some responsibility," she had argued, "the'll never mek out' o' themselves. Sometimes you have to forego your principles an' put y' own family first."

He had finally agreed but, as ever, fired a final shot at Dan.

"He'll more than likely drink hisel' int' an early grave, but you win, a'd better try. A can see that lass o' ours isn't happy an' she's nowt but skin an' bone."

Dan sighed; Sarah's father was finally getting to the news they had be waiting for.

"Hood's managed t' get a place for y't' rent. It's not much; just one up an' one down an' it needs a bit o' work. The folk that had it last must have liked livin' in a midden, but if we all pull together, we can mek somat o' it." Sarah's face brightened and her father thought he saw a glimmer of a smile.

"Somat a haven't seen f' many a moon," he thought.

"Where is it Da, which street?" Sarah asked.

"That's another thing, the' was nowt gannin' here, it's up the hill," he replied, not looking directly at either Sarah or Dan.

Dan and Sarah looked at each other, Dan face showed his anger, but he did not voice his thoughts.

"How the hell does the stupid bugger think a'm goin' t' get t' the pit from there."

Sarah was so exited that at last they were going to have a place of their own; her only doubt was that it would be a trail to get the weekly groceries and she would not be able to see her mother every day.

As if reading their thoughts Sarah's father continued.

"Afore y' say owt, a kna' what y're thinkin'; we'll get y' a bike Dan, it'll put an extra hour on y' day but you'll see, it'll be worth it."

What he did not say was that it would mean one less hour in the pub for Dan and anything to keep him away from his cronies pleased Sarah's father.

"Anyway the's rumours around that a big pit's t' open not three miles from there; y' could try an' get set on an' it should have a canny long life, not like the other little pits round here that's been gannin' down like ninepins f' years now."

Three weeks later Dan and Sarah moved into their new home and, true to his word, Sarah's father worked hard to make the house habitable.

"The's a long way t' go, but it couldn't get any worse than it was three weeks ago so it can only get better." Sarah muttered to herself as she scrubbed the bedroom floor for the third time.

Both of their families had contributed any pieces of furniture they could spare. Curtains, towels and blankets seemed to appear by magic and much to their own and everyone else's surprise Dan and Sarah soon settled into the village way of life. Dan still liked a pint, and a night out with his mates, but it was not a regular occurrence. He acquired an allotment and the other gardeners taught him, 'the tricks of the trade', he told Sarah. He planted potatoes, leeks, carrots and parsnips and could not wait for the day when he could surprise Sarah, and her father, with their own home grown vegetables.

"It'll be fine if a have enough t' give t' the rest o' the family," he told one of his fellow gardeners as they worked the land, sometimes long after the sun had set.

The allotments did hold another attraction for Dan; one that Sarah had no idea about. Most of the men had built a shed in the corner of their allotment, 'for storin' gear,' he had told her. Some had coal boilers and were furnished with old tables and chairs; the sheds were used summer and winter and many a week's wages were lost at a so called friendly game of cards.

Sarah soon had the house 'Ship Shape and Bristol fashion' as her granddad used to say. She black leaded the great shining kitchen range at least once a week. So proud was Sarah of this tiny house that was now their home. She scoured and whitened the hearth, polished the complicated fire – irons, fender, tidy and tongs. Scrubbing the floors and cleaning the knives with emery paper, at first a weekly chore, became a pleasure. The kitchen was beginning to look like a kitchen with the table covered in oilcloth and pushed up against the window to create more space. Her father had bought them a press, a horse-hair sofa and a sewing machine, all second hand but with many more years use in them.

As she often did, Sarah surveyed her morning's work, smiled and muttered.

"Aye, tonight when he comes in from the pit a'll tell him about the bairn."

Sarah was now sure she was going to have a baby and the only person she had told was Hannah.

Hannah lived three doors away, she was ten years older than Sarah, and became a good friend from the very first day they moved to the village. Dan had no problems finding friends. Some of the men from the allotments worked at the same pit and as he liked a pint, or two, the men in the village community quickly accepted him.

At first Sarah thought the day would never come when the villagers would stop and pass the time of day with her; it was always a curt 'good morning, good day or goodnight.'

"My," Sarah would say to herself, "you'd think a was from the other end o` the country not just three miles away."

However, she was settled, the house was much improved and she and Dan were together. Sarah knew Dan had never been happy living with her parents.

Hannah's family had lived in the village for as long as anyone could remember; she knew everyone and everyone knew her. Hannah was loud mouthed; could give as much as she could take and 'swore like a trouper' but her home was a happy one. She sometimes found it hard to make ends meet and Joe, her husband, and their six young children were a lively lot. Joe worked at the pit, like Dan he liked his beer, but he always ensured there was food on the table.

"Claes aren't important," he would tell Hannah if she asked for more money. "As long as the bairns a' well fed the'll survive."

Hannah had promised Sarah she would not breathe a word until Sarah was sure. Well now she was, three months gone, and as Hannah had said to her only yesterday.

"Bustin' t' tell him; scared stiff an' sick as a pig every mornin'."

When Sarah and Dan were first married they had talked about the family they would have one day but Dan had not mentioned it since they had moved to the village and Sarah knew he was disappointed. Every time she tried to discuss it, and voice her fears, he would change the subject or put his coat on, kiss her on the cheek, and go to the pub or the allotments. Eventually she stopped trying to talk to him about it, but she knew it was always there, a barrier between them.

Her father made matters worse when she and Dan made their monthly visit to her parent's home for Sunday tea. After Sunday dinner it was always the same, Dan would go to the allotment while Sarah cleared the dinner dishes and tidied the kitchen.She would be on tender hooks until he returned, always at the last minute and, with some lame excuse. Instead of a leisurely walk to her parents they would hurry, so as not to be late for tea, and end up with an argument which always made the atmosphere worse than it already was at her parents' home.

Sarah's two sisters were married and the conversation was always the same.

"Florrie has a bonnie baby girl," her father told them every month. "An' it won't be long afore our Maisie gi's us another grandbairn. When a' you two goin' to gi' us one?"

Sometimes their visit would clash with one of her sisters and on those occasions she and Dan ended the day with another argument, the reason so trivial, neither of them knowing why they were lying in bed, staring at the wall, both too stubborn to turn over and say sorry.

Sarah had no brothers and her father was bitterly disappointed when, after their third daughter was born, her mother had been told another child could kill her. Sarah knew he looked forward to having a grandson but even if she understood her father's feelings she hated their Sunday teas and her father's constant jibes.

"It's strange," she once said to Hannah, "Dan never suggests we visit his Ma an' Da on a Sunday."

It was not strange really, at least not to Dan. He often visited his mother but only when he knew his father would be at work. He avoided his father like the plague.

"A can't stand him lecturin' me about the demon drink an' gamblin's a sin an' a short cut to meetin' the devil," he told Joe.

But strangely, for all his disapproval of Dan, unlike Sarah's father, Dan's father was a regular visitor to Dan and Sarah's tiny but spotless home.

When Dan was in fore shift he usually went straight to bed after dinner. He hated getting up at one o'clock in the morning, riding his bike to the pit, spending a long shift hewing coal, and then another bike ride before he was back home. No matter what time of day he arrived home, Sarah always had plenty of hot water ready in the tin bath in front of the kitchen fire for Dan to wash away the dirt of each day's labour and today was no exception. Sarah placed Dan's dinner in front of him as he sat, as always, at the same place at the kitchen table.

"A like t' face the window," he had told her on the first day they had moved into their new home, "a like to see what's happenin' in the outside world."

Sarah had smiled, and turning away muttered.

"There's nowt much o' the outside world t' see out there bonny lad."

The view from their kitchen window encompassed the path to the allotments and, dependant on who was on the pathway, Dan would decide whether or not to have half an hours gardening before he went to bed. Sarah sugared Dan's tea and as she placed it down beside his dinner she thought to herself.

"Not t'day me bonny lad a've somat t' tell y', somat more important than all the potatoes in the farmers fields, never mind y' allotment."

Dan ate his dinner, pondering over each mouthful; he was more tired than usual today.

"It's been a hell o' a shift," he said to Sarah.

Sarah poured herself a cup of tea and sitting on the chair at the side of the fireplace she could see the side of his face.

"He does look tired," she thought, "maybe a better wait 'til tomorrow night."

Dan turned to face Sarah noteing the spotless kitchen.

"Too bloody spotless," he thought, "but she's nowt else better t' de."

Sarah spoke first.

"Tired are y' t'day?" she asked as she stared into the fire.

"Aye its bin a rough un," Dan replied, "we hit some stone an' it'll tek a canny few more shifts afore we're through, a think a'll away t' bed as soon as a've finished me dinner."

Sarah cleared the table, he would not be up until six o'clock, how was she going to contain herself for another four hours?

Hannah never popped in on afternoon when Dan was in fore shift. On the only occasion she had, she said she would talk quietly but Dan had not managed to get one wink of sleep. The next time Hannah came, when Dan was in bed, Sarah made an excuse that she was busy and did not have time to gossip. No offence was taken by the good natured Hannah her own husband had the same problem.

When she or the bairns made a noise when Joe was trying to sleep he would bang on the bedroom floor; his way of saying, 'keep quiet down there.' They all knew that if they did not, he would come down stairs, one of the little ones would get a clip around the ear and then there would be silence for the rest of the day. A silence Hannah could not bear; Joe would not speak to her for two days, the whole families bottom lips would be tripping them up, then he would walk in from the pit as if nothing had happened and the merry go round would start all over again.

"At least this way," he told Dan, "a get two days sleep a week."

Dan lay awake, too weary to sleep. He hated the pit especially when it was going badly but he rarely mentioned his work to Sarah even though he knew she was aware of his fears.

"Anyway", he said to himself, "the pits best left at the pit."

But something else was troubling him, Sarah had been different these last few days, something he could not put his finger on, it was if she had something on her mind.

"It can't be somat a've done," he mumbled, "a wonder if any o' her lots been up rubbin' salt in the wounds."

Dan knew she was as disappointed as he was that they did not have a family of their own but for some reason he could not talk to her about it. He knew it was something they should discuss but they never did. Dan turned on his side; his eyes were heavy and every bone in his body ached. As he drifted off to sleep his thoughts were still on Sarah.

"We'll see how the land lies tonight," he told himself, "but a suppose a better try an' find out what's botherin' her."

Sarah sat in front of the fire; she had decided against popping down to Hannah's knowing full well that as soon as she got there she would want to be back. The dishes were washed and the housework finished. She had old sheets and blankets hidden away but she was afraid to get the sewing machine out and start sewing the baby sheets and blankets until she had told him. She heard Dan stirring upstairs and her stomach started to churn. Sometimes, if he could not sleep, he would get up and go back to bed earlier at night.

"This might be one o' those days," she hoped; but it was wishful thinking, there was no sign of Dan coming down the stairs.

Sarah stared at the glowing fire making pictures out of the flames; just as she had done as a child when she and her sisters each tried to see what the other could see. Sometimes the devil; old men with big ears, old women with warts on their noses, dogs, cats and even God himself.

Dan woke with a start; it was dark in the room even though the curtains were not closed. They never closed the bedroom curtains. When they were first married Sarah had closed them before they went up to bed, but Dan had never ever slept with the curtains closed. For the first few weeks it was a ritual, Sarah closed the curtains and Dan opened them before he got into bed. After a few weeks Sarah gave in and now she would not have it any other way. Sarah never let Dan sleep more than four hours on an afternoon and he always relied on her to wake him.

"Where the hell's she' got to, she knows a like two o' three hours on a night afore a go t' work," he grumbled as he pulled on his trousers. "A'll never sleep tonight, if she's down Hannah's gossipin' an` spoilin' them bairns o' hers there'll be hell on."

He ran down the stairs and was surprised to find the kitchen in darkness.

"Even the bloody fire's just about out," he grumbled. "A threw a bucketful o' coal on the fire back afore a went t' bed, she could have raked some down."

As he bent towards the fire, to pick up the rake, he was startled as Sarah stirred in the chair.

"Good God woman," he shouted, "are y' tryin' t' frighten the bloody day lights out o' me? What the hell's the matter? The fires nearly out, y've let me sleep in an' by the look o' it there's nowt ready to eat."

Sarah sat bolt upright and for the first time in their married life told him to go to hell and make his own tea.

Dan was astonished at this new Sarah, one he had never seen before. He stood with his shoulders back, the coal rake in his hand. Sarah was not frightened; she rose from her chair, walked straight past him, through the kitchen door and upstairs to their bedroom. Sarah sat on the edge of the bed; she rarely cried and since marrying Dan she had had very little to cry about. He did not confide in her often; nor did he talk to her about things that, as he thought, did not concern her but Sarah did not mind. Dan never kept her short of money, as many of the miners did with their wives, and as long as his meals were there when he wanted them he rarely ever complained. Staring into the darkness her tears finally came; she cried until she thought her heart would break.

"A hate him," she sobbed, her chest and stomach aching like toothache. " He can mek his own meals from now on or starve t' death, an' he can see t' the fire hi'sel`."

Dan sat stubbornly in the chair that Sarah had so abruptly vacated. The fire was black and he shivered. He could hear Sarah sobbing and he wanted to go and comfort her but it was not in his nature. He would not know what to say and he knew if he tried he would not be able to say what he really felt; one thing would lead to another and he would probably make matters worse than they were.

"Best clean the fire out," he grumbled, "then a'll get the kettle on an' mek' her a nice cup o' tea for when she comes down."

Two hours passed and still Sarah did not come downstairs. Dan thought back to earlier that afternoon when he had decided that he was going to ask her tonight if something was wrong.

"Aye the's somat up wi' her, a best go an' find out."

The fire was now roaring up the chimney; the kettle was boiling and as he put the tea leaves in the teapot and the cups on the table Dan realised that this was something he had never done before. Still grumbling to himself he poured a cup of tea and took it upstairs to Sarah.

When he saw her lying across the bed, seemingly fast asleep, he felt sad but did not know why. She looked so small, her face, which was not beautiful, 'a sensible look' he had heard people say, was puffy and her eyes swollen. He had always thought her pretty, although he had never told her so. Her hair, usually neatly tied back in a bun, had fallen about her shoulders and as Dan gently stroked the sides of her face with the back of his hand he spoke to her.

"What's the matter hinnie, a've never known y' gan on like this afore?"

Sarah did not stir and Dan, feeling confused both with his own feelings, and as to whether she was asleep or ignoring him, put the cup of tea down and turned to walk out of the room. As he crossed the landing he muttered.

"Y're a stubborn bugger Dan."

At the same time Sarah called his name; he turned, rushed back into the bedroom, tripped on the corner of the little clipping mat and ended up face down along side Sarah.

They were often to talk about that night.

"It was fate hinnie," he often told her, "if a'd never tripped on that bloody mat we still might not be talkin'."

As they looked at each other words were not necessary. Dan stared into Sarah's eyes and whispered.

"What's the matter hinnie?"

Twenty minutes later, after they enjoyed the best lovemaking they had ever known, Sarah was in no doubt of Dan's love for her.

"What's wrong hinnie?" Dan repeated.

"A've just been silly," Sarah told him, "a must have just dropped off in front o' the fire, it wont happen again, a promise," Sarah answered; feeling embarrassed not just about the last twenty minutes but her behaviour over the last few hours.

"That's not what a'm on about," Dan chided. "The's somat up, you've been funny f' a few days now, come to think about it f' the last few weeks."

Sarah knew the time was right to tell him. She wished their marriage could always be like this but, as always, decided it was not Dan's fault; the fault was all hers.

34

"A'm, a mean we," she stuttered, as she always did when feeling nervous, "a'm going t' have a bairn."

"You're what?" Dan shouted. "How long have y' known? Are y' telling me you've just let me do, y' kna what, a might have hurt y' or the bairn."

"It's alright Dan," Sarah smiled, "y' won't 'ave done any harm to either o' us."

Dan jumped out of the bed then back in, he was so happy he did not know where he wanted to be or what to say.

"Are y' sure?" he questioned her. "Y' haven't made a mistake?"

"I'm sure Dan, an' a'm alright." She replied as she encircled him in her arms, a show of affection rare for Sarah. "Now let's gan downstairs, a'll wash me face an' brush me hair an' then we'll have a nice pot o' tea."

Dan sat on the cracket beside the fire and as he looked at the clock he shouted.

"My God, Sarah look at the bloody time, it's time a was away to work."

"Can't y' give it a miss f' once Dan? " Sarah asked, as she mashed the tea. "Y've never missed a shift since the day we were wed."

"A daren't miss a shift 'cos from now on we'll need every penny." Dan replied.

But he knew, that for once, he should give Sarah her way, on this night of all nights she wanted him at home with her and he would do as she asked. Speaking softly, he winked at her.

"If a dinna gan now a'll miss the cage, A think a might a've already missed it."

Sarah sighed; this was Dan's way of saying.

"Alreet tonight y' can have y' way."

As she turned away from him she felt the tears prickling behind her eyes, they were tears of joy, and the tone of her voice demonstrated her happiness as she said to Dan.

"A'll mek a bite o' supper an' then we'll have an early night."

It was not to be an early night. It was after midnight when Dan banked the fire and Sarah turned off the lamp. They climbed the stairs together, bubbling over with happiness about their future, closer now than they had ever been. As they lay awake Dan spoke to Sarah about the child that he and Sarah were soon to have.

"If it's a lass a'll work every hour that God sends t' see she doesn't want, but if it's a lad there'll be ne pit f' him. From the day he's born he'll learn that there has t' be a better life in store for a son of ours."

Sarah did not answer but if she had there would have been no mention of a girl; it had never once entered her head that their first child would be anything other than a boy.

Chapter 2

Sarah and Dan spent the following months preparing for the arrival of their baby. Every waking minute Sarah's thoughts were on the day when she and Dan would have a son. Hannah, in her good natured way, laughed at her.

"Y' silly bugger, wait 'til y've as many as me; y'll not have time f' day dreamin`. Y'll not gi' a damn what it is as long as it's alright. Y'll see' it'll just be another bloody mouth t' feed."

Sarah laughed, she knew Hannah loved all of her children and would not be without any of them. Hannah's reply was as ever on the defensive.

"Aye that's right, laugh, a love em now a`ve got 'em, but it was a different story when a fund out a was ganna have em."

Dan was just as happy as Sarah, he had never seen her look so beautiful or to be more contented. Even working down the pit had a new meaning to him. He still feared it, but accepted that it was the only way he could provide for Sarah and the child they soon would have.

Unlike previous visits to his mothers Dan made sure it would be when his father was at home. He wanted them both to hear his good news.

"Me Ma an` me Da are thrilled t' bits," he told Sarah who was waiting anxiously for his return. "Me Ma says she hopes it's a lass, a think she's wantin' t' spoil it wi' bonny dresses an' hats an' things. Even me Da talked t' us about whether it would be a lass o' a lad."

His mother was pleased with their news and was overjoyed that Dan had finally visited when his father was at home.

"Might be the makin's o' y' yet lad," had been his father's first response.

On this occasion Dan's father's attitude towards him did not upset him.

"Aye Da," was his simple reply.

Harry, Dan's brother had married the previous year and lived near to his parents. He and Kate had been childhood sweethearts and both families had always expected them to marry.

"Our Harry's non too happy at the minute, livin' wi' her Ma an' Da, the's those three strappin' brothers o' hers an' her two sisters, it can't be much fun." Dan's mother told him when once more he visited both of his parents.

Dan's parents had offered Harry and Kate a home with them, but George was the problem. Harry much preferred living with Kate's three brothers and two sisters to living with George.

Dan jumped as the back gate clashed but he was not surprised when George walked through the back door and his mother quickly changed the subject. The youngest of the three brothers was now eighteen and the last time Dan had seen Harry he had mentioned George.

"Soft as clarts is our George," Harry had told Dan. "He's courtin' a lass from up the blocks; right under her thumb he is. Me Ma's non too happy but me Da thinks she's the bees knees, teaches at Sunday School; a right little Miss Prim an' Proper. A tell y' what Dan me an' him's not gettin' on these days."

Dan's mother spoke as she struggled to ease herself up in the chair.

"By me pains are bad t'day lad, but never mind about that tell our George y' good news."

His mother had not told George believing that it was Dan and Sarah's business and it was only right for them to have the pleasure of breaking their news. This was the first time Dan had noticed how old his mother looked.

"Not just old," he thought to himself, "she looks bad, a'll have t' have a word wi' me Da when he's on his own an' see what he thinks."

Dan turned to George and with a smile on his face told him about the baby. His smile soon vanished as George curtly replied.

"'Bout time."

Before Dan could answer George turned to his mother.

"A'm not stoppin'," he told her, "Jennie'll be waitin' f' me. We'll be back when we land, a only came in t' get me coat, its cold out there."

As George left, banging the kitchen door behind him, Dan turned to his father who had followed George into the house.

"What's up wi' him?" Dan asked.

As usual his father's reply was in defence of his youngest son.

"Nowt lad," his father looked away as he spoke, "it's just that Jennie an' him'll be ganin't' the chapel. It's her turn this week t' de a bit o' cleanin' ready f' Sunday an' he likes t' help her. Y' na what a good lad he is."

Dan's mother turned away from him and his father. She did not speak; the look on her face confirmed what Harry had told Dan.

Dan left a few minutes after George. George had ruined his visit and there was now an uncomfortable atmosphere between himself and his parents.

"A'd better be off." Dan told them as he put his cap on. "Next time a'll fetch Sarah wi' me, that's if she's up t' it."

Telling his mother to look after herself and nodding to his father, Dan left the same way he had entered by the back door. As he walked down the cobbled back street his thoughts were on his mother. Quietly voicing them he muttered.

"My she looks bad a hope me Da comes up next week, a'll ask Sarah to have a word wi' him an' a'll mention it t' our Harry next time a see him. It'll be no good tryin' t' talk to that other selfish sod, he cares f' nebody but hisel' an' that bloody Jennie."

After a brisk walk home his anger subsided and not wanting to upset Sarah he said very little to her. He told her his mother did not look well and suggested that she go with him on his next visit but thought it best not to mention George other to say he was pleased with their good news.

The next few months could not pass quickly enough for Sarah. By the time she was eight months pregnant she had everything prepared. The house was spick and span, her unborn baby had clothes and bedding, every stitch sewn by Sarah and neatly folded in the new set of drawers demonstrating her love of the expected new addition to their family.

Dan had surprised her with the drawers, she did not think they could afford them but he had insisted. They had seen them in a shop on a rare day out at Durham. Sarah had not asked for them; she only commented that they were exactly the type she would have liked for the baby's clothes if they could afford them. Dan had not   stopped talking about them for a fortnight and now here they were in their bedroom.

"Its t' fetch us good luck," he told her when they arrived. "The first thing we've ever had brand new an' its f' the bairn."

Dan not only surprised Sarah but he surprised himself with his new found skills. He became quite handy with a saw and a hammer and nails.

"A'd never o' thought in a thousand years a could turn me hand t' owt like this," he told one of his fellow gardeners as he put the last touch of paint on the cot he had made.

One of the older men in the village had been only too pleased to demonstrate his joinery skills.

"A'll teach y' a few tricks o' the trade an' then y'll be away," he had told Dan.

Dan now had his own shed in the corner of his allotment and like the others it was used all hours of the day but, unlike the other gardeners, his was to hide the new cot he was making for the baby. Sarah would soon know that he did not waste his time playing cards and gambling, he was a family man and family came first.

"A'm dyin't' see her face in the mornin' when the paints dry an' a tek this along home for her," he shouted to Joe as he passed Dan's allotment.

"Aye marrer, she'll be thrilled t' bits, trouble is Hannah'll be on at me t' get me finger out an' mek somat for her," Joe jokingly replied.

Four weeks later Rob was born. It was an easy birth; Sarah was soon back to normal; a picture of health and proud of her new child who was, as she told everyone, 'peace itself.'

Sarah had wanted to call him Daniel after his father but this was one round Dan intended to win. Sitting on the edge of the bed and holding his son for the first time he gently scolded her.

"No Sarah he'll not be named after me or anybody else, come up wi' a name that's not in my family or yours then y' can choose it."

It seemed to Sarah an impossible task but before she had settled down for the night she had decided on Robert.

"A don't think the's any Roberts in either o' our families Dan so we'll christen him Robert and call him Rob, not Bob mind y', Rob Charlton, a think that has a nice ring t' it don't you?"

Dan smiled the name suited him, his son was a one off, and he was not going to have him called after anyone but himself. Hannah was the first visitor to arrive and Joe soon followed her.

"A've come t' see if he's the little angel Dan's mekin' him out t' be," he told Sarah.

Hannah quickly intervened.

"He is Joe, he's not like our lot, y' can tell he's not goin' t' be a bit o' bother."

Hannah nudged Joe in the ribs and quickly hurried him out of the house.

"What's the rush?" he asked as they hurried next door.

"It's you y' stupid bugger a knew what y'd do, y'll go an' knock all the pleasure out o' it f' them."

Sarah's mother arrived soon after Rob was born and stayed for the traditional two week 'lying in period'.

"A never thought a'd be s' pleased t' see the back o' her," Dan told Hannah, "a never got a look in, every time a went t' pick him up she telt me a was spoilin' him, a don't know how Sarah's puts up wi' her, if she had her way a wouldn't look at him, never mind spoil him."

If it had not been for the deterioration of his mother's health nothing would have spoilt the happiness Dan shared with Sarah and Rob over the coming months. Rob was nine months old when Dan's father told him that not only were his mother's pains becoming unbearable but also she seemed to be losing her mind.

"She's f'gettin' things all o'the time lad, she can remember when you three were bairns but if a've told her once a've told her a thousand times about Rob an' every time a tell her y'd think it was the first. A daren't leave on her own too long so if a'm not up as often y' kna' why.

She's not steady on her feet an' the neighbours keep an eye on her when a'm at work but a can't be too bad an' put on em all the time, so when a'm off a like to see t' her mesel'."

As far as Dan was concerned Rob's first year was the best year in his life.

"That's another rough one ower," he said to his marrer as they crossed the pit yard. "A'll be pleased when a'm in bed tonight."

Even the pit, which he still hated, had a new meaning to Dan, it was work and it provided for him and his family. Dan got on his bike and set off home.

"This bloody bike ride's still a killer," he muttered, "but at least the's money comin' in, an' the's food on the table, an' a'm pleased we sometimes have a bit left ower for Sarah t' buy Rob little bits an' pieces. A've the pit t' thank for that, if nowt else, some poor folk have nowt."

Sarah smiled at Rob.

"Y' Da'll be in soon bonny lad," she told him.

It was Rob's first birthday and he was Sarah's world.

"Never a day's illness an' he's slept right through on a night since he was eight weeks old," she proudly informed her neighbours. "You'd think he knew what shift his Da was on, 'cos he's never once woke him up."

Hannah worried about Sarah.

"One o' these days her bubble'll burst," she confided in Joe, "she's too dammed happy."

Dan arrived home to a familiar scene. Sarah had been up since the crack of dawn, the fire was roaring up the chimney, the water red hot for his bath and his breakfast cooking. Rob was playing on the mat throwing the potatoes, which he preferred to toys, into two large saucepans. As soon as Dan appeared his little arms reached out for him. On fine days Dan often took him to the allotments and he revelled in the attention he received from Dan's fellow gardeners.

"Not t'day me bonnie lad," Dan told him as he took off his pit boots, "y' Da's had a rough un; as soon as a've had a bath an' somat t' eat a'm off t' bed. Birthday or no birthday a need me sleep, your Ma can entertain y', a'll play wi' y' f' an hour when a get up f' me dinner."

Sarah always got up early; she preferred to do some of the housework before Rob was awake, the sooner it was done the more time she had to spend with him. She looked forward to time alone with Rob; singing nursery rhymes, telling him stories, talking to him or just nursing him until he quietly nodded off to sleep while she sang a lullaby.

> "Ride a cock horse to Banbury Cross.
> To see a fine lady upon a white horse.
> Wi' rings on her fingers an' bells on her toes.
> She shall have music wherever she goes."

Rob would gurgle and laugh as Sarah bounced him on her knee waiting for his favourite; Bonnie Bobbie Shafto. Sarah always substituted Rob's name and, although it was his favourite, he would always be fast asleep before she reached the third verse. Today was his birthday but, as far as Sarah was concerned, it was no different from any other day, everyday was Rob's day.

> "Robbie Charlton's bright an' fair," she sang.
> "Combin' down his yellow hair.
> He's my ain for evermair.
> Hey for Robbie Charlton.

> Robbie Charlton went to court.

All in gold an' silver wrought.
Like a grandee as he ought.
Bonnie Robbie Charlton.

All the ribbons flyin' about.
All the ladies lookin' out.
Clappin' their hands an' givin' a shout.
Hurrah for Robbie Charlton."

When Rob was sleeping soundly Sarah said a simple prayer.

"Thanks God for givin' me an' Dan Rob, we might not visit the chapel regular but that doesn't mean we don't believe in y'. Sometimes a think we believe in y' more than them does go every Sunday."

Even though Rob was sleeping Sarah continued her rhyme.

"Robbie Charlton rode a race.
Well a mind his bonnie face.
Won it in a tearin' pace.
Bonnie Robbie Charlton.

Robbie Charlton throws his gold.
Right an' left like Knights o' old.
Now we're left out in the cold.
Bonnie Robbie Charlton.

Robbie Charlton's gone to sea.
Silver buckles on his knee.
When he comes back he'll marry me.
Bonnie Robbie Charlton."

Being careful not to disturb Rob, Sarah raked some coal down from the fire back. She was an expert at holding him in one arm and raking the coal onto the fire without ever having to leave her chair. Afternoons were hers and Rob's; she sang to him and told him stories even when he was sleeping. When he was not she was ever mindful that he was too young to understand much of what she was telling him. Looking down at the sleeping child she spoke.

"When y' Da gets up we'll have a special tea, so one more story an' then it's down y' go, we want everythin' to be ready for when he gets up. We'll have the Bobbie Shafto story again, that's the one a like best mesel'. Aye bonnie lad, you're not fair like Bobbie was supposed t' be but y're my bonnie lad."

Rob had a mass of black curls and green eyes like hers. Apart from that he was the image of Dan. Dan was fair with blue eyes but everything else about Rob was Dan. She had even heard her father, who would not admit it to her or Dan, comment to her mother.

"Aye, a hate t' say it but, he's the pop model o' Dan."

Hannah often listened, as patiently as she could, when Sarah extolled Rob's many virtues but unable to keep quiet too long she would interrupt Sarah.

"Aye the's no mistakin' who his Da is Sarah but when he grows up do y' not think he might be a bit like Bobbie Shafto? He hears y' singin' that ditty often enough."

Sarah's reply would be a firm.

"Aye, Hannah but not exactly like him mind y', a 'm not havin' him gannin' off to sea. His Da says no pit well a say no sea."

Sarah wriggled and made herself comfortable in the chair and snuggling a sleeping Rob close to her breast she continued the story.

"It was well over a hundred years ago that Bobbie Shafto lived at Spennymoor. It wasn't Spennymoor then bonnie lad, at least not as we know it, it was all fields an' Bobbies house was the only one. It's still there today;

Whitworth Hall th'call it. He went wi' a lass from Brancepeth Castle but he left her t' gan to London. She always thought he would come back f' her an' the' say she used t' sing the song a sing to you; wi' Bobbies name mind not yours. The' say he was a flashy feller, wore dandy clothes an' was a bit o' a ladies man; seemin'ly he lost all o' his money gamblin' so he married a rich lady from Yorkshire. That's miles away Rob, me an' y' Da's never been but mebbe one day y'll gan there. Anyway th' say that when the lass from Brancepeth heard he'd gone an' got hisel' married she died o' a broken heart. A don't want you t' be like him in that bit o' the story Rob but the next bit you can be. He brought his wife back t' Whitworth Hall t' live wi' him there an' he finally settled down. The' had a little lad an' Bobby became the Member o' Parliament for the whole o' Durham County. So y' see bonnie lad we've had a famous feller from around here an' all these years after we still sing about him. A wonder if the'll still sing about him in another hundred years?"

That night, much to Sarah's surprise, Dan was up an hour earlier than usual. She heard him moving around upstairs and muttered.

"He's never up 'til a shout o' him".

"Y' dinners no where near ready, y' not usually up 'til five," Sarah shouted up the stairs as she put Rob safely down in his cot and hurried across the kitchen to put the already prepared stew and potatoes onto the fire.

She had not really thought, as far as Dan was concerned, that today would be different from any other. He had to work and sleep the same as all of the other miners. If there was to be anything different to be done then it would be her place to do it. Even her father never altered his routine; no matter what the occasion. The only time she could remember Dan altering his routine was the day she told him she was going to have a baby. Their days were never any different, if it was two o'clock on an afternoon or two o'clock in the morning Dan's meal and bath were ready when he came home from the pit.

Dan came down stairs fully dressed and, as he fastened his muffler, spoke to his sleeping son.

"Watch me vex y' Ma, but dinna worry a'll be back sharpish an' then we'll put a smile on her face."

As he went out of the back door he shouted to Sarah.

"A'm away along t' the allotment." Sarah's eyes prickled as she fought back the tears.

"A thought y' Da was up early 'cos o' y' birthday," she told a now awake and crying Rob. "Never mind bonnie lad, by he's back his dinner'll be ready an' then we'll have some o' them jam tarts an' the little cakes Hannah showed me how t' mek."

Ten minutes later Dan was back and Sarah's face was a picture, at least that's what he told her later that night.

"My but its lovely, lets gi' him a ride, it puts me birthday tea in the shade," she told Dan; thinking as she nervously kissed his cheek, 'he is different from the others.'

Dan lifted Rob up onto the Rocking Horse and as he fastened him on to the saddle and placed his tiny feet into the stirrups he looked lovingly at Sarah.

"A needed a bit o' help 'cos a couldn't have managed it on me own an' it's a bit rough 'round the edges but it's not bad for a beginner is it Sarah? A done most o' it me sel'."

Sarah thought she would burst with happiness and felt more than a little guilty for doubting him.

"That's why a've been out as much lately, mind Sarah, me allotment's suffered so a'll have t' get stuck in there for the next few weeks."

Sarah could not have cared if they if they did not have another home grown vegetable until Rob was two years old. They held Rob, taking it in turn to push the horse, laughing together until Sarah screamed.

"Dan the pans," she ran to the fire and removing the pans with an old jumper sleeve laughed as she told him, "burnt offerin's t'night Dan."

Dan lifted Rob from the horse and carrying him across the kitchen he looked into the pans and joined Sarah in her laughter.

"Never mind hinnie," he told her, "salvage what y' can, a'll fill up wi'y' fancy cakes an' if the's any left the'll de for me bait."

When Dan left for work he was a happy man, he even thanked the Lord for the pit that gave him the means to make a home for Sarah and Rob.

Rob was so excited with his birthday present it took Sarah longer than usual to get him off to sleep. It was a tired Sarah who finally climbed the stairs after tidying the house and preparing the kitchen for Dan's return from work the following morning. When he came home tired and hungry his breakfast and bath would be ready before he climbed into bed for a well earned rest.

Rob's first birthday set the scene for the next two years. Dan and Sarah devoured his every milestone, his first steps, his first words and the mischief he got up to. Her days became busier than ever. When the weather was fine Rob would play in the tiny backyard made safe, by Dan, with a sturdy wooden gate. He liked nothing better than playing with Hannah's younger children while Sarah and Hannah sat and gossiped.

"Puttin' the world t' rights again are y'." Joe would shout over the yard wall.

Rob cried when the older children would not play their games with him but he was the centre of attention when they played 'dressy up' and Hannah supplied their costumes.

"Some o' them's s' dirty an' raggy," Sarah said to Dan one night, when telling him of Rob's perfect day, "y'd think Joe had been down the pit in 'em."

Whatever the children imagined themselve's to be and whatever scene they invented Rob was always the baby and so gained their full attention. It was after Rob's third escape from the backyard a tearful Sarah insisted.

"Y' next job Dan, since you're such a clever carpenter, is the back gate y've been promisin' us."

On one of their happy afternoons Hannah, who had Rob on her knee playing, 'down at the bottom of the deep blue sea', casually remarked to him.

"A think it's about time y' Ma an' Da got y' a little brother or sister to play wi'."

Rob whooped as Hannah continued.

"Catchin' fishes for me tea, by one, two an' a three."

Sarah pretended she had not heard the remark and Hannah, thinking it must be a touchy subject, never mentioned it again. Sarah had not even discussed having more children with Dan. He often playfully said to Rob. "We'll have t' get y' a little sister t' play wi'."

Sarah would pretend she had not heard and busy herself in the kitchen totally ignoring Dan and Rob. Dan was aware that she must have heard and it often crossed his mind that she never talked about having another child but he shrugged it off; he was happy with Rob.

"Everythin's alreet in bed," he told himself, "so mebe she does want another, we'll just have t' wait an' see what happens."

Rob was Sarah's world and at the moment she did not want another child intruding on what she and Rob shared. She knew she was being selfish, and often felt guilty.

"If another little lad comes along Rob we'll love him wont we?" she told him as she put him to bed that night.

Dan's next big project was to build his son a bogey. Looking just a little guilty he told Sarah.

"A found some old wheels in the pit yard."

Sarah made no comment when he brought them home although she thought they looked rather new to be lying around the pit yard. Least said, soonest mended she thought, and left him to get on with making the little wooden cart. As soon as he had finished Dan started to make a sledge.

"F' when the snow comes," he proudly told Hannah.

Sarah's attitude and words to Hannah were different.

"He's goin' t' end up killin' him, expectin' him t' ride bogeys an' sledges afore he can hardly walk."

Dan now visited his parents every Sunday morning and as soon as Rob was big enough to sit on his father's shoulders the three mile walk included him.

"We'll gan an' see y' Grannie", Dan would tell his son. "She mightn't seem as if she knas us anymore but y' Granda says she always picks up a bit after you've been t' see her. Anyway y' Granda likes t' see y' an' he can't come up hisel' much now."

Dan's mother's health was deteriorating and when George and Jennie married they intended to live with Dan's parents to help care for his mother.

"D' y' think it'll be alright?" Dan questioned Harry. "A kna me Ma never liked her much, although she never said so, but a don't suppose that'll make a lot o' difference now. Me Da's always thought a lot o' her an' it'll make his life a lot easier, he'll be able to go t' work wi' an easy mind, an' mebee start t' preach a bit on a Sunday again."

One fine Sunday morning the bogey was displayed in the back yard and Sarah's worries were dispelled. The wood was as smooth as satin and a coat of red paint had created quite a work of art.

"A've fixed a back on it," an excited Dan told Sarah. "A thought he was a bit little yet t' sit straight up all the way. When he's a bit bigger an' he can use it hisel' a'll tek the back off it."

He turned to face Rob as he continued, "an' then y'll have the best bogey in the village, wont y' bonnie lad?"

Feeling pleased with himself and his handiwork Dan looked first at Sarah then turned to Rob.

"Right me bonnie lad, tell y' Ma t' get y' wrapped up we're off for a ride, you're gettin' too bloody heavy for me shoulders. When the snow comes we'll still be able to go 'cos your sledge 'll be ready by then an' y' Ma wont be worryin' about me carryin' y' in the snow 'cos if a slipped wi' y' on me shoulders we' d both come a cropper an' then y' Ma ad have nowt to say."

Sarah scolded Dan for swearing in front of their son but smiled, and waved lovingly to them, as they walked up the small hill towards the village green.

Just as Sarah enjoyed her afternoons with Rob when Dan was at work, Dan enjoyed the Sunday mornings when he had Rob to himself. Climbing the hill they passed two rows of cottages and the chapel before reaching the village green. Rob sat bolt upright on the bogey, looking first to the right and then to the left, and as they approached the village green he turned, as he always did, to wave to his mother.

Rob missed nothing on their outings and every time he asked a question Dan readily supplied him with as many answers as he could. He also used the opportunity to talk to his son.

"A don't begrudge the time y' mother spends wi' y' but the's things a want t' talk t' y' about an' y' Ma would think a was crackers goin' on at y' at your age. It's downhill all the way now bonnie lad, an' it's a lovely mornin', so it won't be long afore we're at your Grannies."

A walk on an autumn morning was Dan's favourite. It reminded him of the walks he took with his father when he was a boy. The road to his parent's house meandered through open countryside and he revelled at the changing shades of autumn leaves and the smell of the damp fresh green grass.

"Every Sunday it looks different," he told Rob. "Not like down the pit where every day's the same, the fresh air's good for me lungs lad, it gets rid o' all that nasty coal dust."

The road was quiet, especially on a Sunday.

"Just you me an' the beasts in the fields Rob," Dan continued. "We can have our talk in peace today. It's like a've told y' afore the's a better life than the pit, but y' need a' education t' get on in this life. Me Da made me go t' school but a took no notice o' him an' a wasn't interested in learnin', mind you it wouldn't have made much difference if a had listened t' him, he couldn't see farther than his nose end, the pit was good enough for him, an' his father, so it was good enough for us. The's only one of us, an' that's our George, who might have got away wi' not gannin' down the pit. Well me lad a'm not your Granda, y're gannin' t' school, y're gannin' t' learn, an' if a have t' break me bloody back down that pit somehow or other we'll get y' a proper education."

Dan laughed as he continued his one way conversation.

"We're goin' t' start y' education early, it's a bit afore y' go t' school so a'll be your teacher. Never mind the daft nursery rhymes y' Ma sings t' y' a've been findin' things out about where we live an' by the time y' start school y'll be able t' tell y' teacher more than she knows about the place. A never knew much about up the hill 'til a came t' live here. A thought it was just another village; a thought the only difference between it an' the others was the weather. Aye that's why a made y' a sledge, we're high up an' we get more snow than th' other places. A've never lost a shift through it mind y', but from what Joe says the time 'll come when a will."

As Dan approached the back streets he thought back to when he was a boy living here. He had loved the houses then, which had been recently built; he could still remember the smell of newly laid stone and fresh wood and paint.

"All y' can smell now is privie middens," he told Rob. "An' the back streets look like th've never seen a broom head for years."

Dan's parents, like the families of the other miners and ironworkers, had been proud of their new homes. But then the men were all in work and their wives worked hard to feed them and keep them clean.

"A day f' everythin'," they said. "Monday's f' washin', Tuesday's f' ironin' an' the rest o' the weeks f' cleanin'."

The cobbled back streets were swilled and broomed every week, and if an area was ever missed the poor occupants of that house were the centre of attention until another bit of juicy gossip gave the women something else to talk about. When they arrived at his parents back gate Dan paused and looked up and down the street as he spoke to his son.

"It's a funny thing, Rob, a've never really noticed 'til today just how run down this place is. But a suppose times have been harder than a thought the' 'ad, an' a lot o' them must have just lost heart in doin' owt. We have t' thank our blessin' s that a'm in work an' y' Ma takes a pride in the house; a notice even y' Grannie's bit's none to clean, it's a good job she can't get out t' see it these days."

As Dan lifted the bogey over the back step he looked proudly at his sleeping son.

"Well bonnie lad," he told him, "how long 'ave a been talkin' t' mesel'? Lets have y' out o' this contraption an' we'll go an' see if y' Granda has somat t' warm us through."

54

Dan's father was, as always, pleased to see his eldest son and, as yet, his only grandchild.

"A've good news an' bad news today," was his greeting. "Y' Ma's ne better, but she's ne worse an' our George an' Jennie's getting' wed. The' ganna live here wi' us; it'll be a weight off me mind havin' somebody here t' look after y' Ma all the time. George seems happy wi' the arrangement an' it keeps him near the pit. Anyway he didn't fancy livin' at Jennies, y' know she goes t' the chapel wi' him but her Ma an' Da' likes a drink; a think her Da likes more than one an' that doesn't gan down at all well wi' our George."

Dan still had mixed feelings about the arrangement but decided it was best to say nothing. He turned towards his mother as he coaxed, the now wide awake Rob, to go and talk to his Grannie. As usual she was sitting on a chair at the side of the kitchen table.

"A can't stand soft chairs anymore," she told anyone who tried to encourage her to sit in, her once favourite, fireside chair.

Dan's father had even bought a second chair. "There we've one each now," he told her as he did his best to make her comfortable.

"Waste o' money," was the only comment she made to her bitterly disappointed husband.

Dan thought his father was right in his assessment of his mother; there was very little difference in her appearance from when he had last seen her. She was oblivious of everything and everyone; her only activity being the constant rolling of her handkerchief, which she held both night and day.

Dan turned his attention back to his father who was obviously anxious to tell him the rest of his news.

"The's a bit o' a problem wi' our Harry Dan," he told him. "He's non too pleased wi' the arrangements. He said after George was married he an' Kate would move in an'

Kate would take good care o' y' Ma, but George says this is his home an' him an' Jennie's comin'. A don't like offendin' our Harry but a' think it's better all round if George lives wi' us; if our Harry's not happy wi' her lot then he'll just have to find somewhere else."

"Aye," Dan thought, "same old story, you're all for that one an' his Jennie but a'll say nowt, it'll only cause more bother."

Instead he tried to hide his feelings and asked.

"When's the big day then Da?"

"Next month all bein' well," his father replied. "A hope you an' Sarah will come an' see him wed. Our Harry says he's not comin' an' a wondered if y' might have a word wi' him. Will y' try an' get him t' change his mind? He might tek a bit more notice o' you than he does o' me. It's not right brothers fallin' out, a never had a wrong word wi' our Jack an' Will."

Dan, once again feeling very uncomfortable in his parents home promised his father he would speak to Harry, and then left abruptly making the excuse that Sarah would expect them back early for dinner.

As he pulled the bogey along the back street Dan, like Sarah, voiced his thoughts to his son.

"A 'm not happy wi' me Da's arrangements for me Ma. A dinna kna why but somats nigglin' at the back o' me mind. The's somat about that Jennie an' a canna put me finger on it. Anyway a'll have a word wi' our Harry next time a see him an' a'll do me best t' get him t' go t' the weddin' for me Ma an' me Da's sake."

Folding the blanket snugly around his son his voice was full of tenderness.

"Warm enough bonnie lad? Let's get oursel's back home an' t' y' Ma. A'll not talk t' y' much on the way back 'cos it's all uphill an' y' na a canna get me wind."

Rob was once more fast asleep before they were half way home. When they reached the top of the hill his father's voice woke the sleeping child.

"Its funny Rob but a think a'm goin' t' like all this learnin' we've got t' de; a've been doin' a bit o' readin' an' a 'm goin' t' practice wi' y'. When y' bigger, mind, a'll expect y't' listen 'cos a don't intend t' be wastin' me time. It's downhill now, so one story afore we get home. Th' say that it's our church that started the custom o' kissin' the bride, but it was the vicar who did the kissin'. A' m not sure a believe it but the' say its right enough."

Dan stopped; tousled Rob's hair then kissed him on the forehead.

"Dinna tell y' Ma that one," he jokingly said as he ran down the bank, to his home and wife, Rob squealing with delight.

Dan stopped a few yards from the house to enjoy a few more private words with his son.

"By it's been a grand Sunday mornin', except f' me Da's news, it makes y' feel good t' learn things Rob. One day when y've got y' sel' a good job an' a fine house y'll not think y' Da was s' daft tellin' y' all o' these things."

CHAPTER 3

It was Rob's third Christmas and Sarah was sure she was going to have another child. She talked to Rob as she put the finishing touches to the paper chains Dan had hung across the kitchen ceiling the night before.

"There bonnie lad them bits o' holly mek y' Da's work a bit more Christmassy. When he gets in from the pit me an' you'll tell him about the new baby we're goin' to get. Won't he be surprised?"

Rob was taking very little notice of his mother, tearing the spare paper chains into tiny pieces and throwing them everywhere was much more interesting.

"A wish y'd stop mekin' a mess Rob, a've just finished tidyin' up, a told y' Da last night y're gettin' to be more hard work every day, but a don't really care bonnie lad you're worth it. Me an' y' Da's really lookin' forward t' Christmas this year, 'cos y'll understand it better."

She then whispered; making sure Rob could not hear her.

"An' y'll love the dog we've got y'."

Sarah talked to Rob throughout the day, whatever her thoughts were she shared them with her son. He copied her every word and move.

"Me do it Ma, me tell him Ma," Rob would shout at her.

Many of the neighbours commented on the extent of his vocabulary; usually by saying.

"My but he is an old fashioned little feller."

Sarah continued the conversation with Rob as she stooped to clear up the paper he had somehow managed to get underneath the dresser.

"Santa Claus comes tomorro' bonnie lad an' if y're good when y' wake up in the mornin' he'll have left y' some presents. We'll hang one o' y' Da's pit socks up on the end o' y' cot tonight, we'll use his 'cos the' bigger, an' Santa'll

58

come down the chimney when y' fast asleep. He'll fill y' sock, an' f' good lads he gi s y' a penny an' very good lads sometimes get two."

Rob's reply demonstrated his confusion with his mother's constant chatter.

"Is me present a new baby?" he asked.

When Dan arrived home a happy wife and son welcomed him with a kiss.

"By a'm pleased a rubbed fore shift f' Christmas week Sarah," was his response to their show of affection. "Home f' me dinner Christmas eve; Christmas Day an' Boxin' Day off an' not back 'til night shift the day after. It must be the best break a've ever had at a holiday time."

Dan quickly ate his dinner and after his bath went straight to bed.

"A'll just have a couple o' hours Sarah, don't let me sleep ower long, a'll have an hour wi' you an' the bairn, when a get up, an' then a'll have a look ower the Bay Horse."

Dan yawned as he spoke and Sarah decided that now was not the time to give him her news.

As soon as Dan had gone to bed Rob climbed onto the fireside chair and curling up into a little ball was soon fast asleep. Sarah's week had been busy, she had finished the housework, done all of the washing and the last of the baking had been taken out of the oven before Dan came home from work. Even though Rob was sleeping she continued talking to him.

"A'm all done but a still haven't got him told, y've gone t' sleep so a've got another two hours on me own thinkin' o' the right words to say t' y' Da when he gets up."

She busied herself in the kitchen, moving the holly from the dresser to the table and then back again, still talking as she carried out her meaningless tasks.

59

"One day Rob we might get a bigger house. If y' Granda's told y' Da once he's told him a thousand times t' try an' get set on at the new pit that's goin' t' open. It's only two miles down the road an' we might get a house there, but y' Da teks no notice o' him, a wish somebody else would say somat, he might tek a bit more notice o' them."

Again, when Sarah first suspected she might be pregnant Hannah was the first to know.

"It's funny Hannah, a wasn't bothered about another bairn but now when a think a 'm havin' one a 'm pleased as punch." What she didn't add was, "as long as it's another lad."

Sarah had often wondered why she felt as she did about having a daughter. Try as she might she could not explain her feelings until one afternoon, when Rob was sleeping, she thought back to her own childhood and in particular to one day she had spent with her Grandmother. Sarah could not remember a time when her own mother or father had kissed and cuddled her, as she did Rob, never mind telling her a story, but she could remember her Grandmother, how she loved her, and the time she spent with her.

Her Grandmother could neither read nor write but she could tell wonderful stories, some so real Sarah could imagine herself there. There was one particular story, she could not recall exactly what it was about but she could remember her Grandmother's words.

"Never have lasses hinnie th'll bring y' nowt but sorrow."

Sarah told herself she was being silly, it probably had nothing to do with her not wanting a girl, but try as she might she could not get it out of her mind.

Two hours later Dan came down the stairs full of the Christmas spirit. They had a special Christmas Eve tea and he joked with Rob as he complimented Sarah on her additional decorations and her Christmas baking.

"We've made a hole in y' bakin' Sarah," he told her. "A hope y've plenty left f' the next couple days, them pies are lovely an' our Rob loves y' jam tarts."

Turning to Rob he winked as he said.

"Y' can eat nearly as much as y' Da these days can't y' bonnie lad?"

As he had promised Dan spent the next hour playing with his son and then he and Sarah carried Rob upstairs to bed, the two of them happily watching him hang a solitary pit sock over the end of his cot.

The dog had been bought on another outing to Durham after Rob had seen it in the toy shop window. It was set on a wooden platform with four wheels and a handle to push it. He had stared in wonder at the toy and shouted,

"Rover, Rover."

From where he had heard the name Dan and Sarah never knew. Rob held his father's hand tightly as he steered him towards the shop door and dragged him into the shop.

"Me want, me want," he shouted.

His excitement filled Dan and Sarah's eyes with tears as the shop assistant, finding it difficult to keep a straight face, asked if she could be of assistance. When they finally persuaded Rob to leave the shop Dan turned to Sarah.

"Somehow a'll find the money from somewhere to buy that dog; if a can he'll have it f' Christmas."

Every week Dan took his pocket money out of his wages before he gave the remainder to Sarah. Although he did not drink as much as he did before Rob was born he still liked to hear the jingle of money in his pocket; just in case he fancied a gill of beer or two. Dan became obsessed with the dog just as he had with set of drawers and so he made a decision.

"Ne more pocket money f' me Sarah 'til y've enough t' pay f' that dog," he told a surprised Sarah.

Each time Joe called on Dan to ask him if he was going for a drink at the Bay Horse his reply was the same.

"It's bloody killin' us but a've telt y' afore Joe, a've signed the pledge 'til Christmas."

Sarah played her part, cutting corners with the housekeeping money and adding, without Dan's knowledge, the small amount she had been saving to give them a few extras for Christmas.

Much to Dan's surprise they had the money to buy the dog three weeks before Christmas and Joe had his drinking partner back earlier than expected. Dan's next problem was where to hide the dog and together they searched for a solution.

"He's only little Sarah," Dan whispered not wanting his son to hear, "but the's only the bedroom an' the kitchen an' back kitchen, he's sure t' find it."

Sarah suggested they leave it at his fathers until just before Christmas.

"If y' bring it up just afore Christmas we can cover it wi' one o' y' old coats; we'll just have a couple days then t' be careful an a'll mek sure he doesn't see it."

As soon as Dan was sure Rob was sleeping he gave Sarah his customary kiss on the cheek; told her he would not be late and left for the Bay Horse and a welcome pint of beer. Sarah settled down, for a quiet Christmas Eve, and staring at the roaring fire she grumbled.

"A'll have t' wait 'til he's in afore a tell him, a hope he's not had too much t' drink."

The heat of the fire made her drowsy and her thoughts, which she voiced as she always did, turned to her family.

"Me Ma an' me Da'll be on the' own this Christmas, an' a bet our Florries hard at it getting' everythin' ready f' tomorro'. It's not easy f' her tryin' t' gi' the two lasses a decent life. Alf doesn't seem t' be able t' hold a job down f' more than a few weeks at a time, the'll never be able t' get on the' feet. Our Maisie still hasn't got ower loosin' the bairn, a kna what she must be gannin' through, it's a bit like when a thought me an Dan would never a bairn, Christmas's' not goin' t' be a very happy time f' her."

Sarah stirred in her chair, she felt cold and as she eased forward to poke the fire she continued talking to herself.

"A feel sorry f' Dan's Da, his Ma's such a handful an' Jennie hasn't turned out t' be the help he thought she would, but a'm pleased about Harry an' Kate at least the've got a place o' the' own now the' should have a better Christmas this year."

Dan had left the house at the same time as Joe and they walked to the Bay Horse together. Joe was always the life and soul of the party and it looked as if there would be a good night ahead of them with plenty of laughter from Joe's special way of telling a good joke. As he attracted the older men from the village into their company there would be plenty of local gossip and reminiscing. Dan was lounging in his chair savouring his beer, and the company, when he felt a tap on his shoulder and was surprised when he heard his brother's voice.

"Shove ower then an' a'll have a seat a side y'."

"What the hell a' you doin' here," Dan asked, rising from his chair to greet his brother, "a thought y' didn't come t' places like this?"

Harry laughed.

"A've been comin' up here f' a few weeks now, a thought a'd bump into y' one weekend but the said y' hadn't been comin' in lately. Dinna tell me Da y' ve seen us mind, if he finds out he's got two o' us drinkin' he'll gan bald never mind you turnin' his hair grey. A started havin' the odd pint when we lived with Kate's Ma an' Da 'cos the pub was the only place a got a bit o' peace an' quiet. A come up here 'cos it's out o' the road, an' a enjoy the walk. Kate knows a come an' she's alright about it. A only stay a

63

couple hours an' t' be honest a think she's sometimes glad t' be rid o' me."

Harry joined in the laughter, enjoying the company of Dan and his friends. When some of the crowd began to drift off home he used the opportunity to ask Dan what he thought about their mother's health. Before Dan had time to answer Harry continued; he spoke quietly not wanting anyone other than Dan to hear what he was saying.

"Have y' noticed the bruises on me Ma's arms? A kna' she's not steady on her feet but honestly Dan, she can't have got them fallin', the' looks like finger marks to me. A don't like accusin' folk but a don't trust that Jennie but if a say owt the'll just say its sour grapes 'cos me Da wouldn't let me an' Kate move in wi' them."

Dan was concerned, he had not noticed anything, but on the other hand he had always had misgivings about the arrangement. He did not like, or trust, Jennie, and Dan knew that Sarah, who could never see wrong in anyone did not get along with her sister in law and avoided her whenever possible.

As Dan assured Harry he would visit his parents as soon as possible, he looked calm on the outside but inside he was furious.

"If the've harmed me Ma a'll kill the bastards," he muttered to himself.

Their conversation then turned to Christmas, Dan telling Harry about the dog they had bought for Rob and their problems to ensure it would be a surprise.

"Aye y've the same trouble as me an' Kate," Harry told him. "Y' want t' come an' see our pokey little hole, a suppose it's better than nowt but, the's not room t' swing a cat. A'm gannin' t' try an' get set on at the new pit that's openin', the' say the' ganna build some new houses f' the miners; the'll be men comin' from all ower so the'll have t' have somewhere f' them t' live."

Harry's words were a hint to Dan but, like Sarah's, he took no notice of them. The two hours in the pub extended to three and as they wished each other a Merry Christmas the evening's conversation was temporarily forgotten.

Dan could hold his drink, but tonight he had had one pint of beer too many, and when he opened the front door he nearly feel flat on his face. Unlike many of his friends alcohol did not make him bad tempered, in fact it had the opposite effect. Sarah made him a cup of strong, sweet black tea while he attempted to walk a straight line across the back yard to the midden. When he returned she guided him to a chair and finally, after numerous interruptions, told him her news.

"Y've made me Christmas Sarah, when's it due?" he questioned her.

His speech had been slurred and his gait unsteady but the news that he was once more to be a father sobered him up as quickly as if Sarah had poured a bucket of cold water over his head.

Excited as he was he found it difficult to sleep and as soon as a happy Sarah stopped talking about the new baby, and the coming Christmas morning, he remembered his conversation with Harry. He made up his mind, with another mouth to feed; he would find about the new pit and maybe get a better job with more money and a bigger house.

As he finally drifted off to sleep his thoughts were on his mother.

"A'll have t' sort out what's happenin' wi' me Ma," he mumbled. "An' woe betide that big headed bugger if the's out gannin' on."

The weather was mild over the Christmas and New Year period. The months of January and the beginning of February were unusually mild but during the third week of

65

February the temperature dropped. Rob was fascinated with the ice on the inside of his bedroom window. Every morning he would stand up in his cot and shout to gain his mother's attention.

"Ma, Ma, Jack Frosts been an' he's made pictures again".

Together Rob and Sarah scratched their names on the ice; Sarah guiding his hand as she, like Dan, tried to educate their son in the only way they knew how.

The frost did not break during the day and on Dan's return from work Rob showed him the pictures he and his mother had drawn on the icy windows.

By the end of the week Dan was walking to work. He had tried continuing to cycle but skidded and fell off grazing his knees and hurting his shoulder.

"A'll break me bloody neck, Sarah, gannin' on that thing," he told her after his second attempt. "The's nowt else f' it, a'll have t' walk, so it's out earlier an' home a bit later 'til the weather picks up."

He was still walking after two weeks and Sarah was worried. He looked tired and, although he did not complain, she knew his chest was bothering him. He made light of his cough when Sarah voiced her concern and he continually reassured her.

"A'm alreet Sarah, all a can say is that it's a good job the bairns not due 'til the summer 'cos y' would have had somat t' worry about then."

During the second week of March the frost gave but it was still bitterly cold.

"We're in f' some snow." Hannah said through chattering teeth.

She shivered as she nudged her large back side nearer to Sarah's roaring fire.

"We'll all be fed up afore this winters out."

The next day she was proved right. It started to snow early morning and continued throughout the day. Dan was cycling to work again and was due in at six o'clock, his usual time when on back shift. Sarah became anxious, when during afternoon, the winds got stronger; her anxiety increased as she looked through the window and watched a blizzard the likes of which she had never seen before. As usual her thoughts were voiced to her son.

"Y' Da'll never manage on his bike in this Rob, a hope he's had the sense t' leave it at the pit an' walk."

She stood with Rob at the window willing Dan to appear but she could see nothing other than the snow swirling in the wind. Sarah told Rob to stay in the kitchen while she looked out of the front door but the wind blew it back against the wall and in seconds she was covered in snow. It took all of her strength to close the door and return to the safety of the kitchen and Rob. Rob did not understand the danger and begged Sarah to take him out in the snow and play with the sledge his father had made for him. She rarely lost her patience but on this occasion the sharpness in her voice soon quietened him.

"No Rob, it's not fit t' let a dog out, let's just hope y' Da's alright, a'll be pleased when he's home safe an' sound."

Sarah breathed a sigh of relief when she heard the back gate slam and ran to open the back door. At first she could not stop laughing as Dan looked so comical.

"A'm pleased y' in," she laughed, "an' a 'm sorry a'm laughing, but y' look s' daft, y' just like a snowman."

Her laughter soon subsided and her mood turned to one of concern. Dan was shivering and his face blue with the cold. Sarah quickly helped him take off his wet clothes and wrapped him in towels and the blanket from the back of the sofa. Even after a hot bath in front of the fire and a pot of hot tea Dan continued to shiver, his teeth chattering as he spoke.

"A'll not bother wi' any dinner Sarah, a think a'll gan straight t' bed, a'm too tired to eat."

Sarah occasionally glanced through the bedroom door that evening but as Dan appeared to be sleeping she did not disturb him. After a frustrating evening trying to keep Rob quiet downstairs when Sarah wearily climbed into bed she was upset to find that the sheets were soaking wet.

Dan felt icy cold and he was still shivering. When she asked him to get out of the bed to change it his reply was incomprehensible. As she attempted to remove the wet sheets Dan struggled with her as if defending himself from an unknown assailant. Sarah was relieved when finally she had him dry and comfortable but her anxiety quickly returned when Dan became so hot, with a raging fever, that within minutes the sheets were just as wet as they had been before.

Throughout the night Dan's temperature swung from hot to cold. When he was hot Sarah sponged him down with cool water, when he was cold she wrapped him in blankets and old coats, anything she could find to keep him warm.

Daybreak brought no improvement to Dan's condition; he was delirious and mumbled constantly about his mother and Jennie.

"Look after me Ma Sarah, keep her safe from our George an' that Jennie," he pleaded.

As Dan had never told Sarah about his conversation with Harry she was at a loss to understand him and all she could do was promise she would.

Sarah quietly whispered to Rob who was still sleeping soundly at the foot of the bed.

"A need help bonnie lad so don't wake up yet."

She did not want to leave them but she had no choice, she needed help and she had to get Hannah. Dressing

68

quickly and then raking more coal onto the fire Sarah fastened her shawl tightly around her head and opened the backdoor to find that the snow had drifted; the back gate had at least three feet of snow lying against it in the backyard and six feet of snow on the outside. Sarah went back into the house and opened the front door to find the conditions were nearly as bad at the front as they were at the back. Her desperation gave her extra strength and using the coal shovel she finally cleared a pathway through the drifting snow to Hannah's house.

Hannah was already up and dressed, her youngest child woke at the crack of dawn and Hannah found her life with Joe to be much more harmonious if she brought the noisy child downstairs. Hannah, as always, was ready to help and took the child back upstairs telling her eldest daughter to care for her. The pathway that Sarah had made was already covered in fresh snow and as they battled through the blizzard they could hear Rob crying. One look at Dan and Hannah knew just how ill he was.

"A'll get Joe t' gan f' the doctor 'cos he'll never get through t' the pit today," she told an even more worried Sarah. "A can de ne more than y've done y' sel' so a'll tek Rob home wi' me; you see t' Dan. Just do what y've been doin'; keep him warm when he's shivering an' try an' cool him off when he's hot. Mek sure he drinks plenty. A'll come back when a've told Joe an' seen to the bairns; our lot'll be only to pleased t' see t' this little un'."

It was early afternoon before an exhausted Joe returned.

"A only saw his missus," Joe told Hannah and Sarah shaking his head as he looked at Dan. "She said he was out on his rounds an' she didn't kna' when he'd be back. She says it'll tek him all day wi' the weather bein's' bad he's got more t' see than usual an it's tekin' him longer t' get 'round. Anyway she's gannin' t' tell 'm but she says she can't promise when he'll come. A said a'd try 'n find him mesel' but she said she had ne idea where he'd be."

Hannah suggested to Sarah that it might be better if Dan was brought downstairs.

"Y' can see t' Rob better if Dan's down here," she coaxed, "an' anyhow you'll all freeze t' death up there."

Sarah agreed and between them they carried Dan downstairs and settled him in the little cupboard bed in the kitchen. Hannah did her best to put on a brave face but she was anxious. Dan and Sarah had become dear friends and she was sure she was about to lose one of them.

"A never thought the first time a'd use the cupboard bed would be f' Dan," Sarah told Hannah doing her best to hide her fears from her friend. "A thought the first time a'd use it would be f' Rob when a'd had the bairn."

It finally stopped snowing shortly after Joe's return and as none of the men in the village had managed to get to work they started the mammoth task of clearing the snow from the fronts of the houses and part of the road.

"The road isn't s' bad now," Joe told Sarah "If he teks care the doctor should get through."

Sarah nursed Dan throughout the rest of the day and night. With the help of Hannah she coped with the endless bed changes, Hannah's eldest daughter taking sheets and blankets home to dry quickly in front of the fire. For the first time in his life Rob was parted from Sarah but he went along happily with Hannah's children to share their bed for the night.

The doctor finally arrived the next day.

"He was s' tired he looked worse than Dan," Hannah informed Joe later in the day.

Dan was still delirious and had a high fever but was no longer shivering. Sarah had feared for his life many times during that long night when she thought Dan's harsh, rasping cough, as he tried to rid his lungs of thick, black coal stained sputum, would choke him to death. After the doctor had listened to Dan's chest and encouraged him to cough he gave Sarah the news she did not want to hear.

"I'm afraid he's got pneumonia; there's little I can do for your husband other than what you are doing for him now. Try and give him this medicine to loosen his cough, keep him propped up on the pillows and don't let him lie flat in the bed. Keep the room warm all of the time, but not too hot, and try to get him to drink. I really can't say what will happen, not until his fever breaks, your good nursing is the only thing that matters now. Just pray to God that when his fever does break it'll be for the better."

Sarah had not slept for more than forty eight hours. She was tired, weary and near to tears but Dan was her main concern. As she busied herself, forcing him to swallow the cough mixture the doctor had left and following the doctor's instructions to the letter, she talked to him.

"Me cryin' won't help y' or anybody else, y're goin' t' pull through bonnie lad, if a never shut me eyes f' a week a'll not let y' die."

Sarah did just that and Rob played his part. After two nights of staying at Hannah's he was missing Sarah and she asked Hannah to bring him home. To Hannah's surprise he did not cling to Sarah as she expected. Once he was safely tucked up in his cot at night he slept through until the following morning going off cheerfully to Hannah's, after his breakfast, for another day of fun. Never once did he vie for Sarah's attention, when she was busy with Dan, or disturb his father when he was sleeping.

During the three days and nights following the doctors visit Sarah never slept. When Hannah offered to sit with Dan, telling her to rest for a few hours, she refused. She would close her eyes for a few minutes but would not leave his side. When Hannah made broth and oxtail soup she ate a little knowing she needed it if she was to carry on caring for

Dan. But most of it was given to Dan who choked on every spoonful as she patiently tried feed him.

In the early hours of the fourth day of Dan's illness Sarah did shed a single tear, he was not getting better; she knew he was much worse. Dan refused his medicine and she could not persuade him to take even a sip of the water she constantly offered him. Sarah prayed to God.

"Don't let him die, let him live t' see his new bairn and t' see Rob grow up t' be a fine man like him."

Dan's speech was incoherent as his fever heightened. He fought her every effort when she tried sponge him down and as she struggled to keep him in the tiny bed she finally raised her voice to him.

"Y've got me black an' blue bonnie lad, but we're not givin' in yet. Y've got t' help me get y' better, y've got t' try 'cos y're ganna get better if it kills me."

At five o'clock Dan fell into an exhausted sleep, the fire raged in his body and Sarah knew all of his strength had left him. Sitting quietly by his side she wept as she had done, over three years ago, on the night she had told Dan she was having a child.

"A dinna kna what else t' do Dan," she told him, "A've tried everythin' a can think of, if y' want t' see the new bairn when it comes and t' see Rob grow up y'll have t' do somat y' sel'."

"Ma, Ma, wake up, me hungry," Rob's cry woke Sarah with a start.

Her first thought was to go to her son.

"What have a been thinkin' about gannin t' sleep," she scolded herself as she looked anxiously at her husband.

Her heart missed a beat; he was alive and sleeping peacefully.

"Dan," she cried, "wake up are y' alright?"

Dan opened his eyes.

"Mek us a cup o' tea hinnie an' open them curtains a canna see the stars."

This time Sarah shed tears of joy and as she kissed him gently on the forehead she said a simple prayer.

"Thanks God, y' answered me prayer an' a'll never forget it, a'll find someway t' repay y', a don't know when but a will."

"A'll fetch Rob down Dan, an' we'll all have a cup o' tea," were the only words she could think of to say to her husband.

She did not care; Dan was going to get better; the two people she cared for more than anyone else in the world needed her even if it was only to give one his breakfast and the other a cup of tea.

When the doctor called the following day Dan was still in bed his legs felt like jelly and his chest was sore. "You did it lass," the doctor told a smiling Sarah. "It was only your care that saved him. Mind you it will be a few weeks before you have him back on his feet but he's over the worst. Feed him up and hopefully we'll soon have him as right as rain." After the doctor listened to Dan's chest he spoke to him but ensured Sarah was listening. "Dan you know you were really ill and I'm afraid you will be left with a weak chest. I would like to say to you never go down the pit again but I know I can't, I know it's your livelihood; all I can do is tell you the facts and hope that you try to be careful." As he left he was deep in thought, this miner had survived, this time, he was one of the lucky ones so many of his patients had not.

"Please don't go Dan, "Sarah pleaded.

"A have t' hinnie we canna live on bread an' water an' the's nowt ready in the allotment yet," was Dan's reply as he kissed her on the cheek and left for his return to the pit.

It had been three weeks before Dan had been strong enough to get out of the little cupboard bed and return to the bed he shared with Sarah.

Spring arrived early and for the following three weeks he spent his time in the allotment, sometimes working, other times, just passing the time of day with his fellow gardeners. Life for Dan, Sarah and Rob soon settled back to normal, but Sarah worried when Dan came home from work exhausted and coughing to rid himelf of the incessant coal dust that settled on his lungs every time he went down the pit he still hated so much. She cared but she knew she must not show him. Sarah, like Dan, was only too aware of how much they needed the pit. Whenever they were alone Dan and Sarah spoke of the new baby they were soon to have and delighted in preparing Rob for the arrival of his new brother or, as Dan insisted, his new baby sister.

"He's off his food an' a can't persuade him t' drink," was the greeting Dan received from Sarah as he put his cycle in the backyard. "He's sickenin' f' somat Dan a can't tempt him wi' owt."

Dan had been back at work for four weeks and was only just coping with the hard work he had to face each day. Tired as he was he nursed his son before going to bed giving Sarah time to catch up on the chores that, for once, she had not completed.

For the next forty eight hours Rob clung to Sarah during the day and was restless during the night. Once again a worried Sarah did not sleep and devoted herself, completely this time, to her son. When Sarah tried to encourage him to play with Hannah's children he refused and he rejected all of Dan's efforts to amuse him. He cried at every attempt to take him from Sarah and the only thing he asked for was more stories.

"If he's not eatin' or drinkin' Sarah," Hannah advised, "then it's more than likely he's got a sore throat. My lot get

74

tonsillitis regular an' flowers o'sulphur usually does the trick."

Sarah tried Hannah's remedy. As Rob cried and kept his mouth firmly closed she tried to blow the yellow powder onto the back of his throat. Finally Rob's resistance frustrated Sarah and she lost her temper as he became more distressed with her every attempt.

"It's no use Rob," she cried, "y' Da'll be home at dinner time an' he'll have t' hold y' down while a have a look at y' throat an' get some o' Hannah's powder on it. Y've got me all worked up an' y na a dinna like shoutin' at y'."

While Dan had his bath Sarah told him of the mornings events. After his bath he held Rob but he still resisted while Sarah struggled to open his mouth.

Sarah sobbed,

"Dan his throats not red, it's all white, like somat's coverin' the back o' his throat."

Both of them knew what this could mean but neither of them was willing to voice their fears.

"A'll not have me dinner Sarah, a'll go straight f' the doctor an' get him t' come," an anxious Dan said as he quickly put on his cap and coat. "A'll go on the bike an' see if he can come straight away."

The doctor arrived before Dan and after looking at, a still struggling, Rob's throat there was no mistaking the diagnosis; Rob had diphtheria.

He turned to Sarah.

"My lass you've had your troubles lately but if you take care of your son the same way you took care of your husband we might just see him through."

He told her that, on this occasion, she and Dan would have to care for their son themselves.

"Strictly no visitors, no help from the neighbours this time, it's highly contagious and we don't want an epidemic. Give him the same care as you gave your husband and keep the room at the same temperature night and day. Keep him propped up to help his breathing and do your best to make him drink. We can only hope and pray the membrane at the back of his throat doesn't get any bigger; his breathing's not too bad at the minute but make sure one of you is always with him and I'll come again tomorrow to see how he is."

Dan arrived just as the doctor was leaving and he did not need to hear his words, the look on the doctor's face told Dan just how gravely ill his son was. As Dan accompanied the doctor to the front door he listened intently to the doctor's advice.

"If the lad shows any sign of choking you get word to me and I'll be back as soon as I can."

As he placed a comforting hand on Dan's shoulder he continued.

"Care for your wife as well Dan, she's had a rough time, first you and now your boy. She's tired and frightened and she can only do so much, especially in her condition, we don't want her coming down with something as well do we?"

For the next forty eight hours Rob showed no sign of improvement. The doctor called twice and on each occasion reassured Dan and Sarah that the membrane was no bigger. Another two days passed and Dan and Sarah were encouraged by the doctor's words.

"The membrane seems to be reducing in size. I think he might be over the worst but he'll still need a few more weeks before he's anything like the little lad he was."

He left giving Dan further advice on Rob's care. I won't be up for another two or three days, a few more little ones in the area have got the same disease and they are keeping me busy. If you need me you know where I am otherwise keep up the good work. When Dan told her the good news Sarah said a silent prayer and when on the following day

Rob asked for a drink she was more than sure her prayers had again been answered.

Rob's improvement continued but he was still very lethargic; sleeping most of the day and fretful and disturbed during the night. Sarah was too afraid to sleep even though the doctor was delighted with Rob's progress and his visits became less frequent. At the end of the second week of Rob's illness he once more developed a fever. He was hot and restless and shuffled constantly in Sarah's arms. Nothing she did could settle him and even his favourite nursery rhymes did nothing to sooth him.

"What's the matter wi' y' bonnie lad?" Sarah asked him. "A thought y' were gettin' better."

"Ma, me legs hurt." Rob replied, in a voice so weak Sarah could hardly hear him. "Cold Ma an' it's dark."

Sarah screamed.

"Dan, Dan get up an' go f' the doctor it's Rob a'm sure he canna see."

The doctor's news was grim.

"I am sorry, but it's not the membrane that's the problem, unfortunately the disease has spread throughout his body, it's a kind of paralysis he's got. If you notice his legs he's not moving them and I've heard of other cases where the eyes have been involved. He's just been unlucky; he's got over the membrane but now has some of the other complications of diphtheria. Usually they get over it in a couple of weeks and, hopefully, his sight and legs will get back to normal. There are two things we have to watch for and that's to do with his breathing and swallowing. If the disease affects the muscles that help him to breath and swallow there can be problems. At the minute he seems alright but watch him carefully."

Sarah and Dan thought the day would never come when Rob would once again be their happy little boy. Sarah was tired but it seemed that no harm had come to her or her unborn child and Dan did his best to comfort her.

"The doctor didn't seem ower worried Sarah, he didn't say when he'd be back, so this must happen a lot wi' diphtheria."

Sarah did not reply; she did not share Dan's optimism, she sat quietly nursing her son praying for his recovery. By the next afternoon Rob had still not improved and Sarah was relieved when the doctor called.

"He didn't say much," she told Dan when he came home from work. "Just that he was pleased Rob wasn't havin' any problems wi' his breathin' an' he seemed pleased when a told him Rob was drinkin' some milk. Apart from that it was just the usual keep up the good work."

That night Sarah's panic was greater than it had been throughout both her husband's and son's illnesses. She was giving Rob a drink, before settling down to another night of dozing in the chair, when he started to choke, the milk ran down his nose and he gasped for breath, his face turned blue and she could not sooth the frightened child. His face was still blue when a terrified Sarah once more screamed for Dan; her urgent cries waking him instantly.

"Get the doctor Dan, he's worse, he's chokin' an' a can't settle him, hurry up an' tell him t' come quick a can't stand t' see him sufferin' like this."

Dan pedalled his bike faster than he had ever done before. His lungs burned, but nothing deterred him,

"Rob must be bad," he said to himself, "Sarah would never carry on like that if he wasn't".

On this occasion Dan and the doctor arrived back at the house at the same time. There was a deadly silence as they entered and Dan breathed a sigh of relief as he spoke.

"A'm sorry doctor a've brought y' up f' nowt, Sarah must have managed to settle him 'cos he was in a' awful state when a left them."

78

The fire was hardly lit and as he crossed the room Dan turned up the lamp.

"She must have nodded off in the chair doctor, an' look at Rob he's sleepin' peacefully now."

The doctor took one look at Sarah's face and new the worst had happened. Rob was dead, she had been helpless; he had choked to death in her arms.

CHAPTER 4

"Suicide's a sin Rob; at least, that's what folk say. Well th' sin wouldn't be mine Rob, it would be God's, that's if th'is one." Sarah knelt at the tiny grave talking to her son as if he was still with her.

The grave was not marked, nor would it be for many a year to come.

"It's funny Hannah but me Da's got me through this, the chapel an' God meant nowt t' me but me Da's talked t' us for hours on end an' it's helped. A miss the lad Hannah, an' it hurts, but a'm begin't' see the's a future wi' the new bairn comin'.'"

Dan was taken aback with Hannah's reply.

"Y' Da might 'ave helped y' lad but he hasn't helped Sarah. A'm pleased y've popped in 'cos a've been wantin' t' talk t' y' about her. A'm worried lad, if we don't do somat she'll end up doin' somat daft."

Dan had been so consumed with his own grief he had assumed that Sarah was coming to terms with hers.

"But she seems alreet Hannah. When a said a was ganin' back t' th' pit she agreed an' she's doin' th' work an' makin' all th' meals now."

"Aye Dan that's th' very thing a'm on about, she's carryin' on if nowt's happen'd. She never slept when Rob when was bad an' a doubt whether she's shut her eyes since. Wake up lad she's sufferin' inside an' a don't think she wants t' carry on. You've got t' get her t' talk, an' most of all she needs t' sleep, she doesn't kna whether it's night o' day."

"Why didn't a listen t' Hannah? Things might a've been different if a had; an' if Sarah dies it'll be my fault." Dan sobbed.

He stared blankly into the fire, the tears rolling down his face. The midwife and Hannah had been with Sarah for ten hours and now the Doctor was with her. Dan had asked the midwife what was happening to Sarah when she came down stairs for more hot water.

"Upstairs's no place f' y', y'll just have to sit down here or gan t' the pub 'till its all ower," was all she replied.

He just wished someone would tell him what was happening.

Dan was guilt ridden; he had not listened to Hannah's warning instead he encouraged Sarah to have a glass of gin each night. She began to sleep again and Dan was pleased with himself; his remedy was working. On the first occasion he had offered her a liberal measure of gin he had been surprised when she accepted it. Sarah never drank alcohol; she always turned her nose up at even a small glass of port at Christmas.

Dan had not just listened to his father to overcome his grief but, when his shifts allowed, he rarely missed a night at the Bay Horse. He drank more than his customary two pints and never forgot to bring Sarah her nightcap; a large glass of gin.

On the nights he was working he had secreted a small bottle in the back of the dresser and poured her an ample measure before he left for work. Dan thought the jug of beer he often brought home for them to share was a good tonic for Sarah, especially as she now slept soundly throughout the night. He never once thought he could harm her.

"A've been a fool," he muttered,"if a'd offered her poison she would have took it."

The previous night Sarah had fallen after he left for the pit and when he came home from work the next morning he had found her lying at the bottom of the stairs. She was conscious but freezing cold and it was obvious, even to him, she was in labour. The baby was not due for another four weeks and, before he tended to Sarah, he ran for Hannah who told him to get the midwife while she looked after Sarah.

Sarah laboured for ten hours before a worried midwife asked Dan to get the doctor. The doctor arrived to find an exhausted Sarah; he administered chloroform and set to work to assist in the birth of the child. Two hours later a blue, apparently lifeless girl was born. Sarah was ill and as the doctor did not have much hope for the child he worked feverishly to restore a flaccid Sarah.

Fearing for Sarah's life his instructions to the midwife, who he knew to be skilled at her job, were given in a manner unusual for him.

"Don't just stand there, see to the child and get two basins, a jug of cold water and a kettle of hot." He quickly glanced at the perfectly formed tiny child and, although he had never known one so small survive, decided they must try. Her body was limp and the cord lay like a broken stem; yet her skin was of a beautiful texture, smooth and tender. Even though the child's head lolled on its thin neck and its limbs seemed boneless he shouted his instructions to Hannah and the midwife.

"You'll have to try, these two have had enough suffering to last them a lifetime. Put cold water into one basin and mix hot and cold in the other until the water is just hot enough for your hand to bear. Now put the baby into the hot water and then the cold until I tell you to stop."

"A'm tellin' y' doctor," the midwife insisted, "she's dead."

"Do what I tell you." He urged. "And every so often press on the child's chest."

He had one eye on the child while he tended to Sarah and the Midwife's cry startled both him and Hannah.

"It might be me imagination doctor but a think the bairn's chest moved by itsel', it did doctor, the bairns breathin'."

As the child gasped a bubble of mucous came from its tiny nostrils, its skin turned pink and then it cried. The girl's tiny arms and legs moved, no longer appearing boneless, and its head now appeared to be obviously attached to its spine.

Dan heard Hannah's cry.

"The bairn's alive."

The doctor's efforts to remove the placenta, that had been so firmly attached, were also rewarded as Sarah's bleeding stopped and her heartbeat strengthened. Another hour passed before he felt confident to leave Sarah and the child in the care of the midwife and Hannah. Before he left he took hold of the bundle and as he opened the towel to once again examine the tiny child he surprised Hannah and the midwife when he thanked them.

"You did well, both of you, she's got a long way to go but at least you've given her a fair chance. She doesn't seem to have anything wrong with her, she's just little."

He looked towards Sarah, who was lying in the middle of a now tidy bed, surrounded by a room full of litter dreaming her way through the anaesthetic, dreams of her new baby, Rob.

Turning to Hannah he smiled, his voice quiet and sincere.

"They need you Hannah. I know you have enough with your own family but try to help them; if this child survives it could be their salvation."

Hannah did not reply he knew she did not have to. Hannah loved Sarah like a sister, maybe her love was a greater love and she knew, as he did, that this little miracle now safe in the midwife's arms might enable Sarah to feel again, maybe even to love again. Hannah returned the doctors' knowing smile, she glanced at the child and then to the drawer which she had quickly prepared, the drawer which was one of the set of drawers bought for Rob and would now be a bed for his sister. Hannah was wise, wiser than the doctor, this child might be their salvation but no child of Sarahs' would ever replace Rob.

The doctor packed his bag and was the first to go down stairs to give Dan the news.

"Don't cry lad it's all over. Sarah's going to be alright; she doesn't know it yet but you've got yourselves a bonny little girl. It'll be some weeks before she's fighting fit, she's so little, but Sarah will be fine and we'll all do our best to pull the little one through. Hannah will help but I think you should ask Sarah's mother to come and stay for a few weeks, the little one will be a full time job and Sarah will not be able to manage for some time yet."

Dan's tears increased as the doctor spoke. As guilt ridden as he was the suggestion of Sarah's mother once more staying in their tiny home filled him with dread. The doctor's final words stirred Dan as he realised how selfish his immediate thoughts had been.

"Pull yourself together lad and go and see your daughter. Let Sarah sleep, sleep and time will do the healing."

Dan loved his daughter from the very first moment he saw her.

"My Jane Ann," he told Sarah as he held their daughter, showing her to her mother for the first time.

Fortunately for Dan, Sarah's mother was ill and it fell to Harry's wife to stay and care for Sarah and the tiny infant who, contrary to the doctor's expectations, took no rearing. She had a strong pair of lungs and knew how to use them. Gradually Sarah's general health improved, she fed the child as it demanded, but she was grateful for Kate who bathed and changed Jane and more importantly gave her the love that Sarah was unable to give.

84

"She's a funny little thing," Hannah told Joe. "She's only little but by she's independent. She sleeps 'til she's hungry an' then she screams. As soon as y' change h' she's off t' sleep again 'til she screams t' be fed again."

Hannah tried to spend as much time with Sarah as she possibly could, passing the time of day and attempting to discuss the progress of the child that everyone described as a miracle.

"Y' should hear th' tales th' midwife's tellin' everybody." Hannah laughed. "Y' wouldn't believe some o' th' stories gannin' round th' village. Bloody miracle worker that doctor was, it was born dead an' he showed her how t' bring it back t' life. A've telt them she has a will o' her own an' it was nowt but a bit o' good doctorin'. She might be little Sarah but she's strong. Anyhow y' kna what th' like Sarah, the'll believe what th' want t' believe."

"Y' can tell me t' mind me own business if y' want Dan but if Kate doesn't go home soon Sarah'll never tek t' th' bairn. She's been wi' y' f' four weeks now, an' anyhow it's not fair on her, she's gettin' to attached t' th' bairn."

Dan was back at the pit, his wife was getting better, his baby girl thriving and although Kate was no substitute for Sarah she saw to his meals and he had no complaints. Dan did not take offence at Hannah's advice, he was only too well aware of how he had disregarded it on a previous occasion.

When Kate finally went back home to Harry, Sarah had little choice but to take over the care of her daughter; the daughter she never wanted and she was not sure if she ever would. She saw to Jane's every need in the same way she cared for Dan and their home. Dan's meals were ready when he returned home from the pit, their home was immaculate, and Jane continued to thrive. Only Hannah was aware that things were not as they should be. Sarah no longer visited her and whenever Hannah visited Sarah Jane was in her cot. The only time Sarah held the child was when she was feeding or changing her.

"Still", Hannah told Joe after every visit, "a'll say nowt, the bairn's thrivin' an' Dan's not complainin'."

As the years passed Dan and Sarah's family grew, another girl and two more boys. The four of them had Dan's fair hair and blue eyes and three of them were blessed with their father's good looks. Unfortunately, Ada, born five years after Jane, was the plain one. No one in the family could make their minds up just who she was like, either in looks or ways. Sarah worried about her; Ada was sly and at times bad tempered and rude to the rest of the family. But, like everything else, Sarah kept her worries to herself. Dan loved each child equally, or so he said, but everyone knew he had a soft spot for Jane and no one knew this more than Jane herself.

After Rob's death Dan had given up his carpentry and his leisure time was spent either in his allotment or the Bay Horse. He didn't completely slip into his old ways but he spent every Friday and Saturday night along with every Saturday and Sunday lunchtime drinking beer with the Bay Horse regulars. His dreams of working in another pit and acquiring a larger house were long forgotten.

When Jane was born Dan still had his dreams but Sarah would not entertain the idea of moving from the village and the little house where Rob had been born. She was often found sitting quietly beside Rob's grave in the village cemetery and there was nothing Dan could say to stop her. She didn't neglect her family and although the house was crowded, with their growing family, she did her best to make room for them all.

Sarah, in her own way, loved all of her children but the loss of Rob made her unable to demonstrate that love.

"It's as if she's frightened that if she shows them she loves them she'll lose them," Hannah told Joe. "There's nowt any o' us can do about it, she'll not change now; the're all well fed an' clothed but a bet sometimes they'd rather have a cuddle. A'm sure Dan realises, but y' can tell he just accepts it all, an' when it gets to much f' him drinks his answer. Mind Joe y' can never tell, but a kna', Sarah still likes a drink an' a think Dan's a bloody fool f' encouragin' her."

When the Great War started Jane was twelve years old, her brother Will was ten, Ada was seven and Tom, the baby, was nearly one. Will idolised his father and could not wait for the day when he could start work at the pit and go to the pub just like him. Tom was a sickly baby and from the day he was born Sarah was forced to give him more attention than the other three, but she was still restrained and limited his care to the bare necessities.

Fortunately, Ada, who in the past never seemed to like anyone took to her little brother and unlike her attitude to her other brother and sister she gave her undivided attention to Tom.

The war brought Hannah her own problems, two of her boys were itching to be off to the war and there was nothing she could do to prevent them. They both worked at the pit but neither of them could accept the work and the pay that was offered. John, the eldest at nineteen, was courting but the thought of a future at the pit and marriage made him even more determined. Hannah knew her boys of old and was acutely aware that whatever John did seventeen year old Bill would follow.

The beginning of the war had little effect on Sarah's mother and father or her sisters. She rarely saw her parents and Florrie had continued to please her father by producing another four grandchildren, all of them boys. Her husband, Alf, was finally doing well and providing handsomely for his family. He worked for Sarah's father, in his now expanding building business, and her father now had plans to include Florrie's sons in the family firm. This was a sore point with Dan as there was never any reference to his sons when his father in law discussed the future of the business and the family. Secretly Sarah was pleased; she had drifted away from her parents and Florrie, and did not want anything to happen that would bring the family close together again. Sarah was well aware that the family knew her secret and they certainly did not approve of her need for a drink. Fortunately one family tie did remain. Sarah's feelings towards her sister, Maisie, were different. After losing her first child, and nearly her own life, Maisie was told that she would never have children. The two sisters shared something that they could never have to put into words but each knew how the other felt.

The passing years had brought many changes to Dan's family. Both of his brothers now worked in the newly opened bigger mines and they each expected the war to bring them more work and greater security. Harry lived and worked only two miles from Dan's home and he was now a pit deputy and had a new terraced house which went with his job. Harry and Kate had three children and Kate visited Sarah at least once a week the two of them enjoying each others company. Kate was non judgemental of Sarah and Sarah harboured no animosity against Kate's rise in prosperity.

Two years after the birth of Jane, Dan's mother died. His father had found her lying at the bottom of the stairs when he came home from work. George was at work at the pit and Dan's mother was in Jennie's care. She told them she had just popped to the shop ten minutes before Dan's father was due in from work but Dan and Harry had their doubts. However, there was nothing they could do or say. They had no proof that anything untoward had happened but the two brothers wondered how their mother could have fallen down the stairs if, as everyone was aware, she could not walk unaided and Jennie, as she told them, had left their mother sitting comfortably in her chair in the kitchen beside the fire before she went out.

Dan and Harry agonised for hours following the death of their mother. How could she have fallen down the stairs if Jennie had left her in the kitchen? She was lying at the foot of the stairs but they were sure she could not have fallen down them. The doctor said the cause of death was from a knock on the head and he presumed she had struck her head on the banister, either from stumbling when attempting to climb the stairs or simply from tripping over the mat. While Dan's father and George accepted the doctor's explanation Dan and Harry did not.

Following Dan and Harry's conversation in the pub Dan had taken more notice of his mother and he was concerned that Harry might have had been right. She always had bruises on one place or another but his father, whenever challenged, made excuses and told the brothers that Jennie had her work cut out caring for their mother.

"Y' should be grateful t' Jennie an' George f' carin' f' y' Ma; an' y' shouldn't be always comin' t' me criticisin' them". He told Dan and Harry when they asked him about the bruises. "Y' Ma wont sit still, every time Jennie turns her back y' Ma tries t' get up by hersel' an' then she falls down," he replied in defence of his daughter-in-law.

Dan thought that strange, as every time he visited his mother she never attempted to get out of chair. But no matter what he or Harry said their father was adamant,

"Jennie's good t' y' Ma an' a can't manage wi' out her an' George livin' here".

They were left with little choice but to accept their father's word and, Harry, who always caused his father to be more defensive said very little.

"It's like holdin' a red rag t' a bull," he told Dan. "When a say owt t' him it ends in one hell o' a row."

The week after their mother's funeral George announced that he and Jennie were moving to the coast.

"A've been offered a job as deputy at one o' the pits on the coast an' a house goes wi' the job so a'm tekin' it. We're movin' next week. Me an' Jennie's done our bit so you two'll have t' see t' me Da."

Knowing that the move must have been planned before their mother's death Harry lost his temper with George but Dan restrained himself knowing that no matter what was said nothing would bring their mother back and in any case, they had no proof that anything had happened to their mother other than what the doctor had told them.

"Best let sleepin' dogs lie," he told Harry. "We'll just upset me Da, its best that the's an end t' the whole sorry affair."

Following his move to the coast Dan and Harry rarely ever saw George. Their father was lucky if he received a visit once a year and he was never invited to George and Jennie's home. After each visit their father insisted on telling Dan and Harry how well their brother was doing. They tried not to upset him by appearing to be interested as he kept them up to date on the progress of his two granddaughters who had been born during the first two years following their move.

George had quickly been promoted to overman at the pit; they moved into a larger house and he and Jennie were supposedly leading lights at the chapel. As usual Harry could not keep quiet when they left their fathers.

"Me Da's mad, our George is all he thinks about, y' wouldn't think me an' you had a job let alone a wife and bairns; as far as he's concerned he's only got two granddaughters an' then he never sees em."

"The're growin' in t' fine young girls, grand young pianists," his father told Dan following one of George's rare visits.

"The' have a lesson every week an' our George has bought a new piano f' them. He's given the old one t' the chapel. Real respected the' are by the folk ower there. Our George was sayin' he thinks the war'll do him a bit o' good.The'll be wantin' all the coal the' can get he says."

Dan said nothing to his father, keeping his thoughts to himself.

"Aye bloody typical, he'll gain out o' other's misfortunes. One day Da, y' might realise just what sort o' man our George is."

CHAPTER 5

Hannah had been on edge all day.

"Them two buggers's up t' sumat Sarah", she told her.

Jane was not at school on that particular day; she had been sick the night before and Sarah had let her sleep on that morning. She was sitting at the kitchen table pretending to read one of her school books but her ears were pricked listening to every word of Sarah and Hannah's conversation. If it was about John she wanted to know. He was her hero and had been since she was a toddler.

He was seven years her senior and was the one person in her life, other than Dan, who pandered to her every whim. He had taken her for walks from the day she took her first faltering steps. He always found the time to listen to her many moans and groans and her love was greater when he told her what a right little smasher she was.

"You'll break plenty lad's hearts in a few years time," he would say when jollying her out of one of her miserable moods.

Jane would look up at him, the adoration shining in her eyes. She was only twelve but she already knew she did not want to break anyone's heart all she wanted was to grow up quickly, then John would love her like she loved him, and then they could get married before he married that lass he was supposed to be courting.

Jane had already told her school friends that John was not really interested in Lily.

"It's just that she runs after him all the time an' he's too kind t' tell her t' push off," she told the girls as they huddled together in the school yard fantasising about their non- existent love lives.

John did love Jane but only in the same way as he loved his sisters. He did give Jane more attention than the others but that was because he felt sorry for her. He had his heard his Ma tell his Da that it was Sarah's fault that Jane was moody and independent. Sarah had never really shown her any love and had always just let her get on with things in her own way.

It was John Jane would run to if she fell and needed a grazed knee bathing. John she would complain to when the teacher at school wrongly accused her of some misdemeanour, or so Jane said, or chattering in class and refusing to do what was asked of her. John would listen to her and laugh with her.

"The teacher's probably right Jane," he would tell her. "D' y' ever de anythin' y' dinna want to?"

Jane was pleased she was off school on this particular day. Hannah was upset and it was because of John and Bill.

"It must be serious," she thought, "a've never seen Hannah cry afore, not even when Joe got lamed at the pit last year."

Jane listened as Hannah continued, crying as she talked and wiping her tears on the corner of her pinnie.

"Our John's in foreshift this week, he went t' work at one this mornin' but our Bill wouldn't get up f' backshift, he said he felt sick. Feelin' sick's never stopped him afore, an' now th' pair o' them's gone off, dressed in the best, wi' out a bye y' leave. The' must think a'm daft o' somat, the pair o' them'll have gone t' Bishop, a kna the' recruitin' there today. A'll swing f' our John takin' Bill wi' him, the'll be tellin' a pack o' lies, pretendin' our Bill's eighteen. A heard the pair o' them whisperin' the other night. The' didn't think a could hear them, but a could. Our Bill was tellin' our John he hoped he got somat to do wi' the hoss's. Bloody hoss's, he must think the' like pit ponies, he has a chance t' run a mile when he sees the size o' them."

93

Hannah was right. At the same time as she was telling Sarah her sorry tale the two brothers were waiting their turn in the queue to see the recruiting sergeant. John went first. The sergeant satisfied with John's answers to his questions did not even look at him as he said.

"Sign or make your mark."

Bill was next. The same questions were asked.

"Age?"

"Eighteen," Bill replied.

The sergeant never once looked at Bill as he questioned him further.

"Sign or make your mark," was all he said.

Bill did just that as quickly as he could, and once outside the two brothers hugged each other.

"We're in," Bill shouted.

"Right lad we're in, but remember we've t' tell me Ma yet an' that'll be a lot worse than facin' the recruitin' sergeant." John told him. "Now let's away home an' face the music."

Both boys left the village within the next six weeks. Neither of them had ever been outside of the county boundaries, a day at Durham or a day at the coast on the chapel trip during the summer was the furthest either of them had ever travelled. John was a little apprehensive before he left unlike Bill who was rareing to go.

Bill upset his mother and father by being unusually belligerent when John received the news that he was the first to go, especially when the night before John left for camp he went to the Bay Horse with his father and mates and Bill was not allowed to go with them. Hannah put her foot down when Joe suggested Bill join them.

"He's not old enough," she yelled at Joe.

Their protests made no difference.

"He should never have joined up in the first place," she cried. "Tryin' to be a man afore he's a boy, I'm havin' nowt else to do wi' it but a tell y' he's not breakin' the law an' gannin' in a pub while he's still under my roof. You're proud o' him now Joe, but mark my words y'll think again when he's gone, an' that's an end t' it, he's not goin' to the Bay Horse wi' you or anyone else."

Two weeks later Bill's attitude changed when his instructions arrived and he realised that he was to be stationed in a camp in a different county from John. However, he put on a brave face and his parting words caused a weeping Hannah even more grief.

"Dinna worry Ma," he joked, forcing a smile on his young face. "Me an' our John are sure t'meet up in France."

As he walked from his home he felt a strange sadness for his mother and that feeling overcame the fears he had for himself.

"A never realised me Ma thought s' much about us," he mumbled to himself, "an' it's a lovely feelin' to kna that when y' gannin' away".

Jane looked out of the bedroom window watching Bill walk up the bank, leaving the safety of his home, and having no idea what the future held for him. She had watched John leave just two weeks earlier and she was not happy. Jane was angry because John was leaving but the fact that Lily was walking up the bank with him filled her with fury. When they reached the village green John put his arms around Lily and Jane could not hide her jealousy as he kissed a weeping Lily tenderly on the lips.

John had kissed Jane the night before he left but the way he kissed her was not in the way he kissed Lily. Jane knew her kiss was just a peck compared to what she had just seen, and telling her to be a good girl while he was away really annoyed her.

"I'll show him," Jane whispered to herself, "when he comes back all show him a'm just as grown up as that Lily."

Jane did just that and while the two boys were fighting in France Jane, like Bill, grew up before her time.

By the end of 1915 John found himself in France along with the many other pitmen who filled the ranks of the 11th battalion of the Durham Light Infantry. There were many occasions when he blocked out the horrors by thinking of home and in particular of the day he and Bill came home from the recruiting office. Bill said he thought his mother was going to have a seizure, first crying then losing her temper and then not speaking to either of them for two days. It was not long before Bill joined John in France.

As usual Sarah did not realise what was happening to her daughter. Jane hardly bothered her mother except to plead for new clothes and so Sarah's life continued as normal throughout the long years of the war. That is until Hannah broke the news.

Everyone knew the war was coming to an end and Bill had been home for nearly three months. He had lost a leg in France and if it hadn't been for him Hannah would not have been sitting with Sarah telling her that her daughter was pregnant.

Bill rarely talked about his experiences in France and Hannah was more than surprised to hear him telling Jane about the events that led up to him losing his leg. She had realised that he and Jane had become very close since his return but she had not realised how close and she had never expected him to confide in such a young girl. Hannah was also aware that Jane had gained quite a reputation since leaving school. Sarah seemed unaware, but Hannah knew Sarah of old. If Sarah did not want to know then it was not happening. It was Joe who told Hannah what the men in the Bay Horse were saying.

"Nebody says owt in front o' Dan, Hannah, but the's many a time 'ave had t' tell some o' th' young uns t' shut the dirty mouths. A dinna kna how much o' it's right 'cos y' kna what young lads are, so don't go sayin' owt t' Sarah yet."

After last night Hannah knew she had to speak. Sarah had to be told no matter what Joe said. The lass was in trouble and needed help. Hannah had stood behind the door and listened to her son and Jane. They were sitting cosily in front of the fire in the kitchen and as everyone else was out Hannah decided to take the opportunity, a rare event, to spring clean the back kitchen.

As Hannah committed what she would have normally said was a sin she began to feel less guilty as she eavesdropped on their conversation. Not only was she hearing Jane's sorry tale, but also at last Bill was showing an interest and talking, something that the doctor had said must happen for him to make a full recovery. Although it was a warm July night Bill sat in his usual chair as near to the fire as he could get with an old wool blanket covering his missing leg. Hannah worried about him. He sat there day in, day out and no matter how uncomfortably hot he appeared to be he never removed the blanket.

It was Jane's crying that first attracted Hannah's attention.

"Bill a'm sure a'm goin't' have a bairn an' a daren't tell me Ma, she'll gan mad an' put me out an' a've ne where t' gan."

At this point Hannah felt like walking into the kitchen and confronting them.

"What's our Bill gone an' done," was her first thought, but she restrained herself as Jane continued.

"He's gone an' married somebody else Bill so a dinna kna what t'do."

Hannah was rigid, she hardly dare breathe, she felt guilty but she needed to know more. The door was slightly ajar and if she stood at the right angle she could just see the couple as they continued their intimate conversation. Bill beckoned Jane over to him and she settled on the floor resting her head on his leg as he tried to calm her.

"Y' Ma wont put y' out Jane, she does love y'. A've heard me Ma say that y' Ma's trouble is she's frightened to show her feelin's, an' y' na y' sel' y' Da thinks the's ne body like y'. It'll all come right in the end f' y' just like it will f' me. Just think o' what me Ma's gannin' through; a bet she wouldn't care if our John had half a dozen lasses havin' a bairn if she thought he was still alive. An' y' kna Jane, he is alive a'm sure o' it. We'll hear about him one o' these days or he'll walk in through that back door as if he was just comin' in from the pit. A'm sure o' him bein' alive Jane, just as a'm as sure y' Ma wont put y' out when she finds out. The war's changin' the way folk think, life's precious no matter what way we come into it. A learnt a lot in France, an' y' kna Jane a think a've learnt a lot more just sittin' in this chair thinkin' an' readin'. When the war's ower, a've made me mind up what a'm gannin' to do. A'm gannin't' mek' somat o' mesel', even if a've only got one leg. A met a fellow in France, a real gentleman he was, an officer. He used to tell me a was a bright young lad an' that a had to get in touch wi' him after the war. His family owns a newspaper an' he said he would get me a job. A told him how a used t' mek' up stories an' how a used t' dream that one day a'd be able to write them down so that other people could read them. He listened to me Jane, really listened, like he was really interested in what a was sayin'; me a bloody pitman who canna speak proper an'wi' ne real education."

The tears rolled down Hannah's cheeks and it took all of her will power to stop her rushing into the kitchen and holding her son in her arms. Bill gently stroked Jane's hair as he continued.

"A've read a lot these last few weeks an' a've learnt a lot more about life since a left the pit. This officer gave me his address, but a lost it when a lost me leg." Bill laughed, "it's a bloody good job a didn't lose me memory as well 'cos a remember the name o' the newspaper an' when the wars ower, a've made me mind up, am gannin' t' find him, that's if he made it back. A wouldn't have dared afore, but a'm goin' t' get in touch wi' that newspaper an' see if the' can help me trace him. A've told y' Jane the war's changed everythin' an' a'm sure y' Ma'll be alright w' y'."

Jane looked up at Bill, the mention of John's name made her momentarily forget her own troubles.

"D' y' really think John's still alive Bill?" she asked.

"Aye Jane a do, he's a lot tougher than a'll ever be, if a'm still alive an' thinkin' o' me future, he'll be somewhere. More than likely he's sittin' the rest o' the war out in some prison camp. You believe me he'll be back one day. A was really scared Jane when a didn't get sent t' the same camp as our John. It never entered me head when we signed up that we'd be split up. How I ended up in a Yorkshire regiment a'll never kna'? But a did an' funny enough a got what a wanted, t' be wi' the hosses. A learnt t' look after them." Bill laughed again. "Mind me Ma was right the' were nowt like pit ponies

99

but a soon got the hang o' it and grew t' love them just as much as a loved the ponies down the pit. A still dinna kna' which was the worse off; the poor pit ponies never seein' the light o' day or them big fine beasts out there in the thick o' the fightin'. Anyway, this officer a was tellin' y' about, he loved the hosses an' he used to spend hours on end just standin' talkin' to them, an' e would go ridin' wi' the other officers when things were quiet. Some o' the other officers were queer, the' looked down on the likes o' us, but he was a gentleman, not like a lot o' the stuck up buggers. I was in C Battery an' our regiment was the only Yorkshire one, the others were from Lancashire. You wouldn't believe it Jane but altogether there was about a thousand o' us. There was only thirty officers but as many hosses as there were men."

Bill's mood changed and as his voice became more of a whisper Hannah had to strain to hear what was being said.

"Just afore a lost me leg there'd been talk gannin' 'round that the Americans were gannin't' join us an' we didn't kna' what to mek' o' it. We didn't kna' if things were gannin't' get better or worse. Anyway, on this particular day, we heard a roar o' aeroplanes. When a looked up a saw them comin' ower the ridge. The' were hardly above the tree tops. A'd never seen as many German planes altogether. A heard the machine guns but the' went right ower the top o' us an' a thanked me lucky stars a was still alive. Not long after that we were told the Boche weren't far away from us an'afore we knew what was happenin' we were under machine gun fire. A can still remember the sound o' the bullets an' the shells fallin' 'round us. The Boche was comin' an' we were told to retreat. We even had to abandon an' blow up our own guns. Our orders were to get out."

Bill paused and sighed as he gently stroked Jane's hair. Hannah was stiff and wanted to move but suddenly Bill began to continue with the story and once again she stood quietly listening to her son.

"A can remember one incident in particular, an' that's probably 'cos it involved another pitman. One o' the guns was stuck in the mud an' this particular fella took it in t' his head that it wasn't ganna be left. The hoss couldn't pull it out an' so he put his great hefty shoulders t' the wheel o' the gun. As fast as he moved it, the gun kept slippin' back. One o' the officers told him t' leave it, but he was determined an' then another two gunners went t' help him. The' got the gun out an' even if everythin' else was left behind that gun went wi' us."

Bill paused again but Hannah knew there was more to come.

"A can remember another incident, when the' was machine gun fire all around us as we were retreating. The' was dead men an' hosses lyin' all ower the road. Then we finally reached a village but we could see the bloody Germans were shellin' it. The' was a crossroads in the middle o' the village and everythin' had to go through it, guns, wagons, lorries, everythin'. The Germans were firin' at the crossroads, big shells, Jane, one every couple o' minutes. Our wagons waited at a safe distance 'til a shell burst then we galloped, like hell, past the danger spot. The' was about half a dozen tryin' t' get through at a time; it was mad an' a was in one o' them bloody wagons when we copped it. It seems somebody dragged me out o' the way o' the other gallopin' hosses but a remember nowt. A wish a knew who it was Jane, he saved me life, an' a'll never be able t' thank him."

Hannah couldn't believe what she was hearing; she was upset but relieved; at last Bill was doing what the

Doctor had said, he was talking about what had happened and maybe now there would be a future for him. Bill had not finished and Jane was a captive audience, the mention of John and the things Bill was telling her were helping her, even if it was only for a short time, to forget her own problems.

"Anyhow, Jane, the next thing a remember is wakin' up in a field hospital. A'd lost me leg but apart from that a had no other injuries an' they told me they would be shippin' me home as soon as the' could. The rest y' kna'. A'm sittin' here an' some o' me mates is still out there fightin'. God knows what our John's been through so you stop y' frettin' an' get on wi' your life. When a look back now a realise most o' the wounded were a lot worse off than me. A saw them in that field hospital an' then when a was in hospital back here. Legs an' arms blown off, blinded an' the lungs burnt out wi' mustard gas. Some o' the poor buggers were struck dumb wi' shell shock an' some o' them had just gone right out o' the minds."

It was not until Joe was home from work and both he and Bill were in bed that Hannah broke down and cried. She cried for Jane but her heart ached for her son. She did not know how she managed to face and talk to Bill when she made him a cup of tea before he went to bed. But Hannah knew she must be strong, or at least appear to be, this was a turning point for him and she would do nothing to prevent him feeling whole and like a man again. Lying in bed awake, there was to be little sleep for Hannah that night, she made her plans.

"A'll open me mouth when the times right," she thought to herself. "Jane needs seein' t' first an' it looks like a'm goin' t' lose our Bill again, but this time he'll be doin' the right thing, an' a'll be pleased t' see him walk

102

up that bank again, even if it's only on one leg, 'cos this time he'll be doin' the right thing."

Hannah's thoughts turned to John, her gentle giant of a son. She had always felt that he had gone off to war never believing that he might have to kill someone. The lad who could not kill a spider, not even a blackclock. He would scrape them up with a piece of paper, throw them over the wall into the back street, and then watch them run safely away. As she eventually dropped off into a fitful sleep she muttered to herself.

"The biggest an' softest o' them all, a wonder if he is alive like our Bill says, an' if he is, a wonder what he's doin' now, a just wish he was back home sittin' playin' the piano in the front parlour."

John was the only member of the family who had inherited her father's love of music. He was only three years old when her father began to teach him to play the piano and her father said he was a natural. As he grew older Hannah's father hands became arthritic and gnarled through years of hard work at the pit and when he was no longer able to play the piano he gave it to John. It stood there, in pride of place, in the parlour. It was the only decent piece of furniture they had but the lid had never once been raised since the day John had left.

During the long years of the war Hannah often dreamt about her boys and tonight was no exception. When she dreamt of John it was always the same dream. He was about two years old and had fallen down a hole. She could never make out where the hole was but she could hear him crying and calling for her. She would walk to the hole, look down and see him, his arms outstretched reaching for her. His frightened face haunted her, but she could never reach him, and she always woke in a cold sweat knowing she could not save her son. Although tonight her sleep was fitful John's terror did not cause her to waken. She slept on to finish the dream and this time she did save him; grasping further and further down until she reached him, pulling him to safety and embracing him in her loving arms.

That night while Hannah slept John lay awake on the wooden boards that had been his bed for many months. He often dreamt of home and his family but that was during the day when he was wide awake. At night his dreams were nightmares. Tonight, like every other night, he woke himself up with his own screams, the sweat pouring from every inch of his body. As he lay shivering in his wet bed he thought back to the time he had first arrived in France.

He was in the 11th battalion of the Durham Light Infantry. Most of the men were miners and they went about their gruelling pioneering duties without any fuss. They knew they could fight as well as the next man but they had no choice but to labour at the heavy work of digging trenches. They were told the job they had to do was just as important as fighting the Germans and as it was not dissimilar to working down the pit they got on with it enjoying the comradeship they had all been used to.

"We'll be alright if this is all that's expected o' us," John yelled at his new found friend as they hoisted sandbags of chalk onto their shoulders, staggering under the weight of them as they carried them to the dump which was a good twenty yards along the trench.

They worked for a full eight hours during the night and were exhausted when five o'clock came and they could file back into the communication trench, wearily trying to find their way back to the point where they could get out and into the open air.

"Aye," Pat shouted back to John, "but a hope we see a bit o' action afore the end comes. A'd hate to go home an' tell them we did nowt different to what we do down the pit."

John was to see plenty of action. He often thought of the horrors he had lived through but his nightmares were always set in those trenches where he had spent the happiest years of the war.

In the autumn of 1917 it rained for days on end and John found himself fighting the Germans in mud so deep it was like a poisonous porridge of uncertain depth. The 15th division of the Durham Light Infantry had suffered a massacre with more than 400 men and 20 officers falling during an advance of a few hundred yards. The Northumberland Fusiliers of the 149th brigade had been sacrificed in an abortive attack through a wilderness of shell holes filled with slimy water.

John had seen the aftermath of the attack, the deep muddy water failing to hide the bodies of the men and mules that had been slaughtered. Shortly after these horrendous events, the infantry, including the 2nd and 14th battalion of the Durham Light Infantry finally experienced a victory while fighting in the great tank battle at Cambrai. Fortunately they had few casualties.

By the end of November the Germans struck back and the conditions became unbearable. It was cold and wet and John as he lay in the mud, with the rest of the battalion, was totally disheartened. He had never felt so hungry in his life. It was the feeling of hunger that he remembered so vividly. They were cut off and struggling to seal the German breach. Even though extra troops were arriving in an effort to stop the Germans moving forward it did not seem that they, or the much needed supplies, would ever reach John and the other weary soldiers.

It was during this battle that John's war came to an end. He could hear the sounds of the exploding shells getting nearer and nearer. He could tolerate that, but what he could not bear was the screaming of his comrades as they were killed or injured. They could not fight back; they were trapped in a hell hole. And there was nothing that he or his fellow soldiers could do to help the injured or dying. John's fear was intensified by the knowledge that it could be his turn next. His last memory of those unforgettable days was a loud explosion, so loud it felt as if his skull had been burst into tiny pieces. Then there was something hard pressing into his ribs and as he opened his eyes, he knew he wasn't dead, looming above him was a German soldier with a bayonet pressing against his chest.

There were many times, during the next few months, when he wished he had been killed. He walked for what seemed to be hundreds of miles and then suffered a long train journey, followed by miles and miles of more walking. He had been hungry lying in the trenches but that hunger was nothing to what he now experienced. Finally he reached his destination, where he was he did not know and he was so exhausted he really did not care. The blisters on his feet had become infected and every step he took he prayed would be his last. Lagging behind brought no comfort it only infuriated the guards, who were just as tired, causing them to kick him back into line. The names of the places they passed meant nothing to him, the only thing he did know was that the rough wooden huts where he was now prisoner was somewhere in Germany. He did not really care where he was, there was nothing but open countryside surrounding them, not another building or landmark in sight.

Italians, British, French and even a handful of Russians all herded together, hardly a thing to eat, and if

106

you were ill you either got better yourself or died. There were no medicines available and it was unlikely there would be. They asked often enough when they saw the Red Cross parcels arrive, but neither extra food nor medicines for the sick were ever distributed.

John had escaped the last typhoid epidemic but many of his new found friends had succumbed. He felt no emotion digging graves and burying his fellow prisoners who had fought so bravely through the horrors of this terrible war only to end up dying of such a stinking disease. It was better not to feel, he was numb, the rest of them, including himself, would die if the war did not finish soon. A bowl of soup and a piece of bread, two or three times a week, was not sufficient for anyone to survive on. Even if starvation or disease did not kill you then just a sideways glance at one of the guards could cause you to be kicked to death. John turned on his side the tears rolling down his cheeks.

"Why do a have to think?" he muttered. "It's easier not to."

Joe's voice woke Hannah with a start.

"Come on Hannah hinnie, are y' gannin't' lie there all day? The's breakfast t' see t' an' bait t' put up. An' y'll never believe it but our Bill's up an' dressed an' he's lightin' the fire. A dinna kna what's happened but he's got a smile on his face an' he's hoppin' around like a spring chicken."

Hannah jumped out of bed and she felt as if a weight had been lifted from her chest.

"Everythin's ganna be alright," she said to herself as she hastily pulled on her clothes. "Out o' bad comes good," she mumbled.

As she walked down the stairs she was still talking to herself.

"A'll do what a can f' Jane, she's been our Bill's salvation. A'll talk t' Sarah today; a'll have t' get it ower with an' the sooner the better by the look o' Jane."

As Bill had predicted Sarah did not show Jane the door. It was Dan who hurt the most and when Sarah broke the news to him he would not believe her.

"She's nowt but a bairn hersel', Hannah must have got it all wrong," he cried.

Hannah had not got it wrong. Sarah had spoken to Jane before she told Dan and there was no doubting it, Jane was five months pregnant.

Hannah had been surprised at Sarah's reaction on the afternoon she had told her. Sarah listened without once interrupting, she asked no questions and did not even ask Hannah how she knew and for how long she had known.

Hannah told Joe about Jane that night but her only reference to Bill was that she had overheard their conversation about Jane being pregnant.

"A couldn't believe it Joe," she told him, "when a told Sarah she said nowt. A think she must have had an inkling, in fact more than that, a think she knew."

Hannah was right, Sarah had suspected and so it came as no surprise to her. At first she had turned a blind eye when Jane was sick on a morning and, more than once, a deaf ear when she walked into the village shop catching the tail end of the gossip, which stopped abruptly, when she entered.

Dan never spoke one word to Jane from the moment Sarah gave him the news. He would not look at her and he was not sure whether he could ever forgive her. He still loved her, that was what hurt the most, but he could not understand how Jane, his little girl, could have acted as she had.

Sarah's reaction to the news was entirely different to that of Dans. She spoke to her; she ranted and raved, called her a little whore, threatened her with the workhouse and then had a few drinks and fell into a blissful sleep.

Ada and Will knew what was going on but were too involved with their own lives to become involved. Will was working at one of the new pits and was working hard, looking forward to the day when he would be doing stonework and earning good money. He was too young to drink or gamble but he could not wait for the day to come when he could start to enjoy himself with his older friends.

Ada was still at school and the older she got the more spiteful and sly she became. She did not have many friends but that did not seem to bother her, her entire life was devoted to her younger brother who at five years of age was still as sickly as ever. Tom was a lovely natured child and strangely enough he avoided inheriting the nasty ways of his sister. Ada ignored Jane most of the time but when no one was listening she would be only too ready to pass some spiteful remark about her sister's predicament.

Sarah knew in her heart, that she would never be able to carry out any of the threats she had made to Jane. When she was not ranting or raving she became quite practical. Eventually she persuaded Jane to tell her who the father of her child was and it was she who set the wheels in motion to ensure that he would have some input into the financial upbringing of her daughter's child. Even Dan had not thought of an alternative solution, Jane would have the baby, no matter what shame it brought on the family, and they would bring it up.

"Y've made y' bed an' y'll lie on it." Sarah told her daughter.

CHAPTER 6

Sarah sat in the corner of the bedroom staring at the bed where her daughter lay sleeping. While others were enjoying their first Christmas dinner, after a long and bloody war, Dan and her other children were down stairs making the best of whatever they could find to eat.

Ada, Will and Tom had never had lavish Christmas dinners and, as far as presents were concerned, they did not expect anything other than a stocking filled with the traditional apple, orange and a few nuts. They were more than pleased with a few extra coppers and every Christmas morning eagerly awaited the arrival of their granda for a 'proper' present. Ada had filled a stocking for Tom, but he was still upset because Santa had forgotten her this year. As far as she was concerned, apart from Tom's stocking, today was no different from any other.

"The's not even owt f' me Granda, our Jane's spoilt Christmas f' all o' us this year," she grumbled to Will.

Will was not interested in his sister's moaning. He was getting ready to go out with his mates and was in a hurry. The one person Will respected was his granda and, although he would never admit it, he was also frightened of him. He would tell lies to his Ma and Da to avoid trouble, but not to his Granda. He would avoid him at all costs. He knew he could not lie to him and the only way was to avoid him. Ada continued moaning and groaning as her Granda prepared to leave and Will muttered under his breath.

"Thank God he's goin', a'd have missed a good session o' pitch an' toss, as it is the rest o' 'em'll have gone wi' out me an' a'll have a job t' catch up wi' 'em. If the' get t' the bloody wood afore me a'll never be able t' find them."

Will and his mates knew how to out smart the police. They gambled every Sunday afternoon and every bank holiday moving to a different part of the wood in an effort to avoid the police. The police knew what they were doing but rarely could find the gamblers. Will had already had a few near misses, running like the wind with the police on his tail. If his father ever found out he knew the trouble he would be in. The thing that annoyed him the most was when he was on a winning streak. If the police disturbed the game he was no better off as all of his winnings were left behind. The last time the police had caught them he had arrived home out of breath, the sweat pouring from him. Dan had accused him of gambling but Will, as usual, denied it; arguing with his father and accusing him of gambling in the Bay Horse. Dan would end the argument in his usual way when he knew he was beaten.

"Y'll de as a say lad an' not as a do."

Sarah walked to the foot of the bed and lifted the sleeping child from the drawer. Settling back in her chair, the child cradled in her arms, she looked down at its tiny wrinkled face. Sarah did not make a sound; she did not want to be disturbed. The tears rolled down her cheeks, she had not felt like this for sixteen long years. It was as if he was back, her beloved Rob. Black curly hair, a beautiful pink face, so peaceful the child was. She too felt at peace sitting holding this child that no one had wanted.

Sarah jumped as the back gate slammed, the child moved in her arms and those few precious moments were gone. This was not Rob. This child was her daughter's, her granddaughter. Memories of her grandmother's words came flooding back to her.

"Never have lasses hinnie the'll bring y' nowt but trouble."

"Aye Grannie," Sarah thought. "Y' never spoke a truer word an' now we' got another."

On that same day John was lying in a hospital bed and once again he was not sure where he was. On the day the Red Cross had arrived he had been with a group of weary prisoners, each of them dipping their stale bread into watery soup. They did not know the war was over and every day came and went just like the one before. No one spoke until the last drop of soup was finished.

"It'll soon be bloody Christmas," John said, not directing his speech at any one in particular.

Direct conversation between the men had stopped some time ago.

"A kna one thing f' sure," he continued, "if the war doesn't end soon the's none o' us'll see another Christmas."

"I doubt if we will see the New Year," was the refined reply from the other side of the filthy hut.

They had all done their best to keep themselves, and the hut, clean but in the end the lice won the battle. Now they were too weak to bother and hopes of an end to the war long since past. There were not many of them left and there had been no new prisoners for weeks. That and the fact that only a handful of guards remained still did not give them hope.

When they heard the sound of a lorry they did as they usually did ignored it, but today curiosity got the better of a young Irish boy who, in the beginning, had always been a butt to the joking of the older prisoners. Recently he had proved his worth to all of them, caring for the sick and dying, offering his own ration of food to those around him who would die whether or not they received his meagre helping.

"It's the Red Cross," he shouted, "and the guards have gone. The war must be over."

Those who could, including John, mustered the strength to run out into the compound. The boy was right, the war was over, but for John there was a further hurdle to cross before he would be back home with the family he so longed to see again.

The Spanish Flu had raged in France during the spring and summer of the last year of the war. Many soldiers on the battlefields, and in the hospitals, having survived the rigours of war had lost their lives to it. As the war ended the Flu struck worldwide and John was its latest victim. The infection ravished his body, as it did all of its victims, showing no mercy. He raved like a lunatic and was unaware of the time, the place or who he was.

Throughout his illness he neither received visitors nor correspondence. The doctors and nurses were not particularly concerned, they knew his family would have been informed, but sometimes the lines of communication were just as slow as they had been during the war. It was to be sometime before John became aware that his family had not received any communication from the authorities informing them that their son was alive, had been a prisoner of war, but was now gravely ill.

Meg was two weeks old and as far as Jane was concerned the whole sordid affair was over. She smiled to herself, she had been right; her mother had taken over the care of the baby. On the day her daughter was born she lay facing the wall neither speaking to anyone nor showing any interest in the child she had given birth to. Neither Sarah nor the midwife could persuade her to feed the baby. Their constant threats that it would starve to death if she did not take the child to her breast made no impression on her. In desperation it was Sarah who gave her granddaughter her first feed. Evaporated milk and honey, which the hungry child readily drank, was to be the means of Sarah's granddaughters' survival.

Because she was so tiny, and the family were afraid she might not survive, Dan's father, in his capacity as a lay preacher, christened her when she was only two days old. Jane would take no part in the simple ceremony that took place in the bedroom. It was Dan's father who chose her name.

"Margaret we'll call her," he said after trying, in vain, to encourage Jane to give her daughter a name.

After Dan's father left Sarah told Dan the baby might be christened Margaret but she was to be called Meg.

"Why?" Dan asked.

Sarah did not give an answer, but everyone knew Sarah's request would be granted.

Sarah was exhausted. It was her turn to help Hannah and her family. The Spanish Flu had arrived in the North of England and Hannah's family were not to be spared. So many families were affected the doctors could only diagnose the condition and advise relatives and friends to apply cold compresses and give their loved ones plenty to drink. Joe was the first, and then Hannah's two youngest came down with the infection. At least Ada was trying to be helpful looking after Dan, the boys and begrudgingly the new baby; she left Jane to care for herself while Sarah spent her time helping Hannah care for her family.

It was a cold January morning and there were many people in the village stricken with the dreadful disease. Sarah was feeling miserable and to make matters worse she and Dan had argued before she had left to go and help Hannah.

"Y' realise Sarah, the's folk dyin' from it an' a dinna want y' catchin' out or bringin' it in t' the bairns," he had told her.

Sarah immediately turned on him.

"How can y' say such a thing, you o' all people, after all she's done f' us these last years?"

Dan realised he had said the wrong thing but he would not give in.

"A'm only sayin' it f' y' own good Sarah; just watch what y' doin', we've the bairn t' think about now."

As Sarah walked down the back street to Hannah's home her thoughts were with her dear friend and of the time when she and Dan had first moved to the village.

"What would we have done wi' out y' Hannah, you an' Joe? What would a do wi'out y' now? No Dan y' wrong, a've got t' help, she'd ave done it f' us an' Joe would an' all."

Sarah was pleased when she first went into Hannah's home and saw that Joe was obviously over the worst. But one look at the little ones and she became concerned, they were much worse. Bill was putting cold compresses on their foreheads and his sisters were in the back kitchen making drinks and sorting the mounting piles of dirty washing.

"Where's y' Ma Bill?" Sarah asked.

"She's in the parlour Sarah," he told her. "She says she's alright, just tired, but a think it's more than that. Will y' gan an' see t' her, we'll manage here?"

Sarah knew as soon as she saw her. Hannah was not just tired she had the flu. There was no point in sending for the doctor, he would see Hannah when he found the time to call and see the others. There was nothing the doctor could do that they could not do themselves. He was just as helpless as they were. The disease would run its course. Instead she sent a message to Dan.

"Tell him the'll have to manage wi' out me," she told Hannah's daughter, "a'm stayin' here t' look after y' Ma."

Sarah stayed for two days and two nights, neither she nor Bill had any sleep. It was the same as when she had cared for Dan and Rob. First she sponged the little ones, then Hannah, changing their beds and offering them drink after drink. At the end of that long forty eight hours Sarah did the last thing she would ever do for her dear friend. She wept bitterly as she lovingly laid out the bodies of her trusted friend and her two youngest children.

The following day the news came that they had all been waiting for. The letter was from John; he was alive and would be home the following week. Bill read the letter to his father. The travel arrangements were made. He was coming by train to Durham station and would arrive the following Tuesday about four o'clock on the afternoon. After the first few sentences Joe's grief was so intense he could not listen. He wanted Hannah here with him, to share in the joy of their son's homecoming. He wanted Hannah, he wanted his children, they should all be here to greet his eldest son, the son he thought dead long ago, the son who Hannah had said was still alive and one day would return home to them.

"Da are y' listenin', Bill shouted, "he's still bad an' we have t' gan an' meet him an' we have t' find some transport t' get him from Durham. He's been a prisoner o' war and since then he's had the flu. Th've only let him home 'cos he's telt them he's got plenty o' family t' look after him."

Bill raised his voice once again. "Da please listen we've things t'de. It'll be the funeral the day after our John comes an' we'll have t' do some organisin' an y'll have to come

116

wi' me to Durham t' get him. You'll have t' tell him about me Ma an' the bairns."

That job was to be Dan's. The station was busy and Dan and Bill were overawed by the number of men in uniform who were either bandaged, missing a limb or being pushed in a wheelchair. The train was one hour late and when it finally arrived and the passengers stepped down from the train onto the platform Dan and Bill were disappointed. Dan feared the worst but could not bring himself to say the words that would only add to Bill's sorrow. Instead he did his best to raise Bill's hopes.

"Somat must have gone wrong Bill," he said with a heavy heart. "He must have missed the train o' somat's stopped him from catchin' it."

As Dan and Bill turned to walk away Bill felt a tug on his coat. He turned and looked down at the gaunt man in the wheelchair, his face was pale with a tinge of yellow and so small, but it was John, a different John and they had not even recognised him. Dan was as surprised as Bill, but when he looked there was no mistaking him, it was John and he was home at last, but to what he thought to himself.

Dan watched the two brothers hugging each other and after a few tears John asked the question he knew would come.

"Where's me Ma an' Da a thought th' would be here wi' y'?"

Dan knew what he had to do. John had to be told now and it was up to him to do the telling. Not a word was spoken on the journey home, a journey that, to Dan, seemed to last a lifetime.

When they arrived at the village they walked down the bank. Dan, pushing John in his wheelchair, Bill, at his side gripping his crutches, head down as always,

117

afraid of stumbling on the uneven ground. Only Dan was aware of the eyes watching them, peering through every window, no one could be seen but every house they passed had the tell tale sign of a curtain pulled to one side.

Dan breathed a sigh of relief when they reached Joe's front door. He lifted a featherweight John from the wheelchair and carried him into the house. Bill followed behind, unable to speak, not knowing what the next few hours would bring. As soon as he had settled John safely in a chair in the kitchen with his father and manoeuvred the wheel chair into the house Dan left.

As he walked to his own home he could see Jane heading down towards Joe's.

"A've been a bloody idiot," he muttered. "What does it matter? What's done's done. She' alive an' a should thank me blessin's f' her an' that bairn she's given us."

Dan had neither looked nor spoken to his daughter since the night Sarah had told him she was going to have a baby but as they approached each other, he turned to face her and spoke as he gently touched her arm.

"Dinna gan t' see him yet hinnie. Gi' him time; come home wi' y' Da an' me you an' y' Ma a'll have a nice pot o' tea."

Jane listened intently, just as she had with Bill, while Dan told Sarah the events of the afternoon.

"It was awful Sarah an' a never want t' have t' do owt like that again."

He kept looking at Jane, including her, trying as best he knew how to show her that she was forgiven. He wanted her to know that he still loved her; he would never be able to tell her that, this was the only way he knew. Jane felt more content than she had been for months. She knew her father well enough, she was his daughter, and now she knew he still loved her. The next

118

time he looked at her she smiled at him. The smile he returned made Jane feel that the last year had never happened.

As Dan continued Jane listened but her mind was on other things.

"A think a might get back t' normal now," she thought.

Dan looked sad as he finished telling an upset Sarah about the afternoon.

"When a telt John he said nowt; he looked bad anough afore but he looks a thousand times worse now. He's never opened his mouth all the way home an' neither did Bill. When a took him int' the house Joe was sat beside the fire, he just looked up at John an' started to cry. A left them there Sarah 'cos a didn't kna what else to do. God knas what it'll be like when he finally goes int' the parlour an' sees the three o' them laid out in th' coffins."

Sarah had, at first, decided to be at Joe's when John arrived home but at the last minute she changed her mind. She knew there was little she could do or say that would make it any easier for the family. Her own experience had taught her that only time can heal and then that healing is never complete.

"Y' did right t' leave them Dan," Sarah told him. "The's nowt we can de f' now. A'll gan down later an' see if the's owt a can de f' the lasses, a think the men's best left on the' own f' now."

Hannah's eldest daughters had left home a number of years before, entering service as soon as they left school. Now they were both married and had their own families' needs to attend to at this tragic time. They were expected to come but not until the day of the funeral and then the telegram they had sent said they would be returning home on the same day. Hannah's two other daughters

119

who were still at home mercifully escaped the flu and although they were grieving as much as their brothers they took on the role of seeing to the family in just the way Hannah had taught them.

Later that night Sarah went to Joe's but she stayed in the back kitchen with his daughters. They had finished the work and were at a loose end. They could not go into the parlour and they did not want to go into the kitchen with their father and brothers. Sarah realised it would be sometime before they really felt the loss of their mother.

John was home now but he was a stranger to them, he had not spoken to them yet, he had not spoken to anyone since his return. Sarah wisely suggested to the girls that they were doing the right thing and suggested they stay the night with her. She was surprised when they jumped at the offer of blankets and pillows on the kitchen floor.

"Gan an' tell y' Da then," was all Sarah said.

Bitter experience had taught Sarah how to cope and hide her sorrow. Her agonies were hidden deep inside of her; hers was a private sorrow that belonged to no one but herself. Hannah's unhappy children would not see it; neither would Dan or anyone else she cared for.

Later that night as Sarah and Dan lay in bed, neither of them able to sleep; they talked about the events of the last few days. So much had happened to others they had had little time to worry about their own lives. Even now Sarah's thoughts were on Hannah's two girls sleeping soundly downstairs in the kitchen.

"It was as if the' couldn't wait t' get away when a asked them t' come Dan, poor bairns, the've been forgotten in all this mess. Even their John comin' home means nowt t' them."

A few doors away Joe, Bill and John still sat in silence. It was late and only Bill had any practical thoughts. He raised his head and spoke the first words to be heard in the house since John's return.

"Let's gan int' the parlour."

Joe did not raise his head; it was if he had not heard Bill speak. Joe was pleased to see John but how could he show that pleasure when his wife and bairns were lying in their coffins in the parlour. Bill was surprised when John slowly heaved himself up from the chair. John was frightened but he knew what must be done. He gripped Bill's arm tightly as the two brothers slowly made their way into the parlour. As Bill hopped on one leg; John mustered all of his strength to face what was to be a long journey; a journey that both he and Bill had to face; a journey without their mother.

Dan had moved all of the furniture out of the parlour. It was the only way they could get three coffins in there. Only the piano and stool remained. The two men sat side by side on the leather stool, neither of them looked towards the coffins, they faced the old piano. Ten minutes passed before either moved or spoke. Bill was the first to speak as he raised the piano lid.

"Play somat f' me Ma John. She lived f' the day when y'd come home an' play the piano again. Play somat f' me Ma."

John looked down at the piano keys, yellow with age. He was not sure if he could remember how, and even if he could, he did not think he would ever be able to play another note.

"Gan on lad," Bill asked him again. "Play it f' me Ma."

John gently ran his fingers over the surface of the keys; he pressed one or two notes and then started to play. After John played the first verse Bill began to sing, starting at the first verse of the hymn, the verse that Hannah loved more than any other.

"On a hill far away stood an old rugged cross,
the emblem of sufferin' an' shame; an' a loved
that old cross where the dearest an' best
f' a world of lost sinners was slain.

So a'll cherish the old rugged cross
'til my trophies at last I lay down;
a will cling t' the old rugged cross
an' exchange it someday f' a crown.

Oh that old rugged cross, so despised by th'world,
has a wondrous attraction f' me;
for the dear Lamb o' God
left his glory above to bear it t' dark Calvary.

So a'll cherish the old rugged cross,
till my trophies at last I lay down;
I will cling t' the old rugged cross
An' exchange it someday f' a crown."

Joe hearing his sons raised himself from the chair and
walked slowly through to the parlour to join them.

"In th' old rugged cross stained wi' blood
so divine, a wondrous beauty a see.
for 'twas on that old cross Jesus suffered
and died t' pardon an' sanctify me.

So a'll cherish the old rugged cross,
till my trophies at last a lay down;
I will cling t' the old rugged cross
an' exchange it someday f' a crown.

T' the old rugged cross I will ever be true'

it's shame an' reproach gladly bear,
then he'll call me someday t' me home
far away; there his glory f' ever a'll share.

So a'll cherish the old rugged cross,
'till my trophies at last I lay down;
I will cling t' the old rugged cross
an' exchange it someday f' a crown."

They were together again in that small room just as they were before the war. John playing the piano, the rest of the family gathered around him, singing and laughing together. But they were not together again, they were singing but there was no laughter in their voices. The family would never be together again. The three men were not only sad but also afraid for the future; their future, how would they ever survive without the support of a beloved wife and mother.

Hannah had loved Sundays, especially after tea when Joe was in from the Bay Horse, the dinner was over and she could relax with her family in the small shabby parlour where for some of the family it was standing room only. The entertainment did not begin until Joe had had his customary two hours sleep after his dinner. He would get up and join them in the parlour; with one eye on the clock Joe would join the family singing Hannah's favourite hymns but when the clock struck seven he would smile at Hannah, quietly leave the parlour put on his cap and coat and go, once more, to join his friends in the Bay Horse.

When the hymn was finished Joe, John and Bill lapsed into a deadly silence. Joe was the first to break it. He looked towards Hannah's coffin that would not be closed until the morning of the funeral and then turning to John he finally spoke to him.

"Y' Ma'll 've enjoyed that John. She'll be pleased y' came home afore she had t' leave us. She'll rest better now, the little ones a' wi' her an' a kna she'll be at peace. She said y'd come home t' her one day an' a didn't believe her. Thanks lad, now lets all away t' bed an' try t' get a bit o' sleep, the's things t' see t' tomorro'."

The funeral over the two families did their best to get on with their lives. Surprisingly Dan and Sarah's family escaped the ravages of the Spanish Flu. As Dan, said to Sarah.

"Our cards musn't have been marked hinnie, he didn't want us yet."

Unlike Sarah, Dan had always believed that when your time was up it was up and there was nothing you or anyone else could do about it.

The following few months were uneventful but there were to be many times in the future when Sarah would wish for the wisdom and companionship of her dear friend. When he was fully recovered Joe went back to the pit and his youngest daughter did her best to fill her mother's place. She cleaned, washed, ironed and baked and soon began to enjoy looking after their home becoming very protective of her father and brothers. Her sister decided to do as their elder sisters had advised. They found her a place in service and she was quickly off to Harrogate to begin a new life and hopefully, as her sisters had done, find a husband.

Bill, after being fitted with a false leg and an amazing show of determination and hard work, finally discarded his crutches. Following numerous letters and disappointments he finally contacted his officer and it was a sad day for Joe when he left for Manchester to take up a junior role in a local newspaper. He wrote to

Joe frequently and his last letter was full of his new life. Joe finished his dinner after a hard shift at the pit and John read the letter to him with Doris sitting quietly, as she always did, on the cracket beside the fire.

30th July,
Dear Da,

I have found a decent place to live now. The lady who runs the lodging house lost her husband in the war. She has two little lasses and I think she has been finding it hard to make ends meet. I'm her second lodger, there's only room for two, and the other one's a canny fellow. I think I've hit lucky, the place is only basic, but it's clean and I couldn't have been luckier as far as the food is concerned, she runs a cracking bait shop.

Don't laugh but I'm trying to write and talk proper. I have been working on the paper for a few weeks now and really I am just the run around. But I love it and I am learning. I am starting night classes in September so I'll not be home for a bit. By a pay me board and then pay for the classes I'll not have much left. I hope I can make it for Christmas. Give my love to John and the lasses and you can show Dan and Sarah me letter if you want to.

Your Loving Son,
William.

Joe laughed when John was finished,
"William be buggered he must be usin' his Sunday name now."
Joe looked towards John and as his son placed the letter on the table Joe looked up at him; he knew Bill would be all right but would John. John's physical health was improving, Doris's suet puddings, broth and

125

dumplings were seeing to that but his mental health was not. Joe had noticed John's periods of depression and the quiet man was now quite bad tempered. As Joe told Dan,

"A'm worried f' him Dan a think he could be violent one o' these days if he doesn't cool that temper o' his."

Joe noticed the sad look on John's face after he had read the letter and did his best to cheer him up.

"Y'll soon be back at the pit lad," he told him.

John was not finding life easy, he still had the nightmares and they were getting worse rather than better. Now his Ma was always down in the trench with him and neither of them could ever find a way out. The doctors had told him the nightmares would fade in time but they were still as vivid as ever and now they haunted him throughout the day.

Lily had tried to renew their friendship but he kept her at arms length, he did not know why but he did not want to renew their relationship. He knew that really he wanted her but the thought of her knowing how he suffered filled him with fear. His father and Doris were the only two people who knew what he was suffering and he did not want anyone else to be involved. Except maybe one person and he was able to talk to her.

"Jane's like a sister," he told himself. "A can talk t' her an' a kna she won't say out t' anybody."

John's reasoning was dangerous. Jane did not look on him as a brother, all of her feelings for him were still alive and she was as determined as ever to have him.

"She flaunted herself, an' a couldn't help me sel'," John reasoned.

John thought back to that night two months ago. How could he have done it?

"She was only a bairn hersel', even if she had one o' her own. The lad who took her down should be horsewhipped an' so should a."

126

Since that night John had avoided Jane like the plague, he did not love her, not like that. He did not want to hurt her, but he knew if they were alone together he would have to tell her the truth. Strangely he slept well the night after they had lain together, no nightmares, but he would not use her, not Jane, the little lass he'd cared for as a child and who was just like one of his sisters.

"Thank God we're back t' normal," Dan said to Sarah as she was setting the table for Sunday dinner, "as least as normal as we ever can be. Joe seems t' be copin' alreet an' he was tellin' me their Bill's settlin' down in Manchester. The only one he seems worried about is their John. He says he's still gettin' them nightmares but he thinks th's somat else botherin' him. Joe says he's sure he's got somat on his mind but he won't say owt."

Joe was right, John did have something on his mind and it was that very morning he had made his mind up to do something about it. He had never expected Jane to get pregnant; after all it was only the once. They had bumped into each other in the village and on this occasion Jane made it quite clear that he was not going to avoid talking to her. After what she told him they arranged to meet for a walk that same afternoon.

"A'm three months gone John an' it can only be yours a've been wi' ne body else. Y'll have t' marry me, me Ma's gettin' suspicious an' a'm sure she's guessed th's somat up."

John could not believe what he was hearing, how could he marry her, she was nowt but a bairn, He did not love her and he realised then that the only girl he loved was Lily, she was the one he wanted to marry and be the mother of his children.

"A can't marry y' Jane it wouldn't be right," he told her. "A'm to old f' y', an' a don't love y', not in that way."

Jane wept bitterly.

"Y' kna a've always loved y' John, ever since a was little," Jane sobbed. "If y' marry me it'll be alreet, a kna y' like us an' when a have y' bairn, y'll see, y'll love both o' us."

They had walked home in silence and he had not spoken to her again since that afternoon. He had seen her often enough, Jane made sure of that, but on each occasion he found an excuse to avoid talking to her, leaving the house when she came to visit or crossing on to the other side of the road whenever he saw her.

John put his coat on as he walked through the back door.

"A'll see y' in the Bay Horse Da," he shouted to his father, "a'm just goin' up t' see Dan f' a couple o' minutes."

When he walked into Dan and Sarah's home he was trembling. He was relieved to find only Dan, Sarah and Jane were in but that did nothing to stop his stomach churning. Ada had taken Meg for a walk in the old pram they had been given and, as usual, Tom was with her. Will was out with his mates planning his afternoon session of pitch and toss and so the coast was clear.

Sarah was surprised to see John; it was not like him to call on a Sunday morning. Joe and John usually met Dan in the Bay Horse at about twelve o'clock.

"So y've come t' collect us this mornin' have y'?" Dan joked.

John felt sick and took a few deep breaths before he spoke.

"No Dan a've come to talk t' you an' Sarah, Jane as well 'cos she needs t' hear what a've got t' say. A'll come straight out wi' it, me an' Jane's ganna be wed."

Sarah stopped what she was doing as Jane jumped out of the chair and ran to John. Together they faced Dan and Sarah. Sarah did not speak she knew immediately why John was going to marry her daughter. Dan's face was a picture as he looked first at Sarah then to Jane. Then turning to John he was the first to speak,

"A never realised th' pair o' y' were interested in each other, not in that way. A kna y've always been friends but a thought that was all it was, y're a lot older than her lad."

As he said the words the penny dropped, the look on Sarah's face said it all. Turning to his daughter his only words were.

"Not again lass, where's it all ganna end?"

Jane did not answer she looked at John and left the talking to him.

"We'll marry as soon as we can Dan. A've a bit put by from playin' in the dance band on a Saturday night an' a'll try an' get set on at one o' the pits. A've already made some enquiries an' th' settin' on at a pit ower Durham way. A'll see if a can get us somewhere t' live ower there. We'll not stay round here, y've had enough t' put up with, a'll bring y' ne more shame."

Jane was horrified as John continued.

"We'll tek the bairn wi' us an' a'll bring her up as if she was my own."

Sarah spoke for the first time.

"Y' can marry Jane, what y've done was wrong an' y' can't undo it but y'll not tek Meg. Jane's never seen t' her since the day she was born, a've done everythin' f' her an' a'll continue t' de it; she'll be brought up thinkin' me an Dan's her Ma and Da an' that's an end t' it"

John turned to leave and Jane followed him into the backyard. She was aghast when a John she did not recognise spoke to her.

"A've telt y' Ma an' Da a'll marry y' Jane but be warned, a dinna love y' an' a never will. Y' needn't

think the bairn'll mek any difference 'cos it wont an a'
somehow think y' life wi' me won't be a bed o'roses."

CHAPTER 7

Meg looked out of the bedroom window; it was still dark but she was too excited to stay in bed any longer.

"Da, Da, wake up y' said we had t' be away early," she shouted.

Dan opened his eyes; he had had a few pints of beer the night before, had just finished a week of fore shift and would have liked to have slept for another couple of hours. Sarah lay beside him, Meg's excited cries had not disturbed her; like Dan, she had drunk more than one beer the night before. Unlike Dan, hers had not been in the Bay Horse but in the privacy of her own kitchen.

Meg jumped on the bed still shouting at the top of her voice.

"Come on Da get up, y' promised, y' said y'd tek us t' Durham an' get us a new coat."

Meg was nearly five and Dan had persuaded Sarah to let Meg have a new coat. "She'll be startin' school an' wearin nowt but Ada's altered hand me downs," he had argued when Sarah refused.

Eventually Sarah gave in to some of Dan's demands.

"A new coat an' a new pinnie an' that's all. The others have had t' mek do an' she'll have t' de the same."

Her Da was taking her to the market and Tom had told Meg that meant they would be going to the big city itself. She had been to Durham before but never to the shops or the market. She had only been to her sister's house and Jane did not really live in Durham, it was somewhere outside the city. All Meg had ever seen of the city was the place where the bus stopped and they got off and on to another. She had only been twice, usually her Da went by himself and on the rare occasions her Ma went with him Meg was left at home with Ada.

Jane and her husband had two boys. The oldest was Dan and he was a year younger than Meg. The second boy was called Joe and he was nearly two. Meg was thrilled when her aunt Jane had told her that she was Dan and Joe's aunty just like their Ada was. She had heard her Ma telling her Da that Jane was going to have another baby so she supposed she would be an aunty again. Meg had been puzzled when her Da replied to her Ma that John was not fair to Jane, he seemed alright to her. He was the one who talked mostly to her when they went and not Jane. She could not understand it when her Da said that Jane should come home and bring the bairns with her. Her Ma had said she was sure that John had hit Jane again even if Jane had said he hadn't. Her Ma had told her Da that Jane would never come home no matter what happened. Meg was never too sure whether she liked Jane or not even if she was her sister, but that did not bother Meg, she did not like Ada very much, Will was alright but she liked John and their Tom the best.

Meg looked up at the man on the horse. Tom had told her about the horse with no tongue, and now she was here, she could see for herself. She was not one little bit tired like her Ma said she would be. She and her Da had walked three miles to get the bus to Durham and when they had gone to see Jane walked another two miles to her house. She was tired then and her Da had to carry her some of the way.

Meg was no longer tired when they reached the city centre; she was starting school on Monday, a big girl now and Tom, who was clever, had told her she had to learn as much as she could.

"Da tell us why th' hoss hasn't got a tongue?" Meg asked, bubbling over with excitement.

"A dinna kna' hinnie," he told her.

Meg was having none of it.

"Y' de kna Da, our Tom says y' telt him and y' kna all sorts o' things but y' telt him y'd forgotten them."

Dan looked down at Meg; she brought back too many memories.

"She's a bonny little thing," he thought to himself.

She was bonny with her jet black hair and green eyes set in an elfin face. Dan thought to himself.

She's little f' her age but as bright as a button, the only thing is she always looks like a little ragamuffin, a new coat an' pinnie 'll mek ne difference t' her she'll have them rotten a muck in ne time."

Dan took Meg's hand.

"Come on hinnie let's away t' the market an' get y' new coat an' pinnie," he coaxed.

Meg was stubborn.

"No Da, not 'til y've telt me about the man on the hoss," she retorted.

"A used t' kna' lots o' things hinnie but our Tom's right a've forgotten most o' them, a've had ne call t' remember them f' a long, long time. A used t' read lots o' books, the'll still be in the house somewhere, that's if y' Ma hasn't given them t' the rag a' bone man. One day a'll have a look an' when y're older y' can read them." He smiled at her and then winked. "Mebee if a try hard a'll remember about the man on the hoss an' then we're gannin' t' get y' coat an' pinnie."

Dan bent down and lifted Meg up to the horse. She wrapped her arms around his neck as he told her the story.

"It's a statue o' the Third Marquis o' Londonderry an' it's stood here f' ower 60 years now. He's wearing his uniform; it's the uniform o' the Grand Hussars."

"What's the Grand Hussars?" Meg interrupted.

133

"Never mind y' questions," Dan scolded, "an' if y' dinna shut up a won't finish telling y'. Anyway he owned lots o' pits 'round here an' he built the port at Seaham so we could ship the coal out. That's why the' did the statue o' him 'cos he mad a lot o' jobs f' us an' his proper name was Charles William Vane Tempest. The story tells us that the man who made the statue killed his sel' 'cos he forgot t' put the hoss's tongue in. But whether that's right or not we'll never kna'. Some folk say that it was a blind man who first found out that the hoss's tongue was missin'. The' say that the fellow who made the statue said that no one would ever kna' what was wrong wi' it, but the blind man felt all ower it an' when he put his hand in its mouth he told them what was missin'."

Dan gently lifted Meg down and smiled. "Right a've telt y' the story now let's away f' y' coat an' pinnie 'cos y' kna' what y' Ma's like, she'll be wonderin' what we up t', an' then tonight a'll be late f' the Bay Hoss."

Meg and Dan had wandered hand in hand on their way to the market. Down North Road and then across Framwellgate bridge to Silver Street. When he lifted her up to look over both sides of the bridge Meg stared in wonder at the meandering river with its weirs. She was only young but Dan had the feeing that she recognised, in her childish way, the beauty of the castle and the cathedral. He had visited Durham on numerous occasions, often to attend meetings in the miners' hall, but this was the first time he had really noticed the buildings which he had always taken for granted.

As they walked up Silver Street Meg stared in every shop window and at last she was quiet, there was so much to see. They passed the shops where Sarah and Dan had bought the set of drawers and toy dog for Rob and it was then that Dan hurried Meg along. When they reached the market place and Meg began to ask Dan questions about the horse he could not help but think of Rob. He had always known just whom this little one was like but today was the first time he had admitted it to himself. As he hurried Meg through the market place his thoughts turned to Sarah.

"A wonder if she thinks the same as me? Mebee one day a'll ask her?"

If the earlier part of the day had been exciting then it was nothing to what Meg experienced when they walked into the indoor market. Apart from the many stalls selling fruit and vegetables there were stalls with food that Meg hadn't known existed. A tired but exited Meg told Tom later that day.

"A've never seen such big lumps o' cheese an' meat. An' Tom the' was a stall wi' pots an' pans, some o' the stalls sold ornaments, lovely ones wi' cats an' dogs on em. A saw a lovely vase wi' flowers painted on it an' y've never seen as many cups, saucers an' plates.

"Da", Meg shouted, "the's as many plates on that stall as ad de all the folk back home."

As they approached the bottom end of the market they came to the second hand stalls overflowing with hammers, saws and just about every type of gardening tool that had ever been invented. As Dan stood talking to the stall holders and looking at their tools Meg became bored. She wandered off ahead of him and what she saw disappointed her. Here were the clothes stalls and they were all second hand, they were no better than the clothes she had on, the altered hand me downs she always had to wear.

Dan became anxious when he realised Meg was no longer by his side but a quick glance to the left and he saw her looking at the second hand clothes stalls.

135

"Keep had a me hand hinnie," Dan scolded, "y'll get lost."

As they walked past the stalls Meg's face brightened, there right in front of her were the new clothes stalls. There were clothes for men, women, children and babies. Suits, hats, dresses, pretty petticoats and nighties and one stall that had just the coat and pinnie she would love to have. She had noticed a stall that sold shoes but Meg knew that she would never dare ask her Da for shoes. Her Ma said boots were the best because they lasted and were better for children's feet.

"Right hinnie let's get y' a coat," Dan told her. "Y' Ma says it has t' be dark, warm an' two sizes too big so it'll last a few years."

Meg did not mind as long as it was new, that was the most important thing, and she wanted it to last because it was her very own coat; it had never belonged to anyone else. As soon as she saw it Meg liked the green one best; she would not try on any other and as it fit Sarah's criteria Dan bought it.

"Can a leave it on Da," shouted a happy Meg.

His reply slightly disappointed her.

"Y' kna y' Ma ud kill the pair o' us if y' walked in the house wi' it on hinnie," Dan explained. "We'll ask the man to wrap it up wi' one o' them white pinnies, then we'll finish the bottle o' water an' the bread an' pie y' Ma put up f' us, an' then we'll have t' be away."

Dan bought two apples and they left the market, each of them happy in their different ways, both munching their apples and Meg chattering endlessly between mouthfuls.

"Da our Tom telt us there was another statue in the market place, a man wi' a bare bum."

Dan laughed at the child; he knew exactly what she meant.

"Aye hinnie, our Tom's right but a think the' must have shifted it. Y' granda telt me about it when a was a little lad an' a think then it had been here f' a couple o' hundred years. What our Tom should have said t' y' was that it was a statue o' the God o' the Sea, Neptune, the' call him. Y' see that square bit o' stone ower there, well he stood on it an' y' could get a drink o' water from the tap stickin' out o' the side o' it."

Meg happy with Dan's explanation finished her apple but was still feeling hungry and also very tired.

"Where we ganna sit an' eat our pie Da?" she asked.

Dan, enjoying his day and Meg's company decided on one further treat.

"We'll get int' trouble off y' Ma f' being late, but since it's a nice day, a think we'll have a walk down by the riverside. We can sit on the grass an' eat our pie and mebee the'll be some boats on the river an' y' can watch them."

It was not far to the river from the market place; a short walk along Saddler Street brought them to Elvet Bridge. When they reached the Magdalen steps Dan pointed out the road that led to the castle and the cathedral. Before Meg had realised it they had arrived at the river. As they approached the bridge Dan's grip tightened on Meg's hand. The steps, which led to the river, were steep and slippery and Meg found that negotiating the bend in the middle was not as easy as she thought it would be.

However, the perils of the steps were worth it when they reached the riverside. They were not the only people out for the day and Meg found it hard to believe what she saw. Many of the people strolling along the riverside were just like her and her Da but others, like the lady who had just passed them, were wearing posh long coats and dresses. Some of the men had smart suits

137

and hats on and some of the younger ladies were not wearing a coat. Their dresses had such pretty colours and fancy lace collars.

"Da," Meg gasped, "some o' them women's got umbrellas an' the've got lace on em."

Dan squeezed Meg's hand.

"The' not umbrellas hinnie, the' parasols, an' the ladies use them t' shade themsel's from the sun."

Meg thought that strange.

"Why would anybody want t' shade themsel's from the sun Da?"

Dan did not answer her question but commented on some of the younger men calling them 'nancy boys.'

Meg did not understand what her Da meant but this time she did not question him she just laughed with him. Dan suddenly realising what he had said turned to Meg.

"Tek' ne notice o' what a said hinnie, it's just that the mek' y' Da laugh wi' their gentlemanly ways wi' the ladies, especially them wi' the straw bengers on an' the sporty shirts an' trousers."

"But Da," Meg asked. "Why have the' all got the best claes on? Are the' goin' t' a weddin' or chapel or sumat? It's not Sunday is it?"

Dan was laughing when he gave her an answer. He could not remember a time when he had laughed so much or enjoyed a day so much.

"No hinnie the' just in the ordinary claes, wait till you're a big lass an' mebee one day y'll get dressed up like that."

Meg's rumbling stomach halted any further questions. They ate their bread and pie and drank their water as they watched, in silence, the young men and women sailing in the boats. Dan watched Meg as she ate her meagre meal, he was proud of his little granddaughter, the child who thought he was her father.

Meg slept on the bus journey home and did her best to walk the three miles from the bus station but it proved too much for her and Dan had to carry her most of the way.

"By that's killed me chest," he told an anxious Sarah when they finally arrived home.

Sarah was concerned, she had worried throughout the day about both of them and Dan was not upset at her welcome, he knew Sarah of old.

"It serves y' right, the pair o' y' an' God only kna's whose been wi' y' Dan," was all she said when they first arrived home.

He smiled knowing there would be more to come later.

As the years had passed Sarah had become increasingly jealous of Dan, he had never given her any cause to feel as she did, but she found herself accusing him whenever the opportunity arose. Dan was still a fine looking man and Sarah knew it. He did not help matters by always taking a great pride in his appearance, his hair was thinning a little, his clear blue eyes still sparkled and, other than his breathlessness, many thought it hard to believe that he had worked underground for over thirty five years. He was not a tall man but he still had the physique of a thirty year old.

The years had not been so kind to Sarah. Each time she gazed at her reflection in the mirror, she noticed more grey hairs. Her face seemed to age every time she looked at it. Sarah could not remember the day when her hair had not been grey. Like Dan she was not very tall but now she was shorter and for some reason, she could not understand why, she had developed a hump on her back. Her back ached which made her bend forward and each time she looked in the mirror she would say the same thing to herself.

"Either this mirror's getting' higher or a'm shrinkin'."

She remembered, when she was younger, her mother would say.

"Straighten up Sarah an' stand wi' y' shoulders back."

But she couldn't, it was natural for her stoop a little.

"Now a stoop lot Ma." Sarah would grumble to herself.

Since Rob had died Sarah had never worn anything other than a black skirt and blouse. She knew her clothes did not help her appearance but, as far as she was concerned, she still mourned him. Black was the only colour she would ever wear. Her only concessions were her pinnies, which she made herself from whatever material she had spare. Like her skirt her pinnie reached her ankles and it was only ever removed if she left the house. If possible they were always grey or brown and wrapped completely around her skirt. Sometimes she would surprise the family by wearing a brighter colour. When they commented her reply was always the same.

"It's only 'cos it's criminal t' waste good material."

They had only been in the house ten minutes when Sarah started.

"Where the hell were y't' this time?" She yelled. "Y' could have had a coat made the time it's took y'. Who've y'been wi'? Who's been t' Durham wi' y'? That's if you've ever been there."

Meg was quick to defend Dan.

"Me an' me Da's been t' Durham, he's got me a lovely coat an' a new pinnie, an' we've been down by the river, an' the's just been the two o' us. We've had a lovely time. Haven't we Da?"

"Bed an' less o' y' mouth", was Sarah's answer to an excited but disappointed Meg.

140

"But Ma," cried Meg, "y've never seen me new things."

Dan turned to Sarah.

"Dinna upset the bairn hinnie," was all said before turning to Meg.

"De as y' telt hinnie gan t' bed y' can show y' Ma all y' stuff tomorro'."

Meg could not resist one last retort.

"A'll get another coat one day Ma, a'll get lots o' claes just like them women down by the river an' a'll wear them all the time, just like me Da says they do."

Meg's first day at school had arrived at last. Tom was ten and he was taking her with him.

"Y'll tek us Tom," Meg had cried the night before, "Me Da's at work an' y' kna me Ma won't tek us."

Meg was pleased it was Tom who was taking her and not Ada. Ada was fifteen and since leaving school stayed at home to help Sarah in the house. She did most of the housework but was not allowed to bake or make the meals. She had only baked once and Dan had complained.

"The sweet stuff's too sweet an' the salty stuff's too salty," he had told Sarah.

Ada went off in the huff when Sarah told her but not before she blamed Meg.

"Meg pestered me, she wanted t' help Ma," she retaliated. "She put the extra salt an' sugar in."

Meg cried and told Sarah Ada was lying. Meg never found out whom her Ma believed, and that hurt her feelings, but she had the satisfaction of knowing that Ada was never allowed to bake again.

Meg was feeling proud of herself. Tom was ten and he was taking her to school. She'd had a bath on Friday night and had tried very hard that weekend to keep herself clean. Keeping clean was never an easy task for Meg, outdoors was always better than indoors for her. She idled her days wandering around the village playing with any of the children who were out at the time.

Sometimes friends would invite her into their houses and if it was larger and 'posher' than hers that was a real treat. An invite to one of their parties was even better. Ada always bathed her and made sure she was washed and dressed each morning. This morning Meg had not needed Ada's help, she had even washed her neck and behind her ears. The only thing Ada was left to do was fasten her pinnie at the back and tie the laces on her boots. She could have managed the laces herself but, as usual, there were knots where the laces had snapped and Meg could not get the lace through the eyeholes in the boots. She was pleased the pinnie was new even if it was too big for her.

"Anyhow Tom", she told her brother. "Me pinnie hides me old dress. A kna' me Ma's altered it an' patched the side and back but a would have hated the others and the teachers to see the patches. But me boots look good, don't the' Tom? Me Da polished them last night an' he showed us how t' mek them shine wi' a spoon handle. He warmed the handle in the fire and then rubbed it on me boots, an' a promised him a wouldn't de it mesel' in case a got burnt in the fire. Now that a've promised him d' y' think he'll de them every week f' me Tom?"

Tom smiled he knew his father would occasionally clean her boots but that job would more often than not be Ada's.

At last Meg was ready to go except for her coat. She had a twinkle in her eye as she put it on. Ada had said it was too warm for a coat but her Ma had took her side when she said she wanted to wear it and she had told

Ada to stop picking on her. Holding Tom's hand they walked together to the small village school.

"A like y't' hold me hand Tom," Meg told him. "A'm not frightened 'cos a want t' start school but you're me best friend, better than all the others. Meg really was nervous and she hoped Tom would not notice. Looking up at him she asked.

"Am a y'best friend Tom?"

"Ay'Meg," he replied and squeezing her hand told her. "Y' me best friend an' me an' you'll always be best friends."

Meg was happy, she felt a lot better now. She loved Tom; he played with her and read her stories but most of all he was her protector. Tom was always there for her, sticking up for her when the other children called her names and stopping the older children from hitting her. Tom was only small and Ada said he was not very strong but Meg knew different. When Ada was not with him he was just as brave as the bigger boys.

More important than standing up for her with the older children it was Tom who always warned her when their Will was in a bad mood. Will drank a lot but he was not like his father after a drink. Meg had often heard Dan arguing with Sarah about Will.

"Y're always givin' him all o' his pay back an' what does he do wi'it? Drink an' gamble." Dan often scolded Sarah.

If Meg got upset during the argument it was Tom who comforted her.

"Our Will works hard at the pit an' meks more money than me Da." Tom had told her.

Meg did not reply and kept her thoughts to herself.

"It's not fair," she thought. "A know me Da telt me Ma that what money he meks does us ne good, an' he's

143

awful t' us after a drink an' when he losses on the hosses o' dogs he teks it out of our Ada an' Tom."

Tom was frightened of Will and as soon as he saw him walking down the bank after a day at the races he would take Meg out or tell her to go to bed. Ada stood up to Will and she would try to protect Tom in the same way he tried to protect Meg. If Dan was out it was always the same; if Will had lost at the races he would get annoyed with Tom; Ada would intervene and she would be the one who ended up with bruises on her arms and occasionally a black eye. Sarah ignored Will's bad temper and Ada would hide her bruises from Dan, always having an excuse ready when Dan asked her why she had a black eye.

It was at these times Tom would tell Meg that she should love her sister. Sometimes Meg thought she did, just a little bit, even if it was Tom she was protecting and not her. Will frightened Meg but he never hit her; she was the only person in the family he bought treats for. It was usually a bag of sweets and she always shared them with Tom. She could not bring herself to offer one to Ada.

Meg thought her first day at school was the best day in her life but she did not tell her Da that, she did not want to hurt his feelings.

"Durham was the best day Da an' school the next," an excited Meg told him as she crossed her fingers behind her back because she was telling a lie.

Meg was pleasantly surprised when she arrived at school; she knew all of the other children who were starting that day. When she and Tom went home for dinner things got even better. Their Ma had made a little leek pudding especially for them to share. There was a big one still boiling in the pan on the fire for her Da and

Will but this was the first time Meg and Tom had their own.

"Isn't school great Tom?" Meg told him with a mouth full of pudding. "An' we're gettin' our own dinner not just a slice o' me Da's or Will's puddin'."

When Meg arrived home at teatime she was just as excited, she could not keep quiet.

"A've got a lovely teacher Ma, she's real pretty an' she telt us all a lovely story afore we came home. She says that every afternoon we have t' have a sleep an' then she'll read us a story. A didn't gan t' sleep Ma, a couldn't, but she never knew 'cos a kept me eyes tight shut."

Meg was so excited she could not keep quiet until an angry Ada upset her.

"Will y' shut up Meg," she shouted."Y mekin' me head ache, we all kna' what school's like."

Meg thought that was the end of it until an angry Sarah turned to Ada.

"Shut up y' sel an' let the bairn tell us." It was enough to make Ada leave the room and retreat into the back kitchen.

Throughout that week Meg found each day to be better than the previous one.

"Ma, Miss says a'm clever, a can nearly say me A B C's but a didn't tell her our Tom had learned us them."

"Da, Miss put me picture a drew o' you an' me Ma on the wall today, a made sure y' had y' best bowler hat on Da an' a even put y' watch chain on it Da."

Meg even spoke to Ada.

"When a fell down today a hurt me knee an' a sat on Miss's knee an' she cuddled me. She was lovely Ada, an' she had a lovely skirt on, it was a good job a had me pinnie on so a didn't mucky it."

That week the Charlton's learnt more about the village school and it's famous Miss than they had ever known. Meg's excitement was so infectious that even Will patiently listened to her chattering. He bought her extra sweets and as usual she shared them with Tom. Ada grumbled to Tom and Meg.

"A never get owt off Will an' he should give me Ma a bit more each week."

Meg for once was not upset; she was too happy to care what Ada said. Saturday and Sunday were never ending and Meg was up bright and early for the start of her second week at school.

When she came home for dinner on Monday her first words were to Sarah.

"Ma, Miss says we've t' tek our birth certificates or somat t' school tomorro'. She says t' bring them in the mornin' an' we can tek them straight home at dinner time."

Sarah ignored Meg's request and told her and Tom to get on with their dinner. Meg did not mention the birth certificate again until she was leaving for school on Monday morning.

"Ma, y've forgotten me birth certificate," she told Sarah.

Sarah did not look up when she replied.

"Y'll have t' tell the teacher a can't find it an' that y'll tek it when a do."

Meg's teacher accepted the explanation but when Friday arrived and there was no birth certificate she warned Meg.

"I want that birth certificate on my desk by nine o'clock on Monday morning or you will be in trouble Meg for not giving your parents my messages."

Meg walked home in silence that Friday and Tom, knowing what a little chatterbox she was sensed trouble.

"What's up Meg?" he asked her. "Have y' been in trouble wi' the teacher?"

The very thought of being in trouble caused Meg to cry.

"Aye Tom an' a haven't done owt wrong, it's me Ma, a keep askin' her f' me birth certificate t' tek t' school an' she says it's lost. A told Miss that me Ma had lost it an' she says things like that dinna get lost. She says a'll be in trouble if a dinna tek it on Monday mornin' an' a daren't ask me Ma again."

Realising how upset Meg was Tom spoke to his mother as soon as they arrived home.

"She'll really get wrong Ma, will y' gan an' tell the teacher it's lost?"

Sarah looked at her worried son and the child by his side who was sobbing uncontrollably.

"It'll mek ne difference lad 'cos a won't be able t' gi' Meg the certificate, a've looked all ower the house an' a canna find it. A must have chucked it in the fire wi' some other papers."

Meg worried all that weekend and when Monday morning came she did not want to go to school.

"Dinna worry Meg," Tom told her. "The teacher'll have t' believe y', if me Ma's burnt it it's not your fault."

If her first day at school was her best then today was her worst. Tom was wrong; Miss did not believe her.

"Miss blamed me," Meg told Tom as they walked home for dinner. "She said ad forgotten t' ask me Ma an' a had t' have the birth certificate on her desk when a came back this afternoon."

Meg started to cry.

"She said a was a scatter brain Tom an' a wouldn't do well at school if a couldn't remember t' gi' me Ma a simple message."

147

As Tom and Meg walked up the back street they could see Dan lifting his bicycle over the back gate step; he had just come home from the pit. Meg tried to stop crying before they went into the house but the tears would not stop.

"An' what's the matter wi' y' hinnie?" Dan asked.

Meg could not speak so it was left to Tom to tell his father Meg's problem with the teacher and the burnt birth certificate. Tom became upset and, on the point of tears himself, spoke to his father in defence of Meg.

"It's not her fault Da, the teacher doesn't believe Meg but a kna' she did ask me Ma."

Dan was surprised; Sarah had not told him that Meg's birth certificate was required at school.

Dan went into the kitchen and told Sarah to get Meg's birth certificate. When she did not respond to his request he raised his voice to her.

"Y' kna' where all the birth certificates are," Dan shouted. "Meg's us in the bible me Da got us when a was twenty one. Y' kna' the're all in there so a can't see what all the bloody fuss is about."

Sarah shouted back at Dan.

"It's not gannin' outside this house."

Dan was tired, he wanted a bath, his dinner and then some sleep and he finally lost his patience with Sarah.

"If y' don't gi' her it t' tek a'll tek the bloody thing mesel'. Fill me bath an' then a'll tek the bairn an' the birth certificate t' the bloody school, an' a'll tell bloody Miss our Meg's no liar."

At last Meg stopped crying; she had never seen her Da so angry and now she was scared.

"Da all the other's have took their own an' brought them back the same day, If y' kna' where it is just gi' us it an' a'll tek it mesel'."

148

Sarah looked at Meg, she wanted to cry just like her granddaughter, she wanted to take the child in her arms but loving Meg brought back such hurtful memories. Instead she spoke quietly to her.

"Y' Da'll tek y' Meg. Go straight int' school an' let y' Da talk t' the teacher by hisel' an' gi' her the certificate. A dinna want it left at the school. Y' Da'll show her it an' bring it back wi' him."

Meg felt much happier as she walked home after school with Tom.

"Me Da must have given Miss me certificate," she told him. "I never got wrong this afternoon, Miss never even spoke t' me. She talked t' the others but she just kept lookin' at me funny like, a think me Da mebee telt her off."

For the rest of that week Meg's teacher ignored her but that was nothing to what happened the following week. Meg was upset.

"Tom, Miss's blamin' me f' everythin' an' it's not my fault." Meg wept. "She blamed me f' talkin' an' a wasn't. She said a'd spilled the paint an' a hadn't, an' then she blamed me for tearin' the pages in a book an' a hadn't."

As the week went on school became worse for Meg. She became so frightened that she sat in her chair as if glued to it. No matter what she did or said she was wrong. Staying in her seat brought the complaint of not standing when the teacher entered the room, standing up brought the complaint of fidgeting. By Friday afternoon Meg was terrified of her teacher.

"A'm not gannin't' school on Monday," she announced to Sarah on Friday night.

Sarah was not surprised; she had known this would happen. She had tried to protect the child but Dan had interfered and done the very thing she had tried so hard to prevent.

"A telt y' what would happen Dan when the teacher found out," she told him after Meg had gone to bed. "If y'd have just let things be the' would have forgotten all about the birth certificate after a few weeks, now the bairns got t' live wi' them knain' f' all her years at school."

Dan knew Sarah was right but he would not give in.

"Sarah, what's done's done so she'll just have t' put up wi' it; at least Meg doesn't kna' why the teacher's pickin' on her."

When Monday morning came Meg cried.

"Y'll have t' gan hinnie," Sarah told her.

But Meg resisted, she kicked and screamed and Tom left the house without her. Eventually a tearful Meg was dressed and ready for school and it was Ada who was given the task of escorting her.

During the next few weeks Meg's life became more miserable.

"It's not fair," she wept to Tom, "Miss picks on us all day and me Ma an' Da an Ada picks on us at home. The' think it's me, an' it's not Tom, it's her a can tell she hates us. Our Ada can bray us as much as she likes t' get us t' go but a'm not stoppin' at school a'll keep runnin' away an' then the'll have t' let us stay at home an' help me Ma an' our Ada."

Tom could not convince Meg that she would not win this battle.

"Y'll have t' gan Meg," he warned her. "The'll send the kiddie catcher out t' me Ma an' Da an' then the'll get int' trouble."

"A'll mek mesel' bad then," Meg retorted. "The'll have t' let me stop off then."

Meg tried everything with no success until one day she had an idea. "A kna what a'll de," she muttered to herself, "a'll run out o' school an' walk t' me Da's pit t' meet him comin' home."

Her escapade ended in total humiliation. As soon as they arrived home Dan smacked her bottom and took her straight back to school. He dragged a howling Meg back into the classroom and her final humiliation was her Da, he was still in his pit clothes.

From that day on Meg knew she had lost the battle and so she made her mind up. She would go to school but if she was going to be blamed for things she had not done she might as well do the things she was being blamed for. She became a fighter; she bossed, bullied and lashed out at anything or anyone in her way. She became the leader and if she could not lead then she would not play; she stood up to everyone, big or small. She often lost the battle but she did not care, she stood her ground, she would show them that she was the best.

The only person she never fought with was Tom. When he tried to lead her away from trouble her answer to him was always.

"A won't fight wi' y'Tom, a promised y' a was y' best friend an' a won't break me promise t' y' "

When Meg refused to get washed for school Ada would scrub her neck and wash behind her ears. She was rough but Meg did not care. She did not even care about her new coat which was ruined following numerous scraps with the other schoolchildren. Sarah had repaired a torn sleeve and patched the areas where the pockets were torn off, Meg hated it but Sarah made her wear it. Nothing deterred Meg; she was coping with her new found situation in the only way she knew how.

Sarah was worried. Meg had not come home from school with Tom and Ada had spent two hours out in the

151

freezing cold looking for her. When she finally found her Meg would tell no one where she had been. Her punishment was the usual, a smacked bottom and off to bed with no tea. Meg still slept with Sarah and Dan and resisted Ada's attempts to persuade her to share with her. Meg loved the comfort her Ma and Da gave her; she loved their smell even if sometimes the smell of beer on her Ma was as bad as on her Da. She was always warm with them and safe. Meg was brave during the day but it was different at night especially if Will came home drunk. He still had never hit her but sometimes lately when she had been cheeky to him he frightened her and she knew he was tempted to raise his fist and strike her.

As Meg lay quietly in the dark she thought back to the day's events and decided that when her Ma came to bed she would tell her where she had been. Meg forced herself to stay awake and as soon as Sarah's head was on the pillow Meg blurted out her apology.

"A'm sorry Ma, a'm sorry a stopped out but it wasn't me fault. A had a fight wi' Lizzie Jackson 'cos she said a was a basket. It's alright 'cos a won an' a telt her it was better t' be a basket then a pig like her."

Sarah did not reply but welcomed Meg into her arms as she cuddled in beside her. Meg was soon asleep and Sarah resolved that she would talk to Dan; things were getting out of hand and there was one thing he could do to help. As soon as he came to bed she told him.

"Dan we'll have t' move; y'll have t' get set on at another pit an' y'll have t' try an' get us another house."

Dan was astonished, ten years ago he would have welcomed Sarah's request, but not now. He was too old, he reasoned, he could not find work in another pit let alone find another house. Sarah continued.

"A mean it Dan, a kna' it was me that stopped y' afore; but if we don't Meg's the one that's ganna suffer.

We've got t' move so nobody kna's she's not ours. Anyhow she's getting older, the' all are, an' the's not enough room here. The's ne sign o' our Will gettin' married so a think the time's come f' us t' move."

A few minutes ago Sarah could not find the words to reply to Meg following her apology. Now it was Dan's turn but there was no cuddle for Sarah. He turned away from her, he did not want to look for work elsewhere and he certainly did not want to move away from the village. He would have to do some serious thinking before Sarah got her answer.

CHAPTER 8

Tom was down on his hunkers watching Meg run around the bedroom making as much noise as she possibly could on the bare floorboards.

"Doesn't a empty house mek' a funny noise?" she shouted.

"Me Ma's hand on y' bare backside'll mek more noise if y' dinna behave an' if y' not careful y'll get a crack 'round the lug ole off our Will when he comes in," he replied.

After Sarah's request to move house Dan had made a few half hearted attempts to move to another pit but after eighteen months they were still in the same house and none of his efforts had come to fruition. He was as content as he ever could be; working at the same pit with his trusted marrers, and then Sarah received her incredible news. Dan was at work when his father came to visit.

"Our Jack's ganna move in wi' us Sarah, he's a canny few years older than me an' he's findin' it hard t' manage now he's on his own," he told her.

Sarah did her best to dissuade him, pointing out the difficulties of caring for an old man and, reminding him of the problems he had faced with Dan's mother. Nothing Sarah said deterred him and he left the house still convinced the move would be as beneficial to him as to his brother. As he left the house he kissed her cheek and told her not to worry.

"It'll have its compensations hinnie, our Jack'll be company f' me."

Dan's father had not been gone half an hour when Sarah's father arrived.

"Somat must be up?" were Sarah's first thoughts. "It's many a moon since me Da's been up here, me Ma must be bad again."

Sarah's mother's health had been failing for some time and she was aware that it would be only a matter of time before her father would be bringing her sad news. Noting the anxious look on his daughter's face Sarah's father was quick to reassure her.

"It's not bad news a've come wi' lass, in fact it's a bit o' good news, s' dinna look s' worried."

Sarah beckoned to her father to sit down at the kitchen table while she lifted the always ready simmering kettle on to the fire in readiness to make him a pot of tea. He spoke as he settled himself at the table.

"Y' remember y' Uncle Lou, Sarah. He moved down south afore y' were married an' a telt y' he died last year. Well seemingly he did well down there. Him an' Elsie only had one lad and he's taken ower the business but what a didn't kna' was that he still had houses up here, the ones we built afore he went. A sold mine, when times were bad, but he's been collectin' rents all this time. He must have had a guilty conscience, or somat, or mebee it's 'cos a stayed behind t' look after me Ma. Anyhow this letter came yesterday, it's from his solicitor, an' he's left the houses up here t' you an' our Maisie an' Florrie.The's nine o' them, that's three each."

When the news sank in Sarah needed a pot of tea much more than her father did. Her father continued talking, reminiscing about the golden days when he worked with his father and his brothers, a time when they were prosperous. Sarah tried to pay attention but she was too busy thinking of the future, maybe she would be able to persuade Dan to move from the village and find new work. This could be their golden opportunity.

When Dan came home from work Sarah was still reeling from the shock of her good fortune. Usually she only discussed anything of importance with Dan when the time was right and that was never when he had just finished a shift down the pit. The right time was when he had a few pints of beer in him. On this occasion she did not care, she was going to have her way. It was years since she had felt so excited and when Dan came home she was adamant.

"Y'll sit down there afore y' dinner an' y'll listen t' every word a have to tell y' Dan."

After she had told him the full story an excited Sarah stood in front of Dan, hands on hips.

"Me Da says he doesn't kna' what the' like, but he's ganna see the solicitor tomorro' an' then we'll all kna' how the land lies."

Dan decided to say nothing and do nothing, at least, not for the moment.

"Nowt's likely t' come o' it," he thought.' "A'll wait an' see afore a say owt."

It was another two weeks before Sarah's father brought any more news. "The three houses y've got are all next door t' each other. One's empty an' the other two have folk in them payin' rent," he told her. "The' only have two bedrooms but the' twice the size o' this place."

Once again Sarah did not choose her time to give Dan the news. He was in bed and as soon as her father left she went upstairs and woke him. As Sarah always ensured the house was quiet when Dan was in nightshift he was surprised when she disturbed him from a deep sleep.

"What's the matter hinnie, has somat happened, a must have only been in bed a couple o' hours," a startled Dan asked.

"Me Da's just been Dan, an' y' kna' them houses me Uncle Lou left us, well the' all next t' each other. Two o' them 'as somebody in em an' we'll get the rent every week but the other had a' old women in it an' she died three months ago so it's empty, that means we can move in it, we'll have ne rent t' pay, an' we'll collect the rent from the other two."

Sarah was disappointed when all Dan said was.

"Right hinnie calm y' sel' down a'll gan back t' sleep f' a couple hours an' we can talk about it tonight."

Dan got no more sleep that day. He needed time to think, time to decide what he should do. He had had his dinner and was getting ready for another night down the pit when he commented on Sarah's good fortune.

"A kna' y' excited hinnie, but we'll have t' think things through. A'm not gettin' any younger an' a'll still have t' gan t' the pit. It'll mek me day even longer an' a can hardly manage me bike now, let alone another two o' three miles each way."

The events of the next few weeks solved all of their problems. Harry was now an overman at a pit less than a mile from the village where the new house was situated. As soon as he heard of Sarah's good fortune he once more offered Dan the job he had been offering him for many months. Will's pit was only two miles from the village and as the move meant less travelling for both of them Dan was left with no choice.

Meg was full of mischief on the day the family first visited their new home. Everything was finalised and the move was planned for the following week. Even Dan was beginning to see the sense in finally accepting that a move to another pit was the right thing to do.

Meg was her usual noisy self and Tom kept close to her side. Although they were still the best of friends he was now twelve and had his own interests. He was no

157

longer around all of the time to protect her, but today was different he was staying close by her side to prevent her ending up with the usual good hiding from Sarah or Ada.

Tom had also noticed that Will was increasingly losing his patience with Meg and he did not want her to end up on the end of his fist, he knew just how much that hurt.

"Tom," Meg shouted, "the's ne gas lights up here, not like the' is downstairs."

Tom and Meg had inspected the house from top to bottom and Tom was pleased with the move even if it meant moving schools. It was only for another two years and his Granda had told him it was a good school with more teachers and he would get a broader education there than in the small village school. His only worry was Meg.

Tom knew it would be impossible to protect her in the way he had done in a small village. In the new school after the age of eleven the boys were separated from the girls, the only time he would see Meg would be as they walked to and from school. He had always been around at playtimes carefully watching Meg and ensuring she did not get into a fight in the playground. He knew only too well what would happen when he was not there. Meg would start to fight with her class mates and even if she was not the instigator it would be her who got into trouble with the teacher. At least that was what usually happened and Tom was not sure that a new school would change anything.

Meg was too excited to care, she was only too pleased to be leaving the village school and the new house was all she could think about for the moment.

"Where d' y' think we'll sleep Tom?" Was one of her many questions. "D'y' think a'll get me own bed?"

158

Tom was patient with Meg answering her questions as best he could. He liked the new house especially as it had gas lights, even if there was only two downstairs, it was better than lamps and candles. He would be able to read his books and do his sums until late, if his Ma let him. He thought she might because the house had two big rooms downstairs, a big kitchen and a parlour, even the back kitchen was big compared to what they had been used to.

It was Tom's turn to talk to Meg.

"D' y' think me Ma'll let us stay up a bit later Meg? If a could go in t' the parlour a could get on wi' me sums wi' out anybody interuptin' us just when a get t' the end. Y' kna how a like to do sums the best an' me Granda says a should stick in 'cos then a might get a job one day wi' figures."

The sound of footsteps on the stairs abruptly ended their conversation. They guessed it would be Ada.

"Will y' both get out o' me way; gan out in the backstreet an' play."

Meg was delighted with Ada's order but Tom was disappointed. He had thought he could do something to help.

As they quickly went down stairs they could still hear Ada grumbling. "A'll never be done cleanin'. The pantry's as big as our back kitchen, an' the back kitchen's as big as our kitchen an' then the's the parlour an' them two big bedrooms. The little bedroom our Tom an' Will sleep in now us only a bit bigger than the pantry here, an' now me Ma says a have to whitewash the netty across the yard."

Sarah was hurrying to heat the water for Dan's bath and she had had a busy morning. Dan's first shift at his new pit was foreshift and he was due in any minute. Tom and Meg had started their new school that morning and they would soon be home for their dinner. Fortunately Will was in back shift so he would not be home until teatime. She was not looking forward to either Dan or Meg coming home.

Dan had been on edge throughout the weekend and she had sent Meg off to school with a good hiding. Thinking of Meg brought a smile to Sarah's face.

"A dinna kna' what wi' ganna de wi' her?" she muttered to herself. "Even a new house an' school'll not mek' her behave hersel'."

Ada had not helped matters. Sarah had insisted that Ada should whitewash the midden that very morning and she had ended up with more white wash on herself than the walls. Then the fire had kept going out. Sarah knew she would eventually get the hang of it but it was trying her patience today.

"A shouldn't have lost me temper wi' our Ada she's worked hard this last couple o' weeks," Sarah muttered as she put more coal on the fire. "But every time a saw her wi'all that whitewash on her a could have strangled her."

Ada and Sarah had worked hard and looking around her Sarah was well aware that their efforts were well rewarded. The house was clean and they had more room there than she had ever thought they would have. Their small amount of furniture made it look bigger than it was but lack of space and money had prevented Sarah buying anything other than the bare essentials.

None of that mattered to Sarah but looking around the house did make her realise the mistakes she had made in the past. It was she who had never wanted to leave the village and the little house where Rob was born. It was her who had been unfair to Dan and the rest of the family.

160

For the first time since Meg was born, she and Dan had a bedroom to themselves. Meg had finally consented to share the desk bed in the parlour with Ada.

It had been a struggle at first.

"It's not right Dan, her sleepin' wi' us, she'll have t' learn; she's seven years old now." Sarah told Dan.

"Everytime she walks up them stairs t' our bed a'm bringin' her back down an' am mekin' her get in the bed in the parlour."

Will and Tom shared the bed in the back bedroom and Tom thought it was wonderful.

"Isn't it great Will?" Tom exclaimed to his brother on their first night in their new home. "Now we dinna have t' climb ower the bottom t' get in."

When Dan arrived home from the pit he greeted Sarah with a smile. He did not mention work but his smile was enough to reassure Sarah that his first shift had not been too bad. As she washed his back Sarah told Dan about Meg's morning antics.

"A could have murdered her Dan, she wouldn't get ready f' school. First it was her dress that was wrong, an' then her coat. Y' kna' what she's like, she wasn't startin' any new school in old clothes. Our Ada had t' drag her t' the sink an' mek' her get washed. She went in the end wi' a bit o' coaxin' from our Tom, but y' should a seen her, what a sight. Her hair wasn't half brushed an' her boots were covered in clarts, but t' be honest Dan a was just as pleased t' see the back o' her."

Dan could not resist having a dig at Sarah when he replied.

"A telt y' didn't a? A telt y' movin' wouldn't solve everythin'. A'll give in t' y' now, a was wrong about the birth certificate but y' kna what she's like an' she'll never be any different."

Dan started to laugh.

161

"A tell y' what though Sarah, a can't help but admire her, 'cos by she's got some guts."

Dan was in bed before Tom and Meg came home for dinner and for the second time that day Sarah was pleasantly surprised when Meg came bounding across the back yard shouting.

"Ma, Ma it was good this mornin' a like it better than the other school an' the rest o' them were dressed just like me. Well most o' them were, some o' them had better coats than me, but a wasn't bothered 'cos a telt them a had two better coats but a didn't want t' mucky them at school."

Meg's fingers were tightly crossed behind her back as she waited for Sarah's reply.

Sarah did not comment but her look told Meg she was not amused at telling lies or as her Da said, make believe. Sarah smiled to herself; she would say nothing this time but woe betide her Granddaughter if she caught her telling any more lies.

Meg continued.

"The teacher telt all the class a was a new starter an' the' had t' show me where t' put me coat an' look after me 'til a got t' kna' what t' de. Our Tom says he liked it an' all an' he thinks he's better at sums than the others."

Finally Sarah interrupted.

"Let our Tom speak f' hisel' Meg a'm sure he can manage wi' out y' speakin' f' him."

Tom looked first at Sarah and then at Meg, he did not care that Meg had spoken on his behalf, he was just relieved that Meg's morning had been trouble free. He could settle down in his new school without worrying about her.

Sarah was pleased with Meg's progress. She was still no angel but the battles, in respect of her attendance at school, had stopped. It was six weeks since they had

162

moved into their new home and Sarah, although having no regrets; found being the owner of their home and two houses next door was not all she thought it might have been. The pittance of rents she received was not sufficient to cover the maintenance of the houses let alone give her a profit to cover their own costs. She knew if she raised the rent the tenants would not be able to afford it and to make matters worse, even though they paid their rent each week, she was a target for their repeated requests for improvements. Every time she went to collect the rent they pointed out the numerous faults within the houses which Sarah knew she would never be able to afford to repair.

This morning her father had visited and the news he brought filled her with dismay. He had told her she had to pay some type of tax on the houses. She did not really understand it; her father had said that it was something to do with death duties. She and Dan had to go and see the solicitor in Durham and from what her father said she would never be able to do any repairs to the properties, it would take all of the rent and maybe a little bit more just to cover the death duties. An anxious Sarah told Dan that night that arrangements had been made for them to see the solicitor the following week.

When the day arrived Dan was in a bad mood. He could not afford to take a shift off from work and so the visit to the solicitor had to be when he was in night shift, and that meant a day without sleep. To make matters worse Meg was on holiday from school and Sarah thought it best for her to go with them. On the morning before they left for Durham Meg was excited.

"It'll be great Tom, "she told her brother. "Just like when me an' me Da went last time."

When they arrived in Durham they went straight to the solicitor's office. Meg was instructed to sit quietly on a chair outside the door of the office. She had been warned by Sarah that she must not be a nuisance but Meg was finding it extremely difficult to sit still. She was tempted to get up and wander around but had second thoughts.

"A better not, "she said to herself. "If a de me Ma an' Da might mek' us gan straight back after th've finished in there, an' a thought a might be able t' persuade me Da t' buy us a new dress while we' here."

When Dan and Sarah finally came out of the office Meg guessed by the look on their faces that something was wrong and her hopes of a visit to the market were dashed when Sarah spoke. To who she was speaking Meg was not sure.

"From what he's just telt us we'll not be gannin't' the market t'day or any other day f' a long time."

Sarah then turned and spoke directly to Meg.

"Y' Da could de wi' a drink an' a could de wi' one mesel' after what he's just telt us. Y're gannin't' have t' mek de wi' what you've got. We might as well gan an' see our Jane while we're here. We'll have t' walk t' save the fare an' we'll have a cup o' tea there an' if John's not at work y' Da can gan an' have a pint wi' him."

Jane now had another two children, a third son and only three weeks ago she'd had another baby.

"A girl this time," Meg had heard her Da tell her Ma.

When they arrived at Jane's Meg could sense there was trouble. The only one not crying was John and as they walked in the front door John walked out of the back door without speaking to anyone. Meg thought he was drunk but it was not until her Da called him, 'a drunken bugger', that she was sure. Her Aunty Jane had a black eye and her blouse was torn, there was a broken plate on the floor and what looked like gravy and potato splashed all over the kitchen wall. For the first time Dan

164

and Sarah's suspicions were proved correct. Meg and the two older boys were quickly sent to the fish and chip shop for bags of chips.

In her usual fashion Jane tried to explain the morning's events to her parents. As usual she made excuses for John.

"He works hard at the pit Da, he never loses a shift an' he plays the piano in the dance band on a Saturday night. He's even began t' give piano lessons an' if he had the time he'd tek' more pupils. It's when he gets them nightmares, he gans out an' gets drunk an' then he teks it out o' me an' the bairns. The bairns daren't breathe when he's had a drink."

Meg and the boys ate their chips in silence. Meg would have liked to play with the boys but they would not leave Jane's side. Even Dan and Sarah's efforts to distract the children had no effect. The three boys sat on the floor holding on to their mother's skirt, too afraid to move.

Meg was pleased to get home that night and even more pleased that she now shared a bed with Ada. Dan and Sarah had had more than their fair share of gin and beer that night. The trip to Durham had not been a good day for any of them. It would be many years before Meg realised why Jane chose to live as she did. But would she really ever understand why?

As the weeks passed Meg settled into her new school and on the whole she appeared to be happy. She still liked to be the dominant one, both at school and at play, and on most occasions that particular trait did not cause many problems. Walking home from school with Tom one day Meg asked him a question.

"Tom the teacher says a'm developin' int' a natural leader or somat like that. A dinna kna' what that means; it doesn't mean a'm bad or somat does it?"

Before Tom had time to answer Meg chattered away.

"She say's a'm good at compositions an' this mornin' she asked us t' read one out t' the others an' then y' kna' what she said?"

Meg paused and at last Tom managed to speak.

"What Meg?"

"She says 'ave got a vivid imagination an' Tom a dinna kna' what that means either."

They were home before Tom had time to reply, the conversation now forgotten by Meg, but not by Tom.

Meg was blissfully unaware of what was happening in her own home. As far as she was concerned Ada looked after the house, Will was as bad tempered as ever and Tom spent more and more time by himself, reading and working at his sums. An invitation to a birthday party taught Meg a lesson she would never forget. It was also the beginning of her awareness of poverty on her family and others.

Meg had been playing on the village green and as soon as she was asked to the party she ran home. She was shouting with excitement as she ran across the back yard.

"Ma a've been asked t' a party can a gan an' can a have a new dress? A'll have t' have a new dress 'cos it's in a pub, Louise lives there wi' her Ma an' Da an' she always has nice dresses on. The others say the're all gettin' new dresses so can a? "

Tom grabbed Meg and ushered her quickly into the parlour.

"Dinna ask me Ma f' owt today Meg," he told her, "me Da an' our Will have just had a row about the pit. Our Will says th' comin' out on strike an' a can remember last time. Y' were only little so y' won't remember but it was awful, we had nowt t' eat hardly. Me Da says he won't gan through that again but our Will says he'll have ne choice an' all the others'll be against him if he doesn't come out wi' them."

The conflict between Dan and Will had been growing for a number of weeks. Today it reached its climax. Will was now active in the union and he had informed his father that he was going to a meeting that was against the coal owners who wanted to reduce theirs wages and make the miners work longer hours.

During the previous two years seventy nine pits had closed in the County of Durham and only five new ones opened. Will had previously attended a meeting which was addressed by A.J. Cooke, Secretary of the Miners Federation of Great Britain and he fired Will's enthusiasm when he prophesied:-

"Before 1925 is out we shall be face to face in Britain with the greatest industrial struggle we have ever had, that will involve not only the miners, but the railwaymen, dockers and engineers."

Later that night Will gave Dan a full account of that meeting but Dan was in no mood to listen to his son, either then or at any time later. He could remember only too well the struggle, not four years before, when they were all locked out of the pits. Dan was quick to remind Will that he did not have the responsibility of feeding a family and that he was only seventeen years of age during the 1921 lock out.

Dan was tired and lost his patience yet again with his son.

"A'm all f' better wages an' shorter hours," Dan argued. "But look what happened last time, the others

167

didn't support us, it was all wind an' piss, an' the same could happen again, the's none o' them kna' what we suffered; bloody Durham Chronicle reportin' that we were non violent. We were all supposed to be workin' in our allotments an' playin' sports. A load o'shite; aye you were alright, y' enjoyed the football wi' out havin' t' worry about where the next bite came from, well it's your turn t' listen t' me now. A sorted this out f' y' the other night; a was that bloody mad a cut it out an' a kept it f' y'."

Dan handed the newspaper clipping to Will and he laughed as he read it.

"With fine weather prevailing the miners have been hard at work in their gardens and allotments. The younger men are indulging in football, while others are practising in their respective cricket fields for the coming seasons."

"Another load o' shite," Dan repeated. "We were left wi' ne choice but t' accept charity an' get int' a load o' debt. Sod bloody charity an' soup kitchens an' sod the bloody food vouchers. A've provided f' me own family all me life an' a'll keep on dein' it 'til the day a die."

Will argued back.

"Aye Da an' what did Peter Lee say? If we failed the struggle we'd have t' gan through it all again."

Dan would not be beaten.

"Aye we failed after three bitter months. We were lucky but some poor sods, after all o' it, had no bloody jobs t' gan back t'. A'm sorry Will, you gan t' y' union meetin's, but a'll not come wi' y'.Y' right if the's a strike a'll have t' gan along wi' the majority, an' a'll support the union, but a'll not be one o' y' that encourages it t' happen."

Even though Tom had warned Meg she could not keep quiet. Before supper she asked Dan first and then

Sarah for a new dress for the party. Her constant badgering caused Sarah to hit her so hard on the legs that the wheals were still there after two days. Finally Dan intervened and Meg was sent to bed without any supper.

The party was planned for the following Saturday and Meg was determined, she was going whether she had a new dress or not. She was not bothered what her Ma said she was going to Louise's party. Unfortunately Meg discovered she had another hurdle to cross before the party could become a reality. She had not thought anything could be worse than not having a new dress until she heard her friends discussing birthday presents. Meg's mind worked overtime. How could she go to the party without a present? Again she pestered Sarah.

"A can't gan Ma wi' out a present; if a canna have a dress then can a have a present t' tek'?"

Meg was forlorn when Sarah answered.

"If y' haven't a present then y' canna gan; y' can't have everythin' y' want Meg."

The day of the party had arrived, Meg was up bright and early still determined she was going to the party. She had a plan and no one, not even her Ma, was going to stop her from going to the party. Ada had a boyfriend, he was her first, and she was keeping it a secret. Meg had spied on her at the top of the street and Ada had warned Meg what would happen to her if she told anyone. She had no intention of telling anyone but Ada's secret could come in useful.

Ada's boyfriend had bought her a lace handkerchief and Meg had watched her hide it under the desk bed, that handkerchief was just what Meg needed. Meg reasoned that Ada would not be able to accuse her of taking it in case she told her Ma about her boyfriend. That morning, before Ada was awake, Meg took the handkerchief and put it in her coat pocket. Before the rest of the family were out of bed Meg was washed, dressed and sitting at the kitchen table reading a book looking a picture of innocence as if butter would not melt in her mouth.

It was not unusual for Meg to be missing for most of the day and on this Saturday, she did as she usually did, and went straight out after breakfast. She returned for her dinner which she ate in silence and then went straight off out again. The party did not start until three o'clock but Meg needed to be out of the house as quickly as possible. If she stayed Ada might give her some jobs to do. She had not washed since the morning and after a day of wandering the roads and playing with her friends she knew she did not look at all like a little girl who was ready to go to a party.

Determined not to miss it Meg decided against going home for a wash, she would be alright; she would go just as she was. Meg waited outside the public house for the others to arrive and was pleasantly surprised. Most of the girls were dressed no better than she was although they were a little cleaner and they did have their hair brushed.

Meg went into the party with the rest of her friends and she was enjoying herself until Louise's mother told them to sit down for tea. It was then that Meg began to feel different from the other children. Her friends started to giggle, they did not include her, and Meg knew they were laughing at her.

"T' pot wi' em," she muttered under her breath. "A'm sure Louise liked me present the best, it was more grown up than the others."

After tea Louise's father started to organize party games, but Meg did not enjoy them, she felt left out and she was beginning to feel guilty about the lace handkerchief. When some of the children started chattering to each other about her dirty hands and face she became upset and when one friend said her hair was

170

like rats tails Meg had had enough. She was relieved when Louise's mother gave them all a packet of sweets and told them it was time to go home. Most of the children were being collected by an older brother or sister and once more Meg crossed her fingers behind her back as she told a lie.

"It's all right Mrs Green, a'll be alright our Tom's meetin' us at the top o' the bank," Meg lied.

That night Meg learnt her lesson the hard way. When she returned from the party Dan asked her where she had been and he accepted her usual reply of out playing with her friends. Sarah made no comment and a relieved Meg was pleased Will was out at he races. One look at Ada and Tom out of the corner of her eye and Meg squirmed in her chair,

"The' kna' somat," she thought to herself.

Since they had moved house Sarah went out with Dan for a drink on a Saturday night. It was not to the public house where Dan drank with his friends but to a quieter public house, the only one in the area where women were served a drink. Women were not allowed in the bar and Dan had to spend his Saturday night drinking in a small room behind the bar. Dan much preferred a night out with his friends but he gave in to Sarah's demands, she enjoyed the company. It was much better, he reasoned, than her collecting her beer from the ducket where there was only room for two people and no opportunity for gossiping.

Sarah had long since tried to hide her drinking habit especially when, after moving house, she realised she was not the only miners' wife who indulged in a glass of beer or a tot of gin or port. Dan had also changed, since their move; he no longer felt guilty about Sarah's drinking. Again he reasoned if she was with him she could not accuse him of being with another woman. She

171

still accused him and tried her upmost to cause an argument with him. Dan did not mind he knew Sarah of old and he rarely ever retaliated to her accusations. They had an unspoken understanding, one that only two people who had shared so much hardship together could ever understand. Sarah knew that Dan would always be faithful to her and she never doubted his loyalty to her and their family. Dan loved Sarah in the same way as she loved him but their love was hidden from the rest of the world, and for most of the time from each other.

As soon as Dan and Sarah left for the pub Ada grabbed Meg and she had never been so afraid in all of her life. Ada held on to Meg and smacked her bottom so hard Meg wondered if she would ever be able to sit on it again. Tom tried to intervene but when he was told about the stolen handkerchief he stalked out into the back yard. As he walked past Meg he spoke to her.

"Y' deserve everythin' y' gettin' off our Ada."

That was the final humiliation, Tom's words hurt more than her bottom, he was her best friend and he always protected her. He was the person she loved more than anyone else in the world. It was later that night as Meg lay on the little desk bed, her face blotchy with tears and eyes so puffed she could hardly see, she realised just how much she loved her Ma and Da.

"A'm scared now," she sobbed. "A love me Ma an' Da just like a love our Tom an' now the' winna want us 'cos our Ada says a'm a thief an' a liar, an' she telt our Tom a was a little blackmailer."

Meg heard Ada leave the house and she guessed she was going to meet Fred; at least she thought that was what he was called. She lay quietly for half an hour willing Tom to come into the parlour. Still crying she said to herself,

"He's not ganna come, he's not me friend anymore, a'll have t' find somewhere t' gan, the' don't want me here."

Meg pondered for a few more minutes.

"A kna' where a'll gan, a'll gan back t' the village t' Joe's house, mebbe he'll let us live there wi' him?"

Meg quietly got out of bed. She dressed quickly and tiptoeing out of the parlour took her coat from the hook in the passage and left the house running as fast as she could up the front street. It took her an hour to walk back to her old village and Meg was frightened as she approached what she thought would be a long, dark, lonely walk. She was pleasantly surprised when she found it to be busy and bustling with people coming and going. As she approached the village green she could hear music and Meg's curiosity made her forget the real reason she was there. The annual fair was in full swing. Roundabouts, coconut shys and roll the half penny stalls, rifle ranges and men throwing darts. Meg's eyes widened when she saw the carousel. Meg was mesmerised by the horses going around and around as she sat on the steps hypnotised by their majestic movement.

Meg yawned, she was feeling tired and finding it difficult to keep her eyes open. The thought of going to Joe's, now it was so late, was worrying her. Under her breath she muttered.

"He might not let me stay when he finds out what a've done, an' then where'll a gan, a better stay here a bit longer 'til a mek me mind up what t' de."

Meg thought she was dreaming. Someone was carrying her and the music was fading away. When she opened her eyes she knew she was not dreaming; it was Will who was carrying her. At first she was frightened but that feeling lasted only a few seconds, she was too

173

tired to care and she felt safe. Meg was safe in the care of her uncle; the uncle who Meg thought was her brother.

"A'll gan an' see Joe tomorro'," Meg thought to herself as slipped back into a deep sleep.

When Meg woke the following morning she could vaguely remember Ada taking her clothes off and putting her to bed the night before. She felt nice, just like last night when Will carried her home, but when she moved her arm hurt and her bottom was sore and then she remembered the events of the day before. Once again Meg was scared.

"Meg come an' get y' breakfast."

It was her Da shouting for her to get up. She knew she would have to face the family but now she wished she had not gone to the fair, she wished she had gone straight to Joe's. Meg ate her breakfast in silence and for the rest of the day only spoke when she was spoken to. She went to Sunday school on the afternoon and came straight home when it was finished, something she rarely ever did. When bed time came Meg could not understand it. Her Ma made her cocoa and still no one had mentioned the party, the stolen handkerchief or her trip to the fair. Meg was never to know whether Ada or Tom had told Dan and Sarah of her misdemeanours or whether Will had told them he had found her asleep on the steps of the carousel. What she did know was that it was wrong to lie, steal or even to think about blackmailing anyone ever again. Meg had learnt her lesson the hard way.

"That's it," Sarah shouted at Meg. "Next week y' can tek a tin one." It was Meg's third Friday at the soup kitchen, where she received a liberal helping of pies and peas, and this was the third plate she had broken on the way home. The soup kitchen was at the chapel and Meg always took the short cut. Unfortunately the high railings she had to climb over proved to be too much of an obstacle for Meg when she had a plate in her hands.

Will had been proved right. By the 3rd of May that year 200 pits had closed in the County of Durham and 150,000 miners were out of work. On that same day the Times newspaper reported.

"The breakdown in negotiations and the threat of a prolonged stoppage has created a feeling of dismay and deepest disappointment in the North."

By the following day nearly all workers in the north East who had been requested to support the miners responded. The Durham Chronicle newspaper reported on the 8th of May.

"The commencement of the General Strike completely paralysed the commercial and industrial activities of the Durham District. In all of the vital industries there was practically a complete withdrawal of labour and citizens devoted their activities to providing maintenance of vital services."

Unfortunately for the miners the General Strike was called off after only nine days and the miners were left to continue their struggle alone. News of the surrender of the T.U.C. to the government was received, in the Durham coalfield, with an incredulity which quickly changed to fury. The Newcastle Workers Chronicle exclaimed.

"Never in the history of worker's struggles, with the one exception of the treachery of our leaders in 1914, has there been such a calculated betrayal of working class interests."

During those long summer months, Meg had her first real taste of poverty and began to understand why Dan and Sarah felt as they did about the acceptance of charity. While Meg and Tom attended the soup kitchens and were never really hungry, the local education authority ensuring that children were fed, Dan and Sarah refused to forsake their principles. They often went hungry for the sake of their children. They occasionally accepted the allocation of free bread and cocoa but their family was just as distressed as many others during those long months. Meg finally understood why there could be no new clothes, why her boots let in water and why sometimes there was not even any soap for washing. She was not overly perturbed as she told Sarah.

"The others at school us just the same as us Ma, s' dinna worry about me an' our Tom."

Will continued with his union activities and joined the picket lines. Fortunately his involvement was limited to stopping transport and although he had a few narrow escapes with the police, he was never arrested. During the month of August the miners in the Midlands began to drift back to work and in October the same happened in the Durham coal fields. Dan was secretly pleased that an end was in sight but, like his son, would not return to work until the union officially called off the strike or an agreement was reached. As the weeks passed life became harder and because of the hardship many miners drifted back to work with the result that miner turned against miner and many who returned were not even safe in their own homes.

After much persuasion Dan finally agreed to attend a union meeting with Will.

"A suppose a better," he told Sarah. "A've refused t' gan back so a suppose a should show me face f' once an' hear things first hand."

He stood side by side with his son listening to local Members of Parliament, Union Leaders and vocal Miners but at the end of it all he only agreed with one statement.

"If there is any feeling that we are done and if there is going to be any going back, for God's sake let's get back to the Miner's Hall at Durham, and let us all go back together."

It was not until the end of that year that Dan and Will finally returned to the pit. They were lucky; for many miners there were no jobs to go back to. Many left the area to find work elsewhere, others left in disgust at the settlement they were offered. Those that did return went back to the very conditions they had rejected. Many were like Will and from their very first day back at work planned revenge on the government and mine owners. It was during their first week back at work that Will read out an article in the Durham Chronicle.

"Listen t' this Da, a telt y', one day we'll beat the bastards."

"The miners are on the bottom and have been compelled to accept dictated and unjust terms. The miners will rise again and will remember because they cannot forget. The victors of today will live to regret their unjust treatment of the miners."

177

CHAPTER 9

The Charlton's were up at the crack of dawn and after a quick but wholesome breakfast set off for a day at the big meeting. The previous year's industrial action had caused the cancellation of one of the most important events in any Durham miner's year. Except for the years of the Great War and industrial action in 1921, 1922 and 1926, Dan had never missed a Gala day. His father took him as soon as he was old enough to walk through the busy streets and often boasted that he had attended the very first meeting in 1871. Dan followed his father's example; the big meeting was a day out for him and his family. Although money was still short, Dan and Sarah had sacrificed their usual Saturday night's entertainment, for the last few weeks, to give the family this one important day out.

Meg could remember the last time she went and like all miners' children she was looking forward to the fun of the fairground. The Gala was the one day of the year when Sarah gave her money of her own to spend.

"An' when it's done it's done," she told Meg.

Meg was happy with the money; she had sufficient for a toffee apple, an ice cream and two or three rides on the shows, but something else was troubling her and it bothered her throughout the journey to Durham.

As they were leaving the house Ada had asked her Ma for some extra money and when her Ma refused Meg could not understand Ada's annoyed retort.

"Meg should only have her own money, not ours. If she did the' might be a bit more f' us then."

Meg was curious as to what Ada meant but for some reason, which was unusual for Meg, she did not want to ask.

"A've nowt o' me own," Meg pondered, "our Ada must have been talkin' about somebody else."

Meg finally convinced herself that she was right and when they arrived at Durham she soon forgot Ada's spiteful remark.

As they walked through the streets of Durham, Meg became more and more excited as the sounds of brass bands got nearer and nearer. Tom was given strict instructions to keep tight hold of her hand and as they approached the city centre they ran ahead of the rest of the family to see the famous spectacle, the miners proudly carrying their pit banners. It was a hot day but the men still wore stiff collars and ties, their clothes sticking to sweaty bodies. They had lost the battle last year but that had not taken away their sense of pride. The thousands of onlookers, who either stood in the crowded streets or marched behind the banners, were as proud of their work and their traditions as the men who marched holding their banners high. The banners were colourful and shone brightly as they swayed in the warm, gentle breeze.

Meg and Tom pushed their way through the jostling crowds, trying to beat each other in reading the name of the lodge on each banner or guess which pit it represented by the picture it displayed. Some of the banners had pictures of people on them and Tom was well informed about the different banners and the reasons for the gala. Will had told him, often enough, about the men who had started the union and the Members of Parliament who supported the miners. It was these men the miners honoured by displaying them proudly on their lodge banners. Some of the banners represented the miners themselves and the pits where they worked and they were the ones Meg liked best. She would pretend that it was her Da or Will carrying their

179

pit lamps, dressed only in a vest and a pair of pit hoggers, knee pads strapped on and feet appearing to be enormous in a pair of heavy pit boots.

Meg thought back to the last time she was at the big meeting when her Da had lifted her onto his shoulders so she could see the bands and the banners over the top of the crowds. But today was better; today she was free; even if they had been warned not to go on any further than the Three Tuns Hotel where Dan and Sarah would meet them. Today she was with Tom pushing through the crowds to reach the front. Will had left the family as soon as they arrived in Durham. He had gone to join his mates and he had told his father they were going to listen to the speeches as soon as the hundreds of banners reached the banks of the River Wear. Tom had wanted to go with Will but Dan refused to let him go.

"It'll be a few more years afore a let y' roam the streets o' Durham on a big Meetin' Day," he told a disappointed Tom. "A kna' our Will, he'll 'ave drunk a few pints o' beer afore the speeches start an' then the's always the chance o' a few rowdy scenes. It's more than likely this year there'll be one o' two fights. The's a lot o' them still got the nasty taste o' defeat in the' mouths."

Dan and Will had argued all the way to Durham and, as usual, Will made sure he had the last word.

"At least Da we'll show 'em we haven't given up. We'll show 'em our solidarity today an' that we're ganna keep fightin' f' better pay an' conditions."

Dan was not impressed by his son's remarks; he had fought too often and seen the hardship caused by the ever increasing shows of solidarity which seemed to get them nowhere.

"A hope y' right an' a'm wrong lad," Dan told him. "One day things might get better but it won't be in my

180

life time. But y' right, enjoy the day lad, 'cos a suppose this is one day in the year when we can all have a bit o' hope f' the future."

It was well into the afternoon before the thousands of miners and their families were congregated on the banks of the river Wear. Meg was pleased there was now just the four of them, her Ma, her Da, Tom and herself. Ada had conveniently met some of her friends and gone off with them but Meg knew better. She had seen Fred lurking behind one of the banners and guessed who Ada was going with. Meg did not like Fred. She knew she had no reason not to like him, she had never even spoken to him, but for some reason she did not like the look of him. When she had whispered to Tom that she had seen Fred he told her to shut up and not let her Ma and Da hear.

"Y'll spoil Ada's day if me Ma an' Da find out," Tom scolded, "an' then she'll tek it out o' us tonight."

The family stood for hours listening to the brass bands and watching the banners being carried through the streets of Durham. At first the banners came in slowly and Meg, quickly becoming bored, was scolded by Sarah for fidgeting. Tom tried to amuse her by telling her to keep quiet and listen to see who could hear the next band first. Soon the banners and bands were following each other one after the other and although Meg was no longer bored she decided she was hungry.

"Ma," she asked, "when a we ganna get somat t' eat, its ages since we had our breakfast?"

It was Dan who answered.

"Right, we'll walk up t' our Jane's an' have a bite t' eat, an' then we'll come back down an' y' can gan t' the shows t' spend y' money afore we watch the banners gannin' back out."

It took nearly an hour to walk to Jane's and Meg was not too happy about going, she remembered only too well her last visit. When they arrived she was pleasantly surprised. John was in and Joe and John's brother Bill were there with Bill's wife and three children. Meg had never met Bill but she had heard Joe and her Ma and Da talk about him often enough. She knew he lived in Manchester and had a good job. As soon as she realised who it was she was quick to divulge her knowledge of the stranger to Tom. Tom told Meg he had met Bill before but that did not deter Meg so he smiled at her and listened.

"A heard Joe, ages ago, tellin' me Ma an' me Da that Bill married a woman he lodged wi' an' she had two lasses o' her own. Joe said that Bill an' her had another bairn an' now he's high up in the paper he works f'. Joe said that Bill wanted him t' gan an' live down there wi' him but he wouldn't gan."

Meg was so busy telling Tom all she knew about Bill that she had forgotten her hunger until she saw the table; it was overflowing with food. There was a ham shank, pork and pickles and even cakes and biscuits for afters.

Turning once more to Tom she exclaimed.

"Our Jane must 'ave been bakin' f' a week by the amount o' pies and cakes that's here."

John told everyone to help themselves and Jane poured everyone a pot of tea. On this occasion everyone in the house, including Jane's children, had a good time. Meg thoroughly enjoyed her meal and noticed that her Ma was laughing with Joe and Bill, something she rarely did. Meg decided she liked Bill and his family even if they did talk different.

"The're a bit posh Tom aren't the'?" she whispered to him.

She thought Bill especially nice and although she did not want to be rude she was dying to know what was wrong with his leg.

After they had eaten John played the piano and Meg's eyes were transfixed on the cigarette in his mouth. She could not keep quiet any longer and nudged Tom.

"Tom 'ave y'seen John's fag, it's burnin' right down in his mouth; it's all ash an'it's not even droppin'off while he's playin'?"

Meg had a fit of the giggles when John lit another cigarette after the first one burnt away. Again he did not smoke it, like the one before, it burnt away in his mouth and not one speck of ash fell from the burning end.

They all left the house together, except for Jane and her children. When Dan asked her why she was not ready to go with them Jane made an excuse.

"A dinna want t' trail the bairns 'round Durham Da."

Meg, for the first time, felt a little sorry for Jane.

"A dinna think its fair," she told Tom as they walked back to the City. "John's comin' wi' us an' Bill's helpin' wi' his bairns an' he has a bad leg, a think John could help her, an' anyhow she's got all that mess t' clear up hersel'."

Tom told her to hush in case John heard her but Meg was not having any of it.

"A dinna think its fair Tom," she insisted. "We've all had our tea an' just come out an' left her. A always liked John better than our Jane 'cos she never seemed t' like me but she talked t' me today an' she never has before. She said a was growin' up an' that me Ma an' Da had telt her a was dein' better at school now we'd shifted. She even asked what lessons a liked best."

Meg soon forgot about Jane once they reached the fairground, especially when John and Bill gave both her and Tom extra money to spend on the shows. It was a tired Meg who marched through Durham with Dan, Sarah and Tom, all of them proud knowing that the banner they marched behind represented Dan's pit.

When they arrived home that night an exhausted Meg fell into her bed. Meg's night in Durham had not been quite as enjoyable as the day. The night was Dan and Sarah's and Tom and Meg had to spend a boring two hours outside one or two rowdy public houses while Dan and Sarah had their usual Saturday night's refreshments.

Meg had thought they would not take her so soon after the Big Meeting. But after only two weeks she was waiting at the railway station with her Ma and Da and they were going to the seaside on the chapel trip. Tom had taken her to the station with him when he went train spotting but she had never been on one. Meg could never understand how Tom could sit for hours watching the trains and then jump in the air with excitement just because he had seen a train with a number he had not seen before. When she went with him she was bored within half an hour and Tom would be annoyed with her because she wanted to go home. If he refused to take her she would run off when he was not looking and then later that night they would both be in trouble, Meg for coming home alone, and Tom for allowing her.

Tom refused to go on the chapel trip, he would have enjoyed going on the train but he knew that all of the children would be much younger than him. Dan, Sarah and Meg walked the three miles to the station and when they arrived most of the other children were already there with there parents. Meg saw her Sunday school teacher and she willed her to come and talk to her Ma and Da but before she stropped talking to the other parents the train arrived. As Meg watched the teacher talking to her friend's parents she noticed, for the first time, that their parents looked much younger than hers, at least their mothers did. They were all wearing coloured dresses and some had coloured coats and hats.

As they sat on the train, chugging along through the open countryside, Meg was distracted. Normally she would be excited at something new but today her thoughts were elsewhere. She was totally engrossed in her Ma and Da, comparing them with the other adults in their carriage.

"Me Da doesn't look much different from the others an' his claes us a lot nicer than some o' the others." Meg mused. "But me Ma looks a lot older than all o' them, an' her claes are awful. A never noticed 'til today but her hair's all grey, some o' the others have grey hair but not all ower."

The lively chatter of two of her friends in the same carriage soon turned Meg's thoughts elsewhere, a game of eye spy and the train was pulling into the station. Her friends had already told her they were having a day on the beach and just like Meg they had brought picnics. Three of her friends made plans to meet with Meg and they planned the different games they would play on the beach.

As they got off the train Meg had her first disappointment of the day. The sky was overcast and it looked as if it was going to rain. Her second disappointment was as they walked to the beach. Her friends and their parents, hoping the weather would improve, decided to still go to the beach. Dan and Sarah walked with them as far as the main street but then turned towards the town centre.

"Come on Meg," Dan said taking Meg's hand in his, "we'll gan t' the beach later if it gets out fine."

After wandering around the shops for a short time there was no improvement in the weather and then Meg had her third disappointment when Sarah said to her,

"Wait outside here Meg, me an' y' Da'll only be a few minutes."

The few minutes lasted an hour and it was a relieved Meg who saw Dan and Sarah waving goodbye to the pub regulars as they came to collect her.

The weather had still not improved although the threatened rain had not materialised. Dan looked up at the sky as he spoke to Meg.

"Y' Granda once brought me here an' the weather was just like this but we walked three miles along the coast an' it was beautiful. We'll not walk today; we'll get the bus an' see if it's the same."

Meg did not care, her day was ruined, and she walked along with Dan and Sarah, saying nothing, but with tears in her eyes. After much searching for the bus they arrived at a much smaller seaside town and Meg's face brightened. The sun was shining and as they neared the bottom of the hill she could see lots of people sitting and playing on the sands. It was not as Tom had told her it would be, the chapel people altogether, adults sitting in large circles chatting to each other and the children playing by themselves. On this beach there were small family groups and the adults were playing with the children.

Meg was to remember that day for many years to come; just her and her Ma and Da and she had a wonderful time. Her Da bought a bat and ball and he played on the beach with her. He took off his coat and her Ma sat on it and when the ball rolled over to her she caught it and laughed as she threw it back to them, especially when she threw it so hard it went in the sea and Meg had to run in to retrieve it. Her Da even took his shoes and socks off, rolled up his trouser bottoms and went plodging in the sea with her.

Meg went with Dan to the stall on the edge of the beach where they had to wait in a long queue but it was worth it. They got a jug of tea and three cups which Meg helped Dan carry back to Sarah The tea was piping hot and her Ma said it was just what she needed as they ate their picnic on the beach.

"Ma a love y' boiled eggs even if me Da says the're covered in sand," Meg told Sarah, "an' y' pies an' cakes us the best 'ave ever tasted."

As Meg watched Sarah meticulously peel her boiled egg, she noticed that a few strands of her grey hair had fallen from the tight bun she wore and they were blowing in the light sea breeze. Sarah talked and laughed with Meg and Dan, pointing at the other families, their antics in the sea amusing her. Even when her Ma did the same as her Da and complained about the sand getting into her boiled egg she said it with laughter in her voice. Meg very nearly spilled her tea when she and her Da had a good laugh at her. Meg was so happy she did not need her friends today; this day with her Ma and Da was one of her best days.

Dan took his watch from his waist coat pocket.

"Right the pair o' y' it's time t' gan back if we t' catch the train."

He cleared the rubbish while Sarah and Meg returned the empty jug and cups back to the tea stall and they set off back, Meg walking proudly between them holding their hands. They all laughed when Sarah said she was getting too old to climb the steep hill in front of them and Meg giggled as Dan pretended to drag Sarah all the way to the top. As they walked to the bus stop Meg listened intently to Dan and Sarah talking about a

187

previous visit. They were not talking to her, in fact it was Dan who was doing all of the talking.

Dan pointed to a large house at the top of the hill and said to Sarah.

"D' y'remember hinnie all them years ago; y' Da paid f' us t' stop there on our weddin' night. It was just one night but a remember it like it was yesterday. A telt y' then y' were bonnie an' y' were the best thing that had ever happened t' me'. Well, a still think y' bonnie, an'y' still the best thing that's ever happened t' me. We had some big plans then didn't we? Who'd have thought the things that have happened would have happened t' us. But the' have an' we're still here together, an' God willin' we'll be together f' a long time yet."

Meg could not wait to get back to the station. When they arrived the weather was still overcast and she could not wait to tell her friends about her marvellous day on the beach.

"A bet, Da, the' aven't had as good a time as us." Meg said as she skipped alongside Dan and Sarah.

They were early back at the station and one of Meg's best days was about to turn into one of her worst.

"Wait outside here," Dan told her as he and Sarah were about to enter the public house beside the station. She was not the only child waiting outside but none of her special friends were there. Then she saw them heading for the station and being afraid that they would see her by herself Meg decided to go into the station.

Meg never had the opportunity to tell her friends about her marvellous day. When Dan and Sarah left the public house they were frantic with worry, Meg had vanished. They found her only minutes before the train was due to leave sitting alone on a bench on the station platform. The laughter of the afternoon was forgotten, a scolding from Sarah, tears from Meg and a journey home in silence.

The rest of the year was uneventful until Christmas Day. Meg's birthday was the day before but it was rarely ever mentioned. She had never had a birthday present; what little there was; was saved for Christmas day. When she was old enough to understand she had cried when no one mentioned her birthday. Her Da had told her she was extra special to have been born at Christmas time and that helped a little but although she never mentioned it she always wished her birthday and not Jesus's birthday could be a cause for celebration.

Last year, Christmas Day had been just like any other day. Her Da and Will had just gone back to work and Tom had told her there was no money so not to expect Santa coming. As it turned out he did come but her stocking had no money in it, only an apple and an orange and worst of all there were no presents. Luckily her Granda came to see them late on Christmas morning and he brought a present. It was lovely doll and Meg did not know how quickly to leave the house to meet her friends and show them her doll.

Unfortunately their Christmas was just as frugal as Meg's; some of her friends had got less than her. Feeling a little sorry for them she let one of her friends nurse the doll. Meg soon realised her mistake when one girl, who Meg had made an enemy of shortly after their move to the village, grabbed the doll and while inspecting it pulled off one of its legs. That Christmas day turned out to be another one of Meg's worst days. When she took the doll home Ada took one look at it, blamed Meg, smacked her bottom and sent her to bed without any tea or supper.

This year, Christmas was differentt; Meg's presents were the best she had ever had. Not only was her stocking full of fruit, but there was nuts and a three penny piece in the bottom of it. She was overjoyed at the two presents at the bottom of the bed. One was a doll's tea set just like the one she had seen in the shop when they were on the chapel trip.

"A wondered why me Da went int' that shop by hisel'," she told Tom later that day. "He made me stand outside wi' me Ma, now a kna' why."

Her other present was a printing set with a stamp and ink. Meg thought that this was going to be one of her best days so to make it even better Meg brought out last years doll, Will had repaired the leg and she had a few presents from previous years that she had not spoilt. Meg displayed them with this year's presents and feeling very pleased with herself she willed her friends to call for her to go out to play.

"A'll ask them in," she muttered to herself, "an' wont th' think Santa's been good t' me this year."

Ada was restless that Christmas morning. She could not sit still; first she tidied the parlour, then the kitchen. As soon as they had finished their dinner she cleared the dishes and washed up and then Meg found out why. Ada was in the parlour when Meg walked in on her and she was putting her best skirt on.

"What y' titivatin' y' sel' up f'?" Meg asked. "Are y'gannin' out? A've never knan y' gan out on a Christmas Day afore."

Ada smiled at her.

"Fred's comin' f' his tea this afternoon; me Da kna's him from the pit an' he telt me Ma it was about time she met him, so she said he could come today."

Ada's information did not please Meg; she still did not like Fred. She had met Fred and Ada in the village the other day and he had tried to be nice to her, but she did not like him and refused when he said she could go for a walk with him and Ada.

Meg decided if Fred was coming she was going out, but as she put her boots on and started to tie the laces, Sarah told them to take them off.

"Y' not gannin' out t'day, y're always roamin' the roads, y'll stay in wi' the rest o' us an' meet Fred." Meg was upset but the arrival of her Granda cheered her up. Her present this year was a drawing book and crayons and Meg started to work on it straight away. The pictures were already drawn but filling them in with the crayons would take quite some time.

"A'll gan in the parlour by mesel'," Meg muttered. "The' can all talk in the kitchen, a dinna want t' sit wi' Fred."

During the winter the parlour was cold and only used as a bedroom for Ada and Meg to sleep in. Tom would brave the cold, sitting with his coat on as he read his books and did his sums, but an hour was usually all he could bear. Christmas day was the only day of the year when the fire in the parlour was lit and Meg could never understand why they all still sat in the kitchen.

"Well t' day," she planned, "a'm usin' it an' am not comin' out f' me tea if he's still here. If me Ma or our Ada say a have t' come out a'll say a feel sick after me dinner."

As always the kitchen and the parlour doors were wide open and as they were adjacent to each other Meg could hear everything in the room next door. When the back door slammed she stopped crayoning and pricked her ears. Ada was introducing Fred to her Ma.

"It'll be our Will's turn when he gets up." Meg grumbled. "A'm pleased a'm out o' the road mebee the'll forget about us."

Meg was happily, kneeling on the floor in front of the fire, crayoning her fourth picture, when Dan came into the parlour with a shovel of coal.

"A' y' ganna come out int' the kitchen an' meet Fred?" He asked.

Without looking up from her book Meg replied.

"Aye Da a will when a finish me picture."

Meg crossed her fingers behind her back and mumbled.

"Please God let them f' get about me."

But then she heard her Da reply to something Fred had said.

"Aye lad, she's in the parlour by hersel', gan an' tek them int' her."

Meg cringed as Fred came through the door.

"A've brought y' a few sweets," Fred said as he knelt on the floor beside her and then he commented on the picture she was crayoning in.

Meg, remembering her manners, thanked him but moved away as he brought his face nearer to hers. She could not help it; she just did not like him.

"Anyway," she thought to herself, "a dinna like the smell o' his breath, he must smoke funny fags 'cos our Will's doesn't smell like that."

As Fred got up he squeezed her shoulder and once more she cringed. Meg knew he had noticed and she turned away as he told her he would see her again before he went home.

When Dan shouted to tell her tea was ready Meg did not reply. Her plan worked and when he came into the parlour she was curled up in a tight ball with her eyes closed. Meg breathed a sigh of relief when she heard her Da telling them all she was sound asleep so he had left her.

That night in bed she was in trouble again.

"Y' upset Fred, he said y' weren't very nice t' him when he gi' y' the sweets. He says he likes y' an' that next time he comes he'll draw y' some pictures t' crayon in. He's a good drawer an' y' better be nice t' him next time 'cos a'm gannin' wi' him proper now, so he'll be comin' a lot."

Meg did not reply and when Ada nudged her she turned on her side and pretended to be asleep. She did not care whether he liked her or not, she did not like him.

CHAPTER 10

Meg was to find that being alone or pretending to be asleep was not the answer to her problems as far as Fred was concerned. She soon realised there was safety in numbers and for the next few years her imaginary protector from all evil was her beloved cat, Topsy.

"Ma, me friend's cats had kittens, can a have two o' them?" Meg shouted across the back yard.

Sarah was adamant.

"No y' certainly can't."

Meg pleaded.

"If a canna have them her Da's ganna drown them t'morro'. He telt Elsie he was ganna put them in a bucket o' water."

Sarah finally gave in.

"Y' can have 'em but y' look after em' y' sel', an' the' not stoppin' in the house on a night, the'll have t' sleep in the coal house."

Meg was delighted and went straight to Elsie's to collect her new friends.

She had only had the kittens three weeks when Blackie went missing. After two weeks of searching the dead kitten was found and Meg blamed Will. He denied it and Meg ended up with the back of his hand across her ear. Meg screamed and wet herself with fright; he had hit her before but never as hard as that. From that day on she never heard another sound in her left ear. Later that night a still weeping Meg told Tom.

"It was Will, he put the last load o' coal in an' he knew the kittens were in the coal house. He should 'ave looked; me Da found it this afternoon when he went out t' fill a bucket a coal. Me Da says a can bring Topsy in the house, a needn't put her in the coal house any more."

Topsy was soon at home in the kitchen and did not seem to miss her brother. She had two favourite spots where she slept for most of the day. The shelf above the oven door was one and the other on top of the mantelpiece. Sarah threatened Meg when Topsy first jumped onto the mantelpiece.

"If that cat knocks any ornaments off it'll be back in the coalhouse."

Meg knew Topsy wouldn't; she could nimbly jump onto one end of the mantelpiece and negotiate the walk to the other end without ever touching an ornament. Sarah grew to love the kitten and when no one else was at home she would laugh at its playful antics. Even Ada could not help but laugh when Topsy, after falling asleep on the oven shelf, would slide off its shiny surface and then scamper away to hide under the kitchen table.

Topsy loved Meg just as much as she loved her. She really was her protector and the cat became one of the reasons that Meg started to get the good hidings from Will that had once been given to Tom. Since the arrival of Topsy, Meg had become a little closer to Ada. It was Ada who stood in front of her and took the blows that were meant for Meg. Will did not like Topsy and the feeling was mutual; she would hiss, spit and extend her claws every time he came near her.

When he thought no one was looking Will often gave the cat a sly kick. Meg often caught him and when she told him to leave the cat alone, calling him cruel, she would end up receiving a good hiding. Meg was defiant; she would pick up the cat and looking Will straight in the eye shout.

A'll set me cat on y' mind."

This incensed Will, especially as on one occasion the cat had jumped out of Meg's arms, landed on his shoulder, its claws piercing through his shirt and, clinging to his skin, caused some nasty scratches.

Just as Ada had told her, Fred became a frequent visitor. At first it was just on a Sunday afternoon for tea but as time passed he would call without an invitation and Meg was always wary whenever he was there. Now whenever he came, Fred and Ada sat in the parlour by themselves and if it was cold Sarah would let Ada light the fire. The arrangement suited Meg but not Tom; it inhibited his studies and caused a rift between him and Ada. He became much closer to Meg and she became as much his confidante as he was hers.

Tom also turned against Fred; he had lost his haven for study because of him and he increasingly took Meg's side no matter with who she was in trouble. He even took Meg's side when Sarah admonished her for her rudeness to Fred. The whole family, including Fred, were now aware of Meg's intense dislike of Ada's boyfriend. He continued to buy her sweets and draw pictures for her to colour in but as soon as he arrived Meg, picked up Topsy and spoke to no one except Tom throughout his visit. She refused to be drawn into conversation with him and grudgingly accepted his sweets only to throw them in the fire when no one was looking. His pictures followed the sweets as soon as he left the house. Sarah scolded her after every visit.

"Y' bad mannered Meg, he seems a nice enough lad an' he really tries hard t' please y'. Will y' not try an' talk t' him next time he comes? Y've got our Tom as bad as y' sel' now."

At first Meg had no answer. Her Ma was right, Fred had not done anything to her; she just did not like him. Meg finally found the words to reply to Sarah.

"A canna help it Ma, a just don't like him an' a canna' talk t' him. Topsy doesn't like him either that's why a pick her up when he comes. She's frightened o' him just like she's frightened o' our Will. An' our Tom always went in the parlour afore but he couldn't have the fire on. Our Ada can put it on when she likes an' the' both sit in there all the time an' our Tom has nowhere t' gan t' de his sums now."

Fred had been coming for two years before Meg understood why she did not like him. One Saturday night she arrived home later than usual having spent an enjoyable afternoon at a friend's house. If she was late and the rest of the family were out she did not worry, she knew the key would be hanging from the string inside the letter box. Meg was used to letting herself in and after a quick supper would be fast asleep in bed before any of them were back home. On this particular Saturday night she was surprised that the door was locked and there was no key on the string. Meg peered through the letter box and could see the kitchen light was on.

"The' must have gone out an' forgot t' put the light out or the' still in," Meg muttered.

She knocked on the door and was shocked when Fred opened it. Her first instinct was to turn round and go back out, but it was cold and dark and knowing Ada would be in she walked passed him without speaking and went into the kitchen. She had expected him to go straight into the parlour with Ada and when he followed her into the kitchen Meg broke her silence.

"Where's our Ada?"

Before he had time to answer she shouted of Topsy who was nowhere to be seen.

"An' where's me cat?" she asked.

"A let the cat out the back an' Ada's gone t' bed wi' a headache," Fred replied. "A brought her home early an' she went straight t' bed. She's asleep now so dinna gan an' disturb her."

When Meg went through into the back kitchen, Fred followed her.

"Where y' gannin'?" he asked.

"T' find me cat," she answered a smiling Fred. "If she ends up havin' kittens me Ma'll gan mad, a'll have t' gan out the back an' find her."

As she pulled the bolt on the back door Fred put his hand on her shoulder as he spoke to her.

"A've some chocolate in me coat pocket Meg, a'll help y' find the cat after so come wi' me an' we'll have some chocolate first."

Fred held Meg's arm tightly and pulled her into the kitchen. She was too frightened to resist. As he sat down on the chair in front of the fire he pulled her onto his knee. She wanted to shout for Ada, but she could not. She knew if Ada caught her sitting on Fred's knee she would be in trouble with her. When Fred cuddled her and asked for a kiss she felt cold and she started to sweat. Meg did not know what Fred was going to do next but she was more than sure that whatever it was, it was something bad.

Suddenly Meg struggled to free herself from his grasp. As his hold tightened her increased terror gave her strength and she kicked Fred and bit his wrist. As Fred cried out in pain he released his hold on her and Meg took the opportunity to make her escape. She ran out of the kitchen, through the back kitchen and into the back yard. Seeing Topsy, sitting on the wall, she grabbed her and ran into the midden firmly bolting the door behind her.

Meg had used the midden as a hiding place before but that was only to hide from Ada or Will to escape a good hiding. On those occasions she had been frightened but

198

tonight was different she was terrified. Tonight Meg did not know from what she was hiding, but there was one thing she was sure of, whatever it was it would be much worse than a good hiding from Ada or Will.

The only other times Meg used the midden, for anything other than what it was intended for, was when she wanted to be alone to think things through. The last time was when she overheard Ada, once more, mention Meg's own money. It was after she had told her Ma her boots were nipping her toes and her Ma had said she could have new ones. All her thinking did not solve the problem and Meg in her usual way muttered to herself.

"A'll have t' ask me Ma what our Ada means about me own money." For days she tried to pluck up the courage to ask but for some reason she never felt able to.

The midden was always a good place to hide; that is if someone else did not want to use it and tonight she wished someone would. Sometimes there would be someone in next door's midden. At those times she kept quiet and still, she did not want the neighbours to know she was there. The sounds Meg could hear through the thin walls fuelled her imagination; she would then feel embarrassed; terrified to leave until her neighbour was safely out of the midden and back into the house.

Their midden was a dry one. It really was just a plank of wood with a hole in it but it had a lid and when the lid was over the hole, Meg found it as comfortable a place as any for her private musing and meditation. The walls of the midden were whitewashed and Meg always took great care not to lean up against them. If she did her clothes would be covered in whitewash and the whole world would know where she had been. While she sat there she would amuse herself by pulling the squares of newspaper her Da had so painstakingly cut into squares and hung on a piece of string on the back of the midden

199

door. It was the only time she ever read a newspaper and was often surprised by interesting pieces of local news. She did not mind reading the births and marriages but the death obituaries she found to be too morbid and these squares of paper she crumpled and threw to the floor ready to put down the midden before she left.

Another amusement for Meg, in the midden; was to make herself comfortable, close one eye, then the other, and, look through the gaps at the top and sides of the door. She could see the washing swaying in the breeze, the kitchen window and sometimes a bird on the back yard wall. Usually it was just a sparrow but if she was lucky she might just catch sight of a pigeon and in the winter a robin. The one thing Meg did not like about the midden was the spiders. If she saw one a battle would commence. Meg would stay completely still and stare at the spider willing it to turn the other way and crawl away from her. She nearly always won the battle.

"If a stare long enough wi'out blinkin'," she thought to herself, "it'll turn the other way."

Meg never killed the spider but she could never understand where the spider disappeared to.

"It must be magic 'cos a never blinked," she thought to herself.

These activities were exclusive to day time; the midden was not a pleasant place in the dark.

It was dark tonight and every sound Meg heard increased her terror. Each time she heard a noise she was convinced it was Fred coming to get her. Fred with a chopping axe coming to break the door down or coming to entice her to come out with a packet of sweets or a present.

After what seemed an eternity, Meg heard the back door bang and then footsteps coming closer and closer. She held her breath; the footsteps passed the midden, the back gate opened and then closed and the sound of foot steps gradually faded away. Meg breathed a sigh of relief; Fred had gone but she was still too afraid to leave the midden. Topsy began to get restless and Meg stroked her as she whispered.

"Keep quiet, he might just be pretendin' t' have gone, wi'stayin' in here 'til me Ma an' Da get in."

Meg shivered as she asked Topsy the questions she herself could not answer.

"What does Fred want wi' me? Why does he want t' kiss me when he can kiss our Ada? A've seen them kissin' when a peeped through the parlour door. Our Ada was lettin' him so why should he want t' kiss me, a'm just a little girl?"

As she sat picking the flakes of whitewash off the midden walls the questions went over and over in her mind. Meg closed one eye and bending her head to one side she could see the sky through the top of the midden door. It was a clear night and the stars were shining brightly and for a few seconds she felt a little better. Again she stroked and spoke to her cat.

"Me Ma an' Da'll soon be back Topsy an' then we'll be safe when a tell them what's happened t' us."

Her Ma and Da were still not home when Meg's thoughts turned to the scavenger.

"What if he comes when we're still in here?" she asked Topsy. "Still we'd better stay, a'd rather the scavenger catch us than Fred."

The scavenger had only once caught Meg in the midden. When the midden hatch opened in the back street and his long handled shovel came beneath her to empty the contents of the midden, Meg catapulted from the midden seat hiding her face in embarrassment, bare bottom exposed. When Tom told her sometime later it had happened to him she was still so embarrassed she

201

would not even admit to him that the same thing had happened to her.

It was sometime later before the midden sneck was raised. "Whe's in there?" Meg heard her Da say.

She felt relieved as she jumped off the seat and quickly pulled the bolt back.But Meg was disappointed when she realised he had obviously had a lot to drink and was in a hurry to use the midden; so still clinging on to Topsy she ran straight into the house. The cat was as cold as Meg and immediately jumped onto the oven shelf. Meg shivered as she looked at Sarah.

"A'll tell her t'morrow, a'm too cold now."

It was a cold but relieved Meg who rolled into bed with Ada who was still sleeping soundly. Meg could not sleep; her mind was still full of the night's events and as she fell into a fitful sleep she spoke to sleeping Ada.

"A want t' tell me Ma an' me Da; if a tell you y'll not believe me an' if a tell me Ma an' me Da th' might say a'm makin' it up, an' if th' de believe me th' might blame us an' say it's all me own fault."

As the weeks passed Meg found it increasingly difficult to mention the incident with Fred. She avoided him like the plague, ensuring she was never alone with him. She did not want to tell lies to the rest of the family but sometimes she had no choice, and these lies always got her into trouble. If Fred was in the house with Ada and the rest of the family were out then was so was Meg. On Saturday nights she would wait at the top of the street waiting for Dan and Sarah to come home. Chilled to the bone Meg would be once more in trouble; this time for stopping out late. She could not defend her actions, she had let too much time pass since the incident with Fred; instead she lied saying she had been to friend's house.

During the next two years Meg changed. Outwardly she lost her aggressiveness but a battle raged inside of her. She felt alone in the world with no one to help or guide her. Her only real friend was Tom, but she could not bring herself to tell him about Fred. Tom had now left school and was working at the local Co-Op store. He did not like the work.

"It's boring Meg," he confided in her. "All a de all day is weigh out flour an' sugar an' cut slabs o' butter int' pounds an' half pounds; a'm not allowed t' serve. When our Ada took us t' get the job the manager said servin' would come later."

It was Ada who had persuaded Dan and Sarah that Tom should work at the store and not go down the pit. He had outgrown his childhood ailments and although not a big lad he was as strong as many of his friends who had started work at the pit. When Tom passed the scholarship for the Grammar school, Ada was as upset as he was when Dan and Sarah refused to let him go.

"The's not the money," was all Dan said when Ada challenged their decision.

Tom's job at the store was presented, by Ada, to Dan and Sarah as a 'fait accompli.'

Meg soon realised that even if she could avoid Fred at home she could not prevent him pestering her when she was out. On two occasions he waited outside while she was buying chips at the fish and chip shop and asked her to walk home with him. Other times he stood outside the school gates watching for her to leave. Each time she made an excuse to her friends and walked home the long way round. Meg did anything to avoid him.

The time soon came for Meg to sit the scholarship and she was surprised when she came home from school one dinner time to find Jane sitting at the kitchen table with her Ma and Ada. The baby and two of the younger children were with her. The elder children were at school and although Meg really liked the two eldest boys she had not seen enough of the younger ones to establish any kind of relationship with them. Joe and Dan visited often especially during the school holidays when they stayed and shared the back bed with Will and Tom. Will complained throughout their stay but Tom and Meg loved having the boys with them; especially Meg, as they were always around the house when Fred was there. The holidays were the only times Meg did not have to worry or stand outside for hours on end.

As soon as Meg sat down for her dinner Jane spoke to her.

"Our Ada says y' good at school an' that the teacher says y've a good chance o' passin' the scholarship f' the high school."

"Aye," Meg told her wondering what it had to do with Jane. "She says a could pass if a'm more careful wi' me sums. She says me sums could let me down so our Tom's been helpin' me. But he says a winna be able t' gan 'cos he couldn't 'cos me Ma an'me Da couldn't afford it. The only reason a'm tryin' is 'cos a'm in the top section an' a dinna want t' be put down."

Jane looked towards Sarah before she spoke again.

"Me an' y' Ma have been talkin' an' she says y' Da thinks y' should gan if y' pass. He says now that our Tom's workin' the' can afford it as long as y' dinna think y' can have everythin' the others get."

Meg could not believe what she was hearing; if she passed the scholarship she could go to the high school.

"Wait till a tell our Tom," she thought.

She knew he would be pleased for her; they had talked about it often enough. Although he had been disappointed when he could not go he still encouraged her to work hard, helping her with her sums and bullying her into working when she did not want to.

As Meg walked back to school, although she was excited with the news, she could not understand why Jane had told her and not her Ma. In her usual way whenever she was alone or had a problem she talked quietly to herself.

"A wonder why our Jane should have owt t' de wi' it? She never said owt when our Tom couldn't gan." Jane was soon forgotten when Meg met her friends. The main topic of conversation was tomorrow's exam and Meg was fired with enthusiasm.

"A can join in wi' em now," she thought, "if a pass a can gan."

When Meg came in from school she went straight into the parlour to do the sums Tom had prepared for her the night before. When he came home from work she told him her good news and after marking her work he gave her several more to do.

"A'm meetin' the lads after me tea Meg," he told her, "but when a come in a'll mark these an' if y' need any help the'll be plenty o' time afore we gan t' bed."

As soon as she had her tea Meg started to work on the sums. She was so engrossed that when the parlour door opened she did not even raise her head. It was not until she felt an arm around her shoulder that she realised it was Fred and she was immediately filled with fear.

"Where's me Ma?" were the only words she was able to speak.

Fred grinned at her showing the yellow teeth that were often in Meg's nightmares.

Fred laughed as he tightened his grip around her shoulders.

"Y' Ma an' Da's gone out an' Ada's gone out t' see a friend who isn't well. Ada says Tom's out w' his mates an' Will's in night shift so the's just you an me Meg."

Meg felt hot then cold and as the panic rose inside of her she started to sweat. Fred held her tightly as he kissed her on the lips, she felt his tongue parting her lips and pressing deep inside her mouth. Meg thought she was going to be sick; the smell and taste of his tobacco making her retch. She tried to scream but no sound came, he was talking to her, telling her everything would be alright and he would not hurt her. As she tried struggle free his hold tightened and his hand, which had been on her knee slowly moved further up her leg. Meg felt his fingers slip through the elastic of her knicker leg. She tried to scream again but Fred placed his free hand over her mouth. Meg was frantic; she had no idea what he was going to do to her but she knew it was something bad and she knew it was her who would be blamed.

Suddenly the back gate slammed and Fred released her and stood up. Meg was shocked to see his trouser buttons were open and as he walked out of the parlour he quickly fastened them snarling at her.

"Keep y' gob shut or it'll be worse next time."

As Meg quickly tidied herself up she could hear him speaking to Tom.

"A've just been helpin' Meg wi' her sums 'til y' got back, when Ada comes back tell her a've gone home f' an early night."

When Tom came into the parlour Meg said nothing, she was too embarrassed to even look at him. Eventually she told him she was tired and would he go into the kitchen because she needed an early night before she sat the scholarship tomorrow. Tom was a little concerned, he thought Meg looked strange, but decided it was probably nerves; Meg had a big day tomorrow.

The eleven plus was a disaster. Meg could not concentrate all she could think about was Fred and the previous night's events. She knew she would fail and she was so ashamed; ashamed about last night; ashamed of her performance in the exam. She had let everyone down especially Tom and Jane.

Meg's feeling of being alone in the world became more intense. The results of the eleven plus were as she expected; she failed, and Meg withdrew into a world of her own. One half of her wanted to feel warm and be happy, to continue working hard at school and be the group leader she had been for the last few years. The other half of her was stronger; it sucked her in leading her into a desolate life where there was nothing to value and nothing worth striving for.

During her remaining years at school Meg fought a raging battle within her, Sarah and Dan often being the recipient of her sometimes aggressive behaviour. At school Meg asked herself.

"Why should a have t' justify what a'm dein'? Where will workin' hard get us? A'll always be on me own an' have t' fight me own battles."

During this period Meg still had nightmares about Fred but now they included Jane. In one recurring dream she would be falling through layers of blackness and there at the bottom was Fred but Jane was there to protect her. Jane would be standing at the top of a long winding staircase and with her stood a man. He was smiling at her; Meg could never see all of his face but she knew he was kind and handsome and if only she could reach him she would never ever be afraid of Fred again. Ada always woke her before she could reach his outstretched arms. As she pulled the bedclothes back over herself Ada would scold Meg,

"Will y' keep quiet y' screams us enough t' wake the dead."

Meg did try to tell Ada about Fred but Ada's response was always that she was making it up to cause trouble. On that particular night Meg had stood for two hours at the top of the street waiting for Dan and Sarah to return home after visiting Dan's father. It was snowing and by the time they got back she was frozen cold and soaking wet. Dan and Sarah took little notice of her. They told her her Granda had died and the three of them walked down the street in silence. That night Meg cried herself to sleep, not only because of her Granda, but when she got in Ada had been annoyed with her for coming home in such a state. As they lay in bed Meg told her about her Fred but Ada was asleep or, as Meg thought, she was pretending to be asleep.

Over the next two years Meg avoided Fred and after the fateful night in the parlour he ignored her for most of the time. The rest of the family had their own problems and Meg was relieved when they did not question her and left her to get on with her own life. The week after her Granda died his brother came to live with them. Sarah had not wanted him to come but Dan insisted and an extra bed was put up in the back bedroom. They were all disgruntled at having a new lodger; Will and Tom because they now had to share their bedroom and Sarah and Ada because of the additional work.

Only Meg was secretly pleased; there would always be someone in the house now. The old man sat all day in front of the fire, smoking his pipe and continually spitting in the fire. More often than not he missed and that meant bother for Meg from Ada who took great pride in the large black leaded fireplace. Sarah complained incessantly about the smell and Dan would be exasperated trying to persuade the old man to wash and change his clothes.

Meg hated the smell in the kitchen and withdrew more and more from the rest of the family. She stayed out of the house as long as she could and would only sit in the parlour when Fred and Ada were out. This caused Meg to feel more resentment towards Sarah when she would not let her light the fire.

"No Meg, y' either sit wi' us in the kitchen or y' sit in the cold," Sarah told her. "A've telt y' afore our Ada can light the fire but just f' her and Fred."

Meg would sit there hour after hour until her fingers and toes were numb with cold. If she was absolutely sure Fred would not be coming back with Ada she went to bed; it was the only place she could keep warm.

Fortunately the old man was just as unhappy living with them as they were having him live with them. After six months he asked Dan to find him a place in a home. It was another six months before Dan's uncle happily left the Charlton's home.

The following year Sarah's mother died and within months her father died suddenly. These events preoccupied the rest of the family and Meg felt more alone and especially isolated from Dan and Sarah. She did not know why, she had never really liked her, but Meg became closer to Jane. Whenever she could persuade Dan to give her the bus fare she would visit her. Will was occasionally generous and she would save whatever he gave her until she had enough for the fare to Durham. Meg's visits to Jane's home never lasted long. She wanted to go but for some reason as soon as she got there she wanted to be back home. Jane now had seven children and Meg often wondered how Jane looked after them.

One day when she came home she said to Tom.

"A dinna kna' how our Jane looks after the bairns; if John's not in whenever a gan she's sittin' in the chair aside the fire and when a leave she' still sittin' there. If he's in she gets up t' mek him somat t' eat an' t' put his bait up. As far as a can see the's not much in the house f' her or the bairns t' eat and the house isn't very clean? A've tried t' tidy up when a'm there but she always tells us t' leave everythin' alone."

Tom seemed interested and so Meg continued.

"The older bairns look after the young uns and the' don't seem t' be at school very much. Sometimes the' tell us the've been bad but once the' said it was 'cos the' had nee claes o' boots t' wear. An' a hate gannin' upstairs Tom. A've looked in the bedrooms an' y' should see the beds; the' not made an' the' have nee beddin' just old coats t' keep them warm. An' a canna stand the bathroom, if me Ma had a bathroom she'd keep it clean, but it stinks in there. A think it's the soap that smells 'cos when a wash me hands a can smell it all the way home."

It was following a visit to Durham that another incident with Fred forced Meg into telling Dan and Sarah about him. Meg was nearly fourteen and in two months time she would be leaving school. As Meg got off the bus in the market place she could see Fred standing outside the sweet shop. She had to pass him but kept her head down, ignoring him when he called her name.

Meg breathed a sigh of relief when he did not follow her and hurried to turn the corner that would lead her to the safety of home.

"If the' all out a'll lock mesel' in," she muttered.

Meg ran down the front street her steps quickening when she heard the footsteps behind her. When she reached the front door it was locked. Meg fumbled in the letterbox to retrieve the door key but as soon as she opened it he was behind her. She was not quick enough to stop him following her into the house but she was older now; she knew what Fred wanted. Meg faced him this time; she did not speak but punched him with all of her strength. When Fred grabbed her hands Meg kicked him so hard he released her hands to protect himself. Taking the opportunity she ran upstairs into Dan and Sarah's bedroom; it was the only room in the house that locked and as she turned the key she heard him running up the stairs.

Meg sat on the bed trembling as Fred kicked the door and shouted abuse at her. Fred was strong and she knew the door would not hold for long. Meg knew she had to stop him.

"A'll tell them all how y' broke the door an' what y've tried t' do t' me if y' dinna gan away," she shouted.

Suddenly there was silence, and then Meg breathed a sigh of relief when she heard Fred cross the landing and go back down the stairs.

After Fred left the house Meg remained locked in the bedroom until she heard Dan and Sarah come in. They were surprised to find the front door unlocked and even more surprised when Meg ran down the stairs to meet them. She cried as she told them what had happened that night but unfortunately for Meg, before she had finished telling them the full story, Ada arrived home. Ada immediately defended Fred; she told Dan and Sarah that Meg had accused Fred in the past and that it was all Meg's vivid imagination. Meg sobbed as she told them that it was the truth, but Ada was adamant.

"Y' kna' what she's like Ma, she's never liked him, an' he only tries t' be nice t' her t' mek' her like him."

Meg knew that was it; Ada had won and once again she was in the wrong. Meg had no choice but to escape to the loneliness of her bed. She could not sleep but when Ada came she pretended she was.

"A'll mek them believe me," Meg thought to herself. "If it's the last thing a de one day me Ma an' Da'll kna a was tellin' the truth."

When Meg left school, just like Jane and Ada, she was not expected to go out to work. Many of her friends were going into service but Dan was adamant,

"Ne daughter o' mine is gannin' int' service; y'll stay at home an' help y' Ma an' our Ada," he told Meg.

Meg was bored, she hated the long days especially as she only spoke to Ada if she had to. There was nothing for her to do in the house and so she took to taking long walks, not really enjoying them, always looking over her shoulder even when she knew Fred would be at work.

Life became unbearable for Meg, she was no nearer to solving her problem than she had been four long years ago, the only difference now was that she knew what Fred wanted from her.

One Saturday while Meg was moping in the parlour Will came home looking very pleased with himself; a few pints, after a good day at the races, had put him in a good mood. He still gave Meg the occasional clip on the ear but usually Meg and Will were quite good friends. It was Will who would enquire as to what was troubling her when she withdrew into herself.

"A fit o' the blues," she would tell him.

Will would laugh and give her sixpence or if he had had a good win a shilling.

"There," he would tell her, "see if that'll snap y' out o' it."

Today Meg was lucky; Will gave her a shilling and that was all she needed for another visit to Jane's.

Meg was pleasantly surprised when she entered the house; it was much tidier. The older children were out and the younger ones, although not very clean, were dressed and playing happily with each other. Jane was making a pie crust and there was a rabbit cooking in the oven. Meg thought Jane seemed pleased to see her as she said.

"Tek' y' coat off Meg; John'll soon be in an' y' can stay an' have some rabbit pie wi' us."

Meg sat quietly by the fire watching Jane roll the pastry for the top of the pie. The kitchen was warm and Meg felt more relaxed than she had for a long time. She noticed that Jane had another black eye but did not mention it knowing that Jane's answer would be the usual one.

"A bumped int' the door."

Jane was smiling as she spoke to Meg.

"What's the matter Meg, y' look like y've the worries o' the world on y' shoulders."

Meg could not help herself; she started to cry and blurted out the whole sordid affair. John arrived home just as Meg was telling Jane what had happened and what he heard from Meg, with the gaps filled in from Jane, outraged him.

"Stop what y' dein' now Jane," he ordered her. "A'll see t' the bairns; get y' coat an' get back wi' her now. Y'll tell them what's gannin' on an' if y' see him y' can tell him he'll have me t' deal with; an' y' can tell Ada if a have t' come through a will, an' he'll be in no fit state t' ever touch another woman when a'm finished wi' him."

Meg had mixed feelings; she was relieved that at last it was out in the open but she was frightened. If they did not believe her, why should they believe Jane? Jane and Meg walked the two miles into the city to catch a bus, the first mile in silence. It was Jane who spoke first.

"It'll be alreet Meg, the'll believe me an' even if the' don't he'll never touch y' again. Once John's finished wi' him he'll wish he'd never laid a finger on y'."

Meg felt a little better but she was curious.

"Why will me Ma an' Da believe y' Jane? An' why did John mek y' come back straight away?"

Jane stopped walking and turned to face Meg.

"A think y're old enough t' kna' Meg; even if me Ma an' Da never wanted y' t' kna'; a think now's the right time t' tell y'. A'm y' Ma Meg; John's not y' Da but a'm y' Ma."

CHAPTER 11

The cold but sunny afternoon did nothing to dispel Meg's misery; so much had happened since she left school and she was so confused. Now she was taking her future into her own hands and doing what she hoped was the best thing for her; she had found a job. She had an eight mile walk in front of her, but she did not care, the farmer at the hiring fair had seemed a nice man and he had told her the job would be mainly housework.

On that day, six weeks ago, Dan and Sarah had been upset when Jane arrived with Meg. Jane had come straight to the point, not only about Fred, but shocking them with the revelation that Meg now knew the truth about whose child she was. There had been a terrible argument and the main purpose of her visit to Jane's was left in the background. As far and Dan and Sarah were concerned, Meg knew and Jane should not have told her.

That night, even if it was dark, the midden became Meg's place of refuge and meditation. Her world was shattered; her Ma wasn't her Ma, Jane was her Ma; her Da wasn't her Da. Jane had told her John wasn't her Da. So who was? Tom and Will weren't her brothers; they were her uncles and Ada wasn't her sister, she was her aunt. That did not really bother her but Tom, he was different. Would he still be her best friend when he found out that Jane was her Ma? Maybe he already knew? Everyone would soon know and she would never be able to hold her head high again.

"A kna' what a'am," Meg cried. "A'm a bastard."

Meg's world crumbled as she thought back to the times Will had hit her, her problems at school, all of the bad times. The good times were forgotten; she could not remember any good times.

"No," she muttered, "the's never been any good times an' th' never will be now. A'm nobody; a dinna belong anywhere an' a canna stay here now wi' me Ma and Da 'cos th' not me Ma an' Da. Our Jane mustn't have wanted me 'cos a would have lived at Durham wi' her? Mebee she did but John didn't want me 'cos he's not me Da? It's funny but 'cos John's always nice t' me an' a wouldn't have minded him bein' me Da, it would have been better than not havin' a Da at all, an' then Joe would have been me' Granda. An' that's another thing, a loved me Granda but he wasn't me Granda. What was he then? He must have been me Great Granda? A wonder who me Da is? Who else does our Jane kna'? John's brother, Bill? Na it canna be him; he's married and lives to far away? He didn't then though, so it could be him? A hope not, a like him but, he lives to far away to be a proper Da. A wonder why Jane didn't marry me Da? Mebee he was rich an' famous an' seduced her an' left her? Yes that must be it; a've got a rich an' famous Da an' when he finds out about me he'll come an' get me an' then a'll be rich an' famous, an' then a'll show them all. But what if me Da was already married an' that's why he couldn't marry Jane?"

So the questions went around and around in Meg's head until she did not know who she was or who she belonged to. Even her fear of Fred faded into the back of her mind.

"What's it matter about Fred?" she cried. "He must have known an' that's why he' been after me, but a dinna care about him anymore an' a'll mek sure one way or another that he'll never touch us again."

Meg had climbed out of childhood and into adolescence with some support from her family now she would have to continue her ascent into womanhood alone.

A week passed before anything else was mentioned and to Meg's surprise it was Will who spoke the first words of comfort to her. As he usually did when he was in foreshift, he washed, had his dinner and then went straight to bed. Meg was dusting Dan and Sarah's bedroom and she was more than surprised when Will called for her to come into his room. Usually after an eight hour shift he was so tired and bad tempered that no one dare speak to him. He had developed a nasty cough, which often kept him awake, but he never lost a shift and Meg had noticed that recently he was looking very tired. His constant drinking and gambling did not help him and his cough was always worse after a day at the races or a night on the booze. The previous Saturday night he had come home with a black eye but that did not surprise Meg or the rest of the family who made no comment. The worse his cough became and the more tired he got so his temper worsened.

Will was in bed when Meg went through into his room and she was even more surprised when he patted the bed and told her to sit down.

"Dinna be hard on me Ma an' Da' Meg, what th' did th' did f' the best, th' were only tryin' t' protect y'."

Will lay back on the pillows and Meg seeing in his eyes that he was exhausted stood up.

"Sit back down Meg," he ordered, "a haven't finished yet. A knew y' were Jane's an' when a was a bairn a wondered why me Ma an' me Da always seemed t' favour y'. Me Ma didn't show it like me Da but a could tell y' were always her favourite. A once asked me Da an' he said the' didn't favour y' it was only 'cos o' the way things were that it seemed the' did. Y' kna' the' had a bairn that died; me Da sometimes mentions him but me Ma never does. Well a fund a photo o' him an' y' kna' Meg, y' looked just like him when y' was a bairn. A dinna kna' f' sure but a think that's got somat t' do wi' the way me Ma an' Da treat y'. Anyhow Meg, even if that's not the reason an' even if y' not me Ma an' Da's, the' dinna show it but the' think as much o' y' as if y' were. An' Meg try an' understand our Jane; she was young when she had y' an' mebee she was wrong but she's paid f' it a thousand times ower since she married John. He's alright wi' us an' give him his due he's been alright wi' you. He's never blamed y' f' what she did but by God he's made her suffer in more ways than one."

Meg did not answer; she did not know what to say to him and as she left the bedroom Will said one final thing to her.

"An' dinna y' worry anymore about Fred. Ada still doesn't believe a word o' it but a kna' me Ma an' Da de even if the winna admit it. John was through last Saturday an' y' see me eye, well Fred's got two like it, an' the' even bonnier than mine."

Will's words brought no comfort to Meg; she felt worse.

"The'all knew," she muttered as she continued dusting. "The' knew all the time, even our Tom must 'ave knan that a'm not his sister. Me sisters an' brothers all live at Durham, an' then the're only half sisters an' brothers, not real ones. Even if the' were a dinna kna them that well; just Dan an' Joe an' then a only see them in the holidays an' they think a'm the aunt so have got nebody that's really mine. A've only got Topsy an' when she gets old she'll die an' then a'll have nebody."

That night it was Tom's turn to question Meg.

"What's up wi' y' Meg, y've been miserable as sin all week. Nebody can get a word out o' y'. Y'd think y'd lost a pound an' fund a hae'penny."

Meg finally lost her temper.

218

"How can y' say that our Tom? Y' knew all along a wasn't y' sister an' y've pretended all the time."

Tom was taken aback, not just by her outburst, but by her words. Meg was sorry for her outburst when Tom replied.

"A dinna kna' what y' on about Meg; what a stupid thing t' say that y' not me sister."

Meg realised immediately that Tom was sincere; he was not aware of the events of the previous week nor was he old enough to have known her to be anything other than his sister. She suddenly felt even closer to him, he had not been part of the conspiracy; Tom had been lied to just like she had.

Meg cried as she told him about Jane and what Will had said to her that afternoon. She said nothing about Fred; that was something she did not want him to know; he was a man, and there was always the possibility he would blame her and then she would lose the one friend she now knew she had. Tom felt like crying himself but held back the tears his voice trembling as he tried to comfort her.

"It might be right what y' say Meg but it doesn't mek' any difference t' me. Everybody thinks y' m' sister an' me Ma an' Da's y' Ma an' Da an' nebody's ganna mek' them any the wiser."

Tom did not realise that his words of comfort only served to make matters worse for Meg. Now she would have to carry this secret with her for the rest of her life; her whole life would be nothing but a lie. Tom's final words brought no consolation.

"Even if y' not me sister y' still me best friend an' a hope a'll always be yours?"

More trouble lay ahead for Meg when she finally plucked up the courage to tell Dan and Sarah that she had found herself a job. At least the trouble started when Dan came home from work and Sarah told Dan. Sarah had little to say when Meg gave her the news but when Dan was told the fireworks erupted. To make matters worse Will came in tired, coughing and bad tempered.

"Y' too young t' work on any farm." Dan shouted. Will joined in the tirade.

"A'm not havin' y' skiviein' f' others; a felt sorry f' y' afore but now y' nowt but an' ungrateful little bitch. Y' place is here wi' us, helping our Ada an' y' Ma. We dinna kna who th' are o' where y' ganin' te."

Meg walked out of the house shouting at them as loudly as they had shouted at her.

"A'm gannin' an' y'll not stop me. The' expect me t' start next week an' if y' try an' stop me a'll find somewhere else t' gan; somewhere where y'll not find me, 'cos a winna tell y' next time."

Leaving home was Meg's solution to her problems and ridding herself of the guilt she now felt. Guilt about Fred, guilt because she was a bastard, guilt because Dan and Sarah had been forced to bring her up and much worse, she was the cause of Jane's unhappiness and the way John treated her.

Meg had found the work herself after one of her friends had told her about the hiring fair. She had no bus fare and was too proud to ask so she had walked to Bishop Auckland. Even if she had asked, Meg knew they would not have given her any money if she had told them what it was for and for some reason she did not want to lie.

When she arrived in Bishop Auckland market place there were lots of other young men and women all standing around with anxious looks on their faces. The farmers stood apart in groups, looking around and eyeing the youngsters up and down. When one walked over to her Meg was startled as he said.

"A' y' f' hire lass?"

"Aye," Meg replied, "a want a job on a farm."

The farmer asked if her parents agreed to her working and Meg crossed her fingers behind her back, as she had done as a child.

"Me Ma an'me Da are dead. Me Da got killed down the pit an' me Ma died straight after."

The look the farmer gave her was sympathetic giving Meg the courage to continue with her lie.

"Me Granda an' me Granma took us all t' live wi' them but th' findin' it hard to keep us an' a'm the oldest so a need t' work t' help out."

"Right," he said, "y're on; y'll be expected t' help in the house an' a hope y' like young uns 'cos wi' got four o' them, an' the' a right handful."

Meg was excited; she had found a job and she could have every Saturday night off and Sunday once a month to go home and visit her grandparents. The farmer left her with instructions on how to find the farm and that she would be expected the following Sunday after tea.

No one mentioned Meg's job again. When she got up on Sunday morning she expected a row but still nothing was mentioned. As she parcelled her few clothes together Sarah came into the parlour. Meg turned to face her and noticed a glimmer of a tear in Sarah's eye as she said,

"If y' must gan Meg y' must; but remember this is y' home an' me an' y' Da'll always be here if y' want owt."

Turning from Meg Sarah walked out of the parlour. Those few words were Sarah's goodbye to Meg and she was to remember them often over the ensuing years.

When Meg arrived at the farm it was late afternoon and she was tired and hungry after the long walk. The farmer introduced her to his wife and four children and then his wife took her to her room. For the first time in weeks Meg smiled; she had a room to herself for the first time in her life and a bed to herself. Before going back downstairs she neatly folded her underclothes and blouses and placed them in the set of drawers and then hung her coat and skirts on the hook on the back of the bedroom door.

She was feeling nervous but when the farmer's wife welcomed her into the kitchen she was soon at ease and found it easy to reply to the farmer's wife's many questions as they drank a welcome pot of tea. As she left the kitchen the farmer's wife gave Meg her first instruction.

"Cut y' sel' two slices o' pork from the joint Meg, an' mek y' sel' a sandwich."

"If this is service," Meg muttered, "a reckon it might not be so bad after all."

Before Meg had time to finish her sandwich the farmer's wife came back into the kitchen.

"We're off t' church now Meg; y' can look after the bairns while we out an' mek sure th' in bed by the time we back. We'll be back be half past seven an' then a'll tell y' all about y' duties."

Meg followed the farmer's wife out of the kitchen and into another room which was similar to the one they had left but much bigger. It had an enormous fireplace which Meg noticed had not seen black lead for many a moon. Sitting in front of the fire were the four children, all of them as much in need of soap and water as the fireplace was of black lead. Meg looked at the clock and realised she had only one and a half hours to carry out her first duty.

Meg failed miserably. When the farmer and his wife arrived home the four children were still sitting in front of the fire. Although they were now clean, they were not in bed as she had been instructed. Meg's first hour with the children was spent pacifying four young children crying for their mother. Washing them and finding their night clothes was a nightmare and the two eldest children took advantage of Meg by being more of a hindrance than a help.

When the farmer and his wife entered the kitchen Meg was struggling with a dying fire and the children looked up to their parents with angelic smiles on their faces. Within twenty minutes their mother had them off to bed and Meg could hardly believe the change in their behaviour; the eldest helping their mother with the little ones; never complaining and doing everything they were told to do.

Meg had not had a lot of experience with young children and she had learned her lesson the hard way. The farmer's wife was quick to show her displeasure and Meg was told in no uncertain terms that if she was to stay with them then she would have to do better the following evening.

The farmer's wife was a large woman and as she proceeded to give Meg her morning duties she stood with folded arms towering above Meg.

"Y'll rise at six every morning, tomorro's wash day so first y'll clean the fire out an' get it ganin' t' heat the water in the boiler. Then y' can lay the table ready f' breakfast, an' then y' can get started wi' the washin'."

The following morning Meg was up at five thirty; she did not want to fail again. The fire was roaring when the farmer and his wife came into the kitchen and Meg was looking forward to her breakfast; she was not prepared for what came next.

"Right lass," the farmer said, "get y' coat an' come wi' me."

Meg would never have dreamt what her next duties would be.

"A'll show y' just this once how to get the cows ready f' milking. A've got a lad who helps on the farm but y' can help me wi' the mikin' every mornin'."

Meg did her best.

"A canna get the hang o' it," she muttered, jumping every time the farmer shouted at her to pull harder.

When the milking was finished the farmer told her to go back into the farmhouse and get on with the housework until breakfast was ready. As Meg lifted the mat in front of the fireplace to take it outside for a good shaking the farmer's wife bellowed at her.

"Stop what y' dein' an' get in the kitchen now an' start mekin' the breakfast, a'll show y' where everythin' is an' then y' can get on wi' it."

Meg was invited to sit with the family for breakfast and she enjoyed every mouthful. She had done so much that morning and was aghast when she looked at the clock to find it was only eight thirty.

After breakfast was over she started the washing, a task she was used to. Meg was pleasantly surprised when an elderly, but obviously robust lady arrived and spoke to her.

"A'm Millie an' a come in three times a week t' de the heavy work so a expect his lordship 'll be wantin' y' t' help him a lot 'round the farm."

Millie was right in her assumption; Meg was only half way through the washing when the farmer called her outside.

"A'll show y' how t' put the milk through the separator an' tek' the cream off. When y've done it tek'

224

it t' bits and wash it thoroughly; then dry it out in front o' the fire ready f' tonights milkin'."

When that was done the farmer's wife gave her the rest of her morning duties.

"Millie's finished the washing so f' the rest o' the mornin' y' can gi' the downstairs a good clean out an' then after dinner some o'the washin''ll be dry so y' can start the ironin'."

Meg listened to her orders but she was so tired she wondered how she would ever finish before bedtime. The farmer's wife continued.

"A want all the oilcloths scrubbed an' mek' sure the parlour mat gets a good shekin' outside. An' when y' dust tek' all the ornaments off, a dinna want y' t' dust 'round 'em. The's plenty washin' soda in the outhouse; that's all a ever use an' a'll show y' tomorro' how t' grind white sand stone t' a powder. A like all the tops in the kitchen and the ceilin' scoured every week an' a like t' see them as white as snow."

As Meg carried out her duties she grumbled to herself.

"She might like them as white as snow but the' not now; the' rotten o' muck it'll tek' weeks just t' get them clean."

By the end of the afternoon Meg was so tired the thought of bed could not come soon enough. At four o'clock the farmer appeared at the kitchen door.

"Right lass it's time f' milkin'."

By teatime Meg felt the tears prickling behind her eyes and was relieved when after tea the farmer's wife said to her.

"Right lass; sit y' sel' down by the fire."

Meg snuggled down in the chair and closed her eyes.

"I hope the' wont think me rude if a gan t' bed early," she thought.

It was only a few seconds later when Meg felt a nudge on her arm and heard a voice in the distance. When she opened her eyes the voice was not in the distance, it was the farmer's wife and she was towering above her.

"Here lass wi' can't have y' sittin' there wi' idle hands, a've put the basket o' mendin' an' darnin' by the side o' y' chair an' y' can get on wi' it while y' sittin'."

The rest of Meg's week continued very much in the same way as her first day and, even though the work was hard, she soon settled into the routine. The food was good; for dinner usually cold lamb or pork left over from the Sunday roast, bacon at the end of the week when the roast was finished and there was always either rice or a suet pudding for afters. She liked having her own room but had not really felt the benefit as each night she was so tired she fell asleep as soon as her head touched the pillow.

As the second week started Meg accepted the hard work but she did not like looking after the children. She even accepted the additional work of helping the farmer with the cows and milking but she could not bring herself to like his children. She knew if she was to stay things would have to improve between her and the children; they behaved like little angels in front of their parents but once alone with Meg they misbehaved, making her never ending chores twice as hard to complete.

Meg was relieved when it was finally her night off. Saturday night could not come soon enough for her; at last an evening to herself. She planned to walk to the nearest village which was only two miles away and there she hoped she might meet someone her own age and ask what they did for entertainment on a Saturday night. She knew it was more than likely there would be a village dance and if there was maybe someone would invite her to go with them.

Meg had only once been to a dance and although Sarah was not too happy for her to go she had grudgingly agreed as long as she knew who she was going with.

"Well," Meg muttered as she got on with the housework, "a'm on me own now an' if a want a can gan every Saturday night an' a dinna have t' ask permission off anyone."

Meg was bitterly disappointed when after tea her employers told her she would be looking after the children that night as they were visiting friends. What was more disappointing they did not even mention that it was her promised night off.

Meg had been at the farm for three weeks before she finally got her night off. As she had planned she walked to the nearest village only to find that it was nearly deserted. A dejected Meg turned around and hurried back to the farm where the farmer's wife's only greeting was another basket of mending.

Meg could not sleep that night; she was miserable and most of all she was homesick. She missed her Ma and Da; she wondered what Tom would be doing, and if Will's cough was any better. Strangely enough she even missed Ada. She got up early the next morning and instead of getting on with her chores Meg quietly packed up her clothes and left the farm before anyone else was awake. As she walked down the farm road she talked to herself as she had always done since the day she had said her first words.

"The' can keep the' five bob a week what a'm supposed t' get after four weeks, a'm gannin' home an' if the' dinna want me a'll walk t' Durham t' our Janes."

227

Ada was in the back kitchen when Meg walked into the house.

"Huh y've finally decided t' pay us a visit," was all she said.

Meg did not reply but walked straight through into the kitchen knowing that on a Sunday morning Sarah would be standing at the kitchen table mixing the batter for the Sunday dinner Yorkshire puddings. Sarah's welcome was not unlike Ada's.

"A see y've got y' claes; come home t' stay have y'?"

Meg looked down at the floor as she replied; she could not face Sarah.

"Aye Ma, a've come back."

She wanted to say a've come home; she wanted Sarah to hold her and tell her everything was alright but she knew that would never happen. Sarah's next words were the nearest Meg would get to knowing that she could stay.

"Y'd better tek y' things through t' the parlour an' put them away then."

Tom was in the parlour when she went through and he greeted her with a smile on his face.

"Eeh Meg a've missed y'," he told her. "Are y' back f' good? Me Da's really missed y' an' so's me Ma even if she winna admit it. Our Will says the house's too quiet wi'out y' an' he's always askin' me Ma if she's heard when y' getting' a day off."

Meg could hear Sarah speaking to someone in the kitchen and wondered who it was,

"Gan in the parlour an' see who's come t' see y'; mebee y'll cheer up a bit an' eat y' dinner now she's back."

It was her beloved Topsy who ran through into the parlour, circling Meg's feet, purring and rubbing her back on Meg's ankles.

"See," Tom exclaimed. "Y' never should have gone off like y' did, the poor cat's hardly had a bite f' three weeks; she just sits all day on the mantelpiece lookin' out o' the kitchen window. Me Ma just said this mornin' if y' didn't come back soon the poor cat 'ud starve to death."

Every Sunday was the same; Sarah, Ada, Tom and Meg had their dinner together. Dan's and Wills'was kept hot in the oven until they came home from the pub. Sometimes they came home together; sometimes Will was much later than Dan but it made no difference to Sarah, each of them had a steaming hot dinner placed on the table before they had time to take their coats off. The dinner was finished and Meg was in the parlour when Dan and Will arrived home together. They had both had a fair amount of beer.

"T'gi' us a' appetite", was the excuse both of them always made.

On the occasions they did eat together the topic of conversation was always the same, the pit, low wages, long hours and the union. Today was no exception and Meg was comforted as she listened to their familiar banter. As usual Will had the chair and Dan only interrupted when he strongly disagreed with his son.

It was now five years since they had returned to work following the strike and the miners were still struggling for better wages and conditions. There had been no improvement and in many instances pay and conditions were worse. Will still believed in the strength of the union and Dan was as sceptical as ever as to what good it would do them. Dan and Will were more fortunate than many of the miners; they still had a job but had to work long hours for very little money. Dan only received the subsistence wage of six shillings and six and a half penny's a week.

Will was slightly better off hewing coal for eight hours a day Monday to Friday and six hours on a Saturday.

"At least wi' better off than the thousands out o' work." Meg heard Dan say to Will. "An' we' not relyin' on handouts all the time. Look at them all; bairns wi' ne boots on the' feet an' nowt t' eat. The've even cut the benefits now an' some o' them get nowt. Look at the folk who've been brought down t' acceptin' food parcels an' claes over the last few years. At least a can hold me head up high, what little we've got a've worked f' it."

As usual Will had a reply.

"Aye Da y'll never see it my way but a'm tellin' y' now, if the coal owners weren't s' bloody greedy we'd all have more money an' we wouldn't be workin' as many hours for a bloody pittance. We've got t' keep on at 'em, it's the only way, an' God willin' one day y'll see, we'll be better off an' a hope the owners a' left wi' nowt."

Meg moved nearer to the door when she heard Will mention her name.

"Look at our Meg, a kna' she left home f' different reasons but y' canna blame lasses like her f' movin' on. A kna' most o' them us just skiviein' f' the owners an' the like but the've knawn nowt but poverty all the' lives. Joe's lasses haven't done s' bad by movin' away. A kna' the' not rich but the' not on the bread line like the' would have been if the'd stayed here an' married a pitman. Why d' y' think a've never wanted t' get married? What can a offer a lass? Nowt but a cough that ud keep her awake all night."

Dan did not reply to Will's outburst and the two men finished their dinner in silence.

"Gan on Meg, gan in the kitchen an' let them see y're back." Tom urged. "Y' kna' the'll be straight up t' bed when the' finish the' dinner. The' winna say out t' y' an' a bet the'll be glad t' see y' back home."

Meg was frightened but she put on a brave face as she walked into the kitchen. Dan's face brightened when he saw her but he did not speak and Will, although it was not the embrace she so longed for, squeezed her shoulder as he spoke to her.

"My lass y' a sight f' sore eyes; y' better not stay away f' s' long next time o' y'll have me Ma an' that bloody cat gannin' int' a decline."

Sarah looked at Meg as she chastised her husband and son.

"Get y' sel's t' bed an' sleep the beer off, Meg's come home t' stay; she'll not be gannin' back there t'night o' any other night."

CHAPTER 12

Two years had passed since Meg had returned home from the farm and for the last six months she had been working at Will's favourite pub. Ever since she had returned Will had realised that she was still as determined as ever to work outside the home and he had got her the job. She worked six days a week but was home most nights by six o'clock and she had every Sunday off. Meg had saved most of her hard earned seven and sixpence a week, Sarah refused to take a penny of it, and she was now the proud owner of a bright red, sit up and beg, Raleigh bicycle. The landlady had given her two hours off that Saturday afternoon and Will had gone with her to choose it.

Since her return home Meg and Will had grown closer to each other; he was still bad tempered but Meg now understood his moods and he became closer to her than any other member of the family even though Tom was still her best friend and Meg knew there would never be anyone who understood her as he did. Ada only acknowledged her when she had to; Fred's visits were few and far between and then only when he knew Will would not be at home.

That was not very often; Will's cough was getting worse and after a shift down the pit all he wanted to do was either go to bed or sit by the fire reading or talking to Meg. He stayed at home most weekends, never admitting he felt ill, and made excuses to Sarah and Dan when they commented on his health or his lack of interest in going to the pub or the races.

Tom now had a girlfriend and Sarah and Dan still enjoyed their nights out together. Ada was often out with Fred and so Will and Meg often found themselves to be the only two members of the family at home on an evening. Each of them began to enjoy each other's company and Meg became more content than she had been for many years. Looking after the Benson's two children at the pub was so different to caring for the farmer's family.

She was grateful to Will for finding her the job because she could work and still live at home. The landlady of the pub needed someone to look after the children and help with the house work while she assisted her husband in running the business and from the very first day Meg loved every minute she spent at the Bensons. They treated her like one of the family, sharing their meals with her and even when they had visitors she never felt like the hired help and they never treated her as such.

It was a Saturday afternoon and Will was going with her to choose the bike. He was in a talkative mood and Meg patiently listened as he told her that he was happy for her.

"A'm pleased things 'ave turned out alreet f' y' at the Benson's Meg; an' at least we've our Ada t' thank f' our Tom gettin' on at the store. She insisted that he wasn't gannin' down the pit an' look at him now. He's just gone twenty an' servin' in the gent's department at the store. A went in the other day an' he really looks the part an' all; swaggerin' around wi' a tape measure 'angin' round his neck. An' that lass o' his seems alreet'; the'll be up the rec' again tonight playin' tennis a bet. Aye Meg, he does reet, an' you see t' it that y' see y' sel' alreet. The Benson's us good folk an' y'll de alreet there as long as y' de y' job an' y' fair wi' them. An' while we' on the subject, 'ave y' noticed the way our Tom's talkin'. He telt me the manager at the store said he had t' talk proper t' the customers when th' came in t' be measured f' new suits." Will laughed. "Mind Meg our Tom didn't say

233

proper he said correctly. Well Meg he's right; if y' want t' get on y' 'ave t' talk proper an' a want y' t' listen t' him an' listen t' the Bensons 'cos they talk proper."

Tonight Meg was not staying in with Will. She had gone back to work after they had chosen the bike and Will had pushed it home for her, but now it was her turn, she was going for a bike ride. As Meg stared at her new bike, which was leaning against the wall in the passage, her thoughts turned to Dan and Sarah.

"Me Ma an' Da are funny, the' have ne money but the' winna tek' a penny o' me pay"

Meg remembered the first day she had received her wages from the Bensons. She had offered it to Sarah but she would not take it from her. When she turned to Dan his response was the same.

"We kept Jane afore she was married an' we've kept our Ada all these years; y' ne different from them so we'll keep you."

"Does that bike have to stay in the passage?" Sarah shouted as Meg tried to manoeuvre it through the kitchen and out into the back street.

Meg did not answer, she knew Sarah did not expect one; it was her way of commenting on the new bike. Meg had cycled on Dan's old bicycle many times in the past and had no fear of riding her new one down the cobbled back street. What she was not prepared for was the sharpness of the brakes and as she picked up speed one squeeze of the brake and Meg went straight over the handlebars.

A dazed Meg looked up into the eyes of the young man who came to her assistance.

"Is me bike alreet?" was all she could think of to say.

"The chains come off an' the's the odd scratch but it seems alreet. But what about you are y' alreet?" he asked

234

smiling down at her. Meg was embarrassed and quickly got to her feet.

"A'm fine," she told him. "A'll tek' me bike up home f' our Will t' fix the chain," she abruptly replied.

As Meg moved to pick up her bicycle the young man moved in front of her and standing the bicycle against the wall proceeded to put the chain back on. Unusually for Meg she did not interrupt him but watched in silence until he handed her the bicycle.

"There, it's fixed," he told her as he turned to walk away. "An' next time be more careful, y've made us late now, a've t' meet me mates up the allotments an' see t' me pigeons."

Meg watched him walk up the backstreet she had just cycled down. She smiled but he did not look back, he was whistling cheerfully and she noticed he had both hands in his pockets.

Meg went straight home, she was more shaken than she thought and after giving the bicycle a thorough inspection she went straight to bed. As she lay in bed she thought of the nice young man who had come to her rescue. She tried to picture his face but she could not put it all together. The one thing she could remember was his eyes.

"Smashin' th' were," she muttered, "brown and just like velvet." Meg giggled. "Just like cow's eyes."

As she drifted off to sleep her last thoughts were of the young man and his face became a little clearer. She remembered his teeth when he had smiled at her.

"Straight and little," she muttered. "The' nice an' white but the's one at the side that's chipped an'that spoils 'em."

Two nights later she saw him again. Meg was outside the fish and chip shop and he was walking down the other side of the street with his mates.

"Give us a chip," he shouted as he and his friends crossed the street.

Meg did just that and it was the beginning of a friendship that would last a lifetime.

Ted was from a large family, he was the fourth youngest of a family of eight, and times were as hard for them as they were for Meg and her family. In many respects Ted's upbringing had been more frugal than Meg's. His elder brother and sister were married and he was the eldest boy at home but as usual Ted was out of work. He had started working at the pit when he left school but after three minor accidents he was frightened and left. His elder brother tried to persuade him to stay but Ted refused. Unwilling to tell anyone why he would no longer work at the pit he often felt guilty that the only work he could ever find was the odd labouring job and they were few and far between. Ted knew that most of his accidents were his own fault; he was so frightened underground and he always seemed to be in the wrong place at the wrong time. He had not known Meg for many weeks but he felt he could trust her and so he confided in her.

"A've a funny feelin', Meg." Meg noticed a serious look on Ted's face; a look she had never seen before. "If a go back down the pit one o' these days somat'll happen t' me an' it'll be more than a bashed finger or toe."

After a few weeks Ted became a regular visitor to Meg's home. He took her to meet his family and Meg was thrilled with the warm welcome she received from not only his parents but from his brothers and sisters. Meg could not help but notice that money was short but the house was clean and they all seemed to be well fed. Meg commented to Sarah after her first visit.

"Eeh Ma the' a lovely family an' the' like us; the' have nowt. A think the' mebbee haven't as much us but the place is so clean y' could eat y' dinner off the floor."

Ted's father was a strict man who had brought his children up to fear but respect him and after meeting him Meg soon had those same feelings towards him. She would stare at this proud man who towered above Ted and think to herself.

"Eeh Ted's him in miniature. Ted hasn't got a bushy grey 'tash an' he hasn't got hairs growin' out o' his ears an' his nose but his eyelashes curl up over his lovely brown eyes just like his Da's."

All was not well at Ted's home tonight. Meg could sense the atmosphere as soon as she walked in. Their walk tonight was to be the banky fields. That's all they ever did, walk to the banky field s, walk to the church fields; walk to doggie wood or to strawberry cot. Ted had once taken her to the allotments but she was not made very welcome. Ted's mates said the allotments were men's territory and the pigeons did not like female company. Meg knew Ted had no money and she also knew that, like his father, he was proud and would be insulted if she offered to pay for a night out at the pictures. He would not even accept a bag of chips from her always saying he preferred to share hers. On many occasions he ate most of them leaving her still feeling hungry but she would not insult him and so restrained from buying more.

As they walked from the short row of houses towards the fields Meg plucked up the courage to ask Ted what was wrong. At first he denied that there were any problems but Meg being naturally inquisitive and not backwards in coming forwards finally got the truth out of him.

"It's me Ma an' Da," Ted told her. "The' twistin' the' faces 'cos a'm out o' work an' a canna' help it. The's nowt t' get; an' our Sam's not helpin' tellin' 'em he can get me set on at the pit again. Me Da says a'm a lazy bugger f' not givin' it another try. Honest Meg a'm not lazy; a'm scared but a canna' tell them that. A dinna want t' fall out wi' our Sam either 'cos he shares his pigeon feed wi' us an' if he stops a canna' afford t' buy any an' then a'll have t' get rid o' me pigeons."

Meg had no answer, no words of comfort. She thought she understood him but apart from Tom and some of her Ma's relations every other man she knew worked at the pit. They continued their walk in silence, Meg still wondering what to say but thinking to herself that even their Tom and her Ma's relations had jobs.

Meg suddenly had an idea.

"Ted me Ma's relations are builders mebee the' can gi' y' a job or the' might kna' someone who can."

Meg's excitement soon subsided when Ted answered her.

"The's ne way y' ganna ask y' Ma o' y' Da about work f' me. A'll find me own job, thanks very much, an' if y' de say owt, that'll be the finish, a'll never tell y' owt again."

They walked home in silence and Meg was upset when she went into the house, she did not even speak to Will who was sitting next to the fire coughing his heart out. Meg went straight to bed; Ted had not even mentioned when he would next see her.

Meg need not have worried, the following evening Ted was waiting for her outside the pub. Meg had spent a happy day with her two charges and was even happier when a cheerful Ted escorted her home and did not mention the previous evening.

The summer and autumn passed and Meg was happier than she had been all of her life. Ted brought out the best in her, even though she still had a temper and liked to win, her tantrums were less frequent and she was learning how to say sorry. At times she could not help herself and lost her temper with Ted. If she tried to cause an argument with him he annoyed her by not arguing back. Meg knew she was on safe ground with Ted, she had found someone with whom she did not have to prove her worth. She could just be Meg and Ted liked her for being Meg. Meg knew she loved him and she was certain he felt the same about her even though he had never told her.

There was one thing that marred their happiness; Ted still could not find work and Meg knew that until he did they would only be friends. Winter was approaching and that would mean the end of their walks for a few months. Meg had enjoyed the autumn evenings much better than the summer. They would sit together watching the sun set and then when it got dark Ted would point out the stars. He would tell her the names of the constellations, his knowledge and apparent love of the sky at night never ceasing to amaze her and draw them closer together.

Unfortunately Meg was soon to realise that knowing Ted did not mean that her life would always be a better one.Ted could bring her just as much unhappiness as happiness.

It was Jane who started the argument. Will was off work; his cough was worse and for the last two weeks he had not left his bed. Jane had come through to see him and brought her two youngest children with her. She went straight up to the bedroom to see Will, leaving the children in the care of Meg and Ted. Ted took them into the back yard to play football and a happy Meg watched them. She laughed as Ted tried to show off his non existent skills as a footballer and the eldest boy easily took the ball from him.

"That's somat else y' not very good at Ted," Meg thought to herself remembering the one and only time Tom had asked Meg and Ted to join him and Nancy for a game of tennis.

"That's the last time a'll ask you and Ted to play Meg," Tom told her the day after their disastrous game. "Showing me up like that in front of Nancy. Neither of you could hit the ball never mind not knowing where to hit it."

Meg just laughed.

"Eeh Tom y' are gettin' high fallutin'. Well just y' wait one o' these days a'll learn t' talk as posh as you an' so will Ted an' we'll learn t' play tennis; mebee we'll be better at it than you an' Nancy."

Meg shivered as she watched the three of them battling for the ball and decided to go indoors and leave them to carry on with their game. As she entered the back kitchen she heard Jane speaking to Sarah; her voice was raised and Meg stood still.

"A see she's still gannin' out wi' him then," Meg heard Jane say to Sarah. "By all accounts from what our Ada says he'll neither work nor want. Spends all day up the pigeon lofts, wi' the other good f' nowts, while our Meg's at work floggin' her wick out an' then he meets her on a night when she's finished. A thought me Da would 'ave put a stop t' it by now? Y're both ower soft wi' her; she gets ower much o' her own way. A mean it Ma, if y' dinna tell her t' stop seein' him a'll tell the lazy bugger what a think o' him."

240

Meg could not hold back any longer, she ran into the kitchen and raised her voice at Jane before Sarah had time to reply to Jane's words.

"He's not a lazy bugger Jane an' you mind y're own business, it's got nowt t' de wi' you who a gan with."

Ted had not heard Jane's comments but he could not fail to hear Meg's raised voice as he rushed into the kitchen.

Sarah quickly intervened.

"It's got nowt t' de wi' y' lad just family business." She told Ted.

But Ted knew, he had heard Meg, it was not family business but he could not defend himself. He looked first at Sarah and then at Jane then lowered his head before speaking.

"Y' right, a best go."

Ted left without saying goodbye to the two boys who were disappointed to see their new found playmate leaving. Meg did not follow him; the old Meg was back and she was ready to do battle with Jane. Once again Sarah intervened before Meg had time to speak.

"Don't start Meg; our Jane's right. Me an' y' Da both feel the same. We didn't say owt 'cos we thought the whole thing would fizzle out, 'cos y' young, but y' gettin' too involved wi' him. It might 'ave been different if he'd had a job an' what y' dinna kna is that our Will offered t' try an' get him set on at his pit but he said he wasn't interested. Y' Da was vexed, he said if it had been a job wi' pigeons he'd have jumped at it an' pigeons cost money, th' dinna mek' it."

Meg was speechless, what could she say in Ted's defence. If she told them why he would not work at the pit she was being disloyal to him so for the first time in her life she let Jane rant and rave, not at her but at Sarah who really could not have cared less. She had too much

241

on her mind; her son was ill and she knew deep down she was going to lose him just as she had lost another son. Meg left the room and went upstairs to Will. Normally she would have told him what had just happened but he was coughing and for the first time Meg noticed the rags that Sarah had cut for him; they were full of thick, black phlegm.

Will had stopped going to the races and to the pub eight weeks ago but he still dragged himself out of bed to go to the pit; coming in after each shift, too tired to eat and after a wash and a pot of sweet tea he would go straight to bed until it was time for his next shift. He surprised them all three weeks ago when he came home from work on the Friday night.

" A'm gannin' straight t' bed Ma after 'ave had a wash but get me suit out will y'? A 'm gannin' t' the races t' morro'."

Sarah begged him not to go and even Meg tried her best to dissuade him. The next morning as he dressed they all tried again.

"A'm gannin' Ma even if it kills me; it's me only bit o' pleasure."

It rained all day and Sarah and Dan were so worried they decided against their usual Saturday night out. When Will finally arrived home he was so weak Dan had to undress him and help him to bed. Sarah sat by his side that night just as she had with Dan when he had returned from the pit in the blizzarding snow. In the middle of the night Sarah woke Tom and Ada; Will had a fever and she was not strong enough to hold him in the bed. The three of them battled with Will until day break when he finally settled into what seemed to be a peaceful sleep. For the next forty eight hours Sarah and Ada nursed him. Ada grumbled about the lack of sleep but Sarah never faltered from the endless task of sponging

242

him down, changing his sheets and offering him copious drinks. Meg did her best to help but Ada grumbled telling her she was getting in their way. Dan was not aware of just how ill his son was until the Tuesday morning when Sarah asked him to go for the doctor.

"I am so sorry," the doctor told Sarah, "but there's nothing I can do. He's got pneumonia and if it was just that I would say he stood a chance but it's the coal dust."

Sarah did not need to hear the doctor's words, she already knew; her son was dying. She had watched her good time boy, the drinker, the gambler, the hard worker slowly die for the last two years. He had become a slave to the pit; too tired to live the good life any more, too tired to eat and finally too tired to go to the pit that Sarah knew was his murderer. She knew the pit had destroyed his lungs; he would never go down that black hole again; he would never get out of his bed again.

That day Meg stayed in the bedroom with Will until Jane had left for home. She pulled a chair along side his bed and sat quietly trying hard not to disturb him. Meg woke with a start and realised within seconds that Will's cough had wakened her.

"A' y' alreet Will?" she asked him.

"It's me feet Meg the' hurt an' the' cold like two bloody blocks o' ice, nowt seems t' warm them up."

Meg looked at this man who she had feared yet grown to love. Who was he, her brother or her uncle? What did it matter? He was Will.

"A'll rub y' feet f' y," she told him.

When Sarah came back upstairs she stood at the bedroom door but did not disturb them. Sarah went back downstairs with tears in her eyes, she would spend the night at her son's side but she would not disturb the two of them; her second son and her granddaughter who was so like her firstborn.

"My that's grand Meg," Will stuttered between bouts of coughing. "A could lie here all night wi' y' doin' that t' me' feet; but away t' bed wi y' y've work in the morning."

"It's alreet Will," Meg told him, " an' anyway the's somat a want t' talk t' y' about."

Will smiled.

"Right bonnie lass, you talk an' a'll listen 'cos if a start t' talk a'll start t' cough an' then me Ma'll be back up an' a'll not hear what y' have t' tell me."

Meg spoke to Will as she walked to the window.

"Can a open the curtains first Will?" Meg asked. "It's cold out tonight but there's a full moon an' y' can see all the stars; there's hardly any clouds in the sky."

Will managed to reply without coughing.

"Aye lass open them, a'm always tellin' me Ma t' open the curtains instead o' burnin' the candles. A've telt her umpteen times, the moon an' the stars 'll light the room, but she teks ne notice."

Meg moved the chair to the foot of the bed and as she rubbed his feet she told him about Ted and what Jane and Sarah had said. Will listened until she had finished but he knew her tale was biased in Ted's favour and Meg would not like what he was about to say. Will stifled his cough he wanted to speak before Sarah came back upstairs.

"A'm sorry lass but our Jane an' me Ma's right. Ted's a canny enough lad but he's never kept a job f' more than five minutes an' he's how old? Twenty one or not a kick o'the arse off."

Meg had no answer; she knew Will was right. It was a dejected Meg who went to bed that night but Sarah was relieved when she went back into the bedroom and Will was sleeping peacefully.

That night set a pattern to Meg's life for the following three months. Work during the day and the foot of Will's bed in the evening. Tom was now sleeping with Dan in the front bedroom; Ada helped to look after Will during the day and Sarah spent the night in a chair at the side of Will's bed. Every night Meg rubbed Will's cold discoloured feet. They were clean, Sarah saw to that, but they were so blue it was as if he had just come in from the pit and had never washed them.

Most of the time Will was quiet as they both gazed out of the window and Meg described the star lit sky. She had learnt a lot about the stars from Ted and this knowledge she departed to Will. She had thought about Ted a lot since the night he had left the house his head down in shame. She had not spoken to him since but she had seen him as she walked home from work. He always kept his distance and never gave her the opportunity to speak to him.

Tonight Will was restless and became agitated when Meg took a well earned rest from rubbing his feet. Will's breathing was laboured and for the last few days he had hardly spoken. Each word was as hard for him to speak as it was for Meg to climb a mountain.

"Meg listen t' me will y'," he gasped. "A've been lyin' here f' days thinkin' about you an' Ted. A kna' y've hardly crossed the doors on a night since y' stopped seein' him. Why don't y' talk t' me Ma? If she had a word wi' her lot the' might find him a job labourin'. A've telt our Tom t' have a word wi' Ted next time he sees him." Will noticed the anxious look on Meg's face. "A've telt our Tom t' tell Ted t' come an' see me, y' silly bugger, not t' talk t' him about a job. A like Ted but 'til he sorts hi'sel' out he's ne good f' y' an' remember what a telt y' afore Meg; promise us y'll learn t' talk proper or y'll never get on in this world."

Will started to cough and an anxious Sarah was soon on the scene to tend to her desperately ill son.

Ted never got to visit Will. The following night while Meg was rubbing his feet he started to cough and as an anxious Sarah ran into the bedroom he lay back on the pillow, the thick black sputum preventing him from breathing. Just as Rob had done Will choked to death but this time Sarah was not alone with her son, her granddaughter was by her side.

CHAPTER 13

Meg saw him that morning as they were leaving the chapel on the day of Will's funeral. There was Ted on the other side of the road leaning on the school gates and looking such a sight. His cap was cocked on one side of his head and Meg recognised the suit. It was one of Sam's old ones and since Sam was two sizes smaller than Ted the sleeves were half way up his arms and the trousers at half mast. In the midst of her grief Meg could not help but smile as she thought.

"It's a wonder he's even got a suit; Sam must 'ave decided t' gi' him it 'cos it's not even good enough t' gan down the pit in."

As family and friends walked to the cemetery Meg's thoughts were still on Ted.

"It's a shame he never got t' see Will. A kna' he liked him an' if things had been different, an' he could o' got a job, the' would 'ave got on well together. Not like our Tom an' him, the' 'aven't much in common. The' get on alreet the two o' them an' the're about the same age but the day we played tennis was enough f' our Tom. Still our Tom kna's nowt about pigeons, o' the stars, so Ted's got one up on him there."

When they reached the cemetery Meg was too upset for any further thoughts of Ted except to wish that he could have been there walking beside her.

Fred had turned up like a bad penny as soon as Ada had told him that Will had died, and he was walking with Ada. John was with Jane and Tom and Nancy were walking at either side of Dan and Sarah. Meg was with Joe at the rear of the little procession. Joe's old pit accident was playing havoc with his leg and over the last few years Meg had rarely seen him. Any news about Joe, or his family, was either through Jane or from Dan on the odd occasion he visited the Bay Horse.

Joe walked with two sticks to support him and he was in his element telling Meg how well he was being looked after in his old age. His youngest daughter had never married, devoting her life to caring for her father. The only time she ever left the house was to do the shopping and even then she never spent any time chatting to the neighbours. She would not even attend weddings or funerals and as Joe had never been a member of the chapel she, like him, did not see the need to attend every Sunday as her old school friends did. When Meg was younger she had told Sarah they called her 'Dottie Doris' and Meg could not understand why she had received a good hiding and had been sent to bed without any supper. She understood now, Joe not only depended on Doris, he ruled her. Ada had told Meg, on one of her rare talkative days, Doris had gone with a lad for years but he had married another lass.

"He was fed up o' waitin'," Ada told Meg with a smirk on her face. "Doris made one excuse after another, always puttin' him off. Everyone knew, except him, it was Joe that was stoppin' her. Poor Doris every time she was ganna get married Joe had a bad turn an' the weddin' was postponed."

Meg was relieved when they finally reached the cemetery and at the grave side she said her final goodbye to Will.

"A promise y' Will from t' day a'll listen t' our Tom an' the Bensons an' a'll try t' talk proper." Meg smiled. "Or like our Tom says, correctly."

The funeral was over; the washing up done and everyone had gone home. Ada had gone out with Fred, and Tom, after making his excuses, was walking Nancy home. Meg sat on the chair at the kitchen table, her head in her hands and feeling so alone. She had read the same page in her book six times and she still could not remember what it was about. Dan and Sarah were in the kitchen with her but, as far as she was concerned, she might as well have been the only person in the house. They were sat at either side of the fireplace, each of them with a glass in their hand drinking themselves into oblivion. Sarah had not touched any beer or gin since the night Will came home from the races; she had not had a drink since he had died but, Meg knew, tonight she would make up for it; tonight Sarah would sleep.

As she got older Meg was beginning to understand her grandmother but that did not dispel her own loneliness. Meg needed someone to talk to; she needed to share her grief. Suddenly she got up from her chair, put her coat on and quietly left the house. Meg walked the village streets, looking from left to right, praying that she would see him.

"A canna gan t' his house; an' in any case he'll not be in. He'll be somewhere wi' his mates chattin' up another lass." Meg muttered.

Meg was not in luck, Ted was no where to be seen and although she had seen some of his friends she was too proud to ask if they had seen him. Meg justified her walk out by calling for a bag of chips before returning home to a dark house that might as well have been empty as far as she was concerned. Dan and Sarah had gone to bed and neither Tom nor Ada had come home. Meg was not at all bothered about Ada but she would have liked to have seen Tom before she went to bed. Even if she had to share him with Nancy, a little bit of his time was better than none. Before she went to sleep that night she thought of Will.

"A'm sorry Will 'ave broken me promise, a kna' 'ave just been talkin't' mesel', but a promise from t'morro' a'll start t' speak proper. A've been practisin' an' a kna' a can. So listen Will; from tomorrow I am going to speak proper. Sorry Will, correctly."

It was three weeks before Meg saw Ted again. She had been thoroughly miserable since Will had died; her only refuge was the Bensons and their happy children. Meg was determined to keep her promise to Will and listened intently to every word they spoke and most of all she listened to their visitors. When the Bensons realised what she was doing they encouraged her and every night she drove Tom to distraction practising the words she had heard throughout the day. He was often annoyed with her as she often caused him to be late to meet Nancy. Meg knew Ada was sniggering behind her back and making fun of her to her Ma and Da, but she did not care; this time she would not break her promise.

Dan had returned to work the day after the funeral and Meg noticed how old he looked; he had completely lost his youthful looks. Not only had his physical appearance changed but he talked and acted like an old man. Meg did not talk very often to Sarah as she always appeared to be in a world of her own. Each evening Sarah sat in front of the fire with a gill of beer in her hand and when Dan's shifts allowed he would join her, constantly topping up their glasses from a jug of beer bought from the nearby pub.

To make matters worse for Meg, Fred was back. The night after Will's funeral he had come to the house and he had been there every night since. He worked at the pit but not underground, he was on bank, and so he did not work shifts, having every evening and every Sunday free. Ada and Fred rarely went out and sat in the parlour every evening and most of Sunday. Fortunately he appeared to have lost interest in Meg and did not bother her except to speak to her as if the past had never happened. Meg felt really sorry for herself spending her evenings sitting in the kitchen with Dan and Sarah who did not speak to each other, let alone her.

Her only pleasure was work and if she could she would find any excuse to stay there long after six o'clock. Some evenings it would be nine o'clock before she finally left their home. The Benson's, being typical friendly publicans, were party to most of the village gossip and knew only to well why Meg lingered each evening and never questioned her motives when she volunteered to stay long after the children had gone to bed. It was on one such night when she was leaving the pub that she bumped into Ted.

As she usually did Meg left by the back door; Mrs Benson would not allow her to use the front door as that meant walking through the men's bar. As she turned the corner there he was, hands in his pockets, sheltering from the raw wind that was howling across the forecourt.

"Where've y' been?" he asked. "A've been hangin' 'round the village since a finished work. A haven't been home f' me tea yet; a was that frightened a'd miss y'."

Meg was tired and though she was pleased to see him she had no intention of letting him know that.

"What do you mean?" She shouted. "Where have a been? It's got nothing to do with you where 'ave been."

Ted was not deterred; he knew Meg's temper and he knew it was worth another try.

"A've come t' tell y' 'ave got a job. It's just labourin' again but this time it looks like it might last. The' building a factory an' a go t' the site in a lorry every day an' a get a ride back on a night. A got the driver t' drop us off here t' night an' a'm frozen standin' waitin' o' y', me feet's like two bloody blocks o' ice. D' y' think the landlady'll gi' us a drink t' warm us up."

Meg laughed at the same happy go lucky Ted.

251

"How will the pigeons survive with out you?" she taunted. Without waiting for an answer she slipped her arm through his. "Come on we'll go down home and a'll make you a cup of cocoa before you go home for your dinner."

As they walked down the cobbled back street Ted's curiosity got the better of him.

"Meg, y' talkin' funny."

"Yes Ted," she replied. "I promised our Will, and a keep forgetting mesel' but a'm learning to talk correctly, an' if a have anything to do with it you will one day."

Her friendship with Ted was resurrected and Meg began to smile again. Ted was working, she was working; she helped at home with the housework and slowly over the next few months every thing got back to normal. That is as normal as they could be without Will.

Meg missed him but Will's death had changed Dan. Sarah appeared to be coping and seemed to miss Will in the same way Meg did, at least that was what Meg thought; only Sarah knew how much she missed him. His loss brought back all the feelings of grief for another son she had lost, the painful memories of a son lost so long ago. Life had taught her to cope and no one was better than Sarah at hiding her feelings. Dan had coped after Rob's death; he had Sarah to worry about and a young family to rear. This time it was different, he had no responsibilities, he wanted a shoulder to cry on; he wanted someone to care for him.

Dan had been Meg's one consolation since she had found out Jane was her mother. He looked so young and Meg knew it was not difficult for everyone to believe he was her father. He had always treated her as a daughter but he had changed. He did not talk to her and the fact that he did not talk to anyone else in the house did not make her feel any better. He started to lose shifts at the pit, drank more and Sarah was trying to persuade him to ask for lighter work at the pit. Eventually he did take Sarah's advice. The wage was less but that had a beneficial effect; less money and different shifts meant less time and money for drink. It was also beneficial for Sarah as she could no longer afford to buy jugs of beer from the local pub and curtailed her drinking to her Saturday night out with Dan and the odd tipple of gin or port when he was in night shift.

Meg decided to keep her relationship with Ted a secret. Dan and Sarah were in on the night she took him home for a hot drink but as he had only stayed for half an hour they did not think it was anything other than a one off. What they did not know was that Ted left early because he knew his mother would be worrying. If he was not home from work in time for his dinner she worried about him coming home from a day labouring, just as any mother did if her son was late home from the pit.

"In any case," he explained to Meg when he said he would have to get home. "It's not just me Ma worrying, 'ave t' be up at the crack o' dawn 'cos if a miss the lorry me job's down the plughole."

Meg was not sure if Sarah and Dan would accept her seeing Ted on a regular basis but after a few months of regular work she decided to chance it. After a Sunday afternoon walk she took him home. Ted, at last, had a little money in his pocket; he gave his full pay to his mother every week and she gave him pocket money every Friday night. They occasionally went to the pictures and on one occasion had gone to Croxdale for a walk along the banks of the river Wear. They still enjoyed their walks on an evening especially now the nights were lighter and warmer.

253

Meg was seventeen and it was on one of their walks when Ted asked her to marry him.

"A gi' me Ma all me pay Meg but she gi'es us a bit back an' our Sam still helps us wi' me pigeons so a'm savin' up t' buy y' an engagement ring."

Some of Meg's friends were engaged, the odd one already married, and as she loved Ted she was happy to say yes.

"I'd like an engagement ring Ted," she told him. "But there's one condition; if we ever get wed you can learn to talk correctly like I am."

Ted laughed and kissed her.

"A will hinnie, if a can, a promise a'll learn t' talk proper after we wed."

It was a week after Ted's proposal that Meg took him home. The house was full. Dan and Sarah, Tom and Nancy, Ada and Fred were all in the kitchen. Poor Meg had the wind taken out of her sails when every one ignored her and Ted might not have been there. It was Ada who dropped the bombshell.

"Our Tom an' Nancy's gettin' wed an' the' movin' in wi' Nancy's Ma an' Da. The' lettin' them a've the front room t' themsel's an' me an' Fred's gettin' wed." As she continued she looked directly at Meg. "Me Ma says me an' Fred can have the parlour t' live in an' y'll have t' sleep in the back bedroom when our Tom's gone."

Meg could not believe what she was hearing. Fred was coming to live with them. All she could say was,

"I'm pleased for y'," as she grabbed Ted's arm and dragged him into the back kitchen and out of the house.

Ted was not at all pleased with Meg's behaviour and as they hurried up the back street he challenged her actions.

"Y' could a said a bit more than y' did t' them, especially t' y're Tom, a could tell he was happy as Larry an' his face dropped a mile when y' dragged us out."

Meg realised she was wrong but she had never told Ted about Fred and, for now, she had no intention of telling him. All she had wanted to do was get out of the house; it was her home and now she would have to share it with Fred. He was the man she feared more than any other; she did not just fear him, she loathed him for what he had done to her and she felt no guilt about her feelings. Will was no longer there to protect her and, from what Ada had said, John would be no help. She had overheard Ada and Fred talking one night.

"All that John's good f' is givin' our Jane a house full o' squallin' kids, playin' the piano an' drinkin' his sel' t' death." Ada had told Fred.

By Meg's eighteenth birthday she had been a bridesmaid for Tom and Nancy and the week before Christmas for Ada and Fred. Meg was happy to be Nancy's bridesmaid; she had not expected to be asked. Even though Nancy had no brothers or sisters Meg had expected that Nancy's best friend would be her only bridesmaid. As it turned out Nancy's parents had saved hard for the wedding and Nancy ended up having four bridesmaids; her best friend, Meg and Nancy's two small cousins. Afterwards Ted, who had stood outside the chapel waiting for them to come out, told her.

"My Meg y' all looked a picture in them dresses an' did y' say Nancy an' her Ma made them all?"

Ted had not been invited to the wedding and if he had he would not have been able to go. He was now working six and a half days a week and had only just managed to get away to see her coming out of the chapel. Meg had been annoyed with him when he complained.

"You should think yourself lucky, theres many a lad would wish he was in your shoes; it's better to be working than standing 'round street corners with no money in your pockets."

Even Dan showed some enthusiasm and before leaving for the chapel he commented.

"By hinnie y' look grand wi' them pink rosebuds in y' hair and y' have such bonny face."

It was Sarah's turn next.

"Y' Da's right lass y' look lovely an' Nancy's done hersel' proud wi' her sewin', that pink satin must o' cost the earth an' she's sewed them bows on perfect."

After the chapel both families crowded into Nancy's parent's small home and a good time was had by all.

If it had not been for Ted Meg would have refused to be Ada's bridesmaid. At first she said no and even Sarah could not persuade her to change her mind. She was not even sure whether she would go to the wedding. Meg wanted to put as much distance between her and Fred as she possibly could.

"A canna understand y' Meg," Ted scolded. "Y'll say yes t' Nancy but not t' y' own sister."

Meg still could not bring herself to tell Ted about Fred and it was not until now that she realised the importance of her other secret. She would have to tell him sooner rather than later that Ada was her aunt and her Ma and Da were really her Granda and Grandma and all of the other complications that went with it. Telling him about Fred was different, no matter how much she cared for Ted she could not tell him; she was afraid that if she did she would lose him.

Instead of explanations she gave in to Ted and it was a reluctant Meg who stood behind Ada and Fred in the

256

registry office. There was to be no chapel wedding for them; Fred had insisted that the registry office was all he and Ada wanted. A chapel wedding would have been some compensation for Meg, she would have been able to wear her bridesmaid dress again, the prettiest dress she had ever owned.

"Sunday best claes us good enough," Fred had told Sarah. Even when she offered them 'a bit o' a do' after the ceremony Fred declined. "A cup o' tea an' a sandwich in the parlour'll de," he told her.

The evening before the wedding Ted asked Meg if she was ready for the big day. She told him she was but that Fred had declined Sarah's offer.

"But what he doesn't know Ted is that me Ma's made them a wedding cake, an' she baked some other stuff for when we get back."

At first it seemed to Meg that Fred moving in was making little difference to her life. In fact it had its compensations; she now had her own bedroom. The first few weeks had been difficult as it was the room in which Will had died. She kept seeing him in the room and the fact that she was now sleeping in the same bed in which he had died did not help. Finally, after constant complaints, Sarah's suggestion did the trick.

"We'll move the bed 'round the other way then y'll be facin' a different wall t' him."

She was right and Meg settled into the room enjoying her privacy. Even downstairs there were no problems. Ada and Fred lived in the parlour, which they did not share with any other member of the family, and again that had its compensations. Just as they did not share the parlour they did not use any other room in the house. Only Ada came into the kitchen; they ate all of their meals in the parlour and Fred only walked through the kitchen if he needed to use the midden.

That suited Meg as she did not have to look at him over the kitchen table. Fred had even put a lock on the parlour door and only he and Ada had a key. The next time Jane came to visit she asked Meg if everything was alright between her and Fred.

"I hardly ever see him," was all Meg replied.

Meg was content, a job she loved, a man she loved and peace at home. As Ada still helped Sarah in the house during the day when Fred was at work, Meg had plenty of spare time to spend with Ted. Even Dan and Sarah seemed happier. Sarah often talked with Meg as she busied herself in the kitchen laughing and sharing a joke with Meg which was usually at Ted's expense.

"Eeh Meg," Sarah would laugh. "What a sight he is when he comes home from work. A wish he'd gan home first an' get changed."

Meg would reply laughing as much as Sarah.

"He can't help it Ma, he has to wear his Da and Sam's cast offs for work he has none of his own. The only suit he's got is the one he always wears and if he went to work in that he'd be a worse mess."

"Still," Sarah answered, "at least he's workin' regular now."

"I've been thinking Ma, now he's working his Ma might buy him a suit but if she doesn't a could get a club out and buy him one. What do you think he'd say if a did?" Meg asked.

"A'm not sure hinnie," was Sarah's advice, "but if a was you a'd shut up 'cos here he is crossin' the back yard."

Meg's short spell of happiness was not to last. It was Easter weekend; she had been given a few days holiday from work and she had bought herself a new dress. Sarah

258

had suggested she invite Ted to tea on Sunday but today Ted was working and Dan and Sarah had gone to visit Jane. They rarely ever visited her but as she had not been through to see them for some time Dan, as ever worried about her and suggested that it being Easter Saturday they should give her a surprise visit. Dan constantly worried about his eldest daughter; he knew his hands were tied as she would never admit to being ill treated by John but Dan knew what was happening and Jane, and his grandchildren's welfare, was a constant worry.

Meg looked at herself in the mirror. She was in Dan and Sarah's bedroom; it was the only room in the house with a long mirror which was part of the front of the wardrobe door. The front bedroom was the best furnished room in the house. A light mahogany wardrobe, a matching dressing table and a washstand were Sarah's prize possessions. Will had bought them for her two years ago along with a new double bed. He had paid the last instalment, on the club he had taken out to buy them, only three weeks before he became unable to work.

Meg thought of Will as she twirled around in front of the mirror, the scalloped edges of her new dress floating up and down, and his words came back to her.

"A'm pleased a've managed t' clear the club off a took out t' buy me Ma's furniture. A think it's the only thing a've ever bought her an' a wouldn't 'ave rested if a thought a'd left them in debt. A never gi' her much o' me pay as it is but she's ganna miss the bit a did gi' her."

The wardrobe faced the bedroom door and Meg was terrified when she saw Fred's reflection in the mirror. He was on the landing, standing quite still, watching her every movement; he did not speak but the look on his face increased her fear. Only seconds passed before he spoke; but to Meg it seemed an eternity.

"Y' needn't ask," he sneered." Ada's out, an' y' needn't worry, she said y'd got a new frock an' a've just come t' gi' y' me opinion."

Meg did not wait for his opinion; she rushed past him but as she turned he grabbed her and she felt a tug on her dress. She had no time to stop and look; she ran down the stairs two at a time and instinct led her to her old place of refuge, the midden. As she bolted the door her tears flowed, tears of fear, tears of frustration. What could she do? Would he come and force the door? Dare she scream for help? Her only solution was to wait in the midden, the midden that no longer held the fear of the scavenger.

Some years before they had a proper lavatory installed and although Meg insisted it was now to be called a lavatory they all, except her, continued to call it the midden. When it was first installed it was a novelty to Meg and something she could boast about to her school friends. Most of them lived in the old colliery houses and were not in the fortunate position of being able to flush the lavatory each time they used it. That was the only compensation of the new lavatory, the spiders were still there and in some respects it was worse than the old midden. It was forever getting blocked up or freezing up in the winter. They had a paraffin lamp in the lavatory and it was left burning on very cold nights but all it did was add a sickly smell to the smells that were already there and the next morning the lavatory was still frozen.

Meg stood in the lavatory her back against the door. She decided against screaming but was determined she would put up a fight if he crossed the yard and came anywhere near her. After a few minutes Meg recognised Ada's footsteps coming down the back street; the episode was over but that did nothing to console her.

How was she going to cope with the constant threat of Fred; she could not say anything to anyone, Fred had not done anything to her, he had not even really said anything wrong. Only Meg and Fred knew what he really wanted from her.

When she finally emerged from the lavatory Meg went straight to her bedroom. As usual Ada and Fred were closeted in the parlour and Meg inspected the damage to her dress without fear of interruption. One look at it and the tears came, it was ruined. If she had been any good at sewing she would have attempted to repair it, but she wasn't, Ada had always taunted her about her lack of skills in that direction.

"Meg canna'sew a button on wi' out it fallin' straight back off." Ada would tell Sarah and Dan.

She had said the same to Nancy when she had seen the beautiful dresses she had made.

Ada never did any sewing for Meg as Sarah, being aware of Meg's inadequacy, did all of Meg's sewing and mending to save her any embarrassment. Meg decided the only thing to do was to hide the dress. She could not hide the tear from Sarah and she was too upset to think of any other possible explanations; the one thing she was sure of she could not tell Sarah the truth.

When Ted arrived for tea on the Sunday afternoon he put his foot in it as soon as he walked through the door.

"Where's y' new dress?" were his first words.

Meg's look was enough to turn him to stone let alone quieten him. Ted's first formal visit to the Charlton's home was a disaster. Only Dan seemed to enjoy his tea, having cut short his afternoon sleep to join them for pineapple chunks and cream which was only ever served if they had guests. As soon as tea was over and the dishes washed Ted suggested a walk. Meg was as relieved as he was to get out of the house; she could not stand the atmosphere that was developing between herself and Sarah. Meg knew Sarah had noticed she was not wearing her new dress and Meg dreaded any more questions.

They walked for more than ten minutes before Ted broke the silence.

"What's up wi' y'Meg. Y' were thrilled t' bits about y' new dress?"

Meg's defence mechanisms came quickly into action and left Ted wondering what he had done or said.

"Mind your own business," Meg shouted. "An' if you've come for a walk just to cross examine me we might as well go home."

They continued their walk in silence until they reached the beck that ran through the path they usually walked along. It was not very wide and very easy to jump across. Ted always enjoyed playing the gentleman by offering her a helping hand. He crossed first and offered his hand, which she did not need, but Meg would take it graciously even though a long step was all that was needed. Today was different and Meg refused his help stepping confidently over the beck. Unfortunately the skirt she was wearing instead of her dress turned out to be her downfall. The skirt was tight; her jump failed and Meg landed in the beck. Ted took one look at her sitting in the muddy water, legs straight out in front of her, supporting herself with her hands, and laughed. Meg was furious, not only because he was laughing at her, but he made no attempt to help her to her feet. When he finally offered her his hand she brushed it aside and shouted as she struggled to her feet.

"I don't need you or anybody else to help me, I'll get up meself just like a've always had to do everything else for meself."

Meg's humiliation was the final straw and for the second time that weekend she broke down in tears. Ted was concerned, he knew Meg so well, and these tears were not from anger, nor were they associated with Meg's bad temper. Ted saw something on Meg's face he had never seen before; she looked so vulnerable and there was something else.

"Yes," he thought. "She looks scared."

He did not understand his feelings but he did know that he wanted to protect her from whatever it was that was so distressing for her. Ted wrapped his arms around her.

"It'll be alreet hinnie," he told her. "But will y' tell us what's wrong wi' y'."

Eventually Meg stopped sobbing and when she could speak her reply was enough for Ted at that moment.

"I'll tell y' Ted but not here, let's walk to our favourite place."

Meg insisted they took the long way round as she wanted to avoid the other people who were out for their Easter Sunday walk. Some of them she would know; others she would not but all of them would be taking advantage of the Easter break. They could see the happy children in the distance rolling paste eggs down the bank, others standing at the bottom, watching their eggs long ago broken and eaten.

Ted tried to cheer her up.

"A bet Meg th' all the same; the'll be just like the ones me Ma an' y' Ma de, boiled in onion skins and all brown inside when y' eat them."

When they arrived at their secluded spot Ted took off his jacket for Meg to sit on. Other than his one comment he had not spoken to her and he was afraid to look at her. When he finally did he was so relieved to see that there were no more tears and he tried to act as if nothing had

263

happened. His first words were enough to make Meg laugh.

"Mek y' sel' comfortable Meg an' sit on me good coat."

The ice was broken and as he held her in his arms neither of them spoke; it was enough for both of them to be together.

It was Meg who spoke first telling him not only about the incident with Fred the previous day but about all of her encounters with him over the previous years. If Ted had found it difficult to understand his feelings earlier in the day he was sure of what he now felt. He never once doubted the truth of what she was telling him and found it difficult to keep quiet until she had finished. Meg saw the anger on his face but asked him not to speak until she had finished.

"Ted a should have told you a long time ago but our Jane's me Ma; a still don't know who me Da is but one day a'll find out."

Meg found it hard to understand when Ted did not immediately reply.

"What's the matter Ted? Are me an' you finished?"

Ted held her closely.

"Don't be daft Meg, it's just that a canna get him out o' me head. A'll kill the bugger when we get home tonight."

Meg was frightened, not for herself this time but, for Ted. She cried once more as she said.

"Don't Ted you know what he's like; he's got a reputation for fighting. It took John and our Will to make him pay last time and you know for yourself you'd be no match for him."

Ted realised Meg was right and his following words took her by surprise.

"We'll get married then."

264

Meg had expected the anger, and she had genuinely thought it might be over after she had told him, but to marry him had never entered head.

"We can't Ted," she responded. "Me Ma and me Da would never let us and a'm not twenty one yet. Anyway we have no where to live."

Ted held her away from him and looking straight into her eyes said.

"If y' Ma an' Da said yes, an' if a could find somewhere f' us t' live, would y' marry me Meg?"

Meg did not have to think before she answered.

"Yes Ted a would."

Three weeks later Ted was outside the pub waiting for Meg to finish work. She could see he was excited and certainly knew why when the told her.

"A've got somewhere f' us t' live. One o' the lads at work telt us today that his Granda had died an' the place he lived in is comin' up f' rent. An' y'll never guess where it is Meg; it's right on the edge o' the fields."

Meg could not get a word in; Ted was so excited extolling the virtues of the house which he had not even seen. Finally he paused allowing her to speak.

"Ted a haven't even mentioned anything to me Ma or Da yet so a hope you haven't said you definitely want the place?"

Ted was not to be deterred.

"A kna' that Meg, that's why a've come straight from work, we ca gan down an' tell y' Ma now."

Meg took hold of his hand as she answered.

"Ted it's not as easy as that; a promise a'll talk to me Ma meself. If we both go now she'll say no. A will ask her but I'll have to catch her in the right mood before a say anything."

Ted was satisfied with Meg's explanation.

"Right Meg," he told her. "But a warn y' if y' haven't telt her be the end o' the week a'll tell her mesel'."

For the rest of the week Meg tried to pluck up the courage to approach Sarah. She wished she could go first to Dan but she knew what his response would be.

"Y' d better talk t' y' Ma afore we decide owt lass."

It was Saturday teatime and she was alone with Sarah and Dan in the kitchen. Dan was asleep in the chair in front of the fire and Meg knew it was now or never, otherwise it would be Ted doing the asking. Every night since he had found out about the house he had pestered her to talk to Sarah and last night he had given her an ultimatum.

"Y'd better have somat t' tell me tomorro' or else a'll definitely ask her mesel'. An' if she says owt a'll tell her a few more home truths."

It was unusual for Ted to be so forceful and what was more unusual Meg was allowing Ted to tell her what to do but she understood his concern and that he was only trying to protect her.

Meg had not expected Sarah to agree to her marrying Ted when she first asked her, usually after an angry response Meg got her own way, but she was not prepared for Sarah's outburst.

"Y' can de what y' want when y' twenty one 'til then y'll stay at home an' dinna ask y' Da t' stick up f' y', a've had me say an' that's the end o' it."

Meg knew it was no good trying, she was not twenty one, and without their consent she could not marry Ted or anyone else.

When Meg told Ted he accepted that there was no point in him trying to persuade Dan or Sarah.

"Dinna worry Meg," he told her. "A kna' a way we can get married wi' out y' Ma an' Da's consent. An' y' kna' what the' like Meg, the'll be alright wi' us after we get married. A just have t' say the word an' the house us ours. Well it's not a house really, it's a cottage an' me mate says it's got a' orchard."

Meg was doubtful; not only as to how Dan and Sarah would react after they were married without their consent, but about the cottage Ted had found for them to live in. She decided to confront him.

"The only place a know where there's cottages on the edge of the fields is where them wooden huts are and I wouldn't call them cottages."

Meg was not at all surprised when Ted replied.

"A dinna kna' exactly where th' are but me mate says it's a grand place an' his word's good enough f' me."

When Meg suggested they go and see for themselves Ted was delighted and asked.

"If we gan an' look does that mean we're gettin' married?"

CHAPTER 14

It was Wednesday night, Tom's half day off from the store, and he and Nancy had just arrived. Nancy could not to wait to take her coat off before telling them her good news.

"We've got one Meg, the letter came this morning, it's one o' the new council houses that's just been finished an' we can move in next week."

Meg was thrilled, if not a little envious. Nancy and Meg had become very close to each other since Nancy had married Tom.

"Y' the sister a never had Meg," Nancy often told her and Meg knew she had a dear and trusted friend in Nancy. As she sat down Nancy was still as excited as she had been when she first walked through the door. "Wouldn't it be great if you an' Ted got one beside us? The've got two bedrooms an' a bathroom an' the've got a back garden an' a little front garden."

" Fat chance of them offerin' us one with Ted out of work again." Meg replied.

Meg and Ted had married exactly one year after Tom and Nancy and although still very much in love, the events that had led up to their marriage and the six months after had not exactly been happy ones. Meg looked forward to Wednesday nights when Tom and Nancy came to play dominoes with them. Tom was her only link with home and she missed Dan and Sarah so much.

Although she was happy for Tom and Nancy Meg dreaded the inevitable; a new home for Tom and Nancy would, more than likely, mean the end of their evenings together. Meg was convinced that their domino nights were an excuse for Tom and Nancy to have an evening out of her parent's home. Nancy's mother was very possessive of her daughter and the offer of the front room had not really been what Nancy's mother had intended. Tom and Nancy had very little privacy, her mother insisting that they all share the house, that she did cooking, and that they all sat down to eat together.

Meg had been right about the cottage. It was one of the wooden huts she thought it would be, and here she was living in one of them. She knew she was being unfair to Ted when she called it a hut. It wasn't really a hut but it wasn't a cottage either. There was one thing Ted had been right about; it did have an orchard, a few apple and pear trees at the bottom of an enormous weed covered garden. In the midst of the weeds was a well which was their only supply of water and the midden was worse than one she had been used to as a child.

Over the years when Meg thought back to their first home there were some happy memories. Ted struggling with the garden; something else he was not very good at. Meg papering the kitchen walls and painting everything in sight bottle green. Tom had got the paint for them at the store and since it was the cheapest, bottle green it had to be. The cottage only had two rooms; a kitchen and a bedroom. The kitchen was dominated by 'Belcher', Ted's nickname for the enormous black stove that was located in the centre of the room. Ted had given it that name the first time he had struggled to light it. Meg laughed when she told him.

"You've used more sticks and paper trying t' light that thing than the bairns use on the bonfires."

When he finally succeeded Meg laughed so much her stomach ached.

"Just look at y' Ted, y' like a black man you'll have to have a bath now, the bloody thing's covered y' in soot. Y' look just like Al Johnson; a black face and two shiny eyes looking out of it."

269

Ted never did master the stove and Meg took over the daily chore of lighting it before cooking their breakfast in the smoke filled room. What their home lacked in convenience, the size of the rooms made up for. The small amount of furniture that had belonged to the old man who had lived there before them was swamped. Fortunately, the amount of rent the owners asked of them each week reflected the condition of Ted's 'cottage' and its furniture. It was the one thing they were thankful for now they were both out of work.

If Ted had not lost his job Meg would probably have waited until she was twenty one to get married but Ted had set his heart on the cottage and losing his job meant losing his dream of a life with Meg. Meg finally weakened the week after he told her the factory was finished and so were the men who had built it.

"A've fund out Meg, if we get married we can gan on the parish an' then we'll still be able t' pay the rent." Ted pleaded.

"Still Ted, what d' y' mean?" Meg asked.

"Aye, a never telt y' but a telt me mate we'd have the place an' 'ave been payin' the rent ever since."

Meg was aghast.

"You stupid fool now what are we going to do?" she asked him.

Ted looked downcast but he was also devious.

"A'm sorry Meg but a thought y' Ma would gi' in in the end. That's why a never got y' an engagement ring an' a never telt y' but 'ave sold me pigeons. If we don't get married a'll have nowt an' loss everythin'."

Meg gave in after his outburst but had she known what living on the parish meant she probably would have told Ted what to do with his 'cottage'. Meg was in the middle of trying to paper the kitchen walls when she had her first but last meeting with the man from the parish. He had come to take their particulars for the mean's test.

"How much did the paint cost?" He barked at her. "Where did y' buy that wallpaper, an' how much did it cost? If y' can afford t' buy paper for the walls what y' applyin' f' money t' live on for? Don't y' kna' the parish isn't here t' gi' y' money t' paper the walls?"

The thin, little bespectacled man from the parish was the cause of their first real argument since they had married. Meg ranted and raved at Ted and there was nothing he could do or say would calm her down.

"That's the finish," she shouted. "You'll never go cap in hand beggin' to that lot again. A've never been so ashamed in all of me life, you'd think it was comin' out of his own pocket. From now on we'll use the bit savin's a've got and then when it's done we'll starve to death before we ever ask for anything again."

Ted, as usual, did not argue and as he went into the garden his only words were.

"Watch it Meg y' slippin' wi' y' talkin' proper."

Meg could not help but smile as she watched him giving vent to his anger in the garden. Ted was worried; winter was fast approaching and Meg's savings might keep them in food for a few weeks but how would they pay the rent and buy coal for the fire? Later that night when they made up Ted's worries were momentarily put behind him especially when Meg made him laugh.

"You'll have to get vexed a bit more often Ted, that's the best bit of gardening you've ever done."

After Ted's first attempt to persuade Meg to marry him without Dan and Sarah's permission Meg contented herself to waiting until she was twenty one; that was until Ted had another bright idea.

"A've been thinkin', an' Meg y' dinna need y' Ma an' Da's permission t' get married. Jane's y' Ma an' it's her permission y' want." Meg laughed at him.

"Ted you must be joking if me Ma and Da won't give their permission you don't think our Jane will, do you?"

Ted was not to be deterred and after his sorry tale about the rent, the pigeons and living off the parish Meg finally was persuaded to go and see the minister at the chapel. That was a disaster so Ted arranged to see the vicar at the church and that was a success; the banns would be read out in three weeks time.

The following week as Meg walked down the back street Sarah was waiting at the gate. Meg thought it unusual but did not worry until she got nearer and saw Sarah's face. Although she was angry she spoke quietly.

"A dinna want y' Da t' hear 'cos he'll only get upset so y' can stand out here while a tell y what 'ave got t' say t' y'. A had a visitor this afternoon, the vicar from the church. A've never met the man in me life afore so a got a shock when a answered the door t' him. He said he'd come t' see about you an' Ted getting' married an' the banns were ganna be read out. A wasn't sure at first what he was on about but then a guessed. Well me lady a gave him me answer, a telt him t' cancel ther banns 'cos you'd changed y' mind."

Throughout the next week Meg could not look Sarah straight in the eye and although Dan had no idea about what had happened she found it difficult to answer him when he spoke to her. That night Meg was not seeing Ted and her evening was spent with her head in a book, not reading, but planning how to tell Ted that the wedding was off. When she saw him the following night she was surprised at his reaction.

"Never mind better luck next time," was all he said.

During the next few weeks Meg was uneasy. Ted seemed the same but he rarely ever suggested doing anything if it cost money.

"A've got it all sorted proper this time," Ted announced. "A've even got the weddin' ring but we'll have t' get an engagement ring later. A've decided we'll de it the other way 'round."

Meg was caught up in Ted's excitement as she allowed him to persuade her that he had everything sorted and, this time, the wedding would not be called off.

"A've seen t' everythin', we get married at the registry office four weeks on Wednesday. Y' only have t' de two things, mek an excuse t' the Bensons t' get the day off an' gi' me y' birth certificate so a can get the paper work sorted."

Meg was dismayed, his first request was easy enough but the second was impossible.

"A can't get me birth certificate Ted and anyhow a'm not sure whether have got one." Meg told him with a quiver in her voice.

Ted was annoyed.

"Dinna be stupid Meg; everybody's got a birth certificate."

Meg continued, head down, not daring to look at him, she was not sure how to explain the predicament she now found herself in.

"When I found out Jane was me real Ma I remembered the carry on me Ma made about me birth certificate when I started school. Ted, I've searched the house and it's definitely not there. I've even searched through me Ma and Da's old suitcase where they keep everything that's important. I asked our Jane about it but she was no help, she said she had no idea where it was, in fact, she said she had never even seen it."

273

Following Meg's explanation Ted calmed down when he realised there could be a problem which would upset his well laid plans.

"Well Meg," he told her. "Birth certificate or no birth certificate we're gettin' married this time."

Ted looked lovingly at Meg.

"Well hinnie we've done it."

They had not gone to the cottage but instead had chosen their favourite place, the place that long ago they had called their own. They had been married that afternoon; no family were present, no friends and the two people Ted had asked to witness their marriage were strangers. A young couple who were standing outside the registrar's office had been only too happy to oblige. Meg was taking some convincing that they were now legally married and looking at her wedding ring she plucked up the courage to ask Ted the question that had been plaguing her ever since they had stepped outside the registrar's office.

"And that's another thing Ted." Meg looked at her wedding ring. "This isn't the ring you bought me. It's a curtain ring like the ones you buy in Woollies."

Ted shuffled on the grass; he was feeling rather uncomfortable at the very mention of the wedding ring and he knew she deserved more than the feeble excuse he had given her when he told her he had no money and could she pay the bus fare to Sedgefield and back.

"A'm sorry Meg a'm not ganna tell y' everythin' but a had t' sell the ring t' get everythin' sorted out. Just trust me when a tell y' we are legally married an' when a get me sel' sorted out a'll sort the cottage out f' us t' move into. We'll just not have t' let on t' anybody yet that we're married. If we both go home t'night, the'll be

274

non the wiser, the'll just think we've been out f' the day."

Meg did trust Ted but she was not sure why.

"A'll have to trust you Ted," she told him. "I haven't any other choice now have I? Just hurry up and get a job and then we can tell them all and face the music."

For the next few hours Meg put her worries behind her. Ted loved her and he was showing her just how deep his love was, there in their favourite place, with the stars shining down on them blessing their union.

It was late when they started the long walk back through the fields and as they neared home Meg began to panic. She had already removed her wedding ring, tucking it away safely in the corner of her purse, but she knew she would not be able to look Dan and Sarah straight in the eye when she went in the house.

"Me Ma will know straight away Ted, she's not daft, she'll know somat's up and anyhow she'll know a look different."

Ted did his best to console her before he left her standing at the front door trying to pluck up the courage to go in.

"Dinna be daft Meg," he replied. "Y' dinna look any different now t' what y' looked this mornin'. We'll tell them t'gether just as soon as 'ave cleaned the cottage up a bit. Y' kna y' sel' we canna live in it in the state it's in, an' 'ave spent all me money. As soon as a get a job a'll have it lookin' grand an' y' Ma an' Da'll be pleased as punch when the' see what a grand place we've got t' live in. The'll not be vexed when the' kna' we've somewhere t' live an' a'm workin'."

Meg believed him but as he left his parting words, once again, made her unsure of their future together.

"A forgot t' ask y' Meg but 'til a get a job d' y' think y'll be able t' gi' us somat f' the rent? A daren't gan t' the parish 'til we tell them all we're married."

They had been married for six weeks and still no one knew. Meg was working but Ted had been unable to find a job. It was lunch time at the Benson's and today Mr Benson had joined them. It was a rare event for him; the pub was usually too busy at lunchtime for him to leave the bar. Meg always enjoyed his company and although he rarely had much to say to her she enjoyed his cheerful banter with his children.

Today he looked annoyed and Meg was not prepared for what he had to say to her.

"You might as well tell us the truth Meg; you've married him haven't you?" Meg was flabbergasted but did not interrupt Mr Benson. "I've had me suspicions for a bit. Ever since a said you could make a bit extra money and wait on in the snug to give Mrs Benson a break he's been in there with a gill of beer lasting him all night. Well I found out last night, you were seen going into the registry office the other Wednesday when you asked Mrs Benson for a day off. You said it was to go to your Jane's with your Ma and Da but I knew at the time you had lied. Your Da came in for a pint at the dinner time and he said your Ma was down home. You've always been a good worker and we've trusted you like one of the family so I said nothing. I thought you deserved another chance and that most probably you had gone to Jane's yourself. Anyhow I know you were there so if you did marry him you'll go straight down home now and tell your Ma and Da. If you don't I'll go down there and tell them meself."

Meg's old self came to the fore; the need to win, the need to be right even when she was wrong. Meg jumped up from her chair knocking it over as she ran across the room to make her escape. This was a side of Meg's nature the Bensons had never seen and as she closed the door behind her she shouted.

"Whoever said it's a liar."

As she ran across the forecourt she took off her apron; all she wanted to do was get away from the Bensons. The tears streamed down her face; if they knew then others must and she had no choice but to face the truth and what was worse, she would have to face her Ma and Da.

Meg decided the truth would have to wait; she needed to see Ted. And she was out of breath when she arrived at his home. Meg knocked on the door praying that he would be in. Ted's father opened the door and one look at Meg's tear stained face told him there was trouble ahead. He ushered Meg into the kitchen and told her to sit down beside the fire. She was cold and wet and it was not until she sat down that she realised she had left the Bensons without her coat. It was unusual for Ted's father but on this occasion he took control of the situation.

"Mek us all a nice pot o' tea," he told Ted's mother. "We'll all have a nice pot o' tea an' then mebee Meg'll tell us all what this is all about. Our Ted's up the allotments seein' t' our Sam's pigeons so he won't be back f' a couple hours yet."

Meg shivered, the pot of hot tea which she held between her hands, as she tried to warm them, giving no comfort. She had not spoken to any one since she had arrived and it was Ted's mother who finally broke the silence. She was worried but also curious as to why Meg had arrived in such a state on their doorstep.

"Come on hinnie drink y' tea an' then if y' want y' can tell us what's wrong wi' y'."

277

Her soothing words did the trick and Meg sobbed as she told them that she and Ted had been married for six weeks. Before she could say another word Ted's father interrupted,

"If that buggers got y' in the family way a'll bloody well kill him." He then left the house as quickly as Meg had left the Bensons.

"You keep her here while a find that bugger. A'll bloody kill him when a get me hands on him," he shouted as he banged the back door shut.

It was a downcast Ted who entered the house not once having defended his actions to his irate father who had had great difficulty in restraining himself from hitting his son. As soon as Ted saw Meg and the state she was in his attitude changed and he held Meg close to him as he faced his father and mother.

"Y've got it all wrong Da, we didn't have t' get married, a never touched her afore we were wed. A married her 'cos a loved her an' it was the only way 'cos her Ma an' her Da wouldn't let us get married. A got a place f' us t' live in but everythin' went wrong when a lost me job an' it was me who persuaded her we should still get married. The's non o' this her fault, it's all mine."

Ted's father shook his head as he spoke.

"Well lad a'll say this f' y'. Y've always been as soft as clarts but y've more gumption than a ever thought y' would. An' you hinnie; well all can say t' y' is y've got guts f' takin' him on 'cos he doesn't kna' what the word responsibility means. Well y've made y' bed an' y'll have t' lie on it. When y've drunk y' tea an' tidied y' sel' up a bit y' can borrow one o' the lasses coats an' the pair o' y' can go t' Meg's together."

Turning to Ted he raised his voice.

"You lad can de the right thing, y'll be the one t' tell her folk just whose fault it is."

Ted and Meg had spent their first night in their new home. They were both cold and miserable; neither of them had slept and Meg's head was throbbing. Ted was hungry but there was not even a piece of dry bread in the house. Meg had not stopped crying since Ted had told Dan and Sarah and it had not turned out as Ted had promised her. Underneath Meg had known it wouldn't; Dan and Sarah were much older than Ted's parents and their values and way of life were entirely different to theirs. Dan did not speak when Ted told him, and seeing the sadness in his eyes broke Meg's heart. Sarah, as Meg knew she would, lost her temper and no matter what Ted said to her, her only response was.

"Flamin' lasses, y' bring nowt but a load o' trouble."

Meg knew she had no choice but to leave. She ran to her room and hastily threw a few clothes into a bag, not even stopping to pack the few items she had been collecting for her bottom drawer. As she left Meg realised she was leaving the place where she had been loved and wanted and as she walked away she knew she had lost, not only her home, but her Ma and Da; the two people she loved as if they were her real parents. Ted and Meg headed for the only place they could go to, the cottage, at least it was theirs and Ted had done as he said he had; he had paid the rent.

By twelve o' clock on their first day Ted was desperate, they needed food, coal for the fire and blankets for the bed. His only hope was Sam and his wife and their first child was due any day. When Ted returned, later that afternoon, he was smiling.

"They tuned up trumps Meg. Me Ma had already telt them an' the've give us some coal an' some blankets an' enough t' eat f' a couple o' days; our Sam's bringin' the coal up on his bike."

Over the next few weeks, with the help of Ted's family and to Meg's surprise, Tom and Nancy, they survived. Meg had some savings which were dwindling rapidly and the few pounds that were left would not last much longer. There seemed little hope that Ted would find a job. He was like many others who had searched for work for months, some for years, until they had given up hope of ever working again.

Meg was singing tonight. Tom and Nancy had invited them to their new house. Unlike Meg had thought their domino nights had not ended, in fact they were now more often. Wednesday at Ted and Meg's, Saturdays at Tom and Nancy's new council house. Nancy always prepared a substantial meal for them and Meg knew that it was the main reason for Ted's love of dominoes. Meg was feeling happier than she had been for some time, trying to put her worries behind her and her fear for the future out of her mind. They were always there looming at the front of everything they did together; spoiling the happiness that she and Ted should be sharing. She loved him but she could not give her love to him completely There was always something to stop her; something to worry about.

"Y' look happy t' night," Ted commented as he struggled with his collar and tie.

"I'm no different tonight than any other," Meg lied as she helped him fasten his collar stud.

She did feel happier tonight and yet there was no reason why she should be other than she had a funny feeling something was going to happen; something that might make life take a turn for the better.

Meg could never have imagined that the events of that night would change their lives dramatically. When they arrived at Tom and Nancy's Meg was shocked to see her Da was sitting at the kitchen table. There were no delicious smells floating around the kitchen and Meg feared the worst.

"What's happened to me Ma?" she cried out.

Dan immediately responded.

"The's nowt the matter wi' y' Ma that y' canna put right hinnie. A kna' y're alreet 'cos our Tom's kept us informed an' y' Ma kna's a'm here tonight. A've come t' ask y't' come home an' bring Ted wi' y'. Y' needn't worry about Ada an' Fred, the've moved int' one o' y' Ma's sisters houses an' the's plenty room f' both o' y'. Y' Ma misses y' an' if the truth be known so do a." Dan smiled, "Anyhow y'd be doin' us a favour an' all, 'cos y' Ma needs a bit o' a hand 'round the house; she's not gettin' any younger an' a'm not much help t' her."

Meg turned to Ted but did not give him time to speak as she answered Dan.

"We'll come home Da, me and Ted. Won't we Ted?" she asked. He didn't speak but Meg knew; the look on his face told her. "We'll come tomorrow Da, tell me Ma we've nowt much to pack and we'll be up in time for our dinner."

CHAPTER 15

Sarah had been watching the clock for the last two hours. She had walked backwards and forwards to the back gate six times, in the last half hour and still there was no sign of them. Just as she decided to make herself a pot of tea Dan, Meg and Ted walked through the back door. Anxious to know the results, and not directing her question to any of them, she asked.

"Well what did the' 'ave t' say at the eye infirmary?" Meg was the one to break the news.

"They told us there was nothing much they could do. When me Da had the stroke the' was damage to the nerves of his eyes an' it's permanent but they don't think it'll get any worse Ma."

Meg and Ted had been living with Dan and Sarah for more than six months and unlike Ada and Fred or Tom and Nancy they were more than happy to share the house with Dan and Sarah. The four of them enjoyed each other's company and it suited Meg and Ted as they were quite content to enjoy the privacy of Meg's old bedroom every night.Ted still had not managed to get a job but Meg was happily back at the Bensons and her wages made all the difference to their lives together.

A word from Dan was all it took to have the Benson's ask Meg to return. They had missed her nearly as much as Dan and Sarah and their children were overjoyed when she returned. Things were even better when Mr Benson told Meg she could wait on three nights a week in the snug. It was only three nights a week but with the help she gave them during the day her wages had risen substantially. She was grateful for the extra money especially since Dan's health had deteriorated and he could no longer work.

Sarah fussed over Dan, helping to take his coat off and then settling him in to his favourite chair. As soon as Dan was comfortable with a pot of strong sweet tea between his hands he spoke to Ted.

"Are y' ganna read the paper t' me then? A might not be able t' see very well but a still like t' kna' what's ganin' on. Is there owt in it about what the government's dein't' the pits now? An' what's that bloody Hitler up te now? Afore a finished at the pit a was contributin' t' get Labour candidates f' Parliament an' now some o' that money's gannin' towards the German an' Austrian refugees. The last thing the' said in the paper was that the' w' ganna de a door t' door collection f' money t' send t' the Czechoslovakian workers."

Ted patiently opened the pages of the paper scanning it for any news that would be of interest to Dan.

"It says here Da that the Executive Committee o' the Durham Miner's Association has forwarded resolutions to the Labour Party, the Foreign Secretary an' the Prime Minister, condemning the brutal an' inhuman treatment meted out by the Nazi Government to the men, women and children of the Jewish Race. The's nowt else about the pits but a think y' were right in what y' said afore, it'll tek' a war t' put right the problems o' the pits an' the bloody owners."

As Dan muttered about the years of trouble he had lived through Ted slowly turned the pages of the paper. Suddenly he jumped out of his chair and put his coat on. As he walked towards the back door he shouted for Meg.

"Meg, Meg, a'm ganin' out, the's a bit in the paper about them a used t' work for. The've won a contract t' build another factory. A'm ganin' up there straight away, y' never kna' a might be lucky an' get set on again if a get in quick."

283

Ted was lucky and the following week he was back in work; his enthusiasm so infectious that even Dan's health seemed to improve. He was so pleased with himself he finally forgave Meg for the loss of his cottage. He had never reproached her, and he knew that they had made the right decision when they came to live with Dan and Sarah, but underneath he yearned for a home of their own.

"Y' were right Meg, y' were so happy that night y' Da asked us t' come an' live wi' em. We've both got a job now an' it's funny the way things work out. A never thought it at the time, but y' Ma an' Da need us now that y' Da's bad an' y' Ma's findin' him hard work," Ted whispered as they lay in bed staring out of the bedroom window; Ted feeling tired but happy and Meg, content to be in his arms with the knowledge that her Ma and Da were sleeping peacefully in the room next door.

Another birthday and another Christmas passed and Meg could not have been happier. Ted was doing well at work, he was learning new skills and, being Ted, he ensured his boss was aware of them. He was determined that this time he would succeed and he did not have to work down the pit to do that.

Meg was busy pulling two pints of beer when Mr Benson walked into the snug with two policemen. She thought the policemen looked solemn but they said nothing to her; it was Mr Benson who broke the news.

"I'm sorry Meg but I'm afraid there's been an accident; it's Ted they've taken him to the County Hospital at Durham."

Meg continued pulling the beer as if no one had spoken.

"Meg, will you listen to me? Ted was involved in an accident this morning. There were only the two of them in the lorry and they are both alive but Ted's in a pretty bad way. Bob here thinks you should get straight through to the hospital so you go and catch the bus and get straight through there. I'll take over in here and than when we close I'll go down and tell Dan and Sarah what's happened."

Meg was numb; she prayed she would wake up and find it was all a dream. As she headed for the bus stop she knew it wasn't and she said a silent prayer.

"Please God let him be alright and don't let the bus be too long a need to get there as soon as a can."

Her prayer was answered; within two minutes the bus arrived. Meg sat on the bus, willing it to go faster, her mind in a turmoil, she was thinking of Ted yet her main concern was that she had not thanked Mr Benson for her bus fare or his kind words.

"Don't worry Meg I'm sure Ted 'll be alright, but I better warn you before you go, Bob said it was a sports car that they bumped and it went straight under the lorry and he thinks the driver was killed,."

When Meg arrived at the hospital she was directed to the ward that Ted and the lorry driver had been admitted to. The ward sister took her into see Ted and Meg was upset when she was told her that he was unconscious and she would only be able to stay for a few minutes. The sister gave the impression that she was too busy to bother with anxious relatives and this annoyed Meg, but for once she said nothing and meekly listened to the sister.

"You'll be able to come at visiting time tonight but just a quick look for now and then it would be better if you went home while we see to him. He won't know you're here and really we're breaking the rules letting you see him now."

285

Meg thought about the ward sister on the bus ride home and as usual she half muttered, half thought to herself.

"That bloody woman not once looked at me when she spoke." Meg even managed to smile to herself. "A wonder if it was her starched collar and cuffs that was the problem. If a hadn't have been so worried about Ted a would have given an answer to what she said."

Meg was pleasantly surprised when she first saw Ted at visiting time; she'd had a quick pot of tea and then caught the bus back to Durham. There was a young doctor in the room when she first arrived and although she was anxious her words to him were full of hope.

"He looks like he's just asleep; he doesn't look bad at all and a suppose when he wakes up he'll be alright."

As she spoke the ward sister walked into the room and Meg totally ignored her as the young doctor offered her a chair. He was an astute young man and began to answer Meg's unspoken questions.

"The only injury he has is to the back of his head; he must have had a hard knock because he was unconscious when they brought him in and I'm afraid only time will tell just how much improvement he'll make. I'm sure sister told you that it's for the best that you go home and we'll let you know each time you visit just what progress he's making."

Meg stayed for a while but when Ted made no movement she felt she had little choice but to do as she had been advised and make the long lonely journey home. Before she left she asked the sister to do one thing for her husband.

"Will you make sure the curtains are kept open at night; if he wakes up in the dark he'll not know where he's at and he always likes to look at the stars?"

The Sister gave Meg a knowing smile and as she left the ward Meg once more muttered to herself.

"A hope she doesn't think it's 'cos he's frightened of the dark."

Meg made that same journey every day sometimes accompanied by Ted's mother or father or by one of his brothers or sisters. By the fifth day the journey became a pleasant one. On the third day following his accident Ted regained consciousness and by the fifth day he was sitting up in bed, upset now that he knew the driver of the car had died, but sharing the occasional joke with his fellow patients. After two weeks he was back home and Meg was told there was no reason why he should not make a full recovery. He was pleased to be home but a dark cloud descended on him when he thought about his job.

"Meg," Ted asked. "If y' gan an' see the boss an' tell him a'm alright he might keep me job."

Meg agreed and it was a happy Ted who received her news.

"He says if you can be at work in a couple of weeks you've still got a job."

On this occasion when the factory was finished Ted did not lose his job, the firm was doing well and so was Ted. He was given a pay rise and offered as much overtime as he wanted. Meg listened as Ted discussed his day with Dan, his dinner was dry and warmed up, but he did not complain; coming home late from work meant more money in his pay packet.

"A dinna kna' what we buildin' these warehouses for an' nebody's saying owt definite but the's plenty o' rumours gannin' round," he told Dan.

Dan enjoyed talking to Ted; he was the only one who listened when he talked about what was happening in

Europe and, what was even better for Dan, Ted always seemed to have his own opinions which often coincided with his.

"It'll not be long afore we have another war," Dan told Ted. "The' say Hitler won't attack Poland but y' can tek my word f' it lad he bloody will an' then we'll all be in a sorry state. Them as can remember the last war dinna want another but mark my words Ted, it'll happen."

The following week the rumours became a reality; on the first of September Germany attacked Poland and two days later France and Great Britain declared war on Germany.

The first few months of the war had little effect on any member of the family, except for Sarah. She was with Dan all day and his constant discussion of the war drove her to distraction; the war had given him a new interest and became his only topic of conversation. Sarah was so grateful to Meg and Ted for a little light relief and she dreaded the day when they would find a home of their home.

The first year of the war was coming to an end when Tom and Nancy arrived for Sunday tea. Usually Sunday tea was a happy event for all of them but today was different; it was obvious to all of them Nancy had been crying. Tom realising that everyone in the house had noticed and wanting to prevent his wife any further embarrassment abruptly gave them his news. It took only two words from Tom for Nancy to break down into flood of tears.

"I've volunteered'."

The tea was wasted as all of the family took Nancy's side telling Tom that he should have considered them all before making such a rash decision. Tom never spoke as they all found reasons why he should not have volunteered. Finally Sarah took control of the situation.

"Well what's done's done; it's like history repeatin' itsel'. Hannahs' two did it behind her back an' you've done the same t' us. All any o' us can de now is pray that y'll get through it safe an' sound an' come back t'all o' us. It's a blessin' y've got ne bairns an' we'll always see t' Nancy an' a'm sure so will her Ma an' Da."

Sarah did not say anything further but she could not help but think of John and Bill.

"Aye," she thought, "Hannah got her two back in a fashion. Neither came back the same two lads that walked up that bank t' gan t' war an' poor soul, she never lived t' see her favourite come home t' her."

It was later in the afternoon, when things had quietened down before Tom explained why he had volunteered. It was a proud, if sad, Nancy who listened to her husband.

"I didn't bother much at first but when France fell to the Germans I realised that we all should be doing something to stop the Germans invading England and I knew it was time for me to do my bit." Tom turned to his mother. "Y' know Ma it was about fighting f' me country but more than that it was about fighting for you and me Da and Nancy and all of me family."

Ted had no intention of volunteering.

"A've listened t' y' Da an' 'ave listened to your Tom. Some of me mates have the same high principles as he has but f' the first time in me life a've got a job wi' decent money," he told Meg later that night. "We've got our names down f' a council house an' ne bloody war's ganna part us now."

Ted did not have to volunteer; seven months after Tom had left the dreaded letter arrived. Meg could not wait for him to come home from work; she knew by the envelope that it was his calling up papers.

"Hurry up Ted and open it; y' know what it is." Meg nearly cried in anticipation and the tears were real when Ted broke the news.

"A've t' report on Monday; a've been called up t' the Durham Light Infantry."

Ted could not believe what he was reading and Dan's comments only added salt to his wounds.

"Y' see what's happened, if y'd stuck t' the pit y' would 'ave been alreet the' need all the coal can get now."

Sarah was weary and trying hard to hold back her own tears as she consoled a tearful Meg.

"It's ne good hinnie the's nowt else we can de f' him. He's pulled through afore, more times than y'll ever kna', but it's like me Grannie always said, when y' times come the's nowt y' can de about it; an' y's Da's time's nearly here. It's like y' Da always says about them fightin' in the war, if the bullets got y' name on it it'll hit y'."

Meg understood what Sarah was saying but it did not help her. Tom had been posted to Malaya and Ted could be shipped abroad any day and now she was losing her Da. As Meg sat by Dan's side holding his cold white hand she spoke softly to him.

"That's what y' are Da. A never knew me real Da and our Jane's never told us who he is, but you're me Da and funny enough I don't really care. You were the one that told us that me real Da had two sons and the' both went in the RAF. You said one of them had been shot down and killed and, it's funny Da, he might be me half brother an' he might be the one that's about the same age as me, an' he's more me brother than our Tom is, but a

290

don't feel a thing for him; as far as I'm concerned our Tom's me brother and like he always said to me, we'll always be best friends."

This was Dan's third stroke and the doctor had told Sarah and Meg that this one would be the last. He had been in bed for over a week and when the doctor had called that morning he gave them the worst news he could have done.

"I'm sorry he's got pneumonia and there is nothing more that can be done for him. Keep him comfortable and try to look on it as a blessing. This last stroke would have left him severely disabled and you know as well as I do that Dan would never have wanted to be dependant on you for the rest of his days."

Sarah knew he was right but that did not make it any easier to bear but as usual she tried to be strong. Meg needed her and she was sure that soon Nancy would need all the care they were able to give her. She understood what Nancy was going through, Tom was her son and she did not just worry about him; she missed him. Nancy acted as though Tom was away on one long holiday and Sarah was only too sure that it would be only a matter of time before she cracked under the strain.

The back gate slammed and Meg looked through the kitchen window to see Ted crossing the back yard.

"A got a days leave so a thought a best mek' the most o' it an' get home t' see how he is today," Ted said as he held Meg tightly in his arms.

She told him what the doctor had said that morning and together they went upstairs to Dan and Sarah's bedroom. Dan appeared to be awake but he did not acknowledge Ted; instead he turned his head towards Meg and smiled. Dan had always enjoyed Ted's short leaves; he was always eager to hear the news of his training and how the war was progressing and Meg was upset to think, that perhaps on this occasion, he had not even recognised Ted.

Ted's first posting was to Brancpeth Castle.

"An easy walk home," he told Meg when he had, 'some time off', as he called it. His next posting was on the coast, it was still near to their home, but Ted was finding that 'some time off' and a longer journey home was not what he had expected; leave was rare and a lift home even rarer. His 'time off' today extended to another two hours and as he left he told Meg.

"If a canna get a lift back a'll have t' walk an' y' kna' what'll happen if a' m late."

As soon as Ted left Meg offered to help Sarah with Dan. His paralysis, after the stroke, made him difficult to manage and Sarah found it difficult to care for him without Meg's help. When they went into the bedroom Dan was agitated, he tried to say something to them but the more he tried the more agitated he became.

"What's wrong with him Ma?" Meg asked Sarah.

As Dan flung his good arm, hitting Meg and upsetting the pot of tea she had brought him, Meg looked at Sarah; she was upset and not meaning to, she shouted.

"We'll have to change all of his bed Ma now he's done that."

Sarah knew what was wrong as Dan mumbled Ted's name, she knew that Ted coming home so often could not go on any longer, she had to speak now.

"Y' Da's tryin' t' tell y' somat hinnie; a'm sorry hinnie but it's time f' y' t' say somat t' Ted. Ne soldier gets as much leave as him an' one o' these days he'll be caught an' y' kna' what'll happen t' him then."

Although Sarah's words haunted Meg and she could not get them out of her mind the events of the following week took priority.

She did as much as she could to help Sarah care for Dan and Ada helped when Meg was at work. The public house had never been busier; the soldiers who were now stationed in the village spent as much time as they were able in the bar ensuring they got as much to drink as they possibly could before being shipped abroad. The Benson's, although understanding, needed Meg to work longer hours as they now had officers billeted in their three spare rooms.

Four days after Ted's visit Dan died and it was a depleted family who attended the service at the chapel. Meg sent a message to Ted informing him of Dan's death and although she needed him more than anyone else she prayed he would not come; knowing his being there would prove Sarah right.

As the small procession left the cemetery Meg breathed a sigh of relief, she was upset but, thankful that Ted had not managed to come. As was the custom when there was a death in the street, the neighbours looked after the house while the family attended the funeral and prepared tea and sandwiches for their return. When they walked into the house Meg could not believe it; there was Ted, warming himself by the fire, a pot of tea in one hand and a sandwich in the other. As he offered his condolences Meg realised that Sarah was right and she would have to confront him as soon as everyone left.

At last Ada had gone home and Sarah had fallen asleep in her chair. Meg knew it was time to challenge Ted and she was relieved when he said.

"Dinna be daft Meg the've given me compassionate leave f' y' Da's funeral. A was late 'cos a couldn't get a lift but a can stay tonight 'cos a've arranged a lift back f' tomorro'."

The Benson's had agreed that Meg should take two days off for the funeral and although the house seemed empty without Dan, Ted helped to ease her sorrow that night. Meg was in tears when she waved goodbye to Ted the following morning as she watched him walk up the back street; turning every few steps to wave goodbye until he was out of sight.

"A'll go up to the market place with you and wait for your lift," Meg had offered as they ate their breakfast.

Ted insisted. "A canna be sure what time he'll come so y' best stay here wi' y' Ma, it's her that needs y' the most now. Me an' you'll have plenty other days together."

The policeman standing at the front door was the same one who had informed her of Ted's accident and Meg shook at the very sight of him.

"A'm sorry t' wake y' at this time of night but a've come t' ask y' if you've seen Ted?" he asked

Meg had been wakened from a deep sleep and all she could think of was another accident.

"A haven't seen him but is he bad this time?"

"He's gone AWOL, Meg, an' if y' kna' where he's at y' better tell us."

Meg should not have been surprised, but she had believed him and now this. What was worse she realised how naïve she had been. Her Ma and Da had been right and Ted being frequently at home after her Da's funeral should have made her realise. Sometimes he had stayed overnight and he always had a good excuse as to why he was on leave. Meg invited the policeman into the passage but there was little she could say.

"A haven't seen him for a few days but a promise when a do a'll let you know where he is."

A week passed before she had any news of Ted and Meg was relieved.

"A knew he wouldn't dare do it, thank God he's gone back," she muttered as she walked home from the Benson's.

She was thinking of Ted when she heard footsteps behind her but each time she turned to look there was no one there. As she turned the corner at the top of the dark back street she heard him.

"Meg, Meg, it's me Ted."

Meg had no doubts, it was him, and the policeman was right, Ted was AWOL. This time she did not believe a word he said and their argument ended with her telling him she would have nothing to do with him unless he turned himself in.

Ted was adamant.

"A will Meg, a promise y', but not 'til am ready. A want t' but a daren't, a kna' what the'll de t' me, an' a'm scared."

Meg knew what he meant and, against her better judgement, decided to give him time before giving himself up.

"A promise y' Ted a'll say nothing to anyone but tell me where you're staying and then I can come and see you."

Ted told her but he also had conditions.

"A'll tell y' where a'm stayin' Meg but y' canna come in case the police is watchin' y'."

During the next week Meg had no further contact with Ted. The policeman called to see her three times, and each time she lied telling him she had not seen Ted, nor did she know where he was. Meg could not sleep, she could not think straight, she had no idea what to do for the best and worst of all there was no one she could turn to for advice.

"A can't ask a soul to tell me what to do for the best," she said to herself. "If a do a'll have to tell them

295

everything and a know underneath what they'll tell me; they'll tell me to turn him in."

Meg got her advice sooner than she expected. She was so tired she could hardly keep her head up and today was the day she had to clean the officer's bedrooms. Mrs Benson rarely helped her but today she was only too ready to help change the bed linen. When they had finished she told Meg to go and make a cup of tea and she would join her in the kitchen. Meg was grateful for a cup of tea and a sit down was just what she needed. What she was not prepared for was Mrs Benson taking hold of her hand and giving her the advice she had so wished for.

"You're not with it Meg, are you?" Meg looked down; she had tears in her eyes and was so pleased Mrs Benson did not give her the opportunity to answer her question. "You needn't explain Meg, I know what's wrong, Mr Benson and I have known for a few days. Ted's been seen"

Meg was relieved; it helped to know that she had someone who shared her secret.

"A feel so ashamed of him Mrs Benson, what will people think of him and what will they think of me? It isn't just Ted either, me money's been stopped from the army, and a think a'm having a bairn; a don't just think, a know I am," a tearful Meg replied.

Mrs Benson took Meg in her arms.

"Try not to worry so much about everything," she told Meg. "We'll help you as much as we can but first you've got to help yourself and you have to help Ted, and you know what that means Meg. If you know where he is you have to tell the police."

"A'll go now, if I don't I never will," Meg told Mrs Benson.

Mrs Benson's reply was exactly what Meg needed to hear.

"You needn't go anywhere Meg, Bob is downstairs in the bar with Mr Benson. We knew you would do the right thing, I'll go for him now and if you want I'll stay with you while you tell him."

Meg was grateful to have a friend in Mrs Benson, she was not just her employer; it would be easier to talk to the policeman when she had the support of a friend.

"Before a tell you where you can find him can I ask you one thing?" Meg asked both Bob and Mrs Benson. "Will you promise me that you will never tell Ted that I was the one who told you where to find him?"

Bob looked sympathetically towards her.

"A promise y' hinnie neither Ted nor the Red Caps'll ever find out where a got me information from."

Two hours later Meg stood in a shop doorway only a few doors from the home of the people who were sheltering Ted.

"Y' so called friends is going to get a shock Ted," she said to herself as she watched the Red Caps march Ted out of the house; his friends following in the custody of the local police.

He turned his head towards the shop but Meg was sure he did not see her. Without shedding a single tear she made a further promise to Ted.

"A've made the stupidest promises to you in the past but this time Ted, a promise you, a never want to see you again."

Four weeks later a letter arrived from Ted. Meg answered it determined that it would be the one and only letter he would ever receive from her again. Her tears fell onto the paper as she told him their marriage was over. Ted replied begging her forgiveness but she did not reply. Many more letters arrived and although she read them she did not reply. He told her of his experiences in the glass house and how it had taught him a lesson he would never forget. He told her he loved her and that it was because of his love for her he did what he did. But Meg had heard it all before; she could not and would not forgive him this time.

It was a terrible winter and Meg was exhausted. She was now seven months pregnant and it was so cold she thought she never feel warm again. It had snowed all night and she had just finished clearing a pathway to get across the back yard for some coal for the fire. She was no longer working for the Benson's and spent most of her time caring for Sarah who had become frail and dependant since Dan had died. Immediately following Dan's death Sarah had surprised Meg; she appeared to be getting on with her life and coping without him but it did not last long. Dan's death had taken its toll; there was no news from Tom and the added worry of Ted, and Meg's pregnancy, proved to be too much for her to cope with.

The coal was wet with the snow; Meg could not get the fire to light and a shiver ran up her spine as she faced the black fire back.

"If you don't light this time, y' bugger, a'll give up an' me and me Ma'll have to freeze to death."

She shivered again, turned and there he was standing behind her; before she had time to speak he put a finger to his lips.

"Shush Meg a've come t' see you before I go abroad. I know you don't want to see me but I want to see you, just this once, and I want you to let me have my say."

Meg turned to face him; the very sight of him caused her to forget her carefully rehearsed words.

"Why did you not answer me letters? Me Ma told us you were havin' a bairn; you could at least have written and told me that." Ted burst into tears. "A'm really sorry f' everythin' I've put you through but a love you and please will y' give me another chance. 'Ave even been tryin' to learn to talk proper."

Meg looked at him, the boy she had loved since she was fifteen years old but there was something different about him and then she knew. She had married the boy she loved and the boy she loved had gone into the army, but it was a man in front of her now; a man begging her forgiveness. She was unsure of her feelings; could she ever love the man as much as she had loved the boy.

CHAPTER 16

"You could have waited a few more weeks Ma; you didn't have to die yet. Why couldn't you have waited 'til I'd had the bairn? I've got nobody now."

A few minutes earlier Meg had raised Sarah's head from the pillow trying to persuade her to take a drink. Sarah refused but as she opened her eyes and looked straight at Meg she struggled to speak her last words. For the rest of her life Meg would treasure but remember with sadness the final words her Ma said to her.

"Me Grannie always said lasses brought nowt but sorrow but a kna' now she was wrong. Y've had a funny life hinnie and it hasn't always been fair t' y' but y' Da loved y' an' y've brought me nowt but joy. From the day y' were born y' put somat back in my life a thought a'd lost f' ever an' a want y't' look in the old case Meg, the's somat in it f' y'."

Sarah had been ill for the last two weeks and when Meg asked the doctor to call she was not prepared for what he had to tell her.

"There's really nothing medically wrong with her Meg. It's just that she seems to have given up the will to live and her heart won't take any more strain."

Meg knew Sarah's time had come. It had been an hour since she had knocked on the passage wall to alert her neighbour. Mrs Johnson came immediately giving her eldest boy instructions to go for the doctor and then to go straight to Ada's with the message she was to come as soon as possible. As she waited Meg wept bitterly; Sarah had died in her arms before either the doctor or Ada arrived. In the precious minutes she had alone with Sarah after her death Meg stroked Sarah's hair as she said her final words to her.

"A'm sorry Ma for how a blamed you all of the time. A realise now it wasn't your fault and I understand why you wouldn't let me have me birth certificate. A know all the other things we used to fight about were just to protect me. A don't think a ever once said to you or me Da that a loved you both and it's only now a realise just how much and how much I'm goin' to miss you. You weren't just me Ma, and I know I always said our Tom was me best friend, but Ma, you were me real friend. You were the one who was always there for me, even if a didn't realise it at the time."

A knock on the door startled Meg and as she gently laid Sarah's head on the pillow the doctor walked into the room and told her what she already knew. When he left Meg was once again alone with Sarah. It was another hour before Ada arrived and as she climbed the stairs a tearful Meg could hear every word she said.

"What the hell d' y' want now; a had t' gi' Fred his supper afore a come an' if he finds out y've sent f' me f' nowt the'll be nowt said?"

Meg did not retaliate; this was no time for an argument with Ada.

"Me Ma's dead Ada; she died two hours ago and the doctors been and gone," was all she said.

Ada was shocked; she had not realised that Sarah had been so ill. Although she called three times a week she rarely stayed more than half an hour always having an excuse to leave and usually it was because of Fred.

"A didn't kna' she was s' bad Meg," Ada snivelled. "Y' should have said. Mind a couldn't have done much 'cos now a'm havin' a bairn Fred says a haven't t' de much f' other folk; y' kna' what he's like, Meg, if his meal's not in front o' him when he comes in."

Meg did not answer but thought of Nancy. It should have been her standing beside her; not Ada. It was

Nancy who had helped her over the past few weeks; it was Nancy who had been more of a daughter to Sarah than Ada had ever been.

However, it was Ada who turned out to be the practical one and Meg was relieved, she did not want to leave Sarah's side, she did not want to face the next few hours of neighbours doing what she knew must be done.

"When you go Ada, will you call at Nancy's and tell her about me Ma?" Meg asked.

Ada was relieved but could not resist asking Meg one question before she left.

"Afore a go Meg did me Ma mention me, an' did she say owt about the house an' things."

Meg answered truthfully.

"No she didn't."

"Right then a'll go f' Mrs Johnson," Ada replied. "A'll ask her t' get somebody t' help her lay me Ma out an' a'll ask if one o' her lot can go f' Nancy. A canna stay much longer 'cos y'kna' what Fred's like, he'll be worryin' about us."

Meg shivered at the mention of Fred.

"An' dinna worry about the undertakers, a'll see t' them in the mornin' after Fred's gone to work," Ada shouted as she went down the stairs.

Meg sat with Sarah until Mrs Johnson arrived and then curiosity got the better of her. Before going downstairs she took the case from the top of the wardrobe and as soon as she settled into a chair in front of the fire she opened it. At first she could not understand what Sarah had meant; she already knew what the case contained; Death certificates, Birth certificates and Marriage lines, Death insurance policies and old photographs, all put away for safe keeping.

"Me Ma must have meant her death policy to pay for the funeral," Meg mumbled and then she found it; a

302

brown envelope marked Last Will and Testament of Sarah Charlton.

Meg opened the envelope and started to read Sarah's will.

"A canna believe it," she said to herself. "Me Ma's left me the house and everything in it. The other two houses are to be shared between our Tom, Ada and Jane."

Immediately Meg realised the trouble that lay ahead.

"Our Tom'll not mind but there'll be hell to pay with our Jane and Ada; well a know what a'm going to do, a'll burn it and then there'll be three houses; one for our Tom, when he comes back, one for Jane and one for Ada."

As Nancy slept fitfully beside her, Meg lay thinking of Ted and Tom.

"If you two had been here you would have cared for me; me husband and me best friend. And Ted if you could have been here lying beside me I might have felt better; but you can't be, you're thousands of miles away; you're stuck in a bloody desert somewhere in Africa."

Meg's thoughts turned to Tom; she had no idea where he was but she hoped he would be alright wherever he was, especially for Nancy's sake who had never once lost faith, even though it was months since she had heard from him. She was so confident he would come home to her; to the house that she so lovingly cared for. She even ensured the gardens were just as Tom had left them; when he returned everything would be just as it was when he had left.

If either of them had known Tom's fate that night their sorrow would have been greater. Sarah had lost her son only hours before she had died. Now there was no one left to carry on the family name. No one left to fulfil

Sarah's ambitions for her first born; Rob, the child she had loved above all others.

Tom had been posted to Singapore in September 1941, his years of experience in the St. Johns Ambulance Brigade directing his fate in his first year of service. He could not believe his luck when he was posted to Singapore. He loved the place and for the first three months he was there it was one long holiday. He often told his comrades.

"If Nancy could have been with me this would have been the happiest three months of me life."

The nights were hot, tropical and airless but to Tom they were not as oppressive as he had been led to believe. There was an absence of winds and dust and there were not as many flies or pests as he had been told there would be. As far as Tom was concerned the warnings about Singapore he had been given were greatly exaggerated.

Unlike many of his comrades he loved to watch the friendly, light coloured little chee cha, a small variety of lizard, chirping cheerfully from the wall showing off its skills; running upside down across the ceilings and then rushing headfirst down vertical walls. Tom used his leave sightseeing in Singapore City and around the island. He visited the Raffles Museum with its fine library and read about the amazing career of the great Englishman who had founded Singapore one hundred and twenty years before. Tom stared in amazement at the famous Raffles Hotel but never plucked up the courage, or had the opportunity, to enter its famous doors.

Tom did not believe, as his comrades did, that anything bad could happen here; every one carried on with their lives as if the war had nothing whatsoever to do with them. He was reassured after overhearing two officers talking and later that night he told his comrades what he had heard.

"A heard what the' said and the' said the Japanese were bluffin' and they would not strike us; the' said Singapore was a fortress."

Little did Tom know that only four months after his arrival, he would witness in his peaceful surroundings the final, tragic two weeks before the surrender of Singapore and for a short time after would ponder his own fate.

Singapore was not the fortress Tom had been led to believe it was. The small detachments of Japanese were incredibly fast and skilled; they were unbeatable. There were insufficient airfields, too few planes and not enough ground troops to guard what airfields there were. Confusion prevailed; field and machine guns were fired without targets and so Tom witnessed the fall of Singapore.

He did his best, using the skills he had been taught in his training to the best of his ability, but he was not prepared for the horrors he would soon encounter. He went without sleep, night after night, as more and more casualties needed his care. There were not only men wounded in battle but there were those who had slept, marched and fought in swamps and jungles, men with fevers, more than half of them having malaria.

During the second Sunday in February Tom's war reached a point he never could have imagined. After a seventeen hours barrage the Japanese landed on the west of the island and the confused fighting lasted until the following Sunday. Tom saw death and bloodshed in numbers he could not comprehend. Not only did he witness the fall of his friends and fellow soldiers but he wept when he saw the horror of the three thousand civilians who were killed in only one week. Tom was spared the torment of weeks, months or years in the hands of the Japanese; two days after capitulation a stray bullet ended his war.

It was ten days since Sarah had died and Nancy was still staying with Meg. Nancy had wanted Meg to stay with her until after the baby was born but Meg refused.

"A want to stay in me own home to have the bairn," Meg told Nancy.

Nancy understood but she wanted to be at home to ensure that everything was perfect for Tom's return from the war.

"What about a compromise Meg?" Nancy asked.

Meg was relieved when Nancy suggested she go home that afternoon but not until she was sure Meg had everything ready for when her time came. The bed was to be brought downstairs and Nancy would call every day and then stay for two weeks once the baby was born.

As Nancy left she reassured Meg.

"The only thing left t' do is t' bring the bed downstairs; promise you won't go up there 'cos a'll get me Da t' come later an' bring it down."

When Meg heard a knock on the door she was surprised it was not Nancy's father, as she had expected, but Ted's brother Sam.

"Can a come in?" he asked. "Nancy called t' ask if a could bring y' bed downstairs 'cos her Da was at work an' a'm on night shift so a've come straight up."

Sam wasted no time in rearranging the furniture in the parlour to accommodate the bed while Meg, in an attempt to hide her embarrassment, busied herself making a pot of tea for both of them. She had not seen Sam or any of his family since she had told Ted their marriage was over. Meg knew she was wrong; she should have gone to see them after Ted came to see her but she was afraid; she still was not sure if she would ever be able to completely forgive or love Ted again.

The work done Meg and Sam sat drinking their tea; Sam, just as embarrassed as she was. Meg knew Nancy's father was not working and suddenly realised just how shrewd Nancy had been. Meg was the first to break the silence.

"My but she's a fly one is Nancy but a'm pleased to see you Sam. A'd really like to see your Ma and Da. Do you think they would make me welcome after all this time?"

Meg knew Sam was a man of few words who rarely showed his feelings and she was more than confident in believing his answer to her question.

"A don't think y' should be ganin' anywhere at the minute Meg, not in your condition, but a can tell y' one thing; y' just have t' say the word an' me Ma'll be up here like a shot. Me Da never visits any o' us but 'ave a feelin' he'd come an all if y'd let him. A kna' y've had a rough time an' a understand now how y' felt. A didn't at the time though, an' a thought y' should 'ave stood by him. Anyhow it's all ower now an' he's had t' gan in the finish so a think it's time f' us all to be a family 'til he comes home."

Meg's reply was simple but sincere.

"You're all welcome Sam, all of Ted's family. Will you tell them for me?"

As Sam left he touched Meg's shoulder.

"A'll tell them the' all welcome," his following words giving Meg a fresh hope for the future. "Y' kna' Meg a dinna kna' y' very well but from what our Ted always said about y' it seems y're a real fighter an' y'll let nebody get the better o'y'. Well y' dinna gi' us that impression now. Lil said t' tell y' that when y've had the bairn y' needn't worry she'll help y'. She'll help when y' havin' the bairn if y' want? An' a'll see to anythin' that Ted would have seen t' if he'd been here."

Meg waved to Sam as he left the house,

"In a way," she said to herself, "it could be Ted walking down there; a bit smaller but they look the same from the back."

Meg's first job after Sam left was to rake some coal from the fireback onto the fire. Sam had thrown a full bucket on to the back before he left and filled another ready for the following morning. Meg was tired but Sam's visit had raised her spirits; the darkness that had hung over her for the past few days had lifted. She put some fresh tea in her pot and settled into the fireside chair. It had always been Sarah's chair and this was the first time Meg had sat in it since Sarah had died. Recently Meg had thought of nothing other than the events of the last few months but now the time had come to think of the future.

"Sam's right," she said to herself. "I've let things get on top of me. I've got no control over the future but it's about time a pulled meself together and got on with me life."

Meg's daughter was two days old when Jane arrived to find her daughter and granddaughter being well looked after by Nancy and Ted's mother. Ted's mother called the day after Sam's visit and never once left Meg during her short and uneventful labour. Nancy was staying with Meg for as long as she was needed and Ted's mother had promised to do as much as she could to help. When it started to snow it was a relieved Jane who excused herself.

"A can see y' dinna need any help; a was ganna offer t' stay but a'll away now an' get the bus 'cos if it sna's

308

much more the'll stop runnin' an' then a'll have ne choice but t' stop wi' y'."

Meg got out of bed to look out of the kitchen window as Jane crossed the yard. While Jane had been in the parlour with Meg Nancy had stayed in the kitchen, only speaking to Jane when she brought her tea. Meg turned to Nancy and laughed.

"Who were you trying to impress? You would have thought the Queen had come for tea. No pot of tea for our Jane; me Ma's best china tea set, dainty little sandwiches and Ted's Ma's jam tarts for our tea. Well Nancy let's get the pots out and let's me and you have a good strong pot of tea."

Nancy laughed but she knew Meg was worried and she was curious as to what Jane had said.

"Never mind the pots Meg; hurry up an' tell us what she said.

"It's alright for now Nancy," Meg replied. "A can stay here; Jane says she's talked to Ada and there's nothing they can do until Tom's back and it's a good job 'cos a don't know where a would have gone."

Nancy was pleased, but still worried; she knew Ada only too well and felt the need to reassure Meg.

"You needn't worry Meg; you know you'll always be welcome with me an' Tom."

Nancy's solution, although reassuring, was not Meg's and as Meg knew, only too well, when Tom returned it would not be Nancy's.

"Thanks Nancy a know you mean well," Meg told her, "but when our Tom comes home you need to be on your own and if I'm honest a think if me and Ted are to have a future we'd need a place of our own to sort things out. Anyhow a'm alright for now except that Jane says that Ada says a have to start and pay them rent 'cos Fred insists the house isn't mine it belongs to them; the

309

greedy bugger. A told her a will but you should have our Tom's share."

Nancy was not amused and told Meg in no uncertain terms.

"How dare they Meg after you've lived here all this time and anyway look at the state of the place. You still haven't got any electric and the back kitchen's dropping to bits. If a see any of them a'll give them a piece of me mind and as far as the rent's concerned a know what Tom would say about that."

Even though Nancy was annoyed Meg was thankful for Jane's visit; at least now she knew where she stood and she still had a roof over her head. She slept well that night wakened only by the hungry cry of her daughter who settled immediately after a feed and a nappy change. The next morning Meg woke early; the house was quiet and Nancy fast asleep in the bed beside her. Her daughter was sleeping soundly in the old cot at the side of the bed and Meg's thoughts turned to Ted and the last time she had seen him.

Following his spell in the glass house he had been posted back to Brancpeth Castle but she rarely saw him, he had learned his lesson. The threat of being posted abroad was soon to become a reality and he had already told her if he stopped coming home altogether it meant he had gone.

"A don't know where the'll send us but a'll write when a can an' tell y' where a'm goin'," Ted had told her.

Meg smiled as she thought of his final words to her.

"An' if a have to talk proper a'll try but a promise a'll de me best to write proper."

Ted's letter came only days before Sarah died; he was on his way to North Africa.

310

Meg was not normally superstitious but if she had known that Tom had died only hours before his mother and Ted had reached his destination at the same time she was giving birth to their daughter she might well have admitted that it was a little more than coincidence.

After an arduous journey via Cyprus and Iraq Ted took his place in the front line just in time to share in the chaos created by Rommel's great out flanking thrust.

As Meg sought to achieve the best life possible for herself, and their daughter, Ted was caught up in a spectacular battle which some said later was nothing more than a miracle of desert navigation in the dark. Ted found himself in the eighth Durham Light Infantry which was part of the fiftieth division which sought its own salvation in a highly original manoeuvre. They broke out through the enemy lines mounted on their own transport and anything else that happened to come along. The eighth pierced the Italian defences and drove south westwards across the German communications for forty miles. Deep in the desert the column turned eastwards and drove back to the Egyptian frontier south of Bir Hachiem. During this time Ted fought as well as the next man shooting the enemy as they went forward.

During the next few weeks Meg heard nothing from Ted, and as Pamela was a loved and contented child demanding nothing but food and comfort, Meg returned to work at the Bensons taking her daughter with her. Pamela slept the hours away while Meg helped Mrs Benson with the never ending rounds of housework and cooking and as their children were now at school Meg's duties were changed to giving Mr Benson help in the snug. The arrangement suited Meg; not only did she need the money but she loved the work and especially the company of the many soldiers who frequented the snug.

311

Meanwhile Ted was playing his part in the bloodiest few months in the history of the Durham Light Infantry. The sixth, eighth and the ninth Durham Light Infantry were badly mauled in an ill conceived attack on a position called Ruin Ridge where they were left unsupported against the Panzers. After being brought up to strength again they were put into the South of the Alamein Line where Ted remained during the opening of the battle. After the initial attack they were bogged down and Ted found himself under the command of the New Zealand Division who were preparing for Operation Supercharge, which was designed to create the conditions for a breakout.

After a four hour march by moonlight Ted arrived at their forming up place covered in dust and sand. After standing shivering for two hours in the bitter cold he was grateful for the warming rum ration given to him and his comrades just half an hour before the assault was due to commence. Ted and his fellow soldiers advanced through a swirling, choking, flame slashed pall of dust and smoke. Over a maze of slit trenches, strong points and craters they advanced. Ted could hear snatches of pipe music in the distance as the highlanders attacked alongside them and occasionally he could distinguish war cries from the Maori Battalion attacking from the right.

For nine days Ted lived through a nightmare; he saw a desert littered with smouldering vehicles, corpses, groups of weary soldiers and scores of wounded soldiers suffering agonies of thirst. Ted lay in the sweltering confines of the narrow slit trenches thinking of Meg, and the child he must now have, as he listened to the sickening sounds that denoted another victim of the battle.

Meg was feeding Pamela who was growing at the rate of knots; or so everyone told her. She was nine months old and taking notice of everything and everyone around her. Meg knew that had her father been at home she would not have received the attention family and friends bestowed upon her. Pamela wanted for nothing; the Bensons and Sam, her surrogate father, looked to her every need. Ted's parents were always ready to give a helping hand but Meg was surprised when his mother and father arrived early one morning. She had not expected a visit from his mother so early in the day and what was more unusual Ted's father was with her.

" Have y' seen the Echo this mornin'?" Ted's father asked.

Meg did not need to answer she knew immediately what he meant.

"Ted's been wounded, his name's here, look his name's right in the middle o' the list."

Ted was wounded on the seventh day of the battle. He was one of the many lying in the trench wondering what would happen next. Fortunately, unlike many of his comrades, Ted was lucky; he was picked up and transported to the nearest field hospital. He spent two hours in the operating theatre, four weeks recuperating and then he was fit for battle again.

The pause in Ted's war gave him time to write home. He had finally received the news that he had a daughter and this was his opportunity to send her a Christmas card and to Meg a selection of photographs, one of which was a fellow soldier whom he had asked to be his daughter's godfather. Unfortunately neither Meg nor Pamela would ever meet the friend of Ted's who had seriously accepted the duties of godfather to Ted's daughter. His war ended on the same day Ted was wounded; he was not as lucky as Ted. It was the New Year before Ted was fit enough

313

to rejoin his regiment; the soldiers had earned a reputation as shock troops and there was plenty more in store for Ted during the following months.

Once the initial shock wore off, Meg's life once more slipped back into its usual pattern. Ted's reassuring letters were a great comfort to her and the rest of his family and together they got on with the pleasurable task of raising his daughter. The war seemed never ending and fearing that Ted may never return Meg became more determined than ever to get on with her life. It was one of her neighbours who gave her the opportunity to widen her horizons.

"Y' never seem t' have any pleasure Meg an' y' certainly a bit young t' have stopped havin' any fun," her neighbour commented.

"If y' want, 'cos a can see the bairns nee bother, a'll mind her f' y't' have the odd night out when y' not workin'."

At first Meg declined but after a little gentle persuasion on her neighbour's part, she accepted.

"Right a will," she told her. "But just once to see how she settles and you'll have to mind her here, a don't want her to go to bed in somebody else's house."

Following her trial night out Meg was only too willing to accept any further offers. Meg's war became fun, she danced, she partied and life became one long merry go round. She still worked hard at the Benson's and gave her daughter all the love and attention she needed, always ensuring that Pamela was fast asleep in bed before she left her in the care of her neighbour. Meg was never unfaithful to Ted but as she told one of her new found friends.

"I might as well enjoy myself 'cos I've no idea what he's getting up to over there and if he's anything like the soldiers billeted in the village he'll be up to no good."

Ted was not enjoying himself. Pamela had had her first birthday before he was back in the battle. A few weeks' extra training gave him time to recuperate and he was as fit as he had ever been when he went back to the front line. During the whole desert campaign of the Eighth Army there was only one natural obstacle to be crossed, Wadi Zigzaou, a ravine sixty feet wide with a stream about thirty feet wide and eight feet deep at the bottom of it. It was liberally defended by mine fields, a network of deep trenches, covered in pill boxes and had anti tank ditches in addition to the geographical hazards. It was here that Ted found himself in an assault by moonlight and as he glanced upwards at a clear sky, for a few seconds, he thought of Meg and said a short prayer.

"Please God if a don't make it make sure Meg and me daughter are safe and they have a happy life. You know who they are God; they're at home and they'll be under the same stars that are shining down on me tonight."

Ted did not end his prayer with a simple amen he had spoken to God as if he was standing next to him.

Despite fierce opposition from the Italians, Ted, with the rest of the Eighth Army, was joined by the Ninth and using scaling ladders they advanced across the Wadi. Throughout the following day they forced their way into the emplacements, some of which they shared with the enemy, while they waited for tanks and anti tank guns to join them. Ted was sure his war was about to end when on the second day a rainstorm swelled the stream and grounded their air support. He could see smoke rising from the wrecked tanks and knew they were losing this battle and it would be more than likely his last. The following day they received orders to withdraw and it was not to be the end for Ted. He began the long weary trek back across the mud flats and the foul smelling waters of the Zigzaou; this time he had been lucky but many of his comrades had not; they had not received the order.

CHAPTER 17

"Will you come and hold these steps for me." Meg shouted through from the parlour to the kitchen. "If it falls off the bairn'll get a bucket full of whitewash all over her head."

"Y'll have t' wait a minute Meg," a harassed Mrs Johnson replied, "a canna de everythin' at once an' the's somebody at the front door."

Mrs Johnson, Meg's next door neighbour, had kindly offered to help decorate the parlour but she was proving to be more a hindrance than a help.

"The door's open," Meg shouted. "It'll be just be our Ada or Nancy an' they can let the' selves in. Will you please come and hold the steps?"

Meg and Mrs Johnson stared in amazement at the young man in uniform who walked into the parlour. There was no mistaking him; a thinner, older Ted from the one who had left three years ago; his brown eyes still sparkled and the grin on his face was as mischievous as ever but what Meg noticed immediately was his shiny white teeth marred only by that single black one.

"What the hell are you doing here?" was all Meg could think of to say as she looked towards Mrs Johnson who was staring at Ted, her mouth wide open and a look of disbelief on her face as if she had just seen a ghost.

Meg questioned Ted as she climbed down from the steps.

"A thought you were in hospital somewhere in South Africa, that's what y' said in your last letter?"

Ted looked down on his daughter who had been playing on the mat at the side of the bed, content to amuse herself until the stranger entered the room. Pamela started to cry and Meg scooped her up in arms and as she turned to Ted her voice was full of anger.

317

"Now look what you've done, you've made her cry, comin' in like that and frightenin' the life out of her."

It was only a few seconds, but to Ted it seemed like a lifetime, before Meg still clutching their daughter flung herself into his arms.

"I'm sorry but a couldn't let you know," he told her. "And a think you're not talking as proper as you should be in front of our daughter after a've worked so hard at it to impress you."

They looked at each other and Meg knew instantly she could forgive him, they would share a lifetime together. There would be plenty time in the future for Ted to tell her what had happened; for now he needed to hold her; to hold his daughter, the child he had tried to picture for three long years.

The decoration was forgotten and Meg busied herself preparing a meal after Mrs Johnson was sent home following a few tactful hints from Meg. Meg was too excited to eat and Pamela refused to leave her side as she rudely stared at the stranger.

"Leave her alone Meg" Ted said. "Don't play war with her, she'll get used to me eventually. For now let's eat our tea and I'll tell you what happened. A nurse at the hospital wrote the first letter t' tell you a had stones in me kidneys and bladder. The' thought it was caused with being so long on the desert; something about the sand had accumulated. The' had to take one of me kidneys out and seemingly it was touch and go whether a would pull through. Well a survived an' they sent me home. They say there'll be no more fightin' for me and a've got a fortnights leave before a report to Nottingham."

Meg cried as she apologised to Ted.

"A'm sorry about the awful reception a gave you Ted, it was just so much of a shock to see you stood there."

She wiped her tears and smiled at Ted as she spoke to Pamela.

"This is your Daddy Pamela, he's come home from the war and he's going to live with us. A think we have something to ask him though. Shall we ask your daddy what them stripes on his arms are for?"

There were further tantrums with Pamela that night.

"Don't like me Daddy, Mammy, an' he's not sleeping in our bed with us," Pamela cried.

Fortunately Ted understood.

"Its alright Meg, if we let her lie in the middle of us she might get used to me after a few nights and then we'll be able persuade her that she's a big girl now and she should be in a bed of her own."

Meg got some time off work and spent two happy weeks with Ted. She quickly realised she could love the man as much as she had the boy and Pamela slowly warmed to his loving nature, but it wasn't always easy and she often ignored him. At first when he took her hand she would leave the house with him but after a few steps Pamela would cry for Meg and she had to accompany them on their walk.

It was the beginning of his second week of leave when Ted finally won her trust. Pamela knew about Uncle Sam's pigeons but she had never seen them. A visit to the allotments was tempting and Pamela finally agreed to go with Ted without Meg. It was a happy Ted who arrived back home two hours later with an even happier Pamela sitting on his shoulders.

That night a major hurdle was surmounted; Pamela was sleeping in her own bed.

"It wasn't the pigeons that did it Meg," Ted told her. "She liked them but we picked some daisies an' a made her a daisy chain. A don't know how but it did the trick, we might have chosen her name afore a went away, but from now on you can call her Pamela but she'll always be Daisy to me."

Most nights Meg and Ted talked until the early hours of the morning; Ted carefully avoiding the bad times of the war and Meg avoiding her good times. One night he asked her about Sarah.

"She seemed fit enough after y' Da died Meg, and you said in your letters she was copin' alright."

The mention of Sarah brought tears to Meg's eyes but she was glad he had asked; the time had come to share her grief with Ted.

"She was at first Ted, but after a few weeks she seemed to stop taking an interest in anything. A don't know what it was Ted, but a'm sure she just died of a broken heart. An' its funny, an' I've often thought about since, but she said somat about our Tom just afore she died. A couldn't understand her, but a've got a funny feeling somat's happened to him. We still haven't heard a thing an' a think Nancy's beginning to feel the same way. Nancy will never admit it but me Ma always said she would crack one day. The other strange thing is, you know how she always kept the house and the gardens immaculate; the garden's always been just as our Tom left it but she hasn't bothered these last few months. The place is clean enough but not like it used to be and she's not her usual self. It's not just me that noticed either, a was talking to her Da the other day and he says she hardly ever calls to see them and before she was hardly ever away."

Two months before the war in Europe officially ended Ted's war was over. He was offered the choice of staying in the forces or of becoming a reserve and working down the mine. To Meg's surprise he chose the latter.

"I'll be alright," he reassured her. "You know yourself a'm different now; a think a've grown up in the last few years. But a'll make you another promise, as well as talking proper, a won't be at the pit all me life, a'll make somat of meself, a'll show you and Daisy and one day we 'll have a lot more than the pit or the army could ever give us."

"Two months at the pit an' he's never lost a shift," Sam remarked as he danced around the room with Pamela.

Ted was dancing with Lil; everyone was dancing family, friends, neighbours and even Ada and her fractious son were smiling. The war was over and it was a time for celebration. There was only one thing that marred their joy; there was still no news of Tom and Nancy was the only member of the family who had declined Meg's invitation to join them.

Meg was surprised when Jane accepted her invitation and she had arrived the night before with John and all of their family.

"You'll all have to sleep on the floor if you're staying," Meg told them.

They did not mind; all of Jane's children were used to making do and none of them were yet married. John and Jane had seven children, the eldest one year younger than Meg and the youngest only two years older than Pamela.

After passing Pamela to Ted, Sam took the opportunity to speak to Meg.

321

"Is it right what a've heard about Ted an' the union?"

Meg knew instantly what Sam was talking about.

"Aye Sam a think you're right."

Meg had overhead John and Ted talking the night before and as they had been celebrating for most of the day Ted, who could never hold his drink, held the chair and his tongue was loose.

"I always said the pit wasn't for me John," Ted slurred. "But by a've had me eyes opened since a came back. Since we got the National Union a think at last the miners might get somewhere. I wasn't interested in politics afore the war but a see things different now and I've decided to put me name up for the union. I'm pretty sure a'll get elected 'cos since a've been back I've said me bit a few times an' a lot of me marrers have said they'll support me."

That night Ted was asleep before his head touched the pillow but the following morning Meg took her opportunity and challenged Ted.

"Hangover or no hangover Ted you'll answer me question. Have you put your name up for the union?" Meg continued before Ted had time to answer her. "If you have you can take it off the list. A thought it was too good to be true you settling down at the pit. You know what the unions are like? You'll bring us nowt but a load of trouble getting involved with that lot."

Ted listened but said nothing; he was determined his future lay with the union.

Ted succeeded and although Meg would not admit it she was proud of her husband. In a short time he had proved to everyone that the man who had come back from the war was not the boy who went to war. He had only been back at the pit for a few months and he had won the vote. Soon their lives began to change; Ted still never lost a shift at the pit but Meg often resented his union work which meant meetings after work, sometimes lasting for hours on end.

"You know Meg," he told her one night when he returned from one of his many meetings. "I think the owners have had it; I think the labour party'll make sure this time the pits are nationalised."

Ted was in fore shift and as usual at the end of his shift had stayed back for a meeting. It was already two o'clock in the afternoon and he had just gone to bed when there was knock on the front door. Meg spoke to Pamela as she hurried to answer the door.

"A've just managed to keep you quiet so your Dad can get some sleep and now somebody's knocking on the door wakening him up."

When she opened the door Meg was surprised to see Nancy's father. She did not have time to ask him in before he gave her the news she had dreaded.

"It's Nancy Meg, it's a good job a called round there first thing this mornin' 'cos a just got there in time."

Meg ushered him into the kitchen as he continued speaking.

"The've taken her to the asylum Meg; she tried t' de away wi' hersel'. When a walked in the front door this mornin' she was lyin' at the bottom o' the stairs. She'd fixed a rope from the banister; thank God she didn't de a very good job o' it. The doctor says she didn't harm hersel' at all but she's snapped Meg; she won't talk an' she's just starin' into space. The doctor was good an' he got her straight in but a hated leavin' her there. Will y' gan an' see her? Her Ma says she can't face ganin't' the asylum."

Meg made Nancy's father a pot of tea and after reassuring him she would visit the following day, told him to go home and see to Nancy's mother.

After Nancy's father left Meg was so upset she woke Ted with the news.

"I'll have to go tomorrow Ted so after work come straight home and mind Pamela."

Ted was as concerned for Nancy as Meg was and he hurried home from work the next day to find Meg waiting with her coat on. It was a hot August day and the bus was full. Meg's concern was momentarily forgotten as she tried to quell the waves of sickness she experienced from the heat and the nauseous smell of stale cigarette smoke. It was not just that most of the passengers were smoking; Meg was used to that from hours of working in the snug, but the gentleman in the seat beside her was smoking pashas, a cigarette smell that Meg abhorred.

As the bus stopped and started at the frequent bus stops Meg listened to snatches of conversation from the other passengers and her ears pricked when she heard an elderly man behind her mention something about the Japanese and a bomb.

"That's the end o' the bloody Japs; the'll have t' surrender now," he told the woman who was sharing a seat with him. "The' say it happened the other day; the Americans 'ave dropped an Atomic Bomb on a place called Hiroshima; the' say it's killed thousands o' them." Meg was not interested in the bomb but the news of a Japanese surrender could mean news of Tom and that was just what she needed to tell Nancy.

Meg was not prepared for what she was about to witness in the asylum and it made a lasting impression on her. After much pleading she was finally allowed to see Nancy and when she finally returned home she told Ted what she had seen.

"At first Ted a honestly wished a hadn't gone t' see her. She didn't seem t' know me; at least a don't think

324

she did. It took me more than hour to find somebody who would take me to see her an' a think a must have walked for miles. It's a massive place and everywhere's locked. The nurse who finally took me to see Nancy was enormous an' she had a great big bunch of keys fastened around her waist. She had to unlock every door we went through and then lock them behind us. I was terrified; I thought I'd never get out of the place. When we finally got to where Nancy was it was awful; there must have been about forty other poor souls there and Nancy was just sat there as if there was not another soul in the place. She didn't say a thing to me; she just stared into space."

Ted made Meg a pot of tea while she nursed her daughter; comforted by the closeness of her. As she drank her tea Meg told Ted about the conversation she had overheard on the bus and he confirmed the events in Japan.

"Aye Meg it's right enough and if that's what's happened, what a bloody end."

The following month it was the end and the newspapers were full of it.

"Are you listening Meg?" Ted shouted through to the back kitchen. "It says here that the Japanese signed the instrument of surrender on board the United States battleship Missouri in Tokyo Bay. That's it Meg, it's really over now and it says it's all over six years and one day after it was started by Hitler's attack on Poland."

The following day Meg visited Nancy. Nancy's father had visited her every day but there was no good news and Meg decided it was time for her to go and see for herself.

"She's no better," she told Ted who was waiting with Pamela when she got off the bus. "The nurse says she won't eat and she never spoke a word all the time a was there. She just sits there staring in front of her as if she was looking or waiting for something."

During the following year Meg continued to work for the Bensons, taking Pamela with her, while Ted became more and more involved with his union activities. Pamela shared her love between them equally; she still enjoyed accompanying Meg to the Bensons but a walk with her father became a priority over any other activity. When he was not at work or attending meetings she accompanied her father on the walks he and Meg had enjoyed before they were married. When it was too cold for walking she would stand in the back yard with him and listen intently as he pointed out the different stars and constellations. Pamela was eager to learn and Ted was proud of his daughter and her growing knowledge of wild life. Her favourite place was one of her father's, Sam's allotment where she exhibited no fear of the pigeons as they returned to the loft, bravely holding them while Sam checked the rings around their legs.

Early the following year Meg accepted the loss of Tom. His body was never found but she knew her best friend would never return.

"He's dead Ted," she told him the night after Ada had called to give her an ultimatum.

"She's as hard as nails our Ada, all she thinks about is getting us out of here. A've told her we'll move as soon as we can find somewhere to go. An' Ted that'll have to be soon 'cos she's starting to get awkward. You know a wish we could stay here 'cos this is me home an' a don't want to leave it. A know it's Fred puttin' the pressure on her, an' a wouldn't walk on the same side of the street as him."

Meg paused as the memories came flooding back to her.

"Even if a thought our Tom might be found, just one look at Nancy and a would be kiddin' meself. He'll never come back and she'll never get out of that place again. They say she doesn't know what's happening but the' wrong. The trouble is Ted, Nancy knew long before us what had happened to our Tom."

Ted wanted to cheer her up but he had other things on his mind and so he decided that tonight he would discuss their future together.

"A always told you Meg that a wouldn't be at the pit forever, well a think a might be. None of us knows what the future holds but for the first time in me life a feel a'm doin' somat important. A can have some influence on the way things turn out by bein' in the union. Things are changin' fast and a want to be part of that change. A've decided that as well as the union I'm goin' to put up for the council 'cos it's not just the conditions at the pit that's important, it's the way people live. We're a good example Meg; we've got our name down for a council house an' it could be years before we get one. I know you said you didn't want to move into a colliery house but I don't think we have much choice and if it's it alright with you a'll put me name down tomorrow?"

Ted had expected an argument with Meg and was pleasantly surprised at her answer.

"You know a've never liked you being on the union Ted; a saw too much of the bother it caused between me Da and our Will. They were always arguing about the carry on with lockouts and strikes and me Ma hated us having to go to the soup kitchens."

Ted interrupted her.

"I understand what you're saying Meg and that's why a want to try an' do somat."

This time Meg interrupted him.

"If you would let me finish what a was saying Ted a think you're right. If we have to we'll move into a colliery house but by all accounts, from what a hear, we might have to wait just as long for one of them as we'll have to wait for a council house. But a suppose anything's better than having our Ada going on at us to get out so she can move in and if you think you can do some good by being on the union and trying to get on the council then good luck to you."

Ted took her in his arms and whispered.

"I've another confession t' make Meg, a've joined the Labour Party."

Meg laughed.

"You're a sly bugger; you know fine well what a would have said if you'd told me."

Pamela held her father's hand as he talked to her; she was happy because he was happy.

"A told you Daisy we were comin' somewhere different this mornin'. Now let's see if you can read the words on that notice."

Pamela's smile vanished as she replied.

"I can't Dad the words are too big. I haven't learnt big words like that at school yet."

Her smile returned and she giggled as Ted scooped her up in his arms.

"Will you read it to me?" she asked her father.

Ted lifted his daughter closer to the notice that was displayed outside the pit yard.

"It says; this colliery is now managed by the National Coal Board on behalf of the people. An' y' see that flag, bonnie lass, well that's the blue an' white flag o' the Coal Board."

Pamela was not at all impressed.

328

"It's alright Dad." she told Ted as she wriggled free from his arms. "But can we go now an' see Uncle Sam's pigeons?"

Ted laughed.

"Right; let's away t' see the pigeons but a promise you one day you'll understand just how important that notice is."

Sam was extolling the virtues of the new kitchen as he spoke to Ted.

"Y' were lucky t' get this place young un. It's a grand place you've got, better than a colliery house, an' Pamela seems to have settled in well. She was tellin' me the other day all about her new friends."

After a long wait on the council's housing list Ted and Meg had finally received the news they had been waiting for. When the letter arrived, Ted assuming it was council business left it unopened until after breakfast.

"Meg," he shouted. "Come here you'll never believe it, we've done it, we've got a council house."

Ted wanted to wait but the following week they moved in to their new home.

"If the bairn comes early we'll be stuck here for weeks an' that means payin' rent on two places." Meg insisted.

Neither Ted nor Sam heard Lil come into the kitchen. She smiled as she spoke to Ted.

"Y' can gan up t' the bedroom an' see them now."

Ted did not know what to expect. He had worried throughout Meg's pregnancy experiencing every symptom long before Meg did. When she laughed at him his reply was always the same.

"It's alright for you you've had a bairn afore; it's the first time I've been around while it's all happenin'."

329

Ted sat on the side of the bed gazing at Meg and the child in her arms.

"Another lass an' this one looks just like you Meg. What are we going to call her?" he asked.

"It's not a lass Ted," Meg smiled as she gave him the news that she knew he wanted to hear.

"It's a boy Ted and his name's Rob. A knew a would have a lad this time, an' his name's been Rob from the first day a knew a was expectin'."

EPILOGUE

A familiar voice outside the room disturbed me. As the light momentarily hurt my eyes, I looked towards the window, it was daylight and there was not a star to be seen in the sky.

"How's Dad?" my brother asked.

"He's slept most of the night Rob and I think I must have," I replied.

Turning to my mother I told her what she already knew.

"Our Rob's here Mam, he's come to let us go home for a while, he'll sit with Dad for a few hours."

Leaning over my father I whispered in his ear.

"Rob's here Dad. Me and Mam are going now but we'll soon be back soon and I want you to listen to me before we go. I know I've told you this for the last few days but I want to be sure you heard me before. You would be so proud of him Dad; Rob's done it. You had to wait years, but Rob did it, he's got your seat. He's won Dad; he's our new Labour Member of Parliament."

Before we left Mam kissed Dad's cheek; she knew the routine just as I did. The nurses would soon be disturbing him, washing him, changing his bed linen, offering him tea. She hated it; the tea dribbling from the side of his mouth, making him cough, distressing him. She had told me last night, she understood they had a job to do but how she wished they would just leave him in peace. She told me she felt guilty but she prayed for God to take him; she knew he would not want to live.

"His time has come Pamela. I've prayed for him to get better, to come home to us, to the house he bought for his family. I wanted him to come back to play with his grandchildren and continue to serve the people he's done his best for. I love him Pamela 'cos he showed

331

them all; he showed them that an ordinary man with a lot of faults can play a part in making their lives better. He gave them so much of himself and there was many a time a resented it. He was away from home for weeks at a time and a know a always said to you and Rob that to give him to them was to love him but if a was honest with meself a did resent it. And it's strange, a thought he'd changed after the war but he didn't really. Your Dad was still the same boy a met when a was fifteen years old. He never settled in a job then and he still couldn't settle; he had to be doing somat different all of the time. He's fought all his life to give people like us a better life. Some folk never find their place in life but he did; it took him a long time but when he did he made sure it counted for somat."

As we drove home from the hospital my mother and I did not speak and my thoughts were elsewhere.

"Would I spend another night at my father's side? Would there be more memories to share? Would we ever be all together again?"

As I turned into the drive of my parent's home, the home where my brother and I had been so happy, I shivered.

"Would I ever be given the opportunity to see any of them again: my father, my grandparents, my great grandparents, their friends and their neighbours?"

As I helped my mother out of the car she looked different, she seemed happier than she had been for sometime. I didn't know why but it made me feel good and as I spoke we smiled at each other.

"Come on Mam we better have some breakfast; you know what me Dad will say if we don't."

"Aye lass," Mam replied. "He'd tell us you'll eat everything in front of you; when a was a lad we were

332

lucky to get a fried egg between us and I haven't fought all me life to watch you lot pickin' an' parkin'."